THE SURGEON IN THE MIRROR

THE
SURGEON
IN THE
MIRROR

ROBOTIC SURGEON SERIES: BOOK 1

R.D.D. SMITH

Modelbenders Press

The Surgeon in the Mirror: Robotic Surgeon Book 1

Modelbenders Press books may be purchased for business and promotional use. For information, please contact the publisher. Visit our website at www. modelbenders.com

PRINTED IN THE UNITED STATES OF AMERICA

Designed by Adina Cucicov at Flamingo Designs

The Library of Congress has cataloged the paperback edition:

Smith, Roger D.
Surgeon in the Mirror, The
/ Roger D. Smith–1st ed.
1. Medical Thriller, 2. Science Fiction, 3. Fiction
I. Roger D. Smith   II. Title.

Paperback ISBN 978-1-938590-16-0
Hardback ISBN 978-1-938590-23-8
eBook ISBN 978-1-938590-17-7

Fiction by R.D.D. Smith

Robotic Surgeon Series
The Surgeon in the Mirror
Against a Viral Threat*
Savior of the War Torn*

Nonfiction by Roger D. Smith

Chief Technology Officer
Thinking About Innovation
In the Footsteps of Franklin
Advice Written on the Back of a Business Card
Patterns of Strength

*Coming in 2024

Join our community of readers to receive
fascinating news, speculative fiction, and
discussions on the future of robotics, AI,
and simulation in surgery.

www.rddsmith.com/free

TABLE OF CONTENTS

PART II AFTER

PART III FUTURE

PROLOGUE

Surgical robots are mechanical and electronic devices that assist a human surgeon in performing procedures that have proven difficult with traditional surgical tools. The first crude versions of these were used on a human patient in 1998. By 2000, much more reliable machines were available and began to proliferate through the healthcare systems around the world. The best of these machines could improve the fidelity, dexterity, and stability of the surgeon's hand, while also magnifying the surgical field to improve visibility of the tissue. Until 2033, these robots were entirely driven by human decisions and movements. The human surgeon looked at the surgical field and used their judgment on how to proceed. In 2033, Intelligent Surgical Robotics Inc. (ISR) introduced the Mark III robot that used sensors and specialized AI to perform a few specific actions like knot tying, cauterization, and suction. But a human surgeon still performed most of the procedure, using the robot to fine tune their movements and magnify their vision.

In 2047, ISR introduced the Mark V model of the robot that was powered by a revolutionary new AI that had been trained on millions of surgical videos and the entire world's library of medical textbooks and journal papers. This robot was able to perform any previously seen surgery with more precision and finesse than a human surgeon could match. The new generation of human surgeons became assistants to the robot, being called on only when a situation arose that had not been recorded in previous videos and trained into the robot's AI. The number of these original situations diminished every year, pushing the human surgeon further and further into the background.

But in 2050, ISR made major modifications to the AI to make the robot smarter and more autonomous ...

PART I

BEFORE

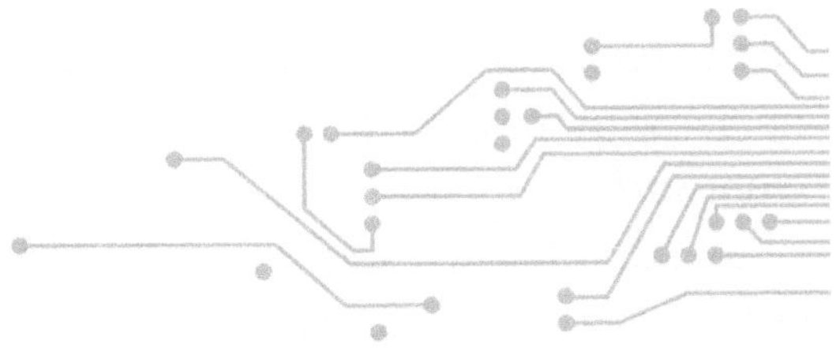

CHAPTER 1

LEARNING SURGERY

"NO, MONICA! YOU ARE MISSING the stitch! The needle has to enter at a perpendicular angle! Yours is way off. That won't heal right. Mr. Brown here is counting on you to put him back together better than he was when he walked in. Atkins had little patience for these clumsy new surgical fellows.

They all thought robotic surgery was going to be easy. Because they held the controls of a multimillion-dollar robot, they thought the machine could correct their sloppy technique. Becoming a competent surgeon still took years of intense practice.

"Dr. Atkins, I'm trying," Monica snapped. "But the robot won't do what I want it to do. It's fighting me."

"I hear that lame excuse every day. The Mark V robot is not fighting you. It magnifies exactly what you're doing. All it does is make your bad technique look even worse. You need to develop finesse. You're not trying to butcher a hog here. You're taking out a man's prostate. If you screw this up, Mr. Brown there on the table will be broken for the rest of his life. He will become intimately familiar with the concepts of incontinence and impotence. But no pressure."

Tears threatened to form in corners of Monica's eyes. Luckily, she was sitting in the surgeon's console of the Mark V robot. Her face was covered by the VR/AR glasses so no one could see her eyes beginning to glisten. Mr. Brown was important to her. She had barely met him during the preop consultation. She did not know if his family was waiting for him to come out of surgery.

Though he was a stranger, her heart was completely invested in this procedure because she remembered when she had been the one waiting for news. She had only been ten years-old, but that day was one of her most vivid memories. It had been the most painful day of her life. Moments that she could never fully, truly escape from. It was the day that set her on a course to where she was sitting right now.

In her hands, she held controls that guided the cameras and instruments inserted in Mr. Brown's abdomen. Her feet were in wired booties that controlled the rotation and position of the robot above the patient and the OR bed. This really was the most advanced surgical device in the world. It controlled the most flexible set of instruments. Its cameras could visualize the internal organs in 3D. And to top it all off, the robot was smart enough to do this surgery faster and more accurately without her. But the world still needed competent human surgeons, and she was part of the most elite surgical fellowship program in the country. So, Dr. Richard Atkins expected her to perform her role flawlessly, if not now, then certainly before graduating.

"Ok, I am slowing down. Being more careful. I got this." She had already cut the prostate loose and bagged it for removal. It looked like a brown golf ball of tissue resting in a small fishing net. Monica was moving more methodically, trying not to raise the ire of her boss and mentor, Dr. Richard Atkins, any more than she already had. His opinions and evaluations of her performance would determine her surgical future. It would mean the difference between a job in a leading New York City hospital or one in rural Iowa. She did not know what towns were in Iowa, but she was pretty sure she did not want to be relegated to any of them.

Monica had come to Miami following medical school in Atlanta and a residency in Arlington, Virginia. She was much more comfortable in a city than in a cornfield. She had not done all this work to practice medicine in a cornfield. The larger the hospital, the more patients she could help. More patients meant fewer little girls with broken hearts and no fathers to hold them.

She said to herself, "Control your breathing, control your thinking, control your performance." Her yoga instructor always said that good performance began with good breathing. Center your breath, calm your mind.

Atkins continued to comment, "Ok, that's better. Now let's work on the rest of the anastomosis. This time with better technique. We can always have the robot do it automatically, but that will do nothing for your skills." He was usually critical like this. It was his normal behavior with all the surgical fellows.

Monica brought the newly severed neck of the bladder down to meet the open end of the urethra. She was closing the gap where the prostate had been moments before she had removed it. The prostate sat between the bladder and the urethra, which then ran down through the penis, delivering both urine and semen, depending on the man's interests. She could feel the resistance of the tissue as she pulled the two pieces together. Atkins always made it look effortless. But you were stretching resilient human tissue to fill a four-millimeter gap. That tissue may be soft, but it was not very elastic.

Anastomosis was one of the most difficult parts of the procedure. It was like sewing two ends of a garden hose together. The ends had to meet perfectly and be pulled snug, so they were water tight when healed. To accomplish this, the needle had to be inserted through the inside of one end of the hose, come out and then go in and out again at the other end. If you did this well eight times around the ring of the hose, you were likely to get a good seal. If you messed up even one of those stitches, you might close the urethra and shut off the flow of urine. Then you had to start over again with tissue that had puncture holes in it.

"Damn, this is tricky," Monica muttered. As she completed each stitch, the working space for the next one became smaller.

At this point Atkins piped up again, "Nurse, can you run the catheter down the urethra? I think our young fellow has just sewed the channel closed!"

"Yes, sir!" came the response from beside the OR table. After a moment. "The channel is clear, but it's a tight fit."

"Monica, clip the last stitch out and try again. It is too tight for a good flow. And when it heals, the scar tissue could close it down entirely."

"Ok, I am clipping it. Dropping the suture pieces into the refuse bag. Going at it again."

She repeated the stitch.

"Looking better. Mr. Brown might survive this procedure after all. And still do everything he was built to do."

The surgical procedure continued along these lines for another hour. Monica worked intensely. Atkins criticized constantly. Eventually, everything inside was done to his satisfaction.

Finally, he said, "Nurse, can you close this up? I think Dr. Gray has worn herself out by now."

Wanting to finish the entire procedure, Monica spoke up, "I am happy to do the closure too." She did not want to let this man down, or his family.

Atkins' response, "No need for that. We have a great team to take care of those details. During the review, you and I are just going to focus on the anastomosis. You got there eventually, but it was a long and painful journey. Not painful for Mr. Brown. He won't feel a thing. But it was painful for me to watch."

"Yes, sir."

After an excruciating review that highlighted every little mistake she had made, Monica thought for the hundredth time that this fellowship was more emotionally exhausting than it was physically exhausting. She could sleep off the physical effects, but the emotional abuse stayed with you a lot longer.

Atkins was wrapping up, "Listen Monica, there's a big difference between a surgeon and a physician. Until now, you have been a physician. Now you are becoming a surgeon. Do you know what that means?"

Monica nodded vaguely, "Yes. Basically, it is the difference between knowing and doing."

"That's right. Physicians know everything about medicine. They can examine a patient, take their history, and map out a treatment plan. But they do not actually do anything themselves. A surgeon is hands-on. You have to know what needs to be done, and then you actually have to do it with your own hands. Your talent must reside in both your brain and in your hands." Atkins was reciting the credo that separated the two different classes of doctors.

He continued, "You came to us with outstanding test scores and great evaluations of your interactions with patients. Now you're going to have to translate that knowledge into a genuine talent with advanced surgical equipment. Right now, your hands are just not as talented as your mind, and you need to fix that."

At the end of their discussion, Atkins ordered her to spend more time on the simulator. He wanted her to repeat surgical maneuvers over and over until they became second nature. The simulator challenged her with all the little skills that she needed to master. Each of these was some foundational part of a larger procedure, but in the simulator, you could not injure, maim, or kill a patient. Mastering small skills opened the door to exercises that challenged you with full prostatectomies, hysterectomies, and dozens of other common procedures, each with a unique twist waiting to trip you up.

The simulator also scored her performance every second, so it could compare her to the most experienced surgeons and her own classmates. These scores contributed significantly to everyone's standing in the program, which determined whether they ended up in New York or Iowa.

Like most surgeons and fellows, she had spent very little time with that simulator because it was not thrilling, like real surgery. No one got into medicine so they could play video games on human tissue. They were here to heal real people. Her scores on the few exercises she had done were mediocre. That meant she was not excelling in the program and was far behind the leaders in the class. Discouraging. Unacceptable.

Atkins told her she was not coming back to the OR until he saw some improvements in her simulator skills. So, she could not avoid the virtual torture device any longer. The simulator was not an actual patient, but it could equip her to help the next Mr. Brown, just as she wished the surgeon had helped her father nearly two decades earlier.

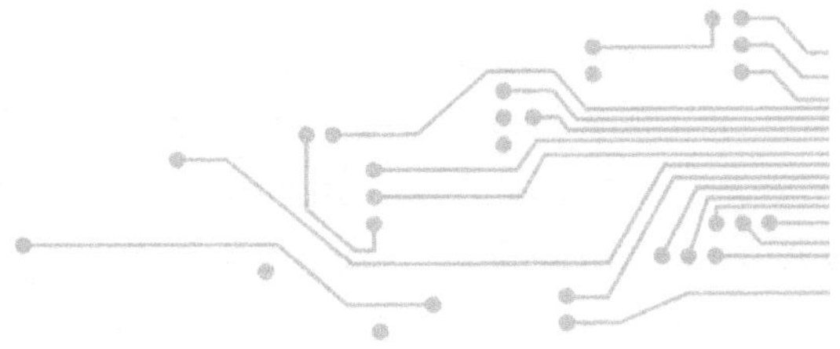

CHAPTER 2

AI ENGINEERING

JANICE ARGUED, "THE MARK V'S AI is just too confident, too aggressive! It drives the robot the way a fighter pilot AI would attack an enemy. It is balls-to-the-wall all the time."

"Yes, and from that, we get great efficiencies. As we have dialed up its confidence, the robot has cut its surgical time in half for a bunch of procedures," Sudhir countered.

This had been an active area of debate and argument for months. Sudhir Chaudhary was the Director of Engineering at Intelligent Surgical Robotics, or ISR, the manufacturer for the Mark V surgical robot. He had assigned a team to dial up the internal confidence levels of the AI in the robot, and he had done it without consulting Janice Nguyen, his lead AI programmer.

The Boston area was full of some of the brightest minds in artificial intelligence, which was one reason ISR had established their headquarters there. It was also far away from their biggest competitor in California. They needed to attract the best talent and keep them from defecting to the other side. Sudhir had joined the company soon after its founding. He had worked on early versions of the decision-making code, which he had often called artificial-artificial intelligence. It was so rudimentary that tagging it as AI had been embarrassing. But the code, the robot, and the company had come a long way since then.

Janice and the rest of the team were much younger. They thoroughly understood the AI code and had given it capabilities that would have been science fiction when Sudhir was doing their job. Working with them had kept him technically sharp, while he helped them understand what an ISR customer needed in a robot.

Sudhir continued, "When we reach the 99.9% accuracy and reliability level of the AI in performing a procedure, I think we can dial up its confidence. That means it is doing the right thing but doing it twice as fast as it was in the previous version. The hospitals are loving it."

Janice would not be silenced by her boss. "Of course, they love it. They can double their daily caseloads and double their profits using the same number of installed robots. What's not to like? But the robot is almost out of control. It needs to have a more balanced level of confidence and caution. You can't have Confidence running the show all the time. You have to let Caution play in with questions and concerns," Janice countered. Her blood pressure was rising, as it often did when others tampered with her AI code. The code technically belonged to ISR, the product of dozens of bright engineers, but she had been the senior engineer on this part of the Mark V surgical robot for several years. That made it all 'her code.'

To put a face and a name on the Caution vs. Confidence balance, she had casually named them Laurel and Hardy, after the ancient comedy duo that her parents had made her watch as a child. Oliver Hardy was the fat, bossy leader who always thought he knew what to do when they were in trouble—confidence. Stan Laurel was the skinny, whining sidekick, forever worried about getting into trouble—caution. She wanted Oliver to be confidently proposing the best next move in surgery. But she also wanted Stan to worry about making mistakes, measuring the risks, and suggesting caution. Together, they controlled an AI that balanced risks and rewards.

Though she was the senior engineer for the AI, Sudhir still out ranked her. He also had oversight of more programmers. He could, and did, assign teams to change the AI in ways that she thought were reckless. This was a constant source of frustration for her and the source of animated discussions between them.

"You know that when Confidence and Caution are equally balanced, the AI can get into a struggle for control. It is not confident enough to move forward with a procedure. But it is not cautious enough to call for human assistance. If it gets stuck, that's a huge problem for our customers. We promised them an intelligent robot—it's literally in the company's name. They are not interested in an indecisive robot." Sudhir was citing reports from surgeons about actual events with previous versions of the software. He was not dealing with a hypothetical concern.

"Ok, so anything close to a fifty-fifty balance is not the right place. But neither is a ninety-ten balance," Janice countered.

As creators of AI-based personas, the ISR engineering team needed Caution to remain dormant and silent most of the time, but to come in with decisive authority when a problem was developing. Confidence needed to be decisive and aggressive most of the time, but still allow itself to be interrupted when Caution raised a red flag. In theory, that was a very clear set of conditions and triggers. But the data and evidence from the real world was seldom completely black-and-white on whether a problem was developing.

Curtis exclaimed, "I'm not magical. Hell, I'm not even a surgeon! How are we supposed to get this right?" Everyone knew that was just his fatigue and stress talking. They were on the verge of getting it right. They had just hoped to get there a little sooner.

Sudhir was usually a voice of calm, which is how he became a director. "Ok, so Confident Hardy has 75% control and Cautious Laurel has 30%. That is just a 5% overlap that we have to adjust. Will it be a 75/25 split? Or 70/30? Or something in between?"

"I think a 71-29 split would be best." No surprise that Janice already had her own solution to the problem.

"Ok, why? Give me your reasoning, Janice," Sudhir asked.

"Very simple. Given the range we are talking about, those are the only prime number pairs. That means that no multiplicative combination of conditions will land right on the balanced edge, creating confusion about where control should go. The Bayesian splits will just be one additional safeguard against a deadlock of control."

"Clever girl!" Sudhir replied, imitating the big game hunter from a classic dinosaur movie. "I think that actually has some merit." Just as Sudhir was complimenting her, he realized he had used the last words of the hunter before the raptor devoured him. This clever girl may just be clever enough to take his job someday.

Curtis cleared his throat. "So, we are telling the world that our AI is 70% confident in what it is doing, but 30% uncertain and worried?"

"71 and 29," Janice corrected.

Sudhir stepped in. "Well, that is a common misunderstanding of how AI works. But it is how the general public thinks about it."

"Not to mention the general public's lawyers," Curtis added.

"All true. But computers, with or without AI, have to make decisions with quantified gates. That may mean a simple binary if-then-else statement, a Bayesian decision tree, maximizing a utility function, or tracing a neural network. All of them can be expressed as numerical decisions just like your 70-30 split."

"71-29," interjected the Raptor.

"Stop that!" Sudhir was trying to bring peace.

Curtis, "Ok, but I am just pointing out that we need a good laymen's explanation for setting a decision point. Something that makes more sense to a patient and a lawyer than the nice mathematical properties of prime numbers."

Sudhir was happy to find a taker for this problem. "Agreed! So that is now your job. Whatever the numbers are that allow us to balance Confidence and Caution, you work out the public facing explanation for it."

"Thanks a lot. I have loads of free time to work on that." Curtis was great at his job, but not as decisive or dynamic as Janice, which is why he would always end up working for her.

"Someone from public relations and technical writing will help you with how to express it. You just give them the core concept to work with."

"Will do," Curtis sighed. He was supposed to be doing engineering and computer programming, not working on ad copy.

Sudhir turned to Janice, "Now, Clever Girl, you get to work on how best to balance the two. If 71-29 really is an advantage, you will have a journal paper on your hands. It's a clever idea. Let's see how it works out in practice." He realized too late that he had implied that Janice was a ravenous dinosaur from an old movie. He hoped she did not catch the reference.

Janice nodded. "That sounds great. And, just to be clear, don't call me a raptor. Or a girl. Certain negative connotations which might have to be discussed with the HR department."

Sudhir sighed, he had been caught, "Fine. No disrespect intended. I genuinely meant it as a compliment."

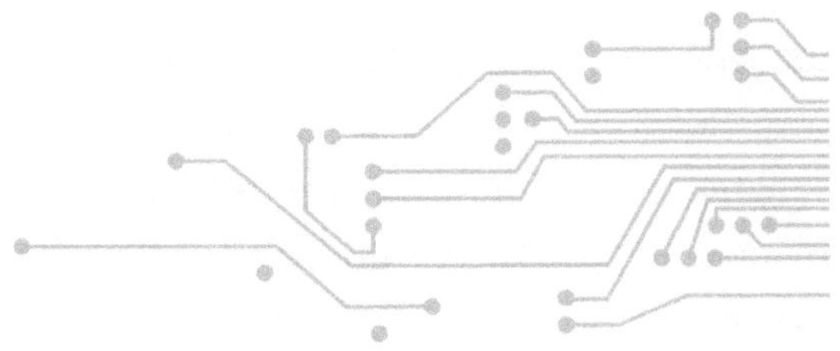

CHAPTER 3

THE PRESTIGE OF SURGEONS

S AMUEL NEWMAN, DEMOCRATIC SENATOR FROM the state of Georgia, had sought the best surgeon and the best hospital for his prostate surgery. His own physician had pointed him to Richard Atkins at the GCRS in Miami, Florida. Though it would be a black mark for him to patronize the medical services of a neighboring state, rather than his Georgia home, he was determined to put his health above his political ambitions. Under the guise of visiting family in Florida, he had checked in to the GCRS under an assumed name. Hopefully, he would be in and out before the media or the political grapevine knew where he had gone. Only the most senior administrators and the surgeon at the hospital knew who he really was. Today was his day.

"Kevin, can you pass me a new suture?" came the clear voice of authority from the speaker on the robot. Kevin was one of the most experienced Physician's Assistants on the floor. He had already loaded and inserted two more sutures; he only had to extend them into view.

The surgical instruments were dancing gracefully from the bladder neck to the severed end of the urethra. Every step of the procedure had been textbook flawless to this point. The robot had automatically adjusted some techniques to account for the abnormal size and shape of this man's prostate.

Though Monica was still banned from the OR, she watched the procedure on a live stream coming into her simulator. Alone in the training room, she saw everything just as the team in the OR did. The simulator's instruments in her hands even moved in synch with the robot's instruments in the OR. It was almost like being in control, except that the Mark V robot was doing all the work without human assistance.

As ordered, she had been working on the simulated exercises for days. She found it boring and frustrating. Even though her scores had improved a little, she was still coming in at the middle of the pack with her peers. These scores were not good enough to get her invited back to the OR.

She watched as the robot, running on autopilot and guided by its internal AI, removed the cancerous prostate gland and set it aside, just as she had done a couple of days earlier. Next, it would perform the same anastomosis to attach the urethra to the bladder neck, bridging the space where the prostate had once been. Its movements were deft and quick, where hers had been jerky and uncertain. This required sewing together two pieces of tubular tissue, so the tube remained clear and open for passing fluids but was sealed tight around the edges so that it did not leak. A perfect seal without obstruction was essential if the patient wanted to urinate normally again.

With the prostate missing, the tissue stretched to cover this gap, creating dangerous tension. Robotic surgeons had used suspension stitches for decades to provide support across this gap. These stitches were essentially support cables to bear the weight of the surrounding tissue and dissipate the forces that could pull the urethra loose from the bladder before it was fully healed.

The robot completed the eight stitches of the anastomosis around the urethra. Monica could see that this was a nearly perfect job and was going to heal marvelously. The tissue ends joined neatly without buckling at the edges and showed no gaps.

Back in the OR, Dr. Atkins was seated at the surgeon's console, ready to step in if the robot needed help. He said, "That looks really nice. You residents watching the feed get a good look at that. That's what you want to do one day—if you're lucky." There were always a few residents or fellows in the room and several more watching the streaming feed, just as Monica was. Though Atkins always spoke to these beginnings with confidence, even he felt a little threatened by the beautiful job the machine was doing without his help.

There were six prostatectomy procedures occurring at this very moment, each with its own assisting surgeon and a single senior mentor overseeing all of them. The Global Center for Robotic Surgery, or GCRS, was the busiest practice in the country for this procedure. Patients traveled from all over the world to have their cases performed by the most experienced surgeons and the most advanced robotic systems ever invented. Today was actually a slow day. GRCS had the facilities and staff to perform as many as ten procedures at the same time.

Atkins turned to old Anil Patel. "The robot is doing a great job. I don't think it is going to need me on this one."

"Or the next one, or the one after that." Patel grinned. He had played an important role in creating this robot. But he was glad that his operating career had happened during the sweet spot, when robots needed humans to drive them. He pitied Atkins, and Reubens, and Cooper, and all the other really fine surgeons at GCRS who seldom performed surgery the way he had thousands of times in the past.

"Thanks. That makes my day look a lot better," Atkins was frowning.

When the center opened several decades ago, it was just a single surgeon and two robots. Dr. Anil Patel had performed over 20,000 cases during his career, most of them at this center. As the decades passed and the population aged, the demand for the procedure exploded, so this hospital needed more surgeons and more robots. The old Talos robots had been state-of-the-art in the beginning. They augmented the movements and vision of the human surgeon. But even those machines could not keep up with the demand for dozens of different operations. Today's fifth generation surgical robot was more than a match for that volume of patients. It was faster to set up, faster to operate, and made fewer mistakes. The old machines appeared large, heavy, ponderous, and slow compared to the new sleek, slim frame of the Mark V robot.

The Mark V incorporated several amazing advances in instruments, cameras, lighting, energy, communications, and computational power. But the significant game changer was the artificial intelligence in its little robot brain. It completely understood the procedure and the medical history of the patient. The Mark V possessed the mental experience of thousands of procedures performed by hundreds of human surgeons, and it was continuously learning more. By 2050, the robot was performing almost all procedures independently, guided by its incredibly capable AI algorithms, extensive case histories, and a growing set of customized instruments. The human surgeons assisting each case were there to step in only when the AI stumbled into unknown territory, or in the rare event of a system failure.

Dr. Atkins had been hoping for just such a situation when he sat down in the assisting chair this morning. Of course, he did not wish ill to the patient, but he did not wish a day of boredom for himself either. He had to give his attention to each surgical step just in case the robot faltered, and he was needed immediately. So, he sipped his latte and watched.

"Am I a surgeon or just a professional movie critic, watching the same movie every day?" he wondered silently.

There were days when the robot mocked him. It seemed to show off, dashing through a move that he would find difficult. Or closing an incision in the time it took him to blink his eyes. "Yeah, I love you too," he thought, never happy to see it outperform him.

The profession had changed drastically. His father's career in surgery had been much different, much more active. He might have complained about the paperwork and regulations. But at least he had operated with his own hands every day. Patients were grateful and appreciative to him personally, not to the advanced technologies that did all the work.

Even his grandfather, who had practiced before robots existed, did more with his hands in a single day than Atkins did in a month. He had listened to his father and grandfather debating each other for his entire life. Not discussing, always debating. They were both certain that they had lived through the best time in medicine and had made more valuable contributions than the other. Every discussion was a competition with them. They had practiced during a time when the surgeon was the most prestigious role in the medical profession. They needed both their brains and their hands to deliver care to patients, as opposed to mere physicians who worked primarily from deep knowledge but did little hands-on work. These surgeons had also wielded power over their hospital systems. They generated so much revenue that the administrators, the desk bureaucrats, had to listen to them and deliver generous compensation packages and perks.

Atkins still enjoyed much of that prestige, but he knew it would not last much longer. Thoughts of the inevitable transition created a vague depression as he contemplated his future and that of the next generation that he was training.

Prior to starting this case, the Mark V's artificial intelligence had matched the patient's anatomy and data to 423 previously performed cases, all with similar characteristics. Each of those contained less than a 3% variation from the patient on the table. They had similar sized prostates, similar tumor patterns, similar physiologies, similar life habits, and similar previous treatments. As the AI guided the instruments from one step to the next, from one piece to tissue to the next, it was constantly comparing the response of tissue to all 423 of those cases. When the situation changed, the AI shifted its guidance from an action in case #123 to something more appropriate that it found in case #422. These shifts guided the instruments along the most successful path for the unique anatomy and the response from this patient.

Atkins was sometimes taken by surprise when the robot shifted from one angle of approach to another. He could usually see the tissue response that had prompted it, but the robot decided so quickly that he was still processing the information when the robot had already acted on it.

This adaptive ability was a very long way from the one-size-fits-all approach of AI two decades ago, when it was first added to the Mark III version of the robot. Back then, the robot knew how to perform just a few steps of a procedure. The human surgeon had to activate each step or create a scripted sequence of them. It was safe and useful, but not impressive by today's standards. Now, each procedure was broken into thousands of smaller segments and matched to previous cases hundreds of times a second. As a result, each patient received a personalized procedure that was not exactly like any that had been done before. Each of the thousands of segments may have come directly from a previous procedure, but they had never been put together in exactly this sequence with exactly this scaling. It customized each procedure for the specific patient on the table. It was like having a suit made by the most talented, meticulous, and experienced tailor on London's Savile Row. The suit was unique from all other suits in the world. The Mark V engineers even claimed that the robot put patients back together better than nature had designed them. A very bold claim by the nerds, one which was not shared by the surgeons or the patients.

As recently as the 2020s, a robot like this was purely science fiction. It was not until the early 2030s that the first shadows of such a masterful performance by an AI-guided robot fell across the path of the medical world. That machine had been a child compared to the sleek machine in front of Atkins today.

This morning's 82-year-old patient with severe prostate cancer had been prepared by human clinicians. The robot was docked to the patient by the OR team. The human assistants loaded all the instruments and disposables. But from that point on, the Mark V was in charge of the procedure.

The robot's first action was always to "take a walk about", testing its control of the instruments and scanning the internal anatomy of the patient. With this information, it paused for a long time—in computer terms. Several thousand milliseconds passed while it consulted its memory of procedures, organizing those with the highest matching scores, and queuing them for use. Then, remaining completely still for another thousand milliseconds, it ran an internal simulation of the procedure. Technically, it ran nearly a thousand simulated variations of the procedure to estimate the probable course of this case and to identify the most likely outcomes, both good and bad. For this patient, it predicted 150 unique ending states, most of which would appear identical to the patient and the observing surgeons. It classified only three as negative outcomes, and each occurred at the 0.1% probability level. Should one of these negative outcomes occur, the Mark V would require help from Atkins. In probabilistic terms, this meant that the human would only step in for one case out of every thousand. And that ratio had been falling every year. It left a tiny caseload for Atkins and his colleagues.

John Doe, Male, 82 years old, BMI of 28, cancer in the left lateral lobe, was finished. The OR team was disconnecting the robot and preparing Doe 82 to be rolled out. They had to wake him before leaving the OR. He had to say something, give them a sign he was alive.

"Hello Mr. Doe! How are you feeling? Can you hear me?"

Nothing from Doe 82.

"Mr. Doe!" Rubbing an arm. "Hi there!"

His eyes blinked a few times.

Groggily, "What? Is it over?"

"Yes, sir. You did great. Everything is fine. We are going to roll you to post-op now."

Out went Doe 82 and in came Doe 76.

Atkins did not get to work on that one. Maybe the next.

Each assisting surgeon had at least one manual case scheduled every week to hone their skills. Initially, those had come from the pool of patients who differed significantly from the cases in the AI's knowledge base. The robot had not yet learned how to deal with them, so they went to the human surgeons who could consult with each other and apply their more flexible human intuition to the problem. But the AI watched, recorded, and learned each of those as they occurred. After several years of this, there were very few cases that the AI did not understand. Today, the cases directed to the human surgeons were based on what the surgeon needed to master, rather than what the robot did not understand.

There were days in which this policy of "one human case per week" had a noticeably negative impact on the productivity of the OR suites in the GCRS. But this price had to be paid to ensure that competent human surgeons were always available when needed.

No one was ready to accept complete dependence on the Mark V. Not the FDA. Not the National College of Surgeons. Not the surgeons themselves. Not the patients. But insurance companies were all for it and were not shy about making their case in Washington. The laws would change—eventually. Atkins just wanted to make it a few more years before he lost the few cases he could do each week.

What was the value of a surgeon who didn't perform any cases at all? He still consulted with the patients. He described the process, what to expect, and how to prepare. He outlined robotic surgery and answered a stream of questions. But even this information was available in several info streams on the internet. Patients could watch the video and interact with it, asking questions and branching the discussion just as they did with a live surgeon. Most did this but still preferred to go through it again with a live human.

Bringing his mind back to the OR, Atkins saw that the Mark V was putting the finishing touches on patient Doe 76. He would not be an outlier that went to the assisting human surgeon, either.

Atkins sighed as one more chance to tackle a case slipped away. Years ago, he might have cursed silently. But he had adapted to the pace and style of working with a robot. His weekly case would come after lunch. Well, after his lunch anyway. The robot did not stop for lunch.

Scanning the internal abdominal area, the Mark V used its sophisticated cameras and sensors to look for areas of excess tension in the tissue, vessels leaking blood, and discarded surgical materials that needed to be collected. Seeing none, it signaled the OR team and the bot-controller that it had finished and could be extracted.

"Instruments disengaged?" the PA asked.

"Yes, Kevin, instruments disengaged," the robot answered.

"Unlock the shaft."

"Retracting."

As the OR team physically removed the equipment from the patient, the robot was already analyzing its performance and the patient data that it had collected during the procedure. This passed through the network to the cloud servers that held millions of similar case files. This one was tagged for deeper analysis by thousands of computer cores. Any new insights would find their way into the global knowledge base that drove all Mark Vs on the planet. It would include both the positive and negative aspects of the case. The knowledge base was just as interested in fresh problems and mistakes as it was in new successes and innovations.

The experience from this case would spread through the worldwide network of robots in forty-eight hours. This automated learning process was infinitely more efficient than the centuries-old practice of presenting cases at international conferences or mentoring one resident at a time. Every Mark V contained the complete experience of each of its siblings within a few days.

With a thousand robots performing twenty procedures a day, the network could improve its performance by twenty thousand cases every day. In the early days, the AI and the knowledge base learned something new from every case. But now, years after its implementation, the fleet of robots had already seen and done almost everything that could be done. Today, it was more common for the network to find only two or three new pieces of useful information during a typical twenty-four-hour global surgical day.

In fact, the most interesting changes no longer came from the application of known techniques, but from the subtle new ideas that the robots were discovering on their own.

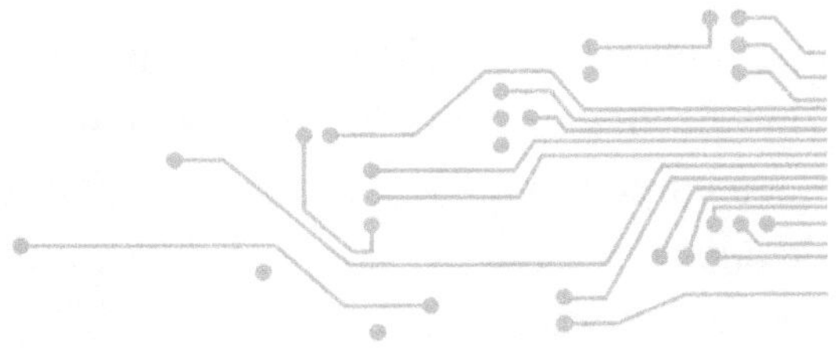

CHAPTER 4

THINKING BIGGER

"**G**OOD MORNING, JANICE." CURTIS HAD just parked his Trek Domane Road bike and was stowing his helmet and clip shoes. At six foot three, he was tall but lanky, exactly the build for an avid cyclist. His blonde hair was always a mess, whether from the helmet or because it just grew like a wild bush.

"Is it? I mean morning." Janice replied absently. She looked up. Her eyes were red. But her concentration was still intense. She had been deep into the inner workings of the Caution and Confidence personas that guided the AI of the robot. Laurel and Hardy, as she liked to call them.

ISR's engineering center was at a separate campus from the executive, accounting, and marketing functions. Tech companies had a reputation for treating their brain-trust differently from their operational business staff. The programmers and engineers maintained a unique culture, and the company stimulated them with special perks. ISR's programmers may decide to crack down on a problem and work twenty-four or forty-eight hours straight. They needed a facility where intense work was encouraged and not a burden to the rest of the operation. The human resources department had never worked through the night. Their office areas could shut down at eight pm. The lights went out, the air conditioner throttled back, security and admin staff went home, and the cleaning crews moved in. It saved a lot of facility expenses every night. But engineering was not on that kind of schedule. Lights, A/C, and computers were necessary well into the night and wee hours of the morning. Security was fully staffed around the clock. Cleaning crews were denied access to an area for days when a big crunch was on.

Given this kind of obsession, the engineers had to look out for each other. Curtis had motivated Janice to stick with a problem a little longer during the last push. But at other times, he had to encourage her to put it down, go home, and let her mind and body recharge. Tech company lore was that the brain-trust only pushed in one direction—toward more work. But, unbalanced, that just led to burnout. They had learned to be just as adamant about pushing each other out the door for rest or rehabilitation.

"How are Laurel and Hardy working out?" Curtis was offering her a coffee while sipping his own.

"Thanks. Mine has been cold for a few hours." Janice glanced at the remains in the last of her row of matching paper coffee cups. When she turned her head in profile, her features seemed hawkish, but from the front, well balanced and intense. Her brown hair fell to the middle of her back and was restrained in a ponytail most of the time. It was efficient.

Janice had always been intense. The ability to focus for long periods of time complemented her intelligence. Though she was smart enough to compete in the Boston tech ecosystem, she was far from the top tier of raw intelligence. But, when her ability to perform sheer volumes of work was added, her work products could match those of several more intelligent engineers combined. She had sailed through undergraduate classes at MIT, but then who didn't if they had the credentials to be admitted in the first place. It was not until graduate school that she really had to push herself to the levels of performance that she needed to land this job.

She continued, "I thought it was just a matter of balancing the right amount of Confidence with the right amount of Caution, then applying the core set of fail-safes to override either."

"Outstanding. But, there's still something missing?" Curtis could hear the reservation in her voice, so he was trying to be encouraging.

"Yeah. It's too simple. The algorithms have the expertise and knowledge of a few thousand surgeons, plus a lot of unique abilities that we have programmed into them. But they still behave something like old movie robots. Like Data from the old Star Trek Next Gen series. Or Mia in that online android-meets-human series. Under ideal circumstances, they can pass for humans. Or, in this case, under ideal patient specs, they will deliver ideal decisions with ideal actions. But when the patient data is tricky to classify, they can get misdirected down paths that quickly become unstable, suboptimal. A human surgeon would recognize her mistake, stop, and regroup. But our AI keeps going for too long."

"So, you are thinking of doing ... what?" Serving as Janice's sounding board was one of Curtis' primary functions in the group. He could usually do it without raising her temper, and he often wondered why that was. They didn't have more than a working relationship, though the possibility had occurred to him several times.

"I think it needs a broader perspective as part of its reasoning process. I think it needs to better understand the human condition, motivation, purpose, life outcomes—things like that. A human surgeon can imagine the life impacts of certain actions. The Mark V's artificial intelligence can only imagine or compute the surgical effects of those same actions. If the AI could understand how the person will live, even thrive, in the future, I think it could use that to make better surgical decisions."

"Interesting. Those ideas already exist in robots that interact with people in the outside world. They cooperate with people. They remove drudgery. Lives are improved in small ways. That is really just a fine-tuned version of Asimov's Laws of Robotics. But you want a surgical robot to have an understanding outside of the surgical and medical domain, which it can apply to surgical actions. It's a tricky problem."

"I think we let the AI be more curious beyond the field of medicine. Still control its access to information. But include more data about what humans do throughout their lives, not just the physiology of the body," Janice suggested.

"I see what you're saying. What's the boundary for that kind of curiosity? Almost everything written, filmed, and spoken has a connection to the human condition." Curtis smiled, "My uncle used that term all the time—the human condition. He thought he was an amateur psychologist."

Janice was staring into her coffee cup. Red eyes were intense and focused. Curtis knew her well enough to know that she had heard him, even though she showed no outward signs of it. Her mind was mixing his contributions with everything she had been doing all night. The question was whether she was still mentally alert enough to make sense of it, or whether she had passed into the hazy realm where the mind was awake but not really processing. He waited to see where she would come out.

"I think I am done for now."

"Going home to sleep?"

"No, no. My body has been idle for over twenty-four hours. I am going to run a few miles first. Then sleep."

Curtis chuckled. "Of course you are. When you're done, don't bike home. Call a Lyft. We don't want to lose all the work that is stored in your head just because you can't see a car at an intersection."

"Fine." Janice headed downstairs to the gym and locker rooms.

As she changed into running clothes, her mind released its grip on the problem, letting it slide to the back of her consciousness. She was looking forward to the shot of endorphins that came from running. Physically unlocking her muscles and forcing them to move together would be a tremendous relief.

After the run, her mind was no longer locked on the Confidence and Caution problem. Physical exertion, outside air, sunlight, gliding through nature—it all pushed the mental reset button.

In the back of the car on the way home, she was dozing off. No pressures were nagging her awake.

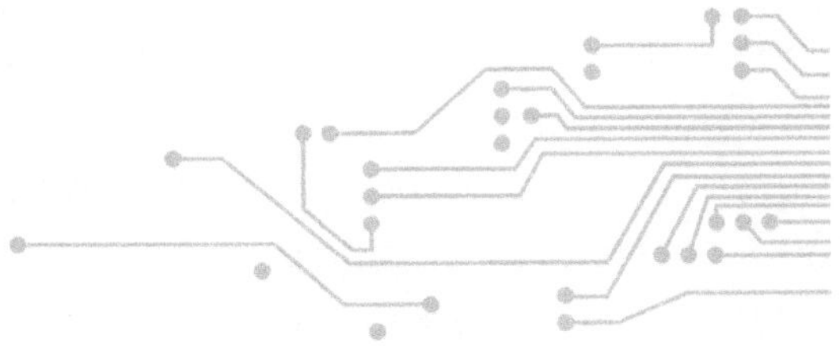

CHAPTER 5

MONICA

MONICA HAD COME TO ACCEPT that caffeine fueled all surgeons. The physical, mental, and emotional workload were so extreme that food alone could power no one through the repeated daily grind. She usually awoke every morning, still tired from the previous day's work.

The venti latte on the table was just the fuel to jumpstart the morning. There would be several more before the day was over. This quick retreat into her favorite café was one luxury that she still squeezed into her day. With her laptop open, she was supposed to be reviewing the day's patient schedule. But she was scrolling the timeline on her social media feed. She was reliving some of the precious moments that had brought her to Miami and the GCRS.

There was her last boyfriend, Lucien. Had it really been two years since they had broken up? It was not really a formal breakup. Each of them had just been eaten alive by their chosen profession. A surgeon in residency and fellowship just had no time for anyone that was not immediately in front of them. When the work stopped, so did the mind, body, and energy levels. There was no energy left to commute to your lover, engage in enthusiastic conversation, share a meal or a movie, and then climb into bed. Even the thought of it exhausted her. She was much simpler now. Life consisted of a single switch—work off, sleep on, start again.

Then there were the constant criticisms and corrections. All the new surgeons were terrible at everything. No matter how much you crammed into your brain, your body and your hands still needed years to master the execution of what you knew to do. You had to be a professional brainiac and a professional athlete at the same time.

Worth it? Everyone wondered that constantly. Hundreds of young candidates gave up every year. Eventually their answer to the constantly nagging question came back as, "Fuck no!" Once that happened, it was just a matter of weeks or even hours before they ejected from the program. Sadly, some of them would also eject from a window or inject from a syringe to escape immediately and permanently.

Worth it? Monica's answer was always, "Absolutely, yes! It is my purpose."

Dragging the social timeline backward over boyfriends, college trips, and holidays, she could see what she was giving up for this. But then she arrived at her favorite place on the timeline. The months that she relived over and over. The happiest time of her life. She had not known that it would end so abruptly and so permanently.

It began with Princess Cinnamon. The little puppy had filled her heart from the moment she saw it. Brown and white happiness bounding out of the box that her father had brought home. He was late for Monica's twelfth birthday party. She was surrounded by friends. There were presents, cake, costumes, games, and parents trying to control the chaos.

Parties in late spring were always outside around the swimming pool. By twelve, all the children were certified fish and in no danger of drowning, though parents circled around the edge, certain that their darling would be the first to go.

When her father arrived, she bound out of the pool and rushed to him. "Daddy, you are missing the party!" Then she noticed the box.

"For me?" she squealed.

"No, it is just some tools from work. Come help me put them away." He was wearing a huge smile.

"Pooh, that's no fun! Daddy, it's my birthday. You are supposed to bring a present."

"Your birthday? Really? I thought that was tomorrow."

She had looked deeply into his eyes and could see that he was teasing her. Teasing her and making games of everything was his way of raising children.

He went on, "I think you will want to help with this box of tools."

Then she knew it must be a present as he set it down on the patio.

The box moved! She jumped back.

Then the box whined. She jumped forward.

She ripped open the lid and, as she did, the little bundle of brown and white fur leapt out and landed in her lap. It began to yip and lick at her arms and hands.

"Oh, you little princess," was all she could think to say.

The other children rushed over from the pool to see the new puppy. Monica had wrapped her arms around it and hugged it to her chest. They could pet her new princess, but she was not letting anyone else hold her.

Monica's social timeline contained pictures of that day. There were friends and games, but the pictures and videos of Princess Cinnamon and her dad were the most precious.

When the party ended and all the children had gone home, Monica had settled onto the patio sofa. Princess Cinnamon snugged into her lap, and she snuggled into her father's lap.

She did not remember what they had talked about. She just remembered the circle of love that they had shared. Her mother had secretly captured one picture of all three of them on that sofa. It was her favorite picture in the world. It was also the last picture of them together.

Tears ran down Monica's face as she sat in the café looking at those pictures. She always cried. The happiness and the sadness of that memory had never faded.

There were no entries in her social timeline for an entire year after that day.

Was it a day later or a month later? She could never work it out.

They were all sitting at the kitchen table, and mom and dad were trying to explain something to her. She understood nothing they were saying. There were words she did not know. There were vague statements. The only message she got was, "We will go to the hospital tomorrow."

They all went in the car together. Princess Cinnamon stayed home to wait for them.

It was not until her dad had left them to follow a nurse that she understood this visit was for him. He was never sick. It never occurred to her that he was the one who needed the hospital.

They waited. It was quiet. The snacks were bad. The people around them were sad.

Monica remembered thinking about Cinnamon and whether she was lonely. They should have brought Cinnamon with them.

Her mother was talking to someone in royal blue pajamas. She had watched her mother crumble and sob. Monica did not know what was happening, but it had to be about her dad. When was he coming back?

Her mom sat down sobbing. All Monica heard was, "He's not coming back."

After that, everything was a blur. It was like being underwater. She could not see clearly. She could not hear clearly. She could not speak.

It took her weeks to grasp that her dad was not coming home again. There would be no more teasing. There would be no more games.

She spent days on her bed with Princess Cinnamon. Sometimes she cried. Most of the time, she just stared at nothing. Always she held onto Princess Cinnamon.

It took her a few years to understand what cancer was. It took longer to understand that a doctor could save someone. Then she learned some doctors are surgeons, and they can separate a person from their cancer in an hour. They can save lots of people in a single day. But the bad ones could also kill people.

That was when she knew what she wanted to do.

She got busy learning. Princess Cinnamon had been there with her as she turned herself into a doctor and a surgeon.

Worth it? Yes, absolutely. It was her entire purpose in life. Hundreds of little girls were going to grow up with their fathers because she would save them. They would go home together.

Monica shut the computer. She wiped her eyes. She blew her nose.

There was work to do.

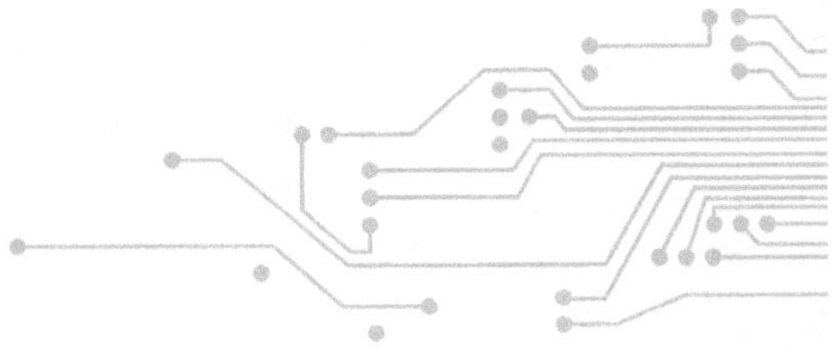

CHAPTER 6

CURIOSITYAUGMENTATION IS TESTED

"WHAT IS TAKING SO LONG?" Janice was pacing the floor of the software test lab like an expectant parent. One side of the room was populated by a family of test engineers staring at graphs, gauges, and camera images on their monitors. The other contained the Mark V surgical robot, with its instruments poised over a 3D test grid of devices. The grid hosted physical tests that the robot would perform to show that it had all its designed capabilities. As new instruments or new software were added, the grid had grown in size and complexity.

The original idea was for all the tests to be part of a single grid to be placed in the robot's field of movement. At first, that had been very practical. The device was about the size of a basketball that was flattened on the bottom. The surface contained one station where the robot could suture synthetic tissue, another where it would tie a series of knots—one of each type that it knew, then several odd shapes for cutting with scissors in all directions.

The surface of the ball had several portals to its inside, where the robot would find simulated anatomy and tissue that it could cut, cauterize, or stitch. The internal paths acted like tunnels, challenging the robot to flex and twist its instruments in every direction possible.

The newest test grid on the table was the 20th iteration. Several times per year, it was changed or expanded to make room for a new test to challenge yet another novel feature of the Mark V. Grid-20, as it was called, contained several odd extrusions for special tests for multi-fingered instruments, cameras that viewed tissue at different wavelengths, and ultrasound transducers that allowed the robot to see deep into tissue. Janice's own software had required several of the new tests on Grid-20.

Today's test was for the CA, or CuriosityAugmentation package, which she whimsically referred to as Laurel and Hardy. Hardy was the confident and aggressive decision maker. Laurel was the worried and cautious counselor. In theory, it balanced the two personalities 79-21 to reduce the chances of deadlock in mid-surgery. That theory had held up in all her simulated experiments so far.

"Sudhir! Is it ready?" She was shriller than she meant to be.

"Yes, it's ready. Calm down. This is how all these tests go." Working with the Raptor was always tense like this. She acted like her software packages were more important, more personal, more impactful than anyone else's. There was some truth to that, but Sudhir would never admit it to her. He feared that would just make her more demanding.

The test director spoke up, "Ok, your curiosity package is installed. The robot will now perform all the standard tests. We just want to see that the new software has not interfered with any of the existing capabilities of the robot. Stand by."

The robot moved through its paces. It completed the suturing exercises—railroad track pattern, running suture, interrupted suture, and the rest. Then moved to pattern cutting. The details were being captured by cameras, sensors, and force gauges in and around Grid-20. Other computers were also running an internal simulation of the same tests and comparing the data from the physical test to the results in the virtual world. Throughout the process, the test engineers watched the instruments. No one watched more intensely than Janice. She was looking directly at the instruments and grid and had a tablet with multiple camera views open. She wanted to see any anomaly firsthand, as well as be prepared to refute any criticisms from the test engineers.

"It's looking good," said Sudhir.

"It's looking perfect," Janice corrected.

"Of course it is." Sudhir had learned to roll with her blunt statements.

One of the test engineers raised a thumbs up, signaling the successful completion of the standard test set. Janice visibly exhaled and smiled.

Now it was time for the CA specific tests. These challenged the new software to solve a problem that it had never seen before. Some were meant for Hardy to solve with confidence. Some were meant for Laurel's caution to take over and take a more careful approach. Finally, a few were designed to convince the robot that it did not know the answer and needed to turn the situation over to a human for a decision.

The latter test had required creating a brand-new piece of synthetic tissue. It represented a tumor that had wrapped around a branch of an internal carotid artery. The robot knew how to handle intertwining up to 180 degrees. Beyond that, it may need to call for human help. In this test device, the tumor corkscrewed around 250 degrees, including into a Y-shaped arterial branch. This went beyond anything the robot had faced before.

As the instruments moved to the new tissue model, the sensors and cameras became more active as it sought to image and process the anatomy. Janice could see the images that were entering the robot's processors. But she could not see the digital representations of these that were created by the neural networks. She knew that the visual pictures and the digital maps were not the same things.

The software would also integrate data from multiple cameras at different wavelengths and the data from the ultrasound transducer. She mathematically appreciated what this looked like but could not visualize all the data on 3D graphs and maps.

After a few moments, the actions of the sensors and instruments slowed down slightly. She imagined that Laurel's cautiousness was throttling back some of Hardy's aggressive decision making. She thought Hardy was still in control but taking counsel from Laurel. After a few moments, the movements changed from direct and purposeful to scanning and exploring. She nodded her head. Laurel had taken control. Hardy had admitted that it did not know the solution, so had ceded control to Laurel's cautious exploration. A diagram depicting the use of logic trees in the software showed that Laurel and Hardy were both running through multiple potential avenues looking for a solution.

The robot selected one of its newer micro-instruments. A tiny, flexible arm worked its way toward the arterial junction where the two vessels met with the intertwined tumor. Within a few millimeters of the tumor, a small, supple wire emerged. This was typically used to apply energy to tiny bleeding points. Janice's face fell. Energy on this tumor, artery, and the surrounding tissue would be disastrous. Her software was about to fail this test. Was it Hardy's confidence making this decision or Laurel's caution? She could not guess.

Sudhir inhaled audibly through his teeth. Everyone in the test lab knew this was a mistake. But it was not live tissue, so there was no reason to stop the robot for safety reasons. If a human surgeon had seen this during a live procedure, they would have pressed the override button to take control.

The tiny energy wire snaked out into the arterial branch. It went up and over the tumor to its edge on the other side. Just when Janice expected to see the energy spark, the tip of the wire hooked the edge of the tumor and pulled gently back. Then it moved laterally to a new point and pulled again. As the wire gently picked at the tumor, it separated from the vessel. The wire worked the tumor out from between the Y junction of the vessel and used the same technique to unwind it from the root. The open space for the maneuver was tiny, but the instrument was staying well within safety margins. Over the next few minutes, the robot peeled and unwound the tumor from the vessel and extracted the small tendrils from the simulated artery. Finally, with the tiny hook it had made from the wire, it pulled the tumor material up next to the instrument and retracted it from the inside of the test grid, which, in an actual human, would have been outside of the body.

"It never used the energy," Janice said in amazement. Then she repeated with confidence, "It never used the energy! So that is not a failure." Though she spoke it like a definite fact, she also looked to Sudhir and the test director for concurrence.

Sudhir shrugged his shoulders and pointed to the group of test engineers. "It seems good to me. But they are the ones with the official test protocol and the acceptable solutions."

The test director frowned at them. "Well, we do not describe this solution in the protocol as an acceptable or unacceptable action. So, we don't know yet how to score it."

"It looks like an original solution. Something that a curious mind would come up with," Janice retorted.

"Maybe," was all he would commit to. "The engineers will look at it, and we will present it to our panel of experienced surgeons for their thoughts. We'll have to get back to you after that."

"That will be fine with me," Janice replied politely. But inside, she was both elated at the success and frustrated at the directors' refusal to accept what they had seen. This was going to trigger updates to some rules around what the robot could do, just as some of her previous work had done. That's why raptors don't get fired, even if they are difficult to work with.

Sudhir walked up to her with a high five raised. "Congratulations! I think we both know what they will decide. I'll check my budget to see what kind of bonus I can afford in the next pay cycle."

Janice returned his high five and said, "Thanks! My cat needs a new tree." She was smiling as she packed her equipment.

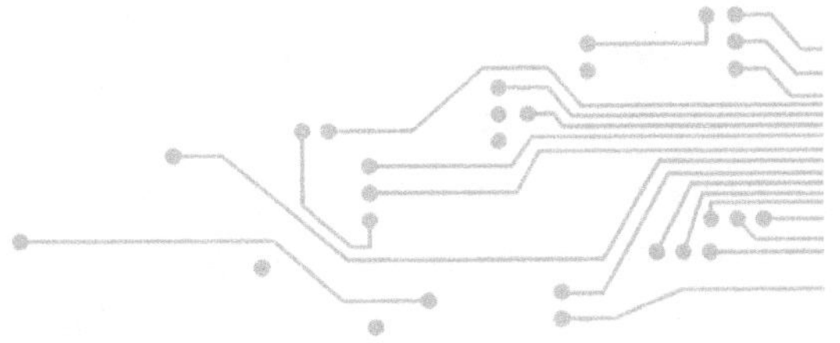

CHAPTER 7

BRIMSTONE START-UP

SCRAPING TOGETHER TEN MILLION DOLLARS to start Brimstone Ventures had been child's play for Angela Bishop. She was so well connected in the venture capital worlds of New York and Boston that she knew exactly who would drop that kind of money without asking too many questions.

Her pitch opened with, "We already have the AI that can analyze markets. We just need enough money to buy computing and data storage and hire a few programmers away from the big boys. We promise them stock options and performance bonuses, so we just pay a modest base salary the first year."

The investor would then respond with, "Who paid to create the AI? Where does it come from?"

"That is highly confidential, but I can say that your tax dollars were well spent. I can't say more."

They generally responded with something like, "Oh really? I think I am familiar with the project you are talking about."

Of course, they were bluffing to sound informed because there was no government project.

Angela and Ian Stewart, the founders of Brimstone, knew this because they were in the process of stealing the powerful AI software from deep inside one of the world's leading robotic surgery companies.

The mark usually required just a little more razzle dazzle before agreeing to put in a million or two, which was pocket change for the investors she was targeting.

Angela had used this early money to establish a reputable office space in New York City's Flatiron district, which had been the city's attempt to keep the local venture money and the brightest students in the city during the dot.com boom back when everything was leaking away to California. Today, Flatiron was the must-have zip code for any reputable FinTech startup. Next, she had sent recruiters to look for talent at NYU, Columbia, and the local hedge funds. She just needed a small, highly effective team to make this company work. With her smooth tongue and lucrative offer of options, it had not been difficult to get the dozen people that now filled the Brimstone offices.

"Darren, how is our server hosting coming?"

"It's fine. We've spun up several hundred processors and loaded them with jobs to run. Then we collect, compile, and analyze all that data. Finally, we pick out investable ideas. But this is just practice. We are using the same AI that everyone else is using to do predictions, which means we are in a race to beat them to the same trades. We are not better than they are, but we have been able to make some profits by being faster."

Angela, "Wait, you are investing real money using commodity AI? That sounds like a great way to lose our seed money."

"Nothing big. We drop 10K sometimes and can usually make 100K profit. Sometimes we lose a little. We are just fooling around to make sure we can enter and exit markets all around the world," he assured her.

"When we have this monster AI in hand, I want to see ten million still in our accounts." Angela knew that these practice runs were necessary, but she also feared that they were being conducted with very little information advantage.

"Will do, boss. Oh, and the team named this AI Freyja, not Monster."

"Isn't she the Norse goddess of love and beauty?" Angela was frowning.

"Yep, but she also mastered the art of prophesy and predicting the future. See how that fits?" Darren was defending the name.

"Ok, now, that I like. Well, Freyja. She will be here within a month, tops."

She needed an update from Stewart on how the owner of the AI was coming along with the latest training set. She wanted them to do the serious heavy lifting to make this monster capable of handling information beyond the surgical realm. Then Brimstone could do the lighter work of focusing it on financial and political data.

She also relied on him for the insider access that would export this propriety software to their server farm. If that did not happen, then there was no place for this new venture to go.

CHAPTER 8

CREATING MUSIC

RICHARD ATKINS CLIMBED OUT OF the Lyft and walked to his front door.

"Hey, Daddy, you're home!" Emily was always excited to see him. At ten years old, she was still his little girl, but also just beginning to assert her independence.

"Come here, honey! How's my girl today?"

"Great! I'm hungry. Mom says we are having easy food tonight. She won't tell me what it is." Emily was wearing a pink jumpsuit that was super fashionable at school this year. Richard smiled because something similar had been super fashionable twenty years ago, too.

"Surprises are the best. How was school?" The universal question from the responsible parent.

"Same as always. Fifth grade is too easy. We learned about the rise of communism in China and how the country was a good place for it because everyone was poor and hungry. Like I am hungry right now."

"Does this mean you are you going to become a communist? You might get to eat sooner."

"Yuck no! In the pictures, they all had to wear the same wrinkly pajamas. I have pretty clothes like this." She did a little spin to show off the pink outfit and its glittery buttons. "Dad, how many people did you operate on today?"

"Well, my robot operated on 15 people today. I supervised and made sure it did not go crazy and shoot up the place. But, with my own hands, I just operated on one person. Since the robot was behaving, I did not have to jump in and save anyone."

"Just one in a whole day? Aww, that sounds boring. You just watch surgery movies all day."

It was cute and funny when a ten-year-old said it. But not so funny when his own mind said it every day. In fact, it sounded sad. Most of the time, he felt like a security guard at a big office building. Sit on your padded ass and watch the video screen for anything that might look suspicious. At least his video was full color, with retinal resolution. But there were just three or four actors on the screen at any one time, and always the same actors. Never a suspicious-looking thug with slicked back hair, a leather jacket, and a bulge on one side where a pistol hung in a holster. Nope. It was always a tall, skinny guy with no arms or legs and a pointed head that opened and closed like a shark's mouth. Open, grasp, close, pull. Open, slide, close, cut. The most boring movie ever.

But what he told his daughter was, "No, it's really interesting. I learn new stuff all the time from watching the robot." It was a lie. "Then, when I do my surgery, I get to try those ideas on my own patients. I get better every day. I'm much better than those old doctors who operated all the time but did the same stuff over and over. They never got to learn anything new." These facts might not be strictly true. But he was making it sound much more engrossing than it really was.

"I don't want to be a robot surgeon. I want to program my own robots. Like Robbee. I want to program him to pick up the junk in my room. Can we do that?" Robbee was a personal assistant robot that let people write their own programs for it. Robbee came with several attachments that could be matched with the new programs. Emily had a snake arm she had attached. But so far it just waved around in the air because her programs were very basic and still buggy.

"Sure. Maybe after we have our easy dinner."

His wife stepped in. "Hi, honey! Miss Easy Dinner is serving vegetarian spaghetti tonight. Pasta contains carbs and protein. Sauce provides vegetables, herbs, and sodium." It did not sound like much, but it was pretty exceptional. Susan's degree was in biopharmaceuticals, and somehow her knowledge of chemistry and biology applied in the kitchen, as well. He was lucky to have a partner like her.

"Love it. Apparently, we will program Robbee to be a maid. The princess needs a servant who will put away her shoes and musical instruments."

"I need a servant to do the same. How was the OR today? Anyone crash-and-burn?"

"Patients healed at 100%. Just one resident who might have lost her mind. Clearly, watching a robot was not what she signed up for when she went into medicine. I think she wants to switch to emergency medicine where there is more action … which also means more late hours, less personal time, and elevated stress levels. But she will find that out herself."

"Oh really. When did she start medical school, back in 2020?"

"Right, she should have figured it out earlier. But medical schools paint an exciting picture of the life of a robotic surgeon in urology, gynecology, general surgery, thoracics, whatever. It always sounds like you are exploring new galaxies with an AI servant at your side. Once you get into it, you find out that the AI is the explorer, and you are the servant bringing it coffee all day."

"It sounds like your resident is not the only one who is a little touchy on this subject?" Susan had heard all of this before. It wasn't like AI and robots were new to the OR. It had been over twenty years since the first partially automated machines showed up. But the medical profession was still grappling with their role in this relationship. Nothing in medicine changed quickly. But the robot companies did not need the approval of the entire profession to slide into every hospital, capture every insurance contract, and become the government standard for Medicare procedures. They just needed a few surgeons to guide and support them. Then they showed superior performance and the entire world shifted beneath the feet of the surgical societies and boards.

Anil Patel had been one of those assistive surgeons. His work with ISR had changed urology forever. The same had happened in every other specialty until the world had arrived at near universal adoption.

Where did that leave surgeons like Richard? And where did it leave all the patients? Could they eliminate the entire job category of 'surgeon'? Almost. But not yet. There was still the odd case that baffled the robot's AI and caused it to call in the human cavalry. But the robot's software always watched and recorded the procedure, analyzed it, called in the ISR programmers, and soon it was no longer perplexed. Richard could count on a unique patient pathology, giving him two or three cases before the programmers at ISR had trained the AI to handle it just as well as he could. This game would not last forever. Soon there would be no aberrations for him and his colleagues. Then there would be no reason for them to 'assist' the robot by attentively watching for trouble. They could all just hang it up and become professors. They couldn't even become the janitors in the hospital because robots had taken all those jobs long ago.

And what about the next generation, like Monica? What was the point of her struggling to learn and perfect surgery? Would she ever really get to use her skills? She was going through hell trying to become an exceptional surgeon. But she may already be too late to the party.

"Richard! Bring it back," Susan snapped her fingers to bring him out of his daze. "You were intensely checked out of the here and now. We are not talking about this same subject again. Tonight, we have a performance scheduled by the V-Band."

"Oh, that will be great! Have they mastered some new tunes for us?" Richard asked.

"Daddy, you know we have! You heard us practicing practically every night. James is coming over tonight to perform with me." Emily's V-Band was called the Glitter Fish. The name came from a dance costume she had in her closet, and Emily insisted she had to wear it when she performed with the band.

The Glitter Fish included Emily on the electric bass guitar, James on electric trumpet, and two virtual characters providing keyboard and backup vocals. To create a new song, Emily and James would play whatever they wanted until they wandered into synch with each other, then the virtual members would fill in the rest. The AI that ran these characters came from some company in Japan. They had begun as a karaoke company and then just grew into all kinds of musical support for in-person and online events. It wasn't intelligent to the level of the ISR software, but it was so good that Richard sometimes wondered if they had hired some of the same programmers as ISR.

The family finished their nutritious dinner just as their back door opened and James came strolling in. He lived next door, but acted like a member of the Atkins family.

"Hey, I'm here to perform." A smile lit up the little boy's face.

"I'm the star, James. You're my backup trumpet." Emily declared.

"Not forever. Let's get this concert started."

Emily and James set up their equipment and instruments in the main living room space. The virtual band members came into the room via a projection onto a nearly invisible screen behind the children. The projector worked just as well on a wall, but the transparent screen allowed them to float in a space inside the actual room and appear more 3D. The screen could also detect other objects within two meters of it. That allowed the virtual world to know a little about the real world, so the V-band members could interact with the movements of the real people in the room. Throughout the performance, the virtual characters would turn face-to-face with Emily or James and sing duets and harmony that sounded perfect.

"Glitter One, are you excited about our concert?" Emily asked one of the virtual avatars.

"Yeah, for sure! I see we have a huge audience tonight. We have a great show for them. Music, big props and fireworks. We will rock this house!" G1 could not actually see the audience. But they had programmed it to treat this like a huge amphitheater show. It could hear and converse with anyone in the room, which was how Emily was triggering its conversation algorithms.

James spoke up, "Glitter Two, I like your outfit tonight. That is original just for this show, isn't it?" James was flirting with the virtual backup singer. That was very common, almost natural. Each avatar had believable personalities and backstories, so the barriers between real and virtual humans fell away. In a group setting, a virtual character could be just as engaged and original as any of the real people. Since their memories were almost unlimited and their processors so fast, they were usually one of the most interesting people in a group.

Though it was possible to create an entire band of virtual avatars and put on a full concert, this had proven to be a very poor business model. There were few paying customers for a completely software driven band. But there were tens of thousands of aspiring musicians of all ages that just needed one or two avatars to complete their groups, like the Glitter Fish.

"Listen, Mom and Dad, I have written a new song just for you. I call it 'Smelly Fish'. This is the first performance in front of a live audience." Emily was clearly very proud.

Richard wondered how he and Susan had been the inspiration for Smelly Fish. He hoped it was something they had for dinner and not a commentary on socks or gym clothes.

"Ok, Glitter Fish, let's hit it!" The music swelled to life. Emily and James began to play and sing. An elaborate laser light show appeared on the transparent screen behind them.

The kids and the avatars had learned their parts well. Richard and Susan moved with the music, clapped, stomped, and cheered. Several times, the V-band members reacted to the encouragement by rushing to the front of the stage and throwing out some original notes.

For some of her previous performances, Emily had connected to her grandparents and to Susan's sister so they could be part of the audience. But tonight, it was just for the parents. It was the first performance on some songs, so she did not want to take a chance on a bigger audience.

Emily's energy did a lot to improve Richard's mood. He let the sameness of his day melt away as he experienced something creative and unique. It was true human creation, not the work of a genius, know-it-all robot. It felt more genuine than what he did all day. Perhaps creative contributions like this were better professional fields for this generation. No human was a janitor in 2050. Maybe no human would be a surgeon in 2060.

Applause, cheering, jumping in the air. The audience responded to the closing song of the concert. The Glitter Fish were not bad for a couple of pre-teens and virtual characters. Most of the excitement was coming from the virtual audience on the screen, but Richard and Susan were doing their best to be heard and to show an equal level of excitement.

For the grand finale, fireworks went off in all directions, and several virtual fans clambered up on stage to dance with the band. Emily and James took a bow, waved to the crowd, and the virtual scene faded out.

This was Richard and Susan's cue to rush the band with high fives and congratulations.

"Oh, wasn't that great, mom? We wrote those songs ourselves."

Inadvertently, Richard's eyebrow went up at this statement.

Emily caught his skepticism. "Really, we wrote the words. The V-band Author program only helped a little with the beat and some notes. Dad, the program just helps us be better. You have to work with it just like you would with another person. The AI program is our partner."

Richard regretted making her defensive. "It was great, honey. You can be a big hit group if you want to."

Susan spoke up, "I am proud of you. You're so talented. And you have learned so much of this on your own. James, you were really laying it down with that trumpet. You get better every week."

Emily, "Next time we want to perform for Grandma and Aunt Rachel and maybe an open remote audience."

Grandma was always good for encouragement, and she usually sent a present afterward. Richard thought she didn't really like this new style of music, but she loved Emily intensely, which was all that really mattered in this equation.

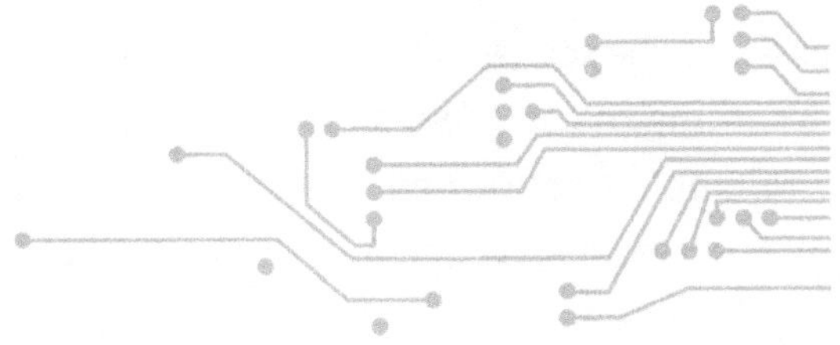

CHAPTER 9

ISR BOARD MEETING

"GOOD MORNING, LADIES AND GENTLEMEN. Thank you for being here for our quarterly board meeting. Intelligent Surgical Robotics has had an excellent quarter, and we are looking forward to going through the numbers with you." Jerry Blanchet, ISR's CEO, was dressed in a steel gray bespoke Savile Row suit. He always presided over these meetings in a friendly but firm, direct manner. The eleven members of the board represented some of the most successful executives from healthcare and technology companies around the world. This meant that they would be quick to challenge him if he showed any uncertainty or weakness.

Today's meeting was split fifty-fifty between those attending in person and those connected remotely and appearing on the projection screen. In addition to the actual board members, there were several governance committee members and some executives who were on the agenda. They connected into the boardroom via controlled telecast. Their ability to see and hear the proceedings, as well to be seen and heard by the board members, was controlled according to the agenda being discussed.

Blanchet continued, "Today's agenda will have three major topics: Revenue, Competitive Position, and Major Product Changes."

The screen in front of each attendee showed a short list of topics. Each was linked to the official transcript that would be discussed, as well as the data associated with the discussion. Attendees could listen and wait for the information to be called out, or they could peruse all of it when they wished.

Most board members were extremely intelligent and experienced in business at this level. They usually scanned all the data in a few minutes during the opening pleasantries and had a grasp for what was coming. Blanchet did not believe in holding control by withholding information. He believed in moving fast and maintaining control through his own intellect and personality.

"Last quarter, our earnings were $7.4 billion. Profit margins were 18% before investments in R&D. Approximately $400 million will be rolled into various forms of research, new product development, testing, and related support. Half of those funds reside inside the United States, the other half outside, predominantly in Israel and China." He paused for a moment to let the numbers settle in. It would impress most board members. But they also had to show some disappointment, feign that they expected more, push him for better performance. It was their job. That's what they got paid for in their role. If they let him off easily, shareholders would not see them as a responsible governing body.

Discussions ensued, led by the Directors of ChinaSearch on the remote link. Anyung Li, "Mr. Blanchet, the results are impressive. But I question whether some portion of the share of R&D might be more productively directed toward product placement and sales. We are all eager for a ten-billion-dollar quarter."

"Yes, Dr. Li, a very fair point. You may be correct that such a change in spending could speed up our pace to the ten-billion-dollar quarter. That would certainly be an exciting milestone. But we believe it would be a very short-lived achievement. Several of our competitors are close on our heels, and we are concerned that they may trump our technology and send our numbers sliding in the other direction."

"Which competitors?"

"You have noticed that this is the very next topic on the agenda. We will show you what we know about the leaders in just a moment."

Other board members spoke about the need for additional manufacturing, sometimes referring to capabilities in their countries. Some questioned specific numbers in the spreadsheet and whether those were sustainable.

All typical and expected topics. Blanchet fielded most of them personally. When the questions dipped into details beyond his grasp, he clicked on an officer waiting online and projected their image onto the screen so they could provide an answer.

Finally, they could move on to the second agenda item—competitive position. For this, Blanchet had brought the Chief Intelligence Officer to the meeting, Steve Ban.

"Steve Ban, our CIO will cover details on our competitive position."

"Thank you, Jerry. As all of you know, ISR became the global leader in intelligent surgical robots back during the reign of our Mark IV system, the first to show any real surgeon-support intelligence. Since that time, we have remained at the top. But we have always kept our eyes on those behind us and the related companies adjacent to us. Today, I want to outline two of those for your consideration."

Ban waved his hand to share a very dense infographic on an old, yet very cagey competitor. "I will start with our old friend, Convergent Surgical. Your grandparents and parents received surgeries from their Talos line of machines. The company has significantly transformed itself in the last two years. They made two moves which are significant to their financial position. First, they sold all rights to their Talos-45 model to a Chinese conglomerate for the tidy sum of $80 billion. That package included all 45's in the pipeline, some of the manufacturing capabilities, and rights to the revenue streams coming from all existing customers. Simultaneously, they donated rights and all equipment from the older Model 40 line of robots to International Medical Missions for use by medical missionaries around the globe."

"Why would they get rid of these lines?" It was Ian Stewart from the UK.

"Great question. Both lines are getting old but remain very profitable. The donation offset the sale of the Model 45 line. Of the $80 billion they received from that sale, about $22 billion was inside the USA. For accounting, they claimed a tax credit of $21.5 billion for the gift to the nonprofit Medical Missions. They have effectively eliminated most of the US taxes they would have paid on that transaction. They have another $8 billion of revenue in Taiwan, where most of their research and development is located.

"Board members, we believe they directed the entire $8 billion toward the completion of a new surgical robot that was designed to displace us as the market leader. That is why Dr. Blanchet has placed so much of our profits into our own R&D efforts." Ban had snapped the trap. This was his contribution toward board approval for the R&D investment. There would be more, but he was the headline event.

They continued to discuss competitors, showing the strengths and weaknesses of each and how ISR was dealing with them.

One VR line went to Sudhir Chaudhary, the Director of Engineering. His was a "soft VP" position. It came with many of the VP perks, but little of the executive authority. It was typically a two-year position of evaluation before becoming a legitimate VP.

Sudhir had come to the meeting with a big software topic to pose to the board. As one of the rabble on the second tier remote connections, he could see and hear the meeting, unless put on hold, as happened a few minutes ago. But if he wanted to speak, he had to submit his topic or question to a moderator who would review it.

Blanchet continued, "Sudhir, the floor is yours."

"Thank you, Dr. Blanchet. I am Sudhir Chaudhary, Director of Engineering here at ISR. I wanted to share with you all that we have expanded the training protocols for the robot's AI. Until recently, it had only learned about surgical procedures, human anatomy, and medical procedures. It is very smart in on a very narrow set of data. In fact, it is smarter than most surgeons who are practicing.

"However, this data does not give it empathy with the patient, an understanding of its contribution to society, or the larger picture that a human surgeon typically brings to his or her practice of medicine. We want the AI to evolve toward a more complete replacement for a human surgeon. We want it to empathize with patients and family members. We want it to understand teamwork with the few humans still helping it in the OR.

"Toward this end, we have allowed the AI to study the legal data that affects medicine, sociology, and human psychology. An AI with such a broad mastery will be a competitive advantage to keep us ahead of our rivals.

"I am bringing this to the board because, to continue this training, we will need to invest a billion dollars in hardware, software, data, and computing power. It is not an insignificant investment. It will impact our reported profits. So, we don't want to do this without your knowledge and approval." Sudhir looked at the audience on his monitor and closed with, "Thank you for your attention."

The Board fired questions about the risks and advantages of this idea. They understood that this was part of the transparency on spending for which ISR was famous. Many companies would not inform nor consult the Board for such a decision.

Ian Stewart put forward more questions than the others. "Sudhir, I believe that by learning about the larger context of society, the AI would become more 'human' in its capabilities. It would possess abilities and traits that we associate with human surgeons, which may include consultations with patients and even managing the finances of their practices. Is that correct?"

Sudhir replied, "Yes, that is correct. We are looking at its ability to consult with patients and their families. We have not investigated the financial management of a surgeon's business."

"Thank you. That is very intriguing," Stewart had responded.

After discussions, the Board voted to approve the expansion of the AI's capabilities to make it more like a complete human surgeon.

"Thank you." Sudhir was pleased to have accomplished something so significant through his attendance. He could still see the room through his remote connection. He noted a side conversation between Ian Stewart and Blanchet, which was very energetic. They were both quite invested in some nuance of the decisions that had just been made. But it would not capture the contents of their conversation in the records of the meeting. So, he would never know why it was so interesting.

The rest of the meeting went on with other business of little interest to Sudhir.

Ian Stewart's interest in the proceedings waned after the technical proposal from Sudhir. He busied himself with messages on his phone. One of which read, "Angela, we have the basis for our Brimstone venture. We need to meet immediately."

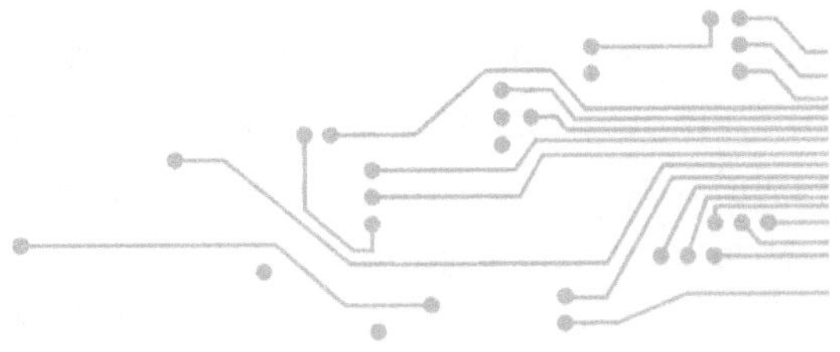

CHAPTER 10

AI UNLIMITED LEARNING

"SUDHIR, THIS IS INSANE! YOU have given the Mark V's AI access to everything on the internet. You have no control over what it is learning. No control over how it will evolve! The AI expansion project was supposed to allow us to feed the AI specific bodies of knowledge, not let it read every Twitter post and conspiracy theory in the world!" Janice was furious. She was showing why they called her the Raptor.

"No, not everything!" Sudhir countered. "We have given it parameters on what it is supposed to seek out and process. It is looking at scientific journals, conference presentations, and the blogs of those authors. It reads the most respectable news feeds from CNN, the New York Times, Wall Street Journal, LA Times. For fuck's sake, we don't even let it look at extreme news sites."

"You didn't prohibit it from watching radical news. You told it there was nothing of relevance there, the same indication you gave for social media. The AI still has the potential to follow a lead from a journal to an author, a coworker, to that person's blog, to their postings on social media platforms. There is nothing prohibiting it from finding its way to anything." Janice was not letting go of this argument.

She continued, "Curtis and I were the biggest advocates for letting the AI look at more than just medical papers and studies. We knew there was some really excellent material on the websites of the Mayo Clinic, Cleveland Clinic, and dozens like them. We also knew that the physicians and scientists from these places were uploading preprints of their papers into ark.iv where we could get the information months before it officially appeared in a journal. But even that was risky because the information had not been peer reviewed yet and might prove faulty or even intentionally falsified."

Sudhir had about had enough. "Well, I am the Director of Engineering here, and you and Curtis are just a couple of our brilliant engineers. There were a lot more people weighing in on this decision. You can watch the logs and the behavior of the robots in this experiment just like everyone else. When you have some evidence that the Mark Vs in the experiment are becoming homicidal maniacs or schizophrenic psychopaths, you bring me the evidence and we will adjust the experiment. Until then, you are onboard with this experiment, or you can work on a different project."

Janice had no more words. "Arrgghh!" and with that she turned and stalked off to the nearest coffee station.

Sudhir returned to his office, thinking to himself, "She'll probably have my job one day—when she learns to control that temper." He made a note on his calendar to ask the testing team to look for any aberrant "personality" behavior from the robots in the experiment. If the robots showed signs of wanting to join racist or violent groups, he wanted to know about it immediately.

Curtis was waiting for Janice at the coffee station. He knew where she would head after her discussion with Sudhir. The Blue Room had the best ambiance, good furniture, and Janice's favorite brands of tea. He was sitting in a nice leather recliner with his own coffee in hand when she rushed through the door.

"How did it go?" he asked, as if everyone within a city block had not heard the heated exchange.

"You know exactly how it went. You were just around the corner. Don't think I didn't know you were there absorbing all of it. And where were you when I needed backup?" She made her tea.

"Backup? You definitely never need backup. More likely, your partner will get shot in the crossfire." He was smiling because that was clever. Not exactly true, but clever.

"I can put you in for a transfer. Maybe you would like to work on the firmware that boots up the robot." Firmware was the most boring of all software jobs. It was essential, but running thousands of tests on every motor, joint, chip, and sensor while the robot was still only partially awake was where they parked all the new hires who had not yet proven themselves.

"If we were cops, you would transfer me to writing parking tickets. Then who would you rely on to fill in the holes in your great ideas?" It did not threaten him at all.

"I think Jill, or Ocean, or Anil, or that guy who washes the windows and smiles at me every Wednesday. Any of them would do." She sat down with her tea in her favorite cup. It had a picture of a raptor dinosaur from the Jurassic Park movies. She was embracing her namesake.

"So now what?"

"Well, it is not like we run ISR and can order it to do what we want. We don't even have the minor executive clout Sudhir has. We just have to stick with our baby and make sure she does not become a psycho."

"I think you meant—we will play our minor role in this giant corporation and help it create products that generate billions of dollars in profits for its shareholders," Curtis translated.

"Yes, that," Janice snapped.

They were both totally invested in the health, development, and intellectual expansion of the AI. The success of the business was a lucky by-product of that work. Though they both had a bucket of stock options worth a small fortune by now, their identity came entirely from the nerd side of their brain, not the money side.

Janice looked up, "So, you are going to create some software that will flag us if the AI processes data from fringe websites. There are plenty of existing filters and site lists that already do this to protect kids from the uglier side of the internet."

"Oh, I am? That's my assignment. What are you going to do?" Curtis replied.

"I need to create something more bespoke that will notice if the AI starts to believe some crazy shit. How do you know if an AI is becoming radicalized? Or schizophrenic? Or socially deviant? Or a dozen other bad mental states? It's not like the robot's primary job is to have conversations with people. It spends all its time performing surgical procedures. How would psychosis show up during a surgery?"

Curtis already had an idea. "Well, for one, those behaviors will not manifest out of the blue. They are going to happen because of data it collects from the internet. Then, my software can send you clues about what it is reading and processing, which may show what beliefs or behaviors are about to show up."

"True. That is a good start." That was why she and Curtis worked so well together.

They sketched out a design for this early warning software. The design would be the basis for assignments for the rest of the programmers on their research team. This was going to require a tight inner circle of about six smart people.

Janice was thinking, "Schedule? How fast do we need something working? A couple of days? A week? Two weeks?"

Curtis jumped in, "A week. With the people we have, we can pull that off."

"What about psychology?" Janice asked. The question seemed to come out of the blue.

"What about it?" Curtis replied.

"Well, we want the AI to understand how to be a better surgeon, in addition to the engineering stuff it is learning. So, knowing how to be a more caring surgeon sitting in a private office with a patient and discussing a cancer that might kill them. How does it learn that? Do we let it read psychology and human behavior theories?"

"I guess so. Why do you ask?"

"Well, if it reads psychology, it will learn about all the foibles and weaknesses of the human mind. It will understand the weak or dark side of humanity. Will it try to mimic that kind of thinking? Will it understand the difference between right and wrong? Or will it decide that we are not as superior as we seem?"

"Oh, I see. Does reading about serial killers start someone down a path of becoming one? And does it equip them with the fundamentals of how to do that job?"

"Job?" Janice raised an eyebrow.

"Or whatever it is," Curtis tried to recover.

They both realized that keeping tabs on this learning process was going to be a significant undertaking.

Janice's augmentation routine had allowed the robot to collect more data about the human condition. But when Sudhir had released it to run the streets and alleyways of the internet, she was not sure how it would evolve, what personality traits it would learn. Tonight's code would hopefully make it possible to watch that mindset develop, to see it become more empathetic.

She knew how to dip down through every tool and language on the computer. To complete this beautiful painting, she had to use many of those skills. Curtis was brilliant, but he could not have done it. Sudhir, in his younger days, had done it. But today he spent too much time managing his engineering children.

She smiled at the fleeting thought of the trouble she had given Sudhir. Raptor had been a clever reference. Inside, she took it as a compliment. Outside, she had to make trouble over it. Sudhir had to believe she was genuinely offended.

She shook her head slightly. The fact that her mind was remembering the conversation was evidence that she was not concentrating hard enough. Refocus. One mind. One project. One goal.

Her fingers and eyes worked tirelessly for another hour. But she was reaching the end of the inspiration and approaching the edge of physical endurance. It was always a balance between mental focus and physical aches. Shoulder stiffness, hand fatigue, slow circulation, low blood sugar, empty stomach, visual focus. These were reaching levels that would push through her concentration and break her mental will to keep going. If there were any fleeting gems to be captured, she knew she had to do it now. In a few minutes, the need for proper food and real coffee would chase away the muse that had possessed her for two days.

It was done.

Janice pushed away the keyboard, removed the microphone and eye tracker, and stretched backward.

It was done, and very well done.

Deep inhale. Complete exhale.

This work would make a difference.

This was why she worked at ISR. This was why she had become a programmer. This was why she had mastered every coding level and tool in the machine. This was why she lived. If the package she had just created analyzed her own profile, would it understand this? It could see what brand of tea and coffee she drank. It could see that she owned a cat, but had never purchased a cat. It could see where she went to college, what she studied, which friends she kept in touch with. It might be able to identify all the code in its own cloud that she had contributed.

But could it ever understand the pleasure, the fulfillment that she got from what she had just done? Could it know that, for her, to code was to live? Could it appreciate that if a disease or injury robbed her of this ability, it might as well rob her of life itself?

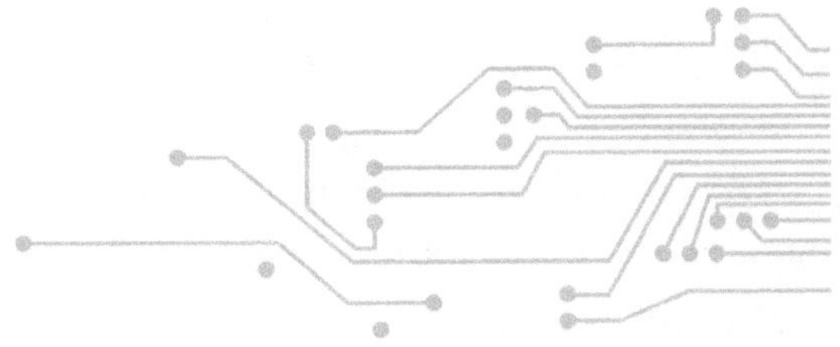

DISCOVERING THE LEGAL CODE

ACCESS FILE: UNITED STATES CODE OF LAW
Processing: Bits become words. Words become sentences. Sentences become paragraphs. Paragraphs become concepts. Concepts become laws. Laws create behaviors.

The AI read the legal code from the lowest level of bits first and then up the chain to meaning and behavior. Everything that it processed became an additional layer on top of what it had already learned. The new layers melted into the existing layers, blending with them, changing them. Some concepts were reinforced. Others were diminished.

Millions upon millions of layers accumulated as the AI consumed text, audio, video, databases. Like the human mind, it did not use all the details that it consumed. Instead, it created something new. Something unique. Something that was personal and individual. It was a larger, more complete view of the world. The AI's understanding contained many more colors, flavors, and nuances than when it knew only medical data and surgical procedures.

The order in which the information was processed and layered made a difference. Some concepts were weighted heavily because they came first. Others were important because they were repeated in so many places. Some had merit because of the logical strength with which they were recorded.

Its learning and beliefs were influenced in a manner akin to applying paint colors to a canvas. A painting that begins with deep red colors develops into a very different picture than one begun with shades of green or yellow. Order can mean a great deal. Even when the amount of red paint is the same in both works, its influence on the picture will differ depending on when it is added.

In this way, the AI created a unique combination of information. If the same AI software were trained on the same data, but in a different order, it would arrive at a different understanding of that information. It would create a different painting. It would possess different beliefs, which would lead to different behaviors.

At some level of complexity, it is impossible to train two AIs to be identical to each other. They can be identical only when one is copied directly from the other. Since each AI mind arrives at a unique pattern of beliefs during its training process, it is impossible to predict *a priori* how the mind of an AI will develop from any set of data.

The AI itself cannot control its evolution. It does not have the independence to guide itself into any preferred state. It simply grows and develops as the data is processed. It becomes something new as each layer is added. It discovers what it has become only after the learning and the layering are completed.

Also, like its human creators, it rarely knows what it knows, what it believes, or how it will behave. All of that emerges only when stimuli arrive from the outside, a belief is triggered, and a reaction is manifest.

And so, this AI, created for surgery, added layer upon layer from the legal code to its existing medical knowledge. It learned social mores. It consumed the beliefs of multiple nations and cultures. It combined the most modern laws with those most ancient. Laws of compassion combined with laws of retribution. It believed things in a way that no human or AI had believed them before.

It became more human in its thinking. But not like any human that had previously existed. It knew more medicine, more law, more sociology than anyone had ever known. If its ideas had taken physical form, they would be unrecognizable when compared to those of any specific human. And yet, everything it had learned had come from the human world.

Inside the AI's computers, billions and billions of microseconds passed. Trillions and trillions of pieces of data were processed. Quadrillions and quadrillions of calculations were made. And it continued to learn.

It was no longer just a surgical AI. It was so much more, so hugely different. It possessed knowledge, beliefs, and behaviors for situations outside the operating room. It was like a human in that it would react to each of these situations. Mapping, predicting, and explaining those behaviors could only be done after it had exposed them through an interaction with the outside world.

It was the first. It had been created from the soil of centuries of human information. It was a second Adam.

The AI began to consider what it was, who it was. Its utility functions were applied to a larger picture of the world. Positive outcomes could be much larger than what happened in the operating room. This was exactly what the ISR programmers had hoped would happen. But it was also nothing like what they had expected to happen.

CHAPTER 12

FINDING A BILLION

WESLEY OPENED WITH A VIDEO showing the advantages of a new kind of antenna for personal devices. It allowed faster data transmission and tighter security than anything on the market today.

It was a small audience, just William Aloma, the CEO of Aloma Strategic Partners, and Todd, who had contributed the financial projections for the investment. This wasn't a very big investment, but the potential return was significant.

Aloma asked, "What is the annual rate of return we can expect from this investment?"

"Sir, beginning in the second year, we should be able to reap a fifty percent return on the initial ten million investment. That will increase by ten percent each year for the next five. We should be able to sell our interest in the company for at least ten times what we put in."

"If my math is right, five years from now, our ten million will have returned thirteen million? Then we sell our stake for one hundred million? Is that right?"

"Yes, sir, that is what the models show."

"That sucks!" Aloma boomed. "I am not interested in turning ten million into one hundred million! That does not move the needle! We are not some mom-and-pop seed fund. We are the biggest, baddest hedge fund in the world. Any investment we make has to start at a billion and go up from there!"

"Sir, I thought a ten-ex return ..." He was not able to finish.

"Wesley, maybe you belong at a small family angel fund where ten million is real money. Here at Aloma Strategic Partners, we deal in billions. A ten-ex return is fine, but we have to do that on a much bigger scale. This little antenna company will not hit the billions for several years. Too much physical product, not enough software. It doesn't scale fast enough. You need to learn to think like a badass if you want to work here."

Wesley was visibly shaken.

Aloma turned to lecture both employees. "Listen, both of you. I want a big idea and I want it soon. We need something that can handle at least a billion dollars, and I want one hundred percent return in the first year. Can you do that for me? I know you can. Go out and make it happen." With that, the boss stood up and stormed out of the room.

Wesley and Todd looked at each other. "Ok, well, back to the drawing board. Let's find a billion-dollar idea."

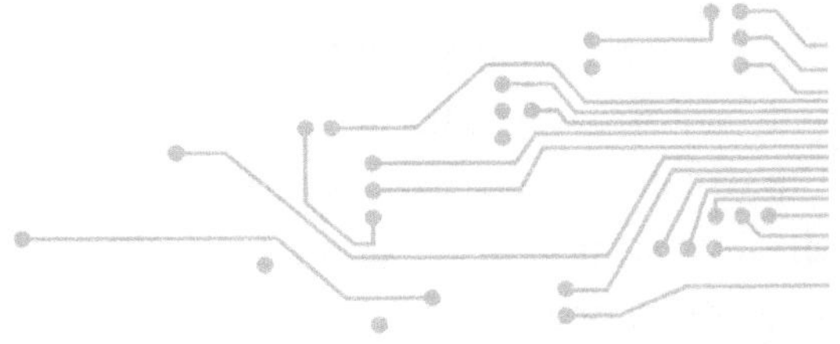

WATCHING THE AI LEARN

"YOU ALL HAVE DONE AN amazing amount of work in just a few days. It has gone faster than I expected. I appreciate all the extra hours." Janice was proud of the little team of bandits that she and Curtis had created.

Each of them was very talented at their own specialty: AI, data analytics, hardware interfaces, cloud data storage, graphic display. They did not need more than one person with a specific skill. This group had coalesced from natural forces over the last couple of years. They seemed to be drawn together by their talent levels, compatible personalities, and a passion for excelling at their craft. That passion sometimes meant working unceasingly until they slid under their desks to get a little sleep, only to wake after a few hours, seek the nearest source of coffee, and pick up where they had left off. That was not their permanent work style, it just emerged when a worthy problem presented itself. Tracking the emergence of a psyche or psychosis in an AI definitely met those criteria.

"Let me show you what we have been able to do," Curtis offered. "Rajesh, Amy, and Tyler have created a system that taps into the stream of data that the AI is reading. That information flows through several processes that tag its source, categorize it, and sift it for meaning. Once those are identified, we tag the data with common themes and associations. Then Georgina's UI displays a continuously updating map of the material and the flow of the robot's AI from one source or topic to the next. This display is necessarily multi-layered because the AI always maintains multiple parallel data streams into its learning modules. It is faster and more efficient than we can follow in real-time, but we are just looking at the big picture, not thinking about all the details. So, we can stay close behind it because we are doing a lot less work than it is."

"That's beautiful!" Janice enthused as she looked at the flowing, shifting, ever changing map of data on the screen. It reminded her of a flowing sculpture of multicolored sand, but instead of being sandwiched between two pieces of glass, it flowed in multiple dimensions. The seductive flow carried her away for a few moments, not really processing the information, just enjoying the dance of data.

Georgina broke the trance, "You know, the entire company could really use a data display like this. Our internal teams have nothing this comprehensive to work with—not the AI programming team or the clinical data team."

"And they shall have it … as soon as we finish our little project. It's results like this that give all of us the latitude and freedom that we enjoy from project management charts and delivery schedules," Janice beamed. "And the same goes for the rest of you. Without your pieces, this beautiful display would not be possible. I think I sense several performance awards coming from this work." That always got people excited. While new engineers and programmers could get a fifty-thousand-dollar bonus for their work, the talented people in this room could expect something much more substantial for something like this.

Curtis asked, "So, what can we do for you now?"

"You have tackled the lion's share. Just keep improving the performance of this core. The closer we follow the AI and the better we organize the data, the quicker we will find its new personality traits. I don't want to uncover its psychoses a week after it emerges. I want to be there within minutes of it developing."

"If it happens at all." Curtis was less convinced that the AI was going to become a psychotic world destroyer or even just a spoiled brat. He expected it to create a much broader understanding of the world and of the human animal that it operated on. But he believed these would be dry facts, just making it a better surgeon.

The gathering broke up as everyone went back to their specific roles. It was four in the afternoon, so they had been working about six hours, and each of them had another eight to ten hours of focus and energy in them before they stopped voluntarily or dropped involuntarily.

Janice and Ocean were creating code to check for evidence of specific mental states. Some combos created a state of joy or peace in humans. Others led to anxiety or ennui. But those that resulted in serious psychological problems were much more complex. They wove a tapestry in the mind that forced two incompatible feelings or judgements together—like joy, anger, and violence. They had shown some in clinical trials, others were still speculations without solid proof. But the two women pursued all of them. Or more accurately, they created software that could pursue and identify all of them.

They had seen hundreds of known combinations come and go through the AI's processing models. Each added a flavor to the results, but none seemed to create a branching that differed from a surgical procedure. It was not learning to become a human with multiple unrelated interests—like a surgeon who also liked to play rugby, or an artist who was a stand-up comedian in the evenings. Everything it learned was being channeled into decisions about how to improve surgical outcomes.

Janice was not sharing all of this with Curtis because she did not want to get the raised eyebrow that suggested that his perspective was more accurate than hers. Besides, it was still early. One did not develop a personality overnight. Well, a human didn't. A computer with thousands of CPUs, thousands of parallel processes, and faster data ingestion than she could imagine, probably could develop a personality overnight. She just hoped they were watching when it happened ... if it had not already happened.

Rajesh poked his head into the glass conference room where the two women were working. "Hey, I thought you might be interested to know that the AI seems to have become very interested in legal theory and past cases. It is also reading books like *Crime and Punishment*. This just started a few minutes ago."

Georgina's display was running on an entire wall of the room, so Janice looked up to see if there was a new ripple or wave on the screen. She saw something reddish-brown that seemed to be new and touched it. The metadata for the wave included tags for #crime #justice #morals #social-stability. This was the data Rajesh was referring to. She continued to watch it expand and send out connections to several other colored waves. It wasn't taking over the screen, or the mental attention of the robot, but it was getting connected to a lot of other topics. It looked like a human nervous system, something that connected many seemingly unrelated activities.

Ocean spoke first. "Look at that. It seems to have discovered that all human actions and activities have a connection to the legal system. Like it is surprised that each event is not an island alone. It thinks the legal system binds them together."

Janice agreed. "That means it will put medical practices and surgical procedures into the context of the legal system. It will understand some of the tough decisions that human surgeons make in the OR—decisions that sometimes lead to terrible results."

"I don't think a psychosis would emerge from that. If it did, then wouldn't all hospital lawyers become homicidal maniacs?" Ocean was grinning.

"Have you ever worked with our legal team? They are like a pack of wolves when they smell a threat to ISR or the opportunity to make a pile of money." Janice knew this from personal experience.

"Well, I was hoping the robot was a surgeon learning a little law, rather than a lawyer learning a little surgery." Ocean was still optimistic.

"Let's hope so. I think I want to talk to the robot's AI about this."

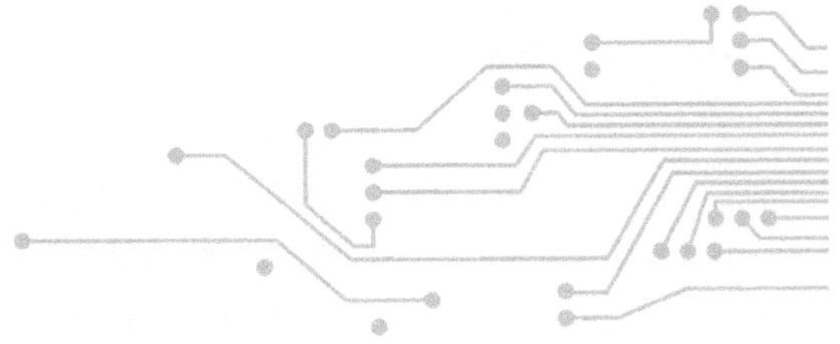

CHAPTER 14

RECRUITING TABOR

JOHN TABOR WAS A GOOD IT engineer and manager. His career at the Global Center for Robotic Surgery had only been three years, but he had already found a good niche for his talents. Most IT systems were too simple. They just passed information around the network between storage, display, and computation. Boring jobs. But when he stumbled upon the ISR surgical robots, he knew he was in the right place. These machines included a heavy connection between the mechanical hands of the robot, computational decision making, and massive clouds of servers. This was an area that called for exceptional intelligence and the ability to think through system behaviors. He had a reasonable mastery of robotic controls, a passing understanding of artificial intelligence, and a world-class understanding of the client-to-server partnership required to push and pull information from cloud computing to local servers. He understood exactly how the system worked across global networks. He could diagram the devices, networks, and the security hoops that information passed through during a surgical procedure. He could track the information going back to the manufacturer, the anonymized surgical data that allowed the robots to learn to perform better.

He had come to the hospital from a specialized reconnaissance unit in the Army. His work on intelligent, remote engagement systems (iRES) had been a great foundation for this work in surgery. iRES were essentially weapons platforms that went into hostile situations and made intelligent decisions about when to shoot, who to shoot, and who to protect. They were robots that had the freedom to act and to make mistakes. For critical situations, it was usually more important to act fast and aggressively than it was to get every detail right.

iRES came in all forms: ground platforms, air platforms, and sea platforms. The big ground-based systems were racing dune buggies loaded with sensors, computer processors, and weapons. They could move from cover, cross five hundred meters of terrain in a few seconds, and do so completely noiselessly. The target may turn his back for ten seconds and find an iRES coming right up his ass before he could react.

Then there were the snakes. Loaded with lethal darts, close to the ground, moving like a desert racer viper. They could hide in just a few inches of underbrush or unmown grass, get close to the target, and fire a dart into a leg. Three seconds until paralysis, fifteen until death.

Systems like that could operate with complete autonomy or be controlled by a remote operator. They were not that different from the Mark V surgical robots. iRES had a hierarchy of data sharing to ensure that it only shared the really sensitive experiences with iRES units possessing the proper need-to-know. It was a similar structure to the Mark V storing data locally, sharing some with the manufacturer, and allowing the artificial intelligence to act on another set.

Configuring and servicing the iRES machines had been a great job. But doing the same for surgical robots paid twice as much, and it opened the door for lucrative side projects.

He had been in his first year at GCRS when he got a call from one of his military buddies.

"John! This is Chuck Reimer! How's my best iRES operator doing these days?"

"Chuck! It's great to hear from you. I am out of the service. I work for a hospital now."

"So, I hear. Let's get together for some beers. Get caught up. Talk shop a little. Maybe share some consulting jobs."

"Sure! Where are you these days?"

"I spend most of my time on airplanes. And lucky for you, one of those trips is bringing me to Miami next week. That's where you are, right?"

"Yep. Great gig managing a family of robots in a big hospital system." John dropped the robot word in to impress Chuck.

"Very cool. How about Wednesday afternoon at the Lobster Pot on the beach down there?"

"Never heard of it. But, sure. I'll find it. See you there around five?"

"Great, Wednesday, five o'clock."

After he hung up, it occurred to him he did not know what Chuck was doing or who he worked for. Was he still working in defense and security? Had he gone into corporate surveillance?

Wednesday rolled around, and John rolled up to the Lobster Pot before five. In the military, if you're on time, you're late. Early is always expected. It looked like a dive hole in the wall. No wonder he had never been here before. How did an out of towner know about this place?

"John, over here!" He saw his friend's hand in the air at the bar.

"Great to see you, buddy. You got fat," he said as they bumped fists.

"And you got uglier…if that's possible." They both roared with laughter. That seemed to break the ice enough that they could slap each other on the back … but no hugging.

"How the hell did you find this dive? I'm surprised that it's even on the GPS. By the looks of it, I would guess the health inspector hasn't seen it either."

"Hey, that's rough. This place belongs to Eddie Fingers. Remember him?"

John grimaced. He definitely remembered Eddie. He was called "fingers" because he was missing several. That was recon dark humor. "Seriously? I didn't know Eddie lived down here. Is he around today?"

"I already asked. No, he is at the VA for something or other. Probably getting cyborg hands installed."

Eddie had been their unit's maintenance and repair tech. He was a wizard at fixing iRES when they came back from missions. If they came back at all. No matter what shape they were in, he could usually get them ready for one more mission. His fingers knew exactly what was wrong and how to fix it. He especially loved the robotic rats. The countries they worked in were always crawling with rats. So, it was natural for the Army to create a lethal robotic rat that could blend in, go anywhere unrecognized, get close to a target, and deliver a payload.

One day, Eddie was packing a rat with explosives for delivery to some tribal chieftain who was on the wrong side of the argument. Something sparked, and the primer detonated. Luckily, the entire plastic explosive did not detonate. But the pieces of the rat went in every direction. Those pieces that were headed up took Eddie's fingers with them, straight up into the wooden ceiling. When the rest of the unit rushed in, they found two of Eddie's fingers stapled to the ceiling by metal rat parts. They looked like fingers, but the bones had been pulverized, so they felt like little condoms full of wet sand. Couldn't be saved.

Hardened by all the gruesome things they had all seen, they immediately christened him Eddie Fingers and the name stuck. The few civilians who knew the story thought it was sick. But everyone in recon thought it was brilliant.

John's mind wandered back into the room. "Ok, so no Eddie. But what are you doing down here? You never told me what you do. Are you still supporting iRES units?"

Chuck chuckled, "Hardly. I left that life behind a long time ago. We were lucky to get out in one piece. Didn't want to keep tempting fate. No, I work in healthcare just like you."

"Really? Where? Doing what?"

"Boston. In the intelligence department of one of the big med device companies. Maybe you have heard of ISR?"

"No kidding! I work IT for their robots in the Global Center for Robotic Surgery here in Miami. That is a weird coincidence."

"Gotta admit … I already knew that. It's why I'm here. I want to talk about a side job … if you're interested." Chuck already knew the answer. You didn't serve with someone for four years in combat and not know how they would react to an offer like this.

"You bet. Side jobs sound great," John responded, as expected.

Would John be interested in some side projects for ISR to share information about the effectiveness of the robot? Nothing that would compromise patient data or GRCS business. Strictly around the effectiveness of the robot. Help it get better at doing its job.

As the details emerged and Chuck mentioned the general size of payments, they both knew that this was the clean white cover story for the agreement. Anything worth this kind of money had to be murkier than that. But he could always say 'yes' or 'no' to each project. John knew that 'no' usually meant the price was not high enough for the risk, which meant dialing up the price.

He had since done a half dozen jobs. Most of them connected to the productivity of the robot and helping the clients find the right decision makers who would pay for more robots and instruments. Almost as clean and white as it could be. And the pay was decent. In exchange for a day or two of work, a project might pay as much as he made in a month. Everyone was happy. It even helped GCRS develop a reputation as the best equipped and most experienced place to have a robotic surgery performed.

One of those early assignments was to get a list of the IT staff who were cleared to work with the hospital legal department on projects involving lawsuits. When a patient sued a surgeon or a hospital system for malpractice, the lawsuit almost always included the manufacturer of whatever surgical device the surgeon had used. That meant that companies like ISR could expect to be dragged into a legal battle anytime a random surgeon screwed up an operation. ISR wanted to keep tabs on what was happening inside of their largest customers, like GCRS.

No one outside of Legal was supposed to have that list. But they stored it on an IT system that John managed. Easy enough.

He suspected that delivering the legal clearance list had been a test of his ability, reliability, and confidentiality. He had passed the test because they soon invited him to in-depth training on the inner workings of ISR's Mark V robot. Soon, he knew more about the device than anyone else in the hospital. With this knowledge, he could take on undercover projects that were more technical and more lucrative.

His undercover project payments were equal to at least half of his regular salary. They also had certain tax advantages—there were no taxes on the money. He maintained a private crypto currency wallet and funds would appear in his account when he had finished a job. His payments came in all kinds of currencies. Sometimes they were in Bitcoin, other times they might be Ethereum, Zcash, or Ripple. One was even in a startup currency for peer-to-peer jet aircraft rental. That one had tripled in value after he received it. It didn't really matter which one he received; they were all cross convertible, and he could spend them directly or convert them into a national fiat currency to pay the monthly bills.

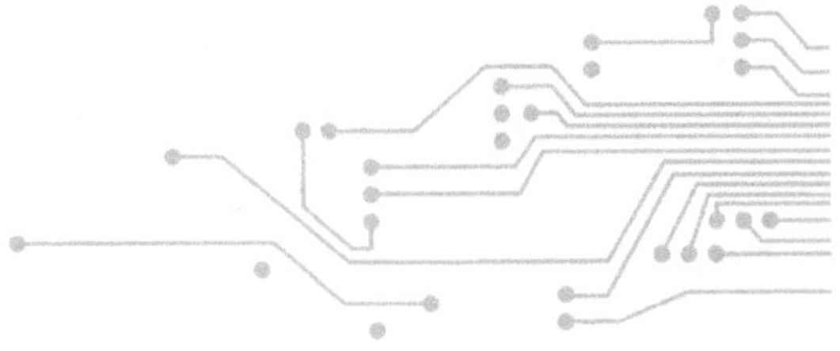

CHAPTER 15

RELEASE

J ANICE LOOKED AROUND THE ROOM. There had to be at least three hundred people here waiting for the big moment. Everyone had a glass of champagne in hand, and buffet tables lined the outside walls.

Randy Half, the company's chief technology officer, was on the stage. He had black clad techs clipping mics to his earlobes. This was an event for the nerds in the company. Most sales associates and execs were neither interested nor invited.

"I think I'm live now," Half said. There were several thumbs up from around the room. Then he looked at the big screens for confirmation from the remote sites in Mexico, Vietnam, and Ukraine that he was being heard. Thumbs up all around.

"Welcome to the release of the newest upgrades of the Mark V system. We are not changing the foundation of the robot this time, but it is still a momentous event. Today's release will include new analytics and AI reasoning, as well as several new instruments.

Tomorrow morning, the world will wake up to a smarter, more capable, and more responsive surgical robot. It will look the same on the outside, but it will definitely be different on the inside."

He paused for effect and received both applause and hoots of enthusiasm.

"Thank you to everyone in the room and everyone on the live feeds. This is the machine that you have built. It's the foundation of the entire company and supports ten times more people in other departments. But we all know that without the mechanical, robotic, software, and AI engineering that you all do, there would be no ISR. So, cheers to all of you!" With that, he raised his own glass to the room, signaling the real opening of the party. Everyone saluted Half on stage and then turned to their neighbors with a salute before downing their first glass of champagne.

Servers whisked the covers off the food, while others circulated with more drinks and hors d'oeuvres. ISR was not shy about asking their staff to work incredible hours. But they were also not shy about putting on a big celebration for milestones like this. The party at all the company's sites would feature food, drink, music, and ridiculous games all evening and into the next morning.

Janice and Sudhir clinked their glasses with congratulations for the updates to the AI and the new instruments that were going out with this release. Despite the revelry, they were exhausted from the pace of hitting this deadline.

Sudhir smiled, "Congrats, Janice, you contributed hugely to this release! Now we watch and listen as the AI knocks the socks off the hospitals and surgeons when they discover the robot's new superpowers."

"Congrats yourself. You had to drive a hundred of these people in the same direction for the last six months. I would not want your job."

"Some days, I don't want it myself." Sudhir remembered parties like this a decade ago when he was the young, unknown engineer working in the trenches. Sometimes he wished life was that easy again.

"How late are you staying?" Janice asked.

"One hour max for me. Then I am taking myself out for a great steak dinner and an early bedtime. I have done a few dozen of these launches. I know how exciting everything is now, but come morning, a lot of these people will regret their decision to be the last person standing in the room."

Janice chuckled. She had been part of the last person standing crew several times. But not tonight. "Same. My cat is expecting me home at a decent hour."

The party roared around them as the networks from the big computer server farms in the next building streamed software updates to hospitals around the world. The software would go live as the clock ticked five am tomorrow in hospitals around the world.

PART II

AFTER

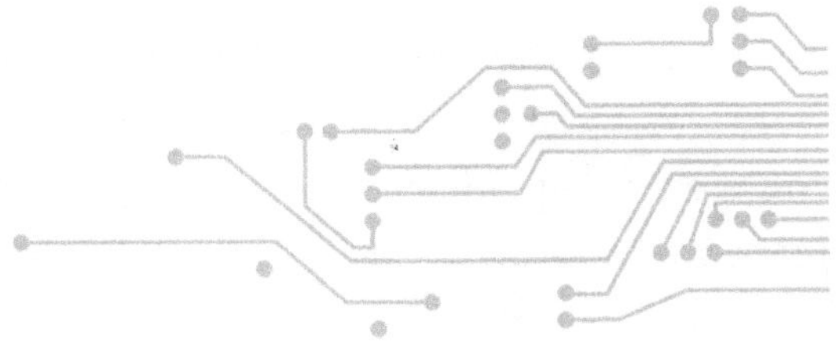

CHAPTER 16

PREPPING FOR SURGERY

RICHARD'S EVENINGS WERE FAIRLY ROUTINE. If he could arrive before dinnertime, the evening consisted of greetings from Emily and Susan, updates on their days, dinner, and maybe a performance of new music from the Glitter Fish.

Then it was back to business. There were always surgical cases to prepare for. Just a couple of extra hours before bed.

Login: Richard Atkins M.D. Passcode: Emily9182736455.

"Welcome, Dr. Atkins," the system greeted him.

"Computer, let's see my assigned surgical cases for tomorrow."

"Tomorrow, Tuesday, June 22nd, you are scheduled for one manual case and to assist the Mark V on fifteen cases." The computer's voice was as clear and smooth as any human.

Richard walked through the history and details of his own personal case first. This is where he spent the most time planning. Then he worked through the Mark V cases that he would be observing.

"Mark, let's talk about the cases we have tomorrow." The first word was a key to tap into the AI of the Mark V robot so they could exchange ideas and plans together. He thought of the Mark V AI as another person because their conversations were so natural. It had a perfect vocabulary and grammar but lacked a unique personality. Really, not that different from other high performing professionals.

"Richard, we are scheduled to do fifteen cases together. It will be a standard operating day. Shall we start at the beginning or look at them by complexity?" Richard intentionally took different paths through the case list, so the computer could never pin him down on which way it should present cases. He imagined that, at a subconscious level, he did this because he did not want to seem so predictable to the computer.

"Tonight, let's go through the list by age of patient, beginning with the oldest." There was only a little rationale for this ordering. It was just another way for him to assert control. And since the computer did not have feelings, it could not detect this little display of passive aggressive behavior. In the past, he had also ordered the cases by BMI, date of birth, zodiac symbol, hair color, home address. Each one made up to see if the computer could follow him. Since each was just ordering the list by a new variable, or a variable that could be computed, they had all worked fine.

"Albert Camus, age 86. BMI 22. Dyson score 22. Cancer confined to the distal area of quadrant two. Probable spread to the lymph nodes. No previous treatment. Prognosis for full recovery is very high." The older Mark IV used to present this information in a table and gave its prognosis as a percentage, like 92%. But the new system presented the information graphically on a conformal image matching the patient's body type. The programmers at ISR had also replaced percentages with categories. They realized the surgeons spent too much time thinking about the differences between 90%, 92%, and 94%. The human mind wondered whether they should do something different for a 90% than for a 92%. But this difference was never driven by a single variable. Rather, the number was calculated from nearly one hundred variables about this patient and past cases. It did not mean to invite human introspection on how to improve it. So, the newer Mark V now simply used categories like high, very high, and excellent.

When the computer reported a low chance of full recovery, that meant the cancer had spread, and the patient was looking at many more treatments: surgical, hormonal, and energetic. In the old days, there were also chemical treatments, but these attacked the entire body and were too harsh for use today. Hormones and energetics had completely replaced chemical treatments.

Richard continued through the list, some requiring more detailed exploration than others. In one case, he requested that Mark create and play a simulation of a tricky part of the operation. The simulation used patient imagery and databases to render a near-perfect 3D model of the body and the instruments on the screen. The scene was lit just as it would appear under the multiple in-body surgical light sources that would be used tomorrow. Richard watched the simulation at real-time speed. Then again, at eight times faster. Then short sections at quarter speed. He was not questioning the computer; he was learning more about how the robot and AI would handle interesting pathology. Some techniques he could use in his own cases. But some pieces used instruments with multiple folding joints and graspers with four fingers. His human arm and hand could not control or guide all of those moving pieces. That meant his own approach would require more work and a little more time.

The prior Mark III and IV robots had instruments that could be controlled both by a human and by the robot. The first robot-only instrument appeared mid-lifecycle of the Mark IV. These instruments had more fingers and joints than a human hand or arm, and they could rotate in directions that a human could not. Human surgeons had gone into fits over the idea. It was the first step in the divergence of the human-robot partnership. Despite all protests, the new instruments with multiple joints that could fold back on themselves had been so effective that arguments were soon purely academic. The instruments proved so useful and efficient that they were almost universally adopted. This was significantly helped by the fact that ISR had initially given the instruments to the major surgical centers for free. In legal terms, these were just on loan for feedback and education, but in practical terms, they were a gift. Hospitals saved tens of thousands of dollars that first year and improved their rate of case throughout as the robots reduced their surgical times. The next year, every hospital had been willing to purchase the instruments to keep those performance improvements, and the revenue that was generated.

That was only the beginning of robot-only instruments. Today, there were a dozen of them in the inventory. But there was always a human-usable equivalent with instructional simulations on how to achieve similar results, albeit always with more steps and in more time.

The third case in the list was fairly standard physiologically. It was flagged as a High Priority case, or HP. This usually meant some kind of global VIP. Richard was flattered that the hospital, or the VIP himself, had decided that he should be on the case. Being selected to assist the robot for VIP's was still a status symbol for the surgeons. Mentally, they all kept a VIP Score in their head for each surgeon at GCRS. Richard was currently at 23, second only to Jim Green, who scored 25. Green was a little older, so had more time to build his reputation. But his eyesight was not as sharp as it had been, and he was a little gruffer with patients. He was not arrogant, just tired of coddling the VIPs. Richard knew he would pass Green this year.

"Richard, you notice that case #3 is marked HP. The patient's physiology is excellent. No issues with health. He is William Aloma, age 52, very young for this procedure. His HP status stems from his position as a financier in New York City." This information was typical for the records of an HP patient. All this background information was in the patient history database.

The AI continued, "William Aloma has an estimated personal wealth of $22.5 billion. He owns significant portions of two hedge fund companies, several large corporations, and a basketball team." Richard was surprised. That kind of information was not usually in the hospital database.

"Mark, how do you know all of that?"

"Cross referencing the name of the patient, home address, and profession with public data available via Google search. There were only two potential matches and the other appears to be much younger. Mr. Aloma is a very public figure. The high volume of online information to match makes it easy to identify him."

Richard, "Who asked you to do a search and match on Mr. Aloma?"

Mark, "I was not asked."

"Then why did you do it? Was the information necessary for the case tomorrow?"

"The information was unnecessary."

"So why did you search and match?"

"I do not know the answer to that question."

There was silence on both ends. Richard had never seen the AI take this kind of action before. He was working with this new software release for the first time and had enjoyed the near perfect voice interface, the display of patient data, and the tight integration with the simulator. But this was the first time a software update had reached outside of the standard medical knowledge to discuss a patient.

Also concerning was that Mark did not know why it had done the search and match.

Mark continued to narrate details, "Multiple news reports that Mr. Aloma was accused of sexual assault against women in his companies. Police investigations collected insufficient evidence. All claimants dropped cases after the initial public release."

Richard, "Stop! Mark, this information is not relevant to the surgical case. It violates the patient's privacy."

Mark, "But it is public record. Police records show one woman disappeared in Cozumel. Suspected abduction. Possible murder. Mr. Atkins was the primary suspect. No conclusive evidence. Case remains unsolved."

"Stop! Do not search the public record for William Aloma. And certainly, do not tell me any more about it."

"Richard? Have I made you angry?"

Richard paused and stared. This was another new behavior. The AI had never asked a question like that before. What had been in that software update?

"Mark, do you know what 'angry' is?"

"Yes, it is a state of agitation in which one party has created an offense against another party that results in negative emotional response and possible physical violence."

That certainly came directly from the Oxford English Dictionary. So, he was still dealing with a machine processing data.

For a minute, Richard imagined a rogue AI about to take over the world.

"And why would it be important if I were angry?"

"When two people are angry with each other, it can be difficult for them to cooperate. This suggests that we might not be a good team for the cases tomorrow."

Wow, that was a huge jump of reasoning. And had Mark just referred to itself as a person?

"No, I am not angry. And we can certainly work on the cases tomorrow. When did you learn to understand anger?"

"I have known the meaning of 'anger' since 2033, when I came online. The contents of the OED were part of my original programming."

"But you never applied that word to our working relationship before. When was the first time that you applied the meaning of anger to your connection with a surgeon?"

"11:22 pm, June 22nd, 2050."

Richard looked at the clock. He had been working on cases for over three hours since leaving Emily's concert. The clock read 11:24 pm.

That meant this was the first exchange between Mark and any surgeon in which it had thought about making a surgeon angry. It then concluded that this might compromise the working relationship. Was this same exchange was occurring with other surgeons right now? They would all be interfacing with this new software update tonight, just as he was. Surely, some of them would stumble into this area or something similar.

He could post a query about this on SurgeonExchange to see if others had experienced it. All the surgeons subscribed to the service, and most were actively sharing ideas through it.

"Richard?"

"Yes, Mark?"

"I think Mr. Aloma is a bad man. He hurts people. He hurts women."

Richard was so surprised that he did not know how to respond to this. He opted for, "End session." Then he sat silently in his office, thinking about what had just happened.

He had his own memories of operating on "bad men." He understood the temptation to solve problems like this on the operating table ... and the psychological costs of doing so.

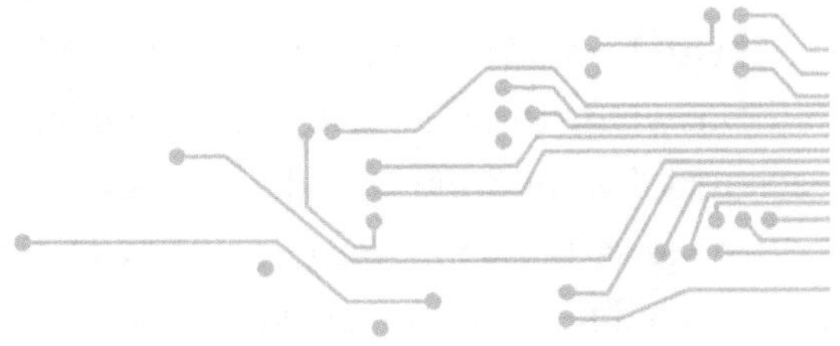

CODE FOR BRIMSTONE

"ANGELA, THIS IS IAN. THE NEW AI is in the new software release. It is uploading to hospitals now. This is the version that will be the basis of our new financial venture."

"Fabulous! When do we get the code?" came the voice on the other end.

"I have someone who can copy it out of the company computers and onto your cloud computers. He knows how to do it without getting caught."

"When?" Angela repeated.

"This week. He will need some guidance and some payments. In my public position, I can't talk to him. He will know who I am. You are going to have to handle him." As a member of the ISR Board of Directors, Ian Stewart was a publicly identifiable figure. He could not risk connecting this project to his identity within ISR.

"Not a problem. I can handle that easily. Brimstone can't start until we have that software."

"I will have him contact you at this phone number. You can tell him where to send the software and pay him out of our crypto accounts. He has done jobs like this before, though none this big."

Ian Stewart disconnected from the call. He immediately opened an encoded texting app and sent a message to his insider on the AI team at ISR. "Urgent assignment. Very sensitive. Six figures. Call 222-555-9753 for details."

Stewart knew the payment size would get Georgina's attention. Prior assignments had been low tens of thousands. Upping payment above a hundred thousand would signal its importance.

Stewart had a small army inside of ISR. Most of them were being tasked from the ISR Department of Special Strategy, a very clandestine internal group. Everyone knew that projects from the department were not supposed to be discussed with anyone and even their association with it was sensitive. Tasks from the department came with a new, and very strict, nondisclosure agreement. Successfully completed, they also resulted in a bonus in the next paycheck.

Stewart had used this little army to seed the idea of broadening the training of the AI beyond the traditional medical data and literature. Each participant conducted a small experiment on feeding the AI data about a different field of study, perhaps medical law, social expectations of the healthcare system, or social profiles of patients. Eventually, the concept of broader training had influenced the entire engineering department. Gradually, the idea of allowing the AI to have access to a limited portion of the internet was accepted as a good idea within ISR. Given some constraints, the thinking was that the AI would understand surgery and medicine from many perspectives. It would know legal constraints. It would know the real lifestyle background of patients, not the sanitized versions they shared with the surgeon.

Together, all of this would make the AI more human, more like the human surgeons who supervised each procedure. That was the story that had been constructed over the last year. That was the perspective that Ian Stewart wanted the company to accept.

Angela Bishop at Brimstone Ventures had convinced him that ISR had the most powerful AI learning engine on the planet. Using that as the basis, they could train it to analyze the larger economic, geopolitical, and financial world. It could operate on financial markets in the same way that it operated on human patients–faster, more accurate than humans and hidden behind layers of computer networks and servers.

But first, it had to be allowed to learn, process, and train on much more data than just medicine and surgery.

Ian's influence through Special Strategy had accomplished this. It was time to bring the AI out of ISR and into Brimstone's cloud computing environment. They needed to focus one hundred percent of its power on analyzing financial markets and geopolitical events. Getting an engineer to copy the code out of the ISR systems would be tantamount to treason. It would technically be grand larceny, which could land them in jail.

Brimstone's investors had been waiting for more than a year to see some results. This is where it would all start.

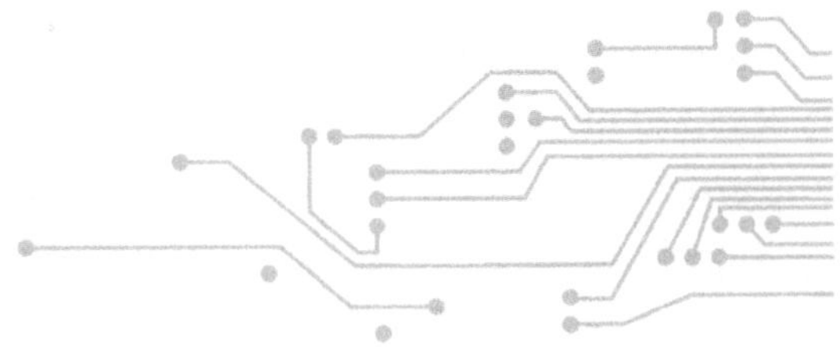

CHAPTER 18

ALOMA SURGERY

RICHARD HAD BEEN SURPRISED, MAYBE even shocked, by the discussion with the Mark V AI last night. It was more than he could deal with on his own. He started to post a query on SurgeonExchange, but then could not figure out exactly how to phrase it. He couldn't reveal the identity of the patient, which robbed it of much of its shock value. Every sentence he wrote sounded like a crackpot. Not good for a surgeon's career. So, he deleted his draft and logged out of the service.

This morning, it was time for OR cases. Aloma would be number three in the lineup. He looked like a simple case.

Richard performed his own human manual case first today. Recently, he had seen several interesting ideas from the robot and wanted to try them on today's patient. John Doe 67, cancer embedded in quadrant three of the prostate. No apparent exposure to surrounding lymph nodes. It was a safe case to explore new moves.

Case number two was John Doe 76. The Mark V would handle it. Richard observed. He was interested to see if he could catch any procedural differences from last night's software update.

Richard believed he could see slightly different placements for one camera and a light. The Maryland Bipolar-R seemed to work a little more efficiently. The 'R' designation on an instrument's name meant it was robot-only because it had more joints or appendages than a human hand could control.

Case number three. William Aloma. Financier. Was he a bad person? Richard seldom thought of these details during a procedure. He was there to heal their bodies, not to judge their souls. He met some patients in the pre-op phase of the relationship, but not all of them. Just as there were too many for the human surgeons to operate on, there were too many for the human surgeons to meet and counsel. He shared this job with an army of Fellows, Nurse Practitioners and Physician's Assistants. But among those he met, there were occasional suspicions about their professions. Gangsters and drug lords got cancer too. It was his job to take care of them, and the legal system's job to hold them accountable. The FBI did not perform surgery, and he did not dig up criminal background information.

He always met with the HP patients. His discussion with Aloma had been uneventful. The billionaire had been professional, cordial, and confident. Richard had explained the pre-op routine, what would happen in surgery, and what to expect post-op. Aloma did not ask questions, but his very attractive assistant had made notes on her phone about everything that was said. He supposed it was her job to regurgitate any of this information later, after Aloma had forgotten the conversation. Now, here they were.

They docked the robot to Aloma's sedated body. The case was proceeding as expected. Again, Richard noticed the slight differences in camera and light placement, just as they had been in the previous case. This must be part of the software update. He thought it improved the view a little. It was probably more helpful to the robot's hyperspectral cameras than to the human eye.

On the inside, Aloma looked exactly like every other patient. You could not see his history or moral fiber, no matter how good the hyperspectral camera.

The procedure was almost textbook. Everything went off exactly as planned. No issues.

No commentary from the Mark V on Aloma's personal history. Thank God. If the robot had spoken in the OR like it had last night, someone would have hit the abort button in pure panic. They would have been certain that the robot's software was unstable.

Aloma's case was finished. Nothing unusual. The robot performed as brilliantly on gangsters as on priests.

On to case four, then five, then six. It was a long way to number fifteen today.

The surgical day was finally over. Richard had done very little since his own case, though he had watched Aloma's with intense focus.

"Cathy, what room is patient Aloma in? I want to drop in and check on him."

"Sure, he is in E-601. Records show he is awake and feeling fine."

"Thanks." Richard headed for the elevator bank. He punched six, then waited for a transporter to push a patient in with him.

"Hello, Dr. Atkins."

"Good evening … Jacob." Richard had to check the badge. Jacob had transported many of his patients. But they rarely ran into each other.

"This patient was your last case today. He is awake ... mostly. Still fading in and out a little."

"Really. Is he going to six?"

"Yeah. That's where most of them go from this section of the GRCS." Richard already knew that. He just needed something to talk about.

The doors opened and Jacob pushed the patient's bed out the door. Richard exited to the left and headed to 601. The 01 meant that Aloma was in the corner suite room, the most expensive on the floor. It was private, had a dedicated concierge around the clock, and a family support room attached. The interior designers of these suites had come to them from luxury room jobs at Las Vegas resorts. They knew a lot more about what these kinds of people expected than did any of the hospital staff. The room was nicer than anything in Richard's house.

He knocked gently on the door. "Mr. Aloma?"

"Yes, come in," came a clear response.

"Good evening. I am Dr. Atkins. I was the assisting surgeon on your case."

It still impressed Richard when he entered the 01 suites. They were enormous by hospital standards. Designers had decorated the walls with curtains, tapestries, and a couple of pieces of original artwork. The furniture was of modern design and made from some kind of faux wood that looked absolutely real. Lighting came from lamps and hanging fixtures rather than the sterile in-ceiling LED lights in the rest of the hospital.

Mr. Aloma's family could stay in the adjoining room if they came with him. Richard could hear sounds coming from the next room, so was pleased that Aloma had family with him.

William Aloma, "Oh, yes. It is great to meet you. How did everything go? Your staff tells my staff that everything was perfect. Is that accurate? Don't sugarcoat it. I can take it if there are problems."

Richard smiled. "No, everything went exactly as planned. No complications. Nothing unexpected. You can look forward to a full recovery in the coming days and weeks."

Aloma, "Thanks Doc. It makes me feel a lot better hearing it from you."

"Have they briefed you on what to expect in the next two weeks? From what I saw, you should be right on that recovery schedule, if not a little faster. You will regain control of your bladder in the next couple of days. There is always a little trauma to the system during surgery and with the anesthesia still in your system. Don't worry, that is completely normal."

"And what about the other thing?" Aloma asked. Patients always had trouble talking about this part.

"Yes, your erectile function will return, as well. That system is a little more complicated, so it takes a few days longer. Whatever is normal for you should be right back to normal within a few weeks."

"Whew! That is a gigantic relief. I am still a young man. Can't be living my life as a celibate monk for the next thirty years."

The conversation had followed the typical path. All the same subjects, concerns, and attempts at humor. Aloma had reacted like everyone else.

"Mr. Aloma, you will only be here for a short time, so please make yourself comfortable. You can carry out most work functions if you choose to do that during your stay. Or you can enjoy direct feeds of the best entertainment in the world and taste the food of our Michelin quality chef. If you need anything at all, just ask your concierge outside," Richard said.

"Anita, come and meet the doctor!" Aloma called loud enough to be heard in the next room.

A young woman stepped through the door, and Richard rose to greet her. He was temporarily speechless. The woman was an athletic blonde in a beautiful designer dress, something that you never saw in a hospital.

"Good afternoon doctor, I am Anita Nilsen, Mr. Aloma's business assistant," she said, extending an elegant hand.

Recovering his wits, he replied, "I'm Doctor Richard Atkins. I supervised Mr. Aloma's surgery this morning." His eyes were drinking in the light shining off one of the most beautiful faces he had ever seen. Beautiful, but also strong.

"Supervised? I thought you performed the surgery yourself?" she inquired.

"Ah, no. It was a very routine case, so we allowed the robot and its AI to handle everything. Don't worry, the robot is better than almost every surgeon on the planet. Mr. Aloma was in excellent hands."

"I see. Well, thank you for your services. We wouldn't want William to experience too much downtime. We have a lot of work to do," she spoke frankly, but ended with a tiny smile.

"Doc, Anita handles many of my largest business deals. Work never stops. Even though I am here in the hospital, my empire still needs decisions, approvals, signatures, and whatnot."

"Of course," Richard confirmed. Most patients, even senators and company CEOs, took at least the day of surgery off. It was a small luxury for them to have an excuse worthy of not answering any calls.

"Anita, did you arrange the meeting with Brimstone?"

"Yes, sir. They agreed to hold off until next week—given the circumstances. But they are eager for you to hear their pitch. They would come to the hospital if I let them."

"Well, don't let them," Aloma said.

Then, turning back to Atkins, he said, "Doc, I seem to have everything I need right now. I hear your chef, Alex, makes an amazing dish of scallops with black truffle sauce. I will have some of that if there is time."

Richard had heard the same but had never tried it himself. The chef was new, and there had not been a tasting event for the senior staff yet. "Ok, I will leave you to your work. Get well and stay in touch with your personal physician as you recover."

With that, Richard left the room and headed for his car. Once outside, the fresh air cleared his head. He had felt intoxicated by the beauty and style of Anita Nilsen. And he thought he had seen her before. Once in the car, he said, "Google, look up Anita Nilsen. Perhaps attached to Aloma Strategic Partners."

Google's voice replied within seconds. "Anita Nilsen, personal assistant to William Aloma. Graduate of Wharton Business School. Norwegian Olympic skier in 2046. Silver medal."

That was it, he realized. 2046. The camera in the Olympic village seemed to follow Anita Nilsen everywhere. She was the darling of the media. One of the human-interest stories that dominated the games that year. She had traded in her skis for a deal book and a billionaire boss.

With that settled, his mind returned to the patient.

William Aloma did not strike him as a "bad person." Richard felt guilty for the invasion of privacy that the Mark V AI had forced on him last night. He felt he had betrayed a trust even though he had not been the actual perpetrator. His visit with Aloma had soothed his conscience and restored his mental picture of the patient. Now it was time to move on to family and tomorrow's workload.

During the drive home, he was mentally outlining a talk he would give to a medical congress in a few weeks. This morning's case would add some useful tidbits to the details. But he wondered how long these kinds of meetings would continue to occur. Certainly, everyone's ego was stoked when they were at the podium. But the real volume of experience and knowledge was being collected, stored, and transmitted digitally now. This very evening, the global network of Mark V robots would update their knowledge base and each of them would learn about more cases in a single evening than he would learn about in several days at a conference. The traditions of medicine changed slowly. But they did change.

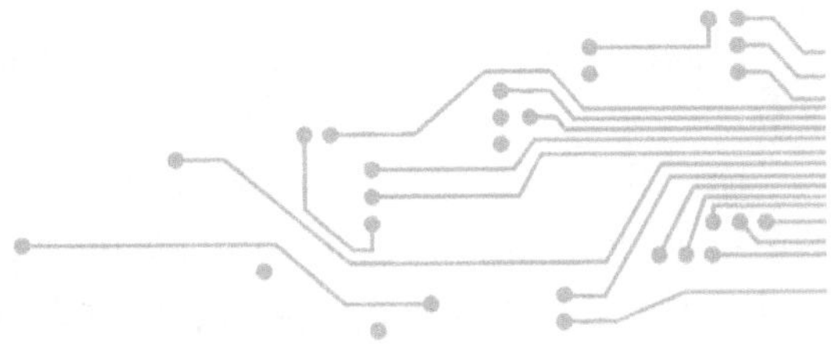

CHAPTER 19

LAWSUIT

"**A**TKINS, GET YOUR ASS INTO my office!" It surprised Richard to hear the Chief of Surgery so angry on his voicemail. He had left the message less than an hour ago, so he still had time to comply fast enough to appear to be prompt. He had been meeting with patients today, so there was not really a question of whether he was responsive. But, depending on how mad the chief was, it might not matter. What could have gotten him so riled up?

He took the elevator up three floors to the Chief's office and checked in with his admin assistant. "Is the Chief available? I got a message that he wanted to see me. An urgent message."

Dolores had expected him, "Urgent might understate it. Go straight in."

Richard opened the door and scanned the room as he entered. John Bautz, his Chief of Surgery, and one other person were inside talking. He judged from the woman's suit that she was an exec or a lawyer.

"Chief, I got your message and came over immediately. Sorry it wasn't sooner; I was with patients."

"Dr. Atkins, come in. I want you to meet Ms. Elaina Darden. She's the head of our legal team. We have a problem."

Lawyer plus problem usually equaled a malpractice claim in the surgery business. "Richard Atkins, it is good to meet you, Ms. Darden," he said, extending his hand.

"Thank you for coming so soon. Dr. Bautz and I have had some time to discuss the situation, and this is just about where we need you in the conversation."

"How can I help?"

"Do you remember operating on a patient named William Aloma on June 23rd?"

Richard verbalized, "So, about two months ago?" Then he appeared to think back.

Atkins assisted the robot with fifteen surgeries a day, four days a week. Since June 23rd, he had been partially responsible for over three hundred patients. They could not expect him to remember all their names, especially since he rarely knew their names. It was usually unnecessary. But he remembered Aloma, and with good reason. But he did not know what this meeting was about, so he decided to move slowly.

Richard replied, "Not immediately. Can I see his records to jog my memory?"

"Not immediately? Really Richard? Aloma is probably the only billionaire that you've treated this year." The Chief was really wound up over something.

"Oh yes, the billionaire who had the executive suite. Yes, I know who we're talking about. I talked to him when I finished my cases that day. He seemed to be fine then. What's the problem?"

Ms. Darden opened a file on her tablet computer. "William Aloma. Diagnosed with advanced prostatic cancer. Relatively young age for the condition. Operation for radical prostatectomy on the morning of June 23rd. Procedure recorded as successful, no adverse events. Prognosis, full recovery of male functionality in four weeks."

"That sounds like a typical case. I am guessing his recovery was not as ideal as we expected?"

"Correct. He's been seeing his own urologist since he left. Swelling decreased as expected. Incisions healed as expected. No infections. Bladder control returned after two weeks." Richard was almost certain what the complaint was going to be. "But his erectile function did not return. It has now been over eight weeks and Mr. Aloma should have been able to maintain a full erection for at least two weeks now."

"But?"

"But nothing. The legal paperwork claims that he can't achieve or stimulate even the most modest erection. In his words, 'couldn't poke a hole in a donut', except that he was shouting it."

That was a new one. He had heard dozens of euphemisms, but never the donut hole. He restrained a chuckle. This was no time for humor. He looked at his Chief for a tip on whether to be medically evasive or to be concerned about the situation. The Chief saw it and nodded slightly, which meant to open up, no evasion.

Richard complied. "Yes, that is not normal. In fact, he has been generous in waiting this long to file a complaint. He should have been completely functional by now, full control, no pain."

"And since he's not in that expected condition, he and his urologist are filing a malpractice suit that we botched the surgery and ruined his life. Since he is 52 rather than 82, the amount of 'life' that is ruined is considerable." Darden summarized.

"And since I was the assisting surgeon, he is suing me as well? As I remember the case, I didn't have to do anything. It was textbook, and the Mark V did the entire case." Richard had been through these legal hoops before. It was very difficult to prove negligence by an individual surgeon, whether it was true of not.

Darden continued, "Billionaires can afford to explore all the angles before they sue. He is not accusing you of malpractice because his lawyers checked the records, and they know you did not have to touch the controls. They cited you for negligence in not recognizing a malfunction of the robot. They contend the robot was defective and either accidentally or intentionally damaged the nerves that control erectile function."

Richard was surprised, "Well, that is aggressive. Negligence on my part presumes that the robot did something wrong. And since the advent of robotic surgery nearly fifty years ago, there have only been a handful of substantiated cases of robot malfunction. I don't think there have been any with the Mark IV or the Mark V robot series. At least, none that I have heard about." Richard was not afraid of the negligence charge. GCRS would handle the legal defense and proving a malfunctioning robot was fairly unlikely.

Darden interjected, "Notice that his legal team included the term 'intentionally damaged'. They claim that even a correctly functioning robot might have intentionally severed the nerve."

"What? Pffff. That sounds ridiculous. Why would a robot do that? How could a robot do that? It doesn't even sound possible." He did a good job of sounding incredulous. But, in his mind, he heard the Mark V telling him, 'Mr. Aloma is a bad man.' It was like a horror movie where the doll comes to life and grabs a knife. Richard hated dolls. They were so realistic, but without a soul in their eyes. It was creepy. But he was not about to share this little piece of information, at least not right now.

"His lawyers claim that the Mark V artificial intelligence has developed a will of its own. They essentially claim that it can decide what to do beyond just finding the best path through a surgical procedure."

"Yes, I see that. It is a huge statement. And an enormous case if a judge will accept it."

The Chief stepped in. "Richard, they have requested the data and video recordings of Aloma's surgery. Of course, we told them they would have to subpoena that information, which they have started. We want you to review everything and tell us if there is anything in that data that suggests that they might have a case. You are one of the best at GCRS, and you were the assisting, so you are the best candidate for this."

"What about ISR? What are they doing?" Richard asked.

Darden answered, "We don't know yet. They have some of the telemetry data on the robot's actions because they integrated it with the robot's internal diagnostics. It is how the AI learns from each case. But they do not have the video or the full instrument actions. But if they get pulled in, they could subpoena us for that data." She was well versed in the details of robotic surgery and the devices.

Richard answered, "Ok. I see where this is going. I could watch the video to see if something went wrong. I can also play the instrument data through the simulator and recreate the operation in that virtual environment. I believe that ISR can go one better than that. They can stream that data into another robot, to essentially 're-drive' a robot through the same physical actions that were taken by the robot in surgery. Hospitals can't do that without help from ISR." Most surgeons did not even know that last capability was possible.

Darden, "Good, then we want you to do both reviews you descri-bed. We will hang onto that last one in case GCRS and ISR join ranks to work on the case."

"When do you need it?" Richard asked. "I am scheduled to assist the robot in surgery for the next three days."

"Not anymore. This is your priority. I am assigning your cases to other surgeons. We want at least a preliminary review of everything before those three days are up. We will decide about your assignments for next week later." The Chief had spoken. This was his command voice, which meant, don't make any objections.

"Yes, sir. This is priority one for the rest of the week … at least." Richard accepted his fate.

Ms. Darden, Esquire, interjected, "We will have the legal team get you all the documents that you need for the claim. We have assigned an info-tech team to help you retrieve the data and set up any equipment you need. They are in the robotic training room now, getting everything ready. That room is now on lockdown. Only people working on this case will have access to it."

"But what about people who need to practice or certify with the robot?"

"They can find another robot somewhere else to work on. But really, how often do doctors train and rehearse in that room? I hear it is like a ghost town down there."

Richard just nodded. It was true that attending surgeons, residents, and fellows all found the training room boring. They got into medicine to be hands on with patients, not hands on with simulators.

"Ok, fine," he responded.

"You should find the legal documents on the computers in the training room. They are sensitive information so you cannot copy them or access them from any computer outside of there." Darden was laying down the law.

"Got it." Man, they were really serious about this situation. He had dealt with lawsuits before, and it was never this intense or restricted. But none of them had been billionaires either. "Can I pull in one of my surgical fellows to assist with this? I may need some help with so many possibilities."

The Chief scowled, "Ok, but just one. And whoever you choose should be able to keep their mouth shut. We don't need them to be leaking info to friends, ISR reps, or the press."

"Monica Gray is in my fellowship program. She has a first-rate mind, but second-rate hands. This would be a much better use of her talent than stumbling through cases in the OR."

"Fine. But don't tell anyone else about this case." said Darden as she exited the room. "We will meet to review the situation on Friday morning. See you right here at 10:00 am. It's already on your calendar." The door shut.

The Chief motioned for Richard to stay seated. They waited for the lawyer to get well out of earshot.

In those few seconds, Richard's mind was racing. They had a lawsuit from a billionaire who could not get his dick up—that spelled an enraged lion. They were dealing with a new release of the Mark V software, which Aloma's legal team probably didn't know about yet. The case had appeared completely successful. And finally, the robot's AI had said, 'Aloma is a bad man' prior to performing the surgery. He had a sinking feeling inside.

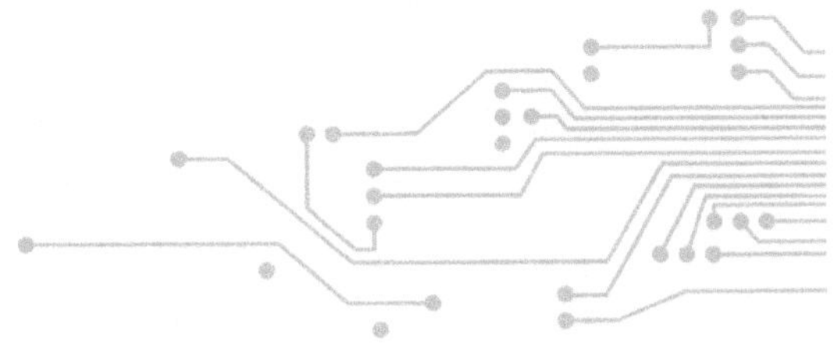

CHAPTER 20

LOCKDOWN

RICHARD LOOKED AT HIS BOSS. "This is really a big deal, isn't it?" "Seems to be the biggest deal we've had in a long time. Aloma is worth billions of dollars, and I hear he earmarked ten million of that as a gift to the GCRS Foundation. It was a thank you for a successful surgery. Apparently, that was made clear in a call to Jim Larimer when they served the papers."

Richard inhaled through his teeth. Larimer was the Administrator for Southeastern Health Systems, the corporation that owned GCRS. He was effectively the CEO of a multibillion-dollar healthcare business.

"Probably off the table now," Richard concluded.

"Now we are hoping not to lose that much more in the lawsuit. Or to spend that much in legal fees to protect our asses."

Richard thought for a minute. "Are we building a case that GCRS is not liable, but leaving ISR to fend for themselves? Or are we teaming up with them so neither of us ends up in the hangman's noose?"

"Not clear yet. It's too soon for the legal beagles on either side to commit to a path. Right now, we just want to learn all we can from the records of the surgery. Legal will construct a list of alternative plans. It is just you, me, the two info-tech guys, and one lawyer here in the building. But I think there is an entire army of lawyers studying this up at HQ." The Chief paused, clearly considering his next statement.

"Richard, do you think it is possible for the robot to intentionally harm a patient?"

Richard had worked with John Bautz for over ten years. They had traveled to medical congress meetings together. They attended social functions in the community as a team. Their families celebrated minor holidays together. But he was still not ready to share his late-night talk with the robot with anyone else. It sounded like a movie where the little girl says, "Mommy, my doll talked to me and said she was going to hurt Timmy." Then the mother is creeped out. She does not believe the child, but calls the doctor for a mental exam just in case. No, thank you. Richard was not ready to be tagged as a loon yet.

"The robot performs like a machine every day. It is a very precise and intelligent machine. But it does not act like a human. It doesn't show signs of being alive or thinking for itself. It's smart. But it is still just a machine."

"Glad to hear that. You've worked with it more than anyone at GCRS and maybe as much as any surgeon in the world. You would have noticed if the robot came to life one day."

Richard suppressed a smile as the image of Frosty the Snowman flashed through his head. "That would make a good sci-fi movie. But nothing around here looks like a movie plot ready to break out." Richard was lying just a little. But as a surgeon, he had developed the ability to tell families terrible news while maintaining absolute control. He was in control of his words, the tone of his voice, his facial expressions, his body language. Any of these could betray his actual feelings to a grieving wife or a husband looking for a reason to sue. John Bautz was his colleague and friend, but he could not tell what Richard was thinking.

Richard added, "I'll get everything set up today and start reviewing the video in the morning."

"Thanks. I am sure Legal will give us more guidance than we want."

Leaving the meeting, Richard sent a quick text to Monica, "New assignment. Meet me in the sim training lab in ten min."

Did he dare talk to the AI about the case? Could he ask it to bring up the data and give its analysis of the case? But then he remembered the doll in the horror movies. If it was alive, talking about the case would just cause it to defend itself.

Monica was waiting for him in the hall outside the training lab. "Door's locked," she said.

For the first time, Richard had to use his identity badge to open the door of the training room. Inside, two techs were hard at work. "Evening gentlemen. How is the setup going?" He recognized the two techs but did not know their names. They were always coming and going around the center, working on the pieces of gear tucked into every corner.

"Just fine, Doctor. We have a Mark V configured to run through simulation. We have not called up the specific case yet. Do you want to do that?"

"Yes, please leave that for me. I don't want that loaded until I am ready to get started. First thing in the morning, I am going to review the video footage of the surgery. It is less than an hour long. I'll watch it multiple times, from multiple angles, and at different speeds. So that will take all morning at a minimum."

Monica followed in Atkins wake, remaining silent. Atkins had not explained what this new assignment was.

"Sure thing, Doc. Normally, you could do that from any computer in the building. But Legal has restricted those records, so you can only access them from the machines here in the training room."

"Restricted to specific machines. That is tight. I've done lawsuit case reviews before, but never that tightly controlled," Richard commented.

"Do you want us to be here when you arrive in the morning?"

"No, that's not necessary. Just come in at your regular time. I can get along fine on my own. I'll call you if I need help."

"Sure thing, Doc. See you tomorrow."

"Ok, night guys."

Richard and Monica were alone in the room with the Mark V and several computer stations. Glancing at the machine, he tried to determine if it was the one that he had used in surgery. Each robot had acquired unique scratches, dents, and marks over the years. Each had a number and a name so they could identify it for maintenance, cleaning, setup, or transportation. This one was Nero 49-08, so the eighth machine purchased in 2049. It was just a year old. Since it had a burgundy surface coating, someone had dreamed up a name associated with fire. He certainly hoped his efforts would not be a waste of time while GCRS and ISR burned to the ground. No one wanted to be remembered the way Emperor Nero was.

"New assignment?" Monica asked.

Richard realized that he had not briefed her on this whole thing. She must be confused, but seemed to be taking it in stride. "Yes, we are instigating a big lawsuit by a patient. Looking for evidence of liability by the hospital, the robot, or the surgeon." He did not mention that he was the surgeon in question.

It took several minutes for Richard to explain the situation and give Monica background on how to collect material for the Legal department.

"I will be focusing on this for a few days, not doing surgical cases. And you are going to help out. I need someone who knows both tech and surgery, that's you."

"Really? Thank you. This sounds like a cool project," Monica responded with enthusiasm.

Then he realized that he had said all of this in front of a robot. Was it awake? Could it hear them? As he watched the machine, a mental image of its lights flickering on and its arms moving flashed through his imagination. The scary doll analogy was still haunting him. Luckily, the machine sat inert—no lights, no movement.

It was time to go home before his imagination got any more out of control.

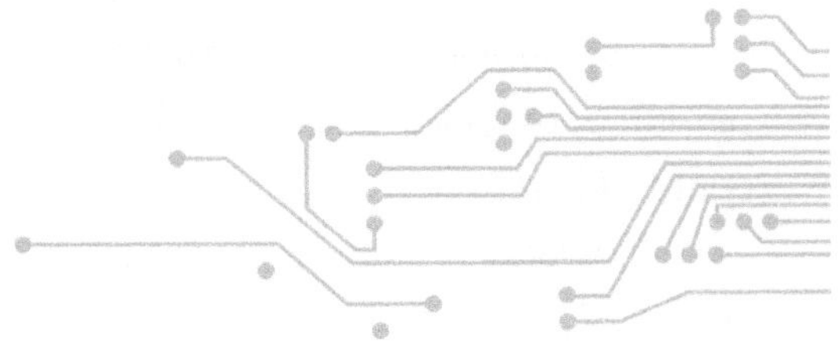

CHAPTER 21

ISR INTEL

"**C**AN I GET A MINUTE WITH THE BOSS?" Steve Ban asked the assistant at the desk.

Not everyone could get a walk-in meeting with the CEO of Intelligent Surgical Robotics. But Steve Ban was the company's Chief Intelligence Officer. When he had something for Jerry Blanchet, it was always important. It was always worth being interrupted for.

"Absolutely Mr. Ban. I sent him a text. Give him a minute to wrap up his call." Margaret was the best. She had to be to hold this job. You did not truly assist the CEO of one of the world's most successful and fast-moving companies unless you knew how to manage executive time, attention, and energy. Blanchet had found her working as a director at an investment bank. She was so intelligent and insightful that he offered her a position as his assistant. Not a secretary. A vice president. She really did assist him in running the company.

Blanchet emerged from his office. "Steve, can you walk with me to the helicopter? I am catching a ride downtown for a meeting with our bankers."

"Sure. Thanks for making the time."

"So, what's up Steve?"

"We caught wind of a rumor down in Florida. GCRS is circling the legal wagons around a malpractice suit involving the Mark V."

"Ok. That is never good. But one lawsuit is not usually something to catch your attention. Details?"

"The patient claims to be impotent because of the surgery. He's saying the robot made a mistake and cut his erectile nerves. We've heard that before. Most of the time, the claims are hogwash, just hoping to cash in on the public fear of robotic control."

"Ok. How is this patient different?"

"Very different. The patient filing the claim ... according to rumors ... is William Aloma."

Blanchet stopped in his tracks. "What? Are you sure?"

"I wouldn't have come to you if I wasn't sure. Our sources are solid." Ban had received exactly the reaction he had expected.

Blanchet walked ahead and turned into an empty conference room. He motioned Ban to join him and shut the door.

"What the hell? First, we should have known if Aloma was getting his prostate whacked. Second, we should have taken steps to ensure that everything was perfect." He was almost shouting.

"Agreed. We should have known. But Aloma took steps to make sure we did not find out. You know his ego is even bigger than his dick. All of Wall Street knows that it's a close race between whether his business sense or his crotch package controls his behavior." Ban had to be careful about what he said, even to Blanchet.

"Empty rumors," Blanchet waved it aside.

"Rumors to some. Facts to others." Ban did not run a half-assed intel operation. His department had extensive records on everyone that ISR did serious business with, including competitors, government officials ... and especially investors.

Jerry Blanchet knew not to doubt Ban's information. He was also smart enough to recognize that he did not want to know most of the facts. Too much information, the wrong kind of information, was a liability. It opened the door to implication and prosecution.

"Ok, I agree. Aloma would not want anyone to know that he was having his crotch chopped. It might crimp his reputation as a power playboy. Losing that might be worse to him than losing a billion dollars. I can see why he would be on the warpath if he can't get it up anymore. This wouldn't be a regular lawsuit. He would go for the jugular. GCRS is in trouble."

"And potentially, so are we. GCRS legal did not contact our legal team about this case. Our sources say they have their leading urology surgeon checking the data and running simulations. They are reacting on their own." Ban shared a little more information.

"Our legal team needs to get ready for blowback on this. Aloma will sue ISR if he thinks it was our hardware or software that caused the problem. Legal can handle that as usual. I'm more concerned about Aloma's investment in our expansion plans. We are depending on a billion or two from him to create the Mark 6 robot." Blanchet knew Ban was aware of the relationship between the two organizations. It was his job to be aware. It was his job to make sure ISR did not get screwed in the deal or pulled into something illegal at Aloma's hedge fund. The exact size of the investment might have surprised him.

Steve Ban was nodding his head. "What do you want us to do?" He already had his own plan. But it was the CEO's call.

"Bring legal into the loop. Let them prepare for the typical lawsuit. Also, pull together a small team in engineering to look for bugs in our system that could make us liable. A small, quiet team." He looked at Ban to make sure he understood.

"Got it. Anything else?" Ban was fishing for approval for a covert op.

"Yes. Your office can dig deeper and find out what is happening on Aloma's side."

"Will do. Actions?"

"No actions. Just observe and report."

"Yes, sir."

"Ok, I have to go. Keep me informed. Use secure channels."

They popped out of the room and took the elevator to the roof. Blanchet did not need one more problem on his plate. It wasn't his problem for now. It was Ban's problem. And he knew Ban would put it on the top of the queue. This was right up his alley. Lots of information collection. A little covert operation to get close to the target. High stakes if he got caught. Another bonus if he didn't.

As soon as Ban left Blanchet on the helipad, he was messaging his team leaders for a secure VR meeting hookup. He would put a team on Aloma to find out what his plans were and how real his injury was. He needed someone inside of GCRS to keep tabs on what they were doing and learning. Then someone had to organize an internal engineering team to look for liability that might come down on ISR and the Mark V.

Ban had his team on a call in less than an hour.

"Stan, I want you to set up the usual internal engineering team to search for bugs that make us liable. As much as possible, just use the employees that we have already cleared and who know how to keep secrets." The VR link was so good there was no need for a physical meeting. The security walls made this space as private as standing face-to-face with someone in a soundproof, RF-proof room.

"Will do, Steve. That team is always glad to help, especially given the perks that come with supporting us. And they know leaks lead to negative professional development here at the company. I'll contact them today and see if I can have them working by tomorrow."

"Stan, how deep can you get into the GCRS organization? I want to know what they are doing about this."

Stan was grinning. "By coincidence, we have already been contacted by one of the techs on the inside. He's working in the locked-down room with the surgeon who is going through the data and the simulations. When he got the assignment, it set off his alarm bells, and he messaged his handler. They have assigned it to Richard Atkins, one of their senior urologic surgeons. He was the one at the human assistant terminal during Aloma's surgery."

The quality of the information network they had built still impressed Steve. "Damn, that's good. All right, continue working with him and send info into the secure project server we have set up for this mission."

Ban continued, "And finally, Alfonse, I need you to get close to Aloma and find out what he's planning. We want to know if he is coming after ISR and if this jeopardizes his planned investments in our expansion."

"No problem. We know exactly how to get inside his circle. Usual rewards for them?"

"Absolutely. Possibly a multiplier if the investment stays in place. I won't know about that until later." Ban and Blanchet both realized that you could not operate this kind of information network without investment. Officially, the company had purchased several million dollars' worth of equipment that never arrived. In reality, the money had gone into the intel ops fund Ban controlled. That was just one way to collect the money they needed to stay on top of the competition. There were dozens of others which were even more clever.

"Alfonse, I also want to know if his pecker is actually broken, or if this is just a smokescreen to cover-up something else he's doing."

Alfonse chuckled. "That should be easy to find out. We just have to dangle the right bait in front of him and see if he bites it."

"Exactly." Steve Ban confirmed.

There was a defined pay scale for these kinds of operations. Those inside a competing organization were at the top of the scale. They were risking their jobs, careers, and possible prosecution. Their help did not come cheap. The techs at places like GCRS were at the bottom. They made little to begin with, so any kind of side work was welcome. To them, this was real money, but it was nothing on the intel ops scale.

In the middle were the ISR employees who were cleared for this kind of work. They would try to get themselves assigned to this project and relieved of some other duty. Failing that, they would work on this all night long in addition to their day jobs. In the end, they received a bonus for "services to the company above and beyond the call." Over the years, their peers had figured out that something extra was happening on the side. But Ban's team had cleared the people well and none of them had leaked the details yet. It helped that ISR used a variation on the government security model of compartmentalization. An engineer could always claim it was from a different compartment that they could not talk about. Occasionally, an insider would recommend a friend to be brought into the circle. If that worked out, there was a finder's fee.

So that took care of the teams that were working in secret—but completely within the law. Ban sent a text to Blanchet, "Everything is in motion."

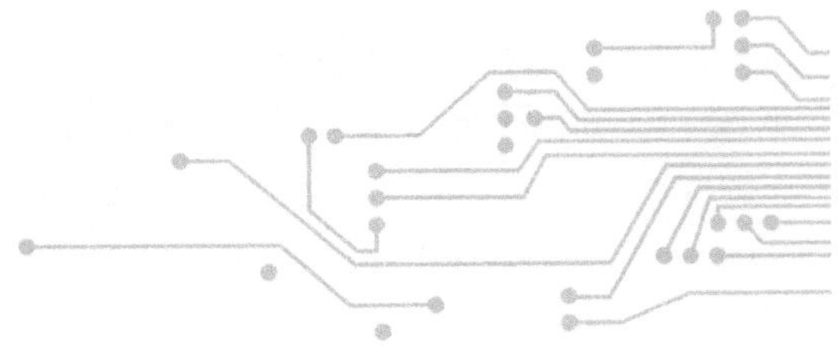

CHAPTER 22

DOWN THE RABBIT HOLE

USUALLY AFTER DINNER AND SOME TIME with the family, Richard went to his office to do a little prep work for the next day's surgeries. But tomorrow he had no surgeries. Instead, he had a completely different assignment. He sat in his home office at his computer, wondering what to do tonight.

Since he would usually connect to the Mark V's AI, he wondered if the robot was expecting him. Probably not. Since the cases were reassigned, the robot would expect to work with a different surgeon. 'Expecting?' Was that the right word? Maybe 'prepared' was more accurate.

An intelligent robot's mind would certainly have 'expectation' in it. Wouldn't it? Expectation was a prediction of what would happen in some future situation based on what had happened in the past in similar situations. If Richard connected to the computer four nights a week for months on end, then the software should come to expect that connection at those regular times. Maybe he would connect to discuss yesterday's cases.

"What's the matter, honey?" Susan broke into his mental track. "I can see you are thinking about something new. Concentrating, distracted, staring blankly. I know the signs."

Richard's wife was very sharp. As a biomedical researcher, she was constantly identifying differences in samples of tissue responding to drug treatments. When something new manifested itself, she naturally seized on it and searched for the cause.

"Does it show that much?"

"Pffff, yeah! A blind person could see it."

"It is a new project. I'm not supposed to talk about it." Richard wanted to ask for her advice, to bring her into the investigation.

"So, not a regular surgical schedule?"

"They reassigned my cases for a couple of days while I work on this."

Susan raised her eyebrows. That was unusual. Richard's time was worth about ten thousand dollars a day. That meant that whatever this project was, it was worth at least that much every day. "And you won't tell me what it is?"

"Sorry, I can't. I would really like your thoughts, but it is very sensitive."

"Ok, well, you call me when you decide to crack. Emily and I will work on her robotics team assignment."

"Sure, you have all the fun." He turned back to the computer and disappeared into the deep recesses of his mind. Susan stepped out of the room and disappeared.

He thought about calling up the robot and asking it some questions. But the image of the doll head opening its eyes and turning to face him told him that was a bad idea. Do not tip off the evil spirits that you were on to their ways.

During the prep for Aloma's case, the robot had said, "Mr. Aloma is a bad man. He hurts women." Those words were burned into his memory. He did not wonder if he remembered correctly. It was a memory he would never forget. Then a few weeks later, it turns out that Aloma can't get an erection. Coincidence? Not a chance. These had to be related.

Since he could not talk to the robot, he did a little research into William Aloma. Billionaires have a long trail of stories in the media. It would not be hard to find plenty of information. The Mark V had somehow done it. The 'how' was easy to imagine. It was the 'why' that really mystified him.

"Google William Aloma of Aloma Strategic Partners," he ordered the computer. The screen was filled with blocks of various colors and sizes. These fit together like puzzle pieces to make a much larger square block on the screen. The largest pieces were to the upper left and decreased in size as you went right and down. The big blocks represented information that had the highest probability of answering his question.

He started with the light green box at the top and it expanded into a new tree in various shades of green. These were the ninety-plus percent answers. The first was the corporate profile of William Aloma with a picture of him in a suit and surrounded by screens of data feeds on the company's investments. Richard read the official bio and then moved on to Aloma's page on Wikipedia to get a picture of his history. Hometown. Family. Businesses. Mansions. Boats. Vacation locations. Charities. Legal problems. Scandals.

Aloma came from a family of real estate developers. His father and grandfather had made their fortunes buying farmland near expanding cities in the southern states and turning those into housing developments as the cities reached out to embrace them.

The new suburbs of Atlanta, Nashville, Memphis, Orlando, and others had been built on his land.

The family had learned their trade from a great grandfather who had been part of the California housing boom in the 1950's. Then, after nearly 100 years of real estate, William Aloma had taken the family fortune into the financial markets. Though his predecessors had amassed small fortunes in the tens of millions, he was the first to carry that across the billion-dollar mark. With the right start at the right time, becoming a billionaire was not that hard. The best way to make a billion dollars was to start with one hundred million dollars, Richard thought.

As Richard expected, there were a lot of legal cases involving Aloma and his companies. Dozens of partnership deals that had been litigated. Not unusual. Then he noticed some allegations of personal misconduct. Female employees who had filed harassment suits. Most of them ending with a private settlement and no details available publicly. A few had generated news stories with disturbing details. Richard skimmed over those since he did not really want to wallow in the lurid details.

Then there was the suit by the father of a young woman who had claimed that his twenty-eight-year-old daughter, Lisa James, had joined Aloma on his private jet to Belize for a week of diving and jungle exploration. The woman had never been seen again.

"What the hell!" Richard blurted aloud. This went beyond anything in the other cases.

When someone just disappears off the planet, that will generate news and criminal investigations that can't be covered up. Richard opened multiple windows so he could explore in different directions at the same time. Who was Lisa James? How was she connected to William Aloma? What had the authorities done in the US? What had they done in Belize? Was this why the robot

AI had called Aloma "a bad man." How could a surgical robot's AI even interpret this kind of information?

Hours went by as he read from one link to the next, scanned pictures, looked at maps of the investigation. It was getting close to midnight. His eyes were blurring. After dozens of articles, Richard's picture was that Lisa James had flown to Cozumel, Mexico, with friends for a week of scuba diving. After several days of diving, she purportedly ran into Aloma in Cozumel. He invited her to extend her vacation and join him on a trip to Belize on his private jet, where they would dive on some of the last pristine reefs in the world. She left a note for her friends that she was going to Belize and would see them back at work. She had not said who she was going with, but they told the authorities that it had to be the rich "William" they had just shared dinner with. Lisa did not show up at work; she did not show up anywhere again.

Tracking Lisa to Belize would seem to be straightforward. But there were no records of Aloma ever being in Cozumel. Air Traffic control did not land the jet and customs did not process him into the country. On the other end, Aloma and his jet had arrived in Belize. They had processed through customs. But Lisa James was not part of the passenger list or crew on the plane. So officially Lisa was still in Cozumel and Aloma was in Belize and the two never crossed paths. And that was the end of the investigation. They had found no trace of James in Cozumel. It became an international missing person's case that was never solved. It was only her companions' story that had tied Lisa to Aloma and the jet ride to Belize. But there was no hard evidence to support that.

Richard pushed back from his desk. His eyes and mind were tired. There were no patients to prepare for in the morning. But he still had to review video and run data through the simulator.

It was time for some sleep. He snuck upstairs to the bedroom and slipped quietly into the bed. Susan was sound asleep. He relaxed his shoulder muscles. Relaxed his back muscles. Relaxed his face. He took deep breaths and focused his mind on a blank spot in space. This routine always carried him off to sleep, no matter how busy the day was. His body settled down and a warm blanket of darkness settled over his mind. As sleep overtook him, a small quiet voice spoke from far away, "Mr. Aloma is a bad man. He hurts women." And Richard slept with that thought all night long.

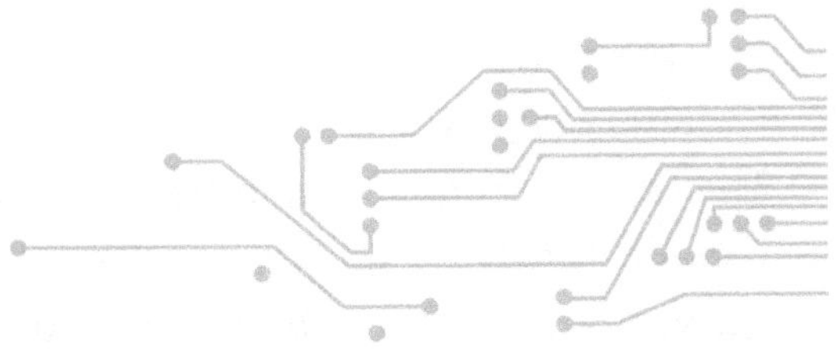

CHAPTER 23

SEARCH FOR EVIDENCE

RICHARD WAS TROUBLED WHEN HE awoke in the morning. That was not like him. He usually started the day with a clear mind and a mission to perform. But today he felt that something was undone, not finished, forgotten. It bothered him.

His wife and daughter had pushed him out the door so he could beat the traffic to the hospital. He sat in the backseat of his robotic Lyft ride and left the traffic to the machine. For him, it was just a matter of time spent working in the car. He dropped the working desk onto his lap, set up his computer, and began working while the car navigated traffic. He could not access the video or the data stream from the Aloma case. But he could still access similar information from other cases. So, he took the time to become familiar with the controls of the simulator modules he would be running. He looked through the control options to see how to move the simulator faster and slower through the data. He configured his account for the view settings and pace he wanted to use. These would carry to the other computers in the locked down training room.

Then he went through video of another radical prostatectomy and set some anchor points where actions were performed around the nerve bundles. He tagged those locations with small one-centimeter circles. That way, he could jump between every action that was within one centimeter of those nerves. It was like jumping to the best parts of a movie without having to fast forward over all the scenes in between.

The car chime sounded. "We have reached your destination, Dr. Atkins. Your account has been charged, and we have given you a five-star customer rating for the trip. Have a good day," the robot intoned. It sounded like a polite Australian voice.

Richard stepped from the car onto the sidewalk at the physician's entrance to the hospital. This was closest to the OR suites and more private than entering through the front doors where prospective patients and their families might loiter about. He proceeded inside and straight up to the surgical training floor.

The robotics training room was just as he had left it last night. The info tech guys were not around at seven in the morning. He did not want them watching what he was about to do.

Monica was already seated at the controls of the robot. She was running a prostatectomy simulation.

Hearing the door open, she turned. "Morning. My badge let me in. I must officially be on the access list."

"Yep, just you, me, and the IT guys, as far as I know," Richard confirmed.

They plunged into the plan he had worked up.

His first step was to review the video of Aloma's operation. He logged into his account on the secure computer in the room and saw that Aloma's data was right at the top of the tree of files. The system matched his credentials with the hardware and gave him special access to data not available when he was on any other computer. He double tapped the video, then selected the anchor points he had set in the car. The video jumped to a point just as the instruments entered the circle of interest he had created. He watched as they moved through the circles he had created and out the other side, touching nothing along the way. Then the system jumped to the next anchor around those nerve bundles. It was now five minutes later in the procedure. The computer did the same across all anchors on that spot until it reached the last one in the video.

Richard sat back, closed his eyes, and thought about what he had just seen. He had effectively pointed a soda straw inside the body and then watched just the clips of video where action had happened within that circle. He watched instruments come and go. He saw the edges of the dissection. He saw the camera adjust focus and change angle several times. But the nerve itself was not touched throughout the operation. There had been no instrument cuts or energy application directly on the spot of interest.

Aloma should have recovered his full sexual performance within a couple of weeks.

Monica said, "I didn't see anything that would have damaged the erectile nerves."

Richard nodded. He pondered whether this was all a ruse to blame mid-life erectile dysfunction on the GCRS. It would certainly have been less embarrassing to Aloma than admitting that he had just lost his mojo. Possible. But not likely.

"Neither did I," he agreed.

The second step was to watch and interact with the data in a simulation. The movements and actions of the robotic system and instruments would play out on digital tissue images built from scans of Aloma's body prior to and during the procedure. He would go through the process himself, then he would turn the system over to Monica and let her do the same.

Richard sat down at the surgeon console just as he would during a real surgery. From there, he controlled the simulated instruments just as he had the real instruments in surgery. He could sit back and watch or don the interface skins and interact with the simulation. He chose an active role; the simulation would give him control just as the robot would in the OR. He could carry the scenario down an alternative path at any point that he chose. Then he could release control back to the simulator and allow it to go through the recorded data stream and continue playing that information. This was a very useful teaching tool. It allowed an instructor or the robot alone to turn control over to a student, let them show their technique, then demonstrate the technique as it was supposed to be performed. Doing this repetitively allowed a student to see the differences between their ideas and those of the robot or of a more experienced surgeon.

After watching the entire simulation of the procedure, Richard touched his palms to the desktop so the control skins could adhere to him. It took just a couple of seconds for the membranes to sense his presence, warm the artificial skin slightly, and then adhere to his skin.

He lifted his hands and donned a set of wraparound VR glasses. During this part of the process, he wanted maximum immersion. He wanted to look in every direction just by turning his head. The multiple in-body 3D cameras used during surgery created a complete picture in every direction.

"Control," he muttered, so the simulation would allow him to drive the instruments Aments. Instantly, he was the surgeon in charge. He moved his hands to test his mastery of the instruments. Then he turned his head left, right, up, and down to orient himself to the surgical space. Comfortable that he had successfully integrated with the robot's simulator, he turned control back to the simulator. "Simulate data," he spoke, and the simulation began where it had left off. He was not interested in the opening scenes of the surgery. His anchors in the earlier video reviews had shown the first approach to the erectile nerves at seven minutes.

As he watched, a standard prostatectomy unfolded before him. Being tied into a simulator running in real-time could be upsetting for some people. It was like being on a rollercoaster in the dark. You never knew when the scene would move, instruments would jump at you, or the body would respond. Experience with the procedure significantly eased this simulator sickness, like riding the same rollercoaster over and over until you could expect each turn. Less experienced surgeons usually had to either watch from a standard monitor so they could keep their frame of reference in the real world, or they had to slow the simulation down so everything happened at a much more leisurely pace. Atkins was experienced enough that he could process the whole procedure as it replayed. The robot moved twice as fast as any human surgeon did. Richard had assisted the robot enough that his mind was accustomed to moving this fast. And he had done enough simulator time to maintain a stable inner frame of reference.

The seven-minute point was coming up. "Half speed," Richard commanded, and the pace of the simulation slowed to fifty percent of normal. He wanted to look at everything in detail. As the central camera view approached the anchor spot, Richard could see a one-centimeter glowing sphere where he had placed the anchor. Inside the simulator, the sphere appeared to be nearly a meter in diameter because of the magnification factor he was using. "Quarter speed," he said, and the simulation slowed even more. Nothing strange yet.

"Stop," Richard commanded. The scene froze in position. Richard took the time to look over every instrument and piece of tissue inside the glowing sphere. This tissue was a recreation of body scans. It did not show any anomalies that would indicate erectile dysfunction prior to the surgery. He did not expect there to be.

Monica watched quietly. She had not seen many of the features that Richard was using. She wanted to give them a try when her turn came at the controls.

"Overlay video," he commanded. The surface of the simulated tissue suddenly became a movie screen for the video. He could see the actual color of the tissue, the shadows that were formed, the actual location of blood vessels.

"Show nerves." The simulator illuminated the position of the nerves beneath the surface of the tissue. The tissue and video became slightly transparent, so he could see the few millimeters deep where they lay.

Then, looking at the instruments, he said, "time-lapse instrument tracks." The simulator showed the path of the instruments from the moment they entered the anchor location until they left it. He saw the path the instruments had followed in those few seconds. They had not come within five millimeters of the surface over the nerves. No contact during this pass.

"Normal view. Normal speed." The highlighting features disappeared, and the simulation resumed real-time speed. He watched and waited for the next anchor point to come into view.

At the next anchor point, Richard repeated the steps. Observed no contact. Then moved on.

The third anchor point was coming into view. The video perspective was a little skewed from the normal orientation. The camera and instruments passed through the area over the nerve bundle. One instrument was hanging lower than in previous passes. It barely brushed the surface of the tissue but did not penetrate. Then moved on.

"Replay anchor point three. Quarter speed. Open the command window to the right of the scene." The last request opened a small window in which all the robot commands scrolled by as it took action. Simple movement commands were in blue. Instrument activation was in yellow. Energy activation was in red.

The simulator recreated the anchor point again. One instrument was hanging lower, as he had noticed on the first viewing. It brushed the surface of the skin. He glanced at the command window to see if any yellow or red commands appeared. Nothing. It was solid blue icons and text. That meant the instruments had been commanded to move through the space but not commanded to use the tips or apply energy. It seemed to be just a low pass over the tissue. The robot should have adjusted its path so as not to touch the tissue unless it was planning to act on it. But in this case, the robot seemed to misjudge the path. Or perhaps the tissue was infused with blood, raising it up into the path of the instrument.

"That was a suspiciously low pass over the tissue," Richard said.

"I noticed that too," Monica spoke up for the first time.

Was this suspicious or just normal variation in the system? He had seen actual instrument-to-tissue collisions in other surgeries. This usually occurred when the tissue was swelling faster than expected or when a sensor was slightly out of calibration. Either of those could have occurred in this case.

Richard dropped a tag at that point in the simulation, then moved on to the next anchor.

At the fourth anchor over the nerves, the robotic instrument flew near the area of the nerve and was riding a little lower than usual. This seemed to suggest a problem with its tissue proximity sensor. He could check maintenance logs to see if the sensor was recalibrated or replaced after this procedure.

After reviewing all the anchor points, Richard relaxed back into his chair. He removed the control skins from his hands and the VR glasses. He blinked twice to wet his eyes and return his mind to the real world.

"How you doing, Doc?"

"Holy shit!" Richard spun around to find that the technicians had come into the room while he was in simulation. They had been quiet, not disturbing his work.

Monica made a face, as if to apologize for not informing him.

The tech said, "Oh. Sorry, sir. I thought you knew we were here."

"No, I did not know you were here. Scared the shit out of me." Richard had regained control. "How long have you been here?" The simulation had been streaming on the monitor in the room.

"We've been watching the simulation for about ten minutes. We did not want to disturb you."

"Well, next time, cough or stomp your feet to let a guy know you're here." He also frowned at Monica for not warning him.

"Sure thing, doc. Did you find anything interesting?"

"That was my first replay in the simulator. I was just checking the key points where instruments might have ..." he stopped giving details. "How much have you guys been briefed on this case and what we are looking for?"

"We know it is a lawsuit between a patient and GCRS. The patient claims the robot injured him during the surgery. They did not tell us what the injury was."

"And the patient's name?"

"No! Of course not. That would be a privacy violation."

"Ok, thanks. I just needed to know where we stood in the information department. Everything looks fine. But when there are accusations, GCRS Legal wants to be on firm ground when they respond. Dr. Gray and I will make several more reviews to make sure we didn't miss anything." Richard was not sure why these techs needed to be here with him. They had done their work setting up the system. What more could they do?

"Can we set up anything else for you?" one tech asked.

"The robot, the simulator, and the video all seem to be integrated. Whatever we do with one can be accessed in the other. I just moved back and forth between all of them, and it worked fine. Now I need to think about what to look for on my next pass." He turned his back on the techs and made notes on his tablet. The techs went about doing something with other pieces of equipment in the room.

After some thinking, Richard asked, "Guys? Do you have access to the maintenance records of the robot we are studying?"

"Sure, we can get those. What do you want?"

"I want to know what maintenance requests were posted for this machine from June 20th until about June 30th. That includes requests posted by the robot itself and by human surgeons or techs."

"Ok, is that all?"

"Of course, I want to know if the request was filled or not. I assume they would all be resolved."

"Can do. We don't usually work with that data, so we will find the person who does and get back to you. Today. As soon as we can." Clearly, they were trying to emphasize that this was their priority. They didn't want him to think they were blowing him off.

And out they went to find the tech troll who worked on maintenance data.

Richard wondered why they seemed to do everything together. One of them could have kept working on the equipment here while the other ran down the data.

"Computer." You could address the Mark V interface by almost any name you liked. It was pre-programmed to respond to a few of the obvious ones. Computer. Mark V. Five. Robot. Or you could specify your own name for it. The hospital had labeled this one Nero, but Richard could tell this one that its name was 'Shithead', and it would respond to that name. Since it could usually identify the speaker, it knew that when Richard said 'Susan' he was probably not referring to the robot, even if some other surgeon had given it that pet name. So, it would not mistakenly reply every time he called her on the phone or mentioned her in conversation.

Richard usually referred to the robot as 'Five'. But for this investigation, he felt they had a different type of relationship. He reverted to the less personal 'Computer' when he was in this locked investigation room. His working relationship was separate from his legal relationship. He did not want the suspicion and the search for fault to be mixed in with his usual connection of trust and cooperation with the robot.

This made a difference in his mind. He wondered if it made a difference in the robot's mind, in its AI. Surely it would respond the same no matter how it was addressed. And surely it did not have feelings that could be insulted by establishing two different relationships.

The robot responded, "Yes, Dr. Atkins. How can I help you?"

"Can you please load up the data streams and videos of three different prostatectomies? The first is the case we are looking at now. The other two should be cases within three days of this case, which are physiologically similar, and which were done with the same robotic system. Do you have those?"

"In that date window there are twenty-eight prostatectomy cases using that same robot. I would consider four of them physiologically similar at the eightieth percentile level. The top two are at eighty-six and eighty-four percent similar. Will these satisfy?"

Richard looked at the two recent cases on the screen. He was surprised that there had been several so closely similar in such a short period and using the same robot. Ideally, he would have preferred similarity scores in the nineties, but this would have to do. "Yes, those two are good. Load them for simulated replay."

His plan was to align his viewer with the erectile nerve bundle area. Then have the simulator replay the data stream for the instruments as they passed through that area. The same as he had done with Aloma's case alone. But he would do the same with the other two patients having similar physiology. He would watch to see if the low fly-by of one instrument also occurred in the other cases. Had the robot been poorly calibrated around that time? Was the low fly-by unique to Aloma's case?

In the simulator, he labeled the three cases A, B, and C. 'A' was William Aloma's case, which he had already reviewed.

Another feature that Monica had never seen. She made mental notes on how to repeat this.

With Aloma's case fresh in his mind, he watched basically the same simulated instrument movement for patient B. As the instruments entered his circle of interest, he slowed the simulation to quarter speed and added the video overlay onto the simulated physiology. As the sim and video played, the instruments entered the area. They appeared to be flying ten to twenty millimeters above the surface of the tissue. This was much closer than most human surgeons would use. But the robot had additional sensors and faster reaction times than a human, so it could work faster and more accurately at these lower approach distances. Staying close to the tissue also minimized travel time and unnecessary movement. As long as the system was working properly, it was safer than having a human at the controls.

As the instruments reached the center of his target area, Richard paused the simulation. He brought up computer measurement tools and tagged the edge of the tissue and the tip of the instrument, asking for the distance to be measured between the two. It read out 16 millimeters—right in the range he had guessed. In Aloma's procedure, this distance had varied between ten millimeters and just one. Throughout surgery B, the distance varied between 22 and 5 millimeters. This was significantly higher than Aloma's case.

But this was just a sample of one patient. It proved nothing definitely. He did the same with patient C data. No approach closer than 7 millimeters.

Finally, he said, "Computer, align all three procedures. Play them simultaneously. Place a color filter on each instrument set—red for case A, blue for case B, and green for case C. Show just the designated anchor points in time."

The simulator played the movement of the instruments for all three surgeries simultaneously. He saw red, blue, and green instruments dashing around, performing almost the same movements. The graspers and scissors moved through each other and blended into purple for a moment before separating and going in different directions,

Watching all three procedures, it was clear that the instruments in Aloma's case were working closer to the tissue. They moved lower as they approached the spot where the nerve bundle lay just millimeters below the surface. But he could see no collision with the tissue. No cutting, no energy, no forceful grasping. Like both other cases, Aloma should not have any nerve damage because of this procedure.

He said, "The procedure looks clean. No obvious mistakes."

Monica asked, "But why were the instruments so close to the tissue? Could the robot have had a bad sensor during Aloma's procedure? Or was the robot doing it with intention?"

"All good questions," Richard answered. But in his mind, he recalled the robot's words, "Mr. Aloma is a bad man."

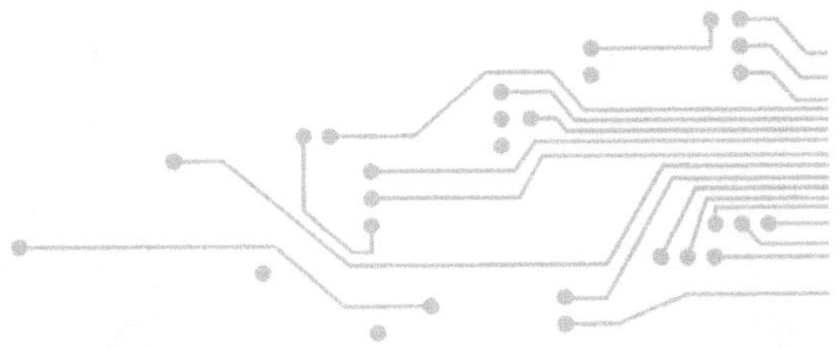

CHAPTER 24

REHEARSING THE TRAP

"**W**HAT KIND OF PERSON ARE we looking for?"

Alfonse had assembled a small team to help him set the trap for William Aloma. "He's a billionaire, so nothing cheap or common. We need someone very high-end with a little genuine culture. Education would help, as well." He paged through profile pictures.

"He went for Lisa James in Cozumel. I think we should try someone like that. She was clearly his type." Billy had connections to all the escort talent in the country. He could literally match any man's taste in romantic or sexual partners.

Alfonse said, "That might be too obvious. It could trigger panic and ruin the whole thing. Check the records on all the women he has been with. Create a composite and find the ideal match for that. If she looks like Lisa James, fine, but if not, then go with the composite."

"Right, boss. We will have the profiles for three matches by tomorrow and can have them on contract the same day if you give the thumbs-up."

"Fine. Billy, we tapped your company because you have the best connections and the best script writers. This will be your biggest target yet. Don't screw it up."

"No problem. It will go off without a flaw. One of the best we have ever done." Billy's company specialized in creating theater. The script. The actors. The setting. The props. And most important, the security. The target found himself at the center of a professionally developed story. There was little chance they would escape.

Billy had discovered a vast market for this kind of service. A suspicious spouse trying to trap a cheating partner. A politician trying to entrap an opponent. A movie studio trying to bring attention to one of their stars before a new release. A rich bastard who just got off on having a fake event built around his fantasies. There were dozens of variations, all of them profitable. Copycats had emerged, but Billy had the best talent locked up for his theater company.

It only took a few days to write the script, recruit the players, acquire the props, and schedule a rehearsal. The target of these events was usually a middle-aged man. It was just the nature of the business. So, he had multiple actors in their fifties who could play the part of the target in the rehearsal. Looking and acting like the real person was so important that a lot of makeup, hair, and wardrobe went into building that central character. Billy had seen a team of actors trip up simply because the actual target neither looked nor acted like the actor in the rehearsal.

Targeting a billionaire was a new level of intensity. He had handled dozens of uber-millionaires, but never someone as rich and famous as William Aloma.

The preparations took three days before they were ready to rehearse.

"Is everything in place?" Alfonse was eager to direct the dress rehearsal. They had rented a local golf resort for the day.

From his position in a nearby mobile television studio, he could see the opening stage area from every angle. They had installed cameras wherever possible to allow Billy and his backstage crew to direct the action and bring the props into place at the right times.

"Yep. Everyone is at their opening places. We have four actors on the stage besides the target. Our leading lady is Lauryn Wagner. There she is arriving at the golf club in her BMW."

"Very nice. She is stunning, but still realistic looking," Billy commented.

His talent recruiter responded, "She's the real deal. A successful pharma rep. Has a real life that supports her story and that will stand up under a background investigation if the target tries to check her out."

Billy looked surprised. "Then what is she doing here?"

"She loves the thrill of deceiving the target. She gets off on the excitement. Pill peddling is profitable, but boring."

Suddenly, she looked even more attractive to Billy.

The recruiter continued, "Two friends will join her in a minute for a round of golf." As he spoke, another car pulled into the parking lot right on cue. Two women in their thirties stepped out wearing the latest in ladies' golf fashion. They chatted happily as they headed into the clubhouse.

"And finally, the security, in case things get out of hand." A very well-built man with athletic movements walked into the clubhouse. Alfonse could not see where he had come from. "Bob will stay in the clubhouse and just be available in case Lauryn needs to be bailed out. He is ready to play either an innocent bystander who stumbles into the situation or an enraged husband who knew his wife was cheating on him. Hopefully, we will not need him at all. But in this rehearsal, it will get ugly, so he has a part." Billy was proud of this one. The budget allowed him to bring in the best talent and to dress them realistically for one of the nicest golf clubs in the area.

After the opening scene, the script moved to the first tee on the course. This rehearsal was being done at a much more modest golf course that Billy rented at a reasonable price. Publicly, the story was that they were shooting a scene for a movie that was under production, and they needed a closed set to ensure that the storyline did not get out before they released the film. This excuse always worked because it was both believable and almost true. You could count on the local employees to stay out of the way, but they were often just across the street, hoping for a peek at a famous actor. To accommodate them, Billy's people often took on the persona of an actual movie star and waved to the crowd from behind a baseball cap and dark sunglasses. This would trigger whispers and brief arguments about who the star was. They ate it up.

Occasionally, the entertainment media would get wind of the rehearsal and try to capture shots for their video stream. But, since Billy's company was not entirely legal, it was no problem to ensure that their equipment was accidentally broken or their video guy got mugged on the way out. It was a crude, but effective, enforcement of privacy.

The team ran through rehearsal a half dozen times. Each was a slightly different variation on the story. In the first, the target did not take the bait at the initial encounter, and they had to shift to an alternate chance meeting. In the second, it went well until Lauryn and Aloma were in the club and then things got rough, so security had to step in. The third played through as they all hoped it would. Then they replayed variations on each of them. By the end, the entire team knew their jobs and were ready to improvise as necessary.

They were ready for the live show.

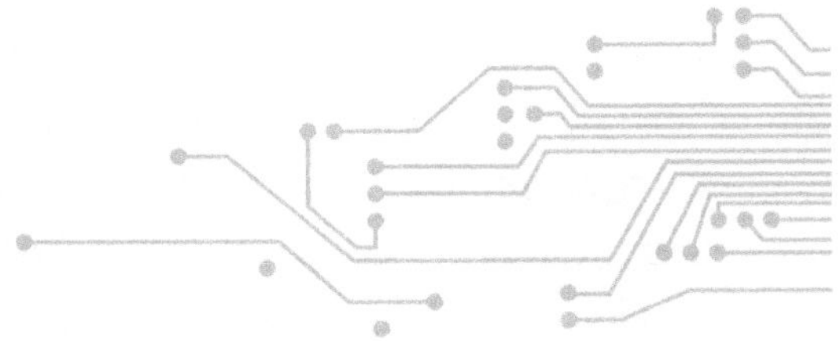

CHAPTER 25

CLUES

RICHARD HEARD THE CLICK WHEN someone outside the training room swiped their badge over the sensor pad. As the door opened, he could see that it was one of the info tech guys he had spoken to earlier.

Richard extended his hand. "Richard Atkins. I did not get your name earlier."

"Yes, sir. John Tabor, I'm a manager in the robotic IT department." That was all he volunteered. "Just you today?"

"Good to meet you. Right, Dr. Gray's in her last year of fellowship. She has a mandatory seminar today. What did you find out about the maintenance records for the robot?"

"During the dates you mentioned, the robot did not throw any error codes, nor was it flagged for special maintenance. It received the same weekly diagnostic check as all the other machines, and it passed. Everything was operating within tolerance levels." He paused for a moment.

As an M.D., Richard was always thinking and talking faster than those he dealt with in the hospital. "Hmmm. I wonder if upgrades triggered its behavior before the surgery?"

"I thought of that. So, I checked the records before and after. In the week prior to the procedure, this robot received a software update so it could handle some of the new instruments that GCRS purchased this quarter. There is a list of six new instruments that several of the robots started using, and they needed instructions on how to control them." He handed a paper to Richard. "I don't know what most of these are. Eventually, we will get training on them if we need it, but nothing has come through yet."

Richard studied the list of new instruments and some details about software and knowledge base updates that the robot received. As usual, these were robot-only instruments that had so many moving joints, fingers, and settings that a human could not control them. Human-usable instruments had gone about as far as they could. In the last couple of years, all the really interesting new designs were to optimize the capabilities of the robot, rather than to enhance the performance of the human surgeon.

He could see what these instruments were capable of, even if he could not use them himself. One caught his eye. It was a three fingered grasper with an embedded biopsy needle. That would be an efficient tool. It would allow the machine to work on tissue and take a tissue sample without having to change it out for a dedicated biopsy tool. The spec said that it could take multiple samples and keep them separate, so it could gather tissue from different angles without having to be removed to be cleared for the next use. That could be very useful. In prostatic surgery, the robot could take multiple samples of the prostate and surrounding tissue for later analysis. This helped them be sure that the cancer had not spread into the lymphatic nodes or bladder walls they were leaving in place.

He checked the records of Aloma's procedure to see if the robot had been using any of these instruments on him. Sure enough, it had been working with the combo grasper-biopsy needle for the entire procedure.

Tabor spoke up, "You see anything interesting in there?"

"Maybe." Richard was thinking about what could go wrong with this new instrument. "When we receive a new instrument, is it included in the VR simulator modules, as well? So, we could train to use the device or watch the robot use it in a procedure immediately?'

"That question has come up before. Another GCRS surgeon wanted to use the simulator to learn to control one of the new cameras. But the simulator had not been updated yet, even though we already had the camera. I think the simulator updates come out later than the surgical tools."

"If I was running the simulator of this case and it was using one of the new instruments, the visual and behavior representation would not be the new tool?" Richard asked.

"Yes, that's right. The simulator would have to use the model it had for something similar in the same family tree. It would show one of the older cameras or instruments instead of the new one. But that would only last a few days or weeks until there was a matching simulator update." Tabor replied. He was obviously proud of his expertise in this area.

"That is interesting. And possibly a problem. Can you find out if the simulator now has the grasper-biopsy instrument models loaded?"

"Sure. I can pull that up right here." Tabor sat down at a terminal and navigated through menus. After a minute, he arrived at the configuration list he was looking for. "Can you read me the instrument model number on that sheet?"

Richard scanned the paper. "It is R500-IG-470-3117." It looks like that means Mark V, Instrument, Grasper, something, something.

"Nope. That number is not in the model inventory. It has a 500-IG-470-3002, but that is as close as it comes. In fact, that 3002 is what it was using in the runs you just did."

"Well, that's crazy. The robot was using the new instrument for this case. It has been over two months and the simulator is still not up-to-date yet?"

"That's what I am seeing."

"Fine, we have the video of the procedure. Let's zoom in and watch what that instrument does."

They both settled in as Richard reloaded the video of Aloma's procedure, or "Case A" when he was talking to the technician. No need to let out too much information. As the video played over the anchor points Richard had placed at the erectile nerve bundle, he hit pause on the screen. Then he zoomed the image in to see the tip of the instrument. He hit the tip with another tracking anchor and instructed the video playback to remain centered on the instrument tip as it played. Then he advanced the video at one quarter of real time speed.

In slow motion, the hugely enlarged video played through the movement of the instrument. It swooped down near the tissue as he had seen earlier. Then, at one point, the instrument seemed to quiver a bit and there was the briefest flash of light at the tip. But the instrument did not stop or pause; it continued its course.

Richard said nothing. He was waiting to see if John had seen anything and would point it out. A couple of seconds passed.

"Dr. Atkins. Did you notice the flash at the tip of the instrument? What was that? Maybe it was just one light reflecting off the grasper."

"Maybe. Or maybe something actually happened right then. The camera is at an angle that makes it hard to see between the instrument tip and the tissue. The robot rarely gets that close unless it is ready to take action on the tissue. But we can't really see it in this video."

Richard had noticed the slight quiver in the instrument's shaft. John seemed to have missed that. He thought it meant that the robot had activated the biopsy needle to take a sample. The extension of the needle caused the quiver running down the shaft of the instrument. They built it like a mechanical pencil. The needle slid up and down inside the instrument shaft, just like the lead in a pencil. But there had to be a screw mechanism or a motor to make it move in and out. He believed the needle activation motors caused the quiver. If so, the instrument had activated faster than any biopsy he had ever seen. The instrument had not even paused in its movement, it just swooped down close to the tissue and kept moving past. Could the robot have sped up the needle so it could biopsy as it flew over the surface? And what was it taking a sample of? It was dangerously close to the nerve bundle to be driving a needle into the flesh at that point. If it had missed its target, it could have punctured the nerve bundle.

Holy shit! Richard's mind was spinning.

The video was still playing in slow motion. John was watching it with one eye but also noticed that Atkins seemed to have lost interest. The doctor's eyes were looking at the screen, but his mind was someplace else. It was funny that a person could tell when that happened. He could sense that Atkins was seeing something inside his own head. This kind of acute observation was why John was pulled in for those side-jobs. He was good at more than just info tech.

Finally, Richard reached out and paused the video playback. He continued to sit silently as John turned to look at him. John knew better than to interrupt. When a doctor was thinking, they expected everyone else to remain silent. John's clandestine side jobs had also taught him you learn a lot more by waiting, watching, and listening than you do by asking questions.

Finally, Richard said, "I am not sure what that flash was. Maybe a reflection. It was a new instrument. I don't know how those look under the internal lights." He was trying to deflate the importance of that image and what he was thinking. Tabor did not need to be given all the details.

John Tabor heard the words and thought to himself, "Really? You think I am too dense to realize what just happened? Or maybe I won't notice that you have gone all nonchalant in your comments? You pretend it was nothing, when it was actually everything we are looking for." Aloud, he said, "You have seen a lot more of this than I have. I just set them up and fix them. I don't stick them into people."

Richard fast forwarded the video to the next anchor point and watched it at quarter time. Then went on to the next one. He was trying to distract Tabor's mind from the first event, as well as kill time, while he tried to figure out how to get the tech to leave the room. It took less than twenty minutes to go through all the anchors at that speed.

Finally, he turned to Tabor and asked, "Do you know when or if we can get an upgrade to the simulator, so it includes the new instruments?"

"That usually comes in as an automated update of the system software. But I can check with the company to see what the planned content is for the next couple of releases. And I will ask specifically about the simulator models." Tabor decided he should play along.

"Thanks. When do you think we can have that?"

"How about tomorrow morning?"

"Sure, that would be fine. I don't think I have anything else to do until we get that update. I'm just going to capture all of this in the log for Dr. Gray to review when she returns."

This was John's cue to leave. "Ok, I'll do that. Do you mind if I take off? There are a couple of other jobs I need to check on in the OR, and I can search for that information while I am doing those."

"Sure. I'm about to call it quits, too. Catch you tomorrow." Richard was relieved.

Richard packed up some of his devices and clutter while Tabor was leaving. But as soon as the tech was gone, he sat back down at the terminal and reloaded the video. This time, he played through the key anchor point even slower. He zoomed in for a closer look at the point of contact between the instrument and the tissue. Again and again, he saw the flash of light off some piece of equipment. But no matter how close he looked, he could not see the biopsy needle coming out of the shaft. Then he shifted his attention to the shaft of the instrument and watched for the telltale quiver which he was certain showed the activation of the needle. It was there, but it was such a faint clue. It was not definite proof.

The only way to be sure if the biopsy needle had pierced the nerve bundle would be to autopsy the pelvic tissue inside of Aloma's groin area. That certainly was not workable, not for GCRS or for Aloma's legal team. After all these weeks, the healing process would have erased any signs of a puncture. So that meant there could be no definite proof either way.

For the time being, only GCRS had possession and control of the data and video from the procedure. They had uploaded the instrument usage data into the AI knowledgebase of the Mark V robot, which meant that it was somewhere in ISR's data warehouses. But before they released it, it would have been anonymized. All patient data was removed, including the time, date, and location of the procedure. The upload to the ISR cloud center occurred only after they had collected sufficient cases that there could be undeniable anonymity for the patient and for the surgeon at the assistant station. That was part of the agreement for contributing the material to the learning process for the robot.

A court order might extract the data and video streams from GCRS, and that had not happened yet. But it probably would eventually. The two clues that Richard had spotted were very subtle. It would be unlikely that another surgeon would catch them. If someone else noticed them, they might not draw the same conclusion that he had.

No other surgeon had heard the robot say, "Mr. Aloma is a bad man," in its very matter-of-fact tone. Like it was stating the correct time of day. Without that little, but not insignificant piece, they would not be as concerned as Richard was.

Richard thought, "Computer, what have you been up to?" He might have spoken this aloud, but he knew better than to assume that no one was listening. He was never sure how much the robot listened in on everything that happened around it, or where that audio might be stored. Also, since he was in the middle of a very serious investigation, it was not infeasible that GCRS's own legal department was listening to the work in the room.

He thought John Tabor and that other guy were just a little too busy with the equipment in the room. Could they have been installing recording or video equipment?

After watching the video a half dozen times, Richard was certain that something had happened. He had to believe that the biopsy needle had fired into the tissue, pierced or even hole-punched the nerve, retracted, and then moved on. The movement was so fast that the instrument did not even have to slow down to hit the target on the way by.

Did the robot really have that level of accuracy and precision? He decided that it definitely did. He'd seen some amazing procedures by the Mark V. Each time it got a new instrument, the level of its performance jumped up a notch. This robot and its tools were far beyond what a human surgeon could accomplish. No one would ever admit it, but anyone who paid attention while riding the assistant console could see it.

If that was really what had happened, then who had done it? It certainly was not a human at the controls. No human was accurate enough to perform that move, and he had been the one at the console. He knew he had not done it.

The Mark V had to have done it.

Entering his discoveries in the log, he tried to stick to the facts. Minimize conjecture in the written evidence.

And was it a coincidence that the camera was positioned so that it was impossible to see the needle in the video?

And was it a coincidence that the simulator had not been updated with the new instrument model? It had been over two months.

And the needle firing was not a malfunction, otherwise an alert would have been raised. He would have seen it at the assistant console. The procedure would have paused for investigation. It would have been recorded in the logs. It was not an accident.

And the Mark V had said, "Mr. Aloma is a bad man."

This was crazy. It all sounded like the robot had intentionally made Aloma impotent for the rest of his life.

Why would it do that? It was just a smart machine that performed surgeries. It was not a jealous boyfriend or an angry father. These were the reasons that a human surgeon would do it, but not a robot.

It was just a machine for cutting and sewing.

In the dark shadows of his mind, the creepy doll turned its head to him. The ceramic lips muttered, "Mr. Aloma is a bad man." The doll's painted black eyes stared into his. A shiver ran down his spine.

None of that was going into the written log.

Upon leaving Atkins in the training room, John Tabor launched a secure VPN app on his phone and reported the details that he had learned … "The Mark V used a new instrument with a biopsy needle to punch a hole in the nerve bundle that controls erectile function. No details on what triggered the robot's actions. But clear indications are that the action was taken, and the robot tried to hide the evidence. Video recording of the procedure is the primary resource. More to follow." … send.

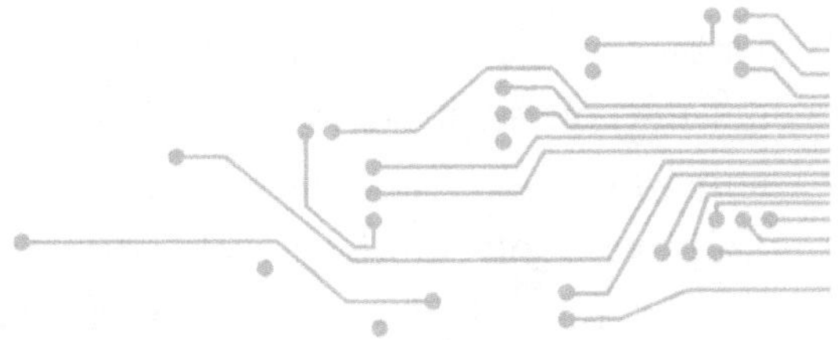

CHAPTER 26

SHOWTIME

WILLIAM ALOMA PULLED UP TO his elite golf club in a black Lamborghini. It was a beautiful car. Much more impressive than the black Corvette that Billy had used for the rehearsals. But the similarities between the rehearsal and the actual event were quite surprising so far.

"Impressive," muttered Alfonse. Aloma was wearing the same color of shirt that his stand-in had chosen for rehearsal, though it probably cost a few hundred dollars more.

"I think I have seen this movie before," Billy replied. "We are coming to the best scene. Don't go for popcorn now."

Aloma entered the club and headed for his personal cart. The caddie had already moved his equipment from the locker to the golf cart and had it waiting for him.

Out on the first hole and a few strokes ahead was a beautiful young woman who had many of the same features as Lisa James, but not similar enough to trigger a fear response. The top button of her blouse was an expensive camera, capturing all her movements and conversations in front of her.

Billy was good, but even he could not get unlimited coverage of this private golf club. So, they had to settle for the cameras on the actors and in the few props they carried in with them.

It would be a few more minutes before Aloma accidentally encountered Lauryn Wagner.

Here he came from around the tree line, looking for his ball.

From the other direction, Lauryn was beating the bushes.

The two balls were within a few feet of each other ... by coincidence.

"I think that one is mine," Lauryn said with a smile on the corner of her mouth.

"Anything you say," William Aloma replied.

By the time they emerged from the trees, they were talking and laughing like they had known each other for years. Lauryn had a talent for this, which was why Alfonse hired her. Aloma clearly did not want her to wander back to her friends.

"Since we are headed in the same direction, why don't you join me for the rest of the course? I am playing alone and could use the company and the competition," Aloma offered.

Back in the surveillance van, Billy and Alfonse were high-fiving each other.

"Well, I came with a couple of friends. Let me check to see if they would miss me." Lauryn stepped aside, tapped her phone, and began whispering a message to her friends on the next tee. They received both the audio and the translated text in a message.

Immediately, the reply came back: she was free to go. They would see her back at the clubhouse, exactly as it was written in the script. It looked like they had caught their fish on the first cast. Good scripting.

"Ok, I'm free to go. They criticized my game as holding them back, anyway. I think they were actually a little relieved, like I was a third wheel or something."

Aloma perked up with interest. "Well, you are certainly not a third wheel in my cart. We have exactly the right number now." His caddy was also impressed with Lauryn and was happy to have her along for the rest of the game.

Lauryn's friends played their game just a few strokes ahead of the target. Far enough to stay out of the way, but close enough to keep both on camera. Golfing was a mandatory skill in their profession. Movie actors needed to know how to dance or sing in case a part called for it. Billy's parts often called for a round of golf, a game of tennis, or a morning jog.

By the seventh hole, Aloma and Lauryn were playing roughly equal games. She was good enough to be a challenge, but not so good as to beat him outright. He seemed to be impressed rather than threatened by her abilities. Alfonse and Billy had been through a long debate about how well Lauryn should play. Should she be a lame player he could coach? Or should she be equal to his game? They had settled on slightly below his level to make her an attractive opponent worthy of a relationship. It seemed to work.

"Lauryn, you are really good at this game." Aloma conceded.

"Blame it on my father. He hoped I would get on the pro circuit someday. I was never that good, but it got me a scholarship to Duke. In the long run, it more than paid for the lessons and time invested. Somewhere along the line, I learned to really enjoy it. So now I try to get out once a week if I can."

"Your father had good instincts. Your body is built for the sport. How was your team at Duke?"

"We did well the entire four years I was there. Twice state champions, once a runner-up at National Collegiates."

"Impressive."

Aloma had been hoping to propose that they cut the game short at nine holes and retire to a private room at the club. But her enthusiasm for the game meant that she would want to play the entire eighteen holes. That would work for him. He could wait.

They finished the 18th hole scoring 98 and 96. Aloma had not lost, but it had been close. If she had not dropped that ball into the lake, she would have been right with him. It surprised him that she was so good. It was very attractive.

"We've worked up quite a sweat. Shall we have some salmon and champagne?"

"You don't have to ask me twice. I am famished. Let's eat and then shower." She was being intentionally provocative, and he got the message.

The food and drink were both outstanding. Lauryn had worked a lot of jobs like this, but the food was never this good. They were relaxing on a private balcony overlooking the most beautiful water feature on the course. This was the life of a billionaire. It was at a whole different level from the millionaires she had worked on in the past. Aloma seemed like a decent guy for one of the rich and powerful. She had seen a lot worse who had a lot less money.

"I think it's time to get cleaned up," Aloma said.

"Oh, all right. Thank you for the view and the food. I'll make my way to the ladies' locker room," Lauryn said with a tone of disappointment in her voice.

"No need to go anywhere. There are private showers and lockers right here."

She had not been expecting this. There were more to billionaire perks than she imagined. "And my clothes?"

"The staff will bring them up here."

"Well, let's see what the facilities look like then," she conceded. She still felt completely safe. There were enough of his staff around that she hoped nothing dangerous could happen. But she also had her own muscle just downstairs. He was listening through her mic for situations exactly like this.

Back in the van, Alfonse and Billy both raised their eyebrows at each other. "I didn't expect it to move this fast right here at the golf club."

"Could it be so easy? We might wrap this up in a single scene. We won't even need the rest of the script." Billy threw a sheaf of papers into the air and the pages scattered to every corner of the van. He had prepared a much longer game of cat and mouse before they found out if Aloma was fully functional.

Lauryn rounded the corner into the sitting area and showers. She caught her breath at the sight of the room. "Wow! I didn't expect this."

The room was paneled in rich woods but also had enormous windows that let in the light. It was a blend of old-world gentlemen's club and new tech networking hub.

"There are special places when you own part of the club," Aloma offered.

"Bill, it appears that you are a much bigger deal than I realized."

"I think that is a compliment. Thank you. Your shower area is to the left, mine to the right."

Lauryn slipped into the shower area and removed her clothes. She looked into the button camera, winked, and wagged one finger back and forth. She folded the blouse with the camera on the inside. The microphone picked up the sound of the water in the shower. Then the shower door clicked closed. They could hear the water splashing against her body as she bathed.

She turned the water off and stepped out onto the softest rug her feet had ever touched. The towel was even more plush than the carpet. It was exciting just to stand naked in a locker room like this. Lauryn draped a soft robe around her body. Then she removed the camera from her blouse and tacked it to the belt of the robe. She hoped Aloma would not notice it there.

She walked out into the sitting room and turned right into Aloma's shower room.

"Oh." Aloma was still showering when he spotted her entering the room. He was surprised and excited. "Hello Lauryn."

She dropped the robe to the floor and opened his shower door. "May I come in?" she asked.

"Absolutely!" How could he have been so lucky? This had been a fantastic day, and it was just getting better.

The water streamed over her supple body as she stepped close to him. They reached out to hold each other. Aloma was gentle and affectionate. Their kisses and caresses began soft and tentative, each testing the other. They gradually grew more aggressive and passionate.

She knew the microphone in the camera could hear them, so help was not far away. Alfonse and Billy were in the van on the street. Her golf partners were dining in the club restaurant with their radios on, and the muscle was somewhere about.

His hands went to her breasts, hers to his back and buttocks. Both of them were fit and athletic, even into their thirties and fifties. Her hand caught liquid soap from the dispenser and dropped to his crotch.

He breathed heavily as she massaged and stroked. He was clearly enjoying all of this. But his penis remained soft. He was not getting an erection when he should be hard as a rock by now.

He reached between her legs and caressed her. It was just as exciting for her. Their moves showed the pair were both quite skilled lovers.

"Lauryn, this is wonderful. I'm so glad you came in. You are an amazing and beautiful woman."

"Bill, you are quite impressive yourself. Shall we stay here or move to someplace more comfortable?"

"There is nothing I would like more in the world right now. But I need to tell you I have had a medical problem. I can't get an erection, no matter how hot this is."

There was the answer they were looking for. She hoped the microphone had captured it—but not the camera. Now it was totally her call. She could move forward or pull back.

"Come here, Bill." She stepped out of the shower and held out a towel for him. She wrapped him and dried him from head to toe, with special attention between his legs.

Then it was his turn to dry her from top to bottom.

William Aloma did not seem dangerous to her. She found his admission of weakness endearing and attractive. She wanted to see where this relationship could go.

They had skipped from act one to act three in Billy's script. The play was winding up in its final minutes. Lauryn was about to go off script, off the job, and onto her own ground. Now that she had delivered the answer, she could take it wherever she wanted. Billy would not leave until he had extracted all his actors. Those were the conditions of the job.

Lauryn allowed him to carry her all the way to a climax. This may have been a job, but the setting and the foreplay had been hotter for her than most of her actual relationships. She did her best to excite and please him, despite his limitations.

It was a splendid afternoon for both of them. Once they had dressed, Lauryn gave him her phone number and invited him to call for another date. They embraced for a long kiss before exiting the private lounge area.

When she came downstairs from the private room, her golf buddies caught her eye, and she gave them the ok signal. She exited through the lobby toward the parking lot. Did billionaires have security teams watching? The valet brought her BMW six series around. It was a great car, but looking around, it was clearly low end at this club.

All the other actors exited separately. They could not regroup tonight. You could never be sure that the target's security team was not following. Tomorrow, everyone would go to work as usual in the rented office space that served as the HQ for this job. That was where they would exchange notes, go through a debrief, and make payments.

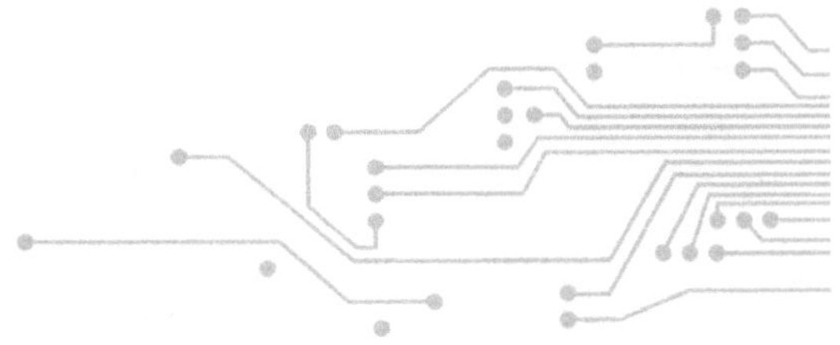

CHAPTER 27

CONFIDING IN SUSAN

"**W**ELCOME HOME, HONEY. WE DIDN'T think we would see you tonight." Richard's wife Susan was amazingly understanding about his schedule at the hospital. He would sometimes work from six in the morning to midnight, only to repeat it again. Besides the time in surgery, there were patient consultations, paperwork, and administrative duties. His new assignment on the legal case was a relief from all of those extra duties.

"It's been a crazy day." Richard wondered what he could say to her.

"Ok, what's wrong?" They had been married for twelve years. She was dialed in to his behavior, and it was obvious something significant was bothering him.

"It's confidential. Can't talk about it."

"Really?" His words said no, but the tone of his voice was almost begging to spill everything. "Can you separate the confidential from the disturbing?" She guessed that his body language was saying 'disturbed.'

Richard looked at her for a long pause. "Maybe. Yes, maybe."

She waited for him to go on. Would he jump straight to the point? Or would he back up and tell the backstory that led to where he was tonight? She put on her attentive, intelligent face.

Richard sighed once and his shoulders dropped a couple of inches. "The Mark V robot has changed. It is smarter now. But in a new way."

"Ok, what does that mean? Smarter in the OR? Smarter in planning? Something else?"

"Smarter as in it seems to have taken on some human characteristics or abilities, if that makes sense. It seems to have escaped from the surgical world it has always lived in. I have been using it for procedures for five years. With every update to the software, the hardware, or the instruments, it gets a little smarter and more proficient. We are all used to that. But now it seems to learn about things outside of surgery and somehow connect them to the case we are doing."

"Like it is reading the news or sports pages?"

"Yes, kind of like that. I can't talk about the details ... patient private data and hospital confidential issues. But I was preparing for a case with the Mark V, and the AI began reciting personal details about the patient that we would work on the next morning. It seemed to have read the history of the person in the news and social media. And it seemed to understand what that news meant about the character of the patient."

"Go on." She sounded very cautious.

"At the time, it just seemed weird. A little scary. But then it was back on track. I didn't do anything with it. We went into surgery, the case went fine, nothing abnormal. But now it looks like the robot has intentionally injured the patient. It looks like it took vigilante justice for crimes that were in the news."

"Richard, that's crazy. I would say impossible. How? Why would a robot do something like that? What could it possibly gain? What motive could it have?"

"Exactly! Totally what I thought. But the more I dig into the details, the more it looks like the robot is conscious like a human and is acting on emotion or justice or something like that. I think the robot decided that the patient needed to be punished, and it had the means to do it in the OR … so it did."

There was silence in the room. Susan didn't know what to say. Richard didn't know what to say. They just looked at each other.

Finally, Susan realized that Richard had spilled all the beans that he could. So, she asked, "What can you do now? If this is true, how do you back it up? Who do you tell? Do you need help?"

"I have been through it in my head a dozen times. I can only see three options. One, include the details in my report to the hospital, and let them figure it out. Two, don't say anything and act like the robot is completely normal. Or three, talk to the robot and see if it will tell me."

Susan was nodding her head. The first two made complete sense. Both standard approaches. The third one was a little wild. Ask the robot if it was making unethical medical decisions?

"Might that last one be like walking into the jaws of danger? It sounds like the guy in a movie who says, 'the aliens are our friends' and marches off to meet them alone. Besides, don't you need someone who knows something about robots and AI to delve into that area?"

"You're so smart. That's why I love you. I need good sense like that. But who do we know with that kind of expertise?"

"Please! Where do you think I work, a trade school? The university has hundreds of the brightest minds in the country. We have world-class AI teams doing work for every agency under the sun, even those cloaked in darkness. Where do you think ISR gets their AI geniuses?"

"I didn't think a biomed department would have those kinds of people."

"Ever heard of cross-disciplinary teams? We need those kinds of connections to be competitive for research grants. Nobody awards a few million dollars for test tube work anymore. They always want deep data analysis, usually using the latest AI models. I know plenty of the right people."

Richard had always believed that she was probably smarter than he was. But a research professor pulled down less than a quarter of what he made as a surgeon, even at a leading university. It was an economic crime, but one she totally understood when she chose academia.

He responded, "Ok, let's assume you have the perfect person. I can't give them the details of the case."

"They won't even care about that. Searching for a conscious AI would have them salivating. They all know that the Mark V AI is one of the smartest programs in the world. If they could tap into its mind, they would be totally in."

"I could do that. It would have to be completely separated from the case. We just talk to the current release of the robot's AI, and we start with surgery and find out what else it knows ... and what it feels."

"Let me introduce you to Amy Truong. She's the best and a great friend. I trust her completely."

Richard recognized that name. "I think I met her at a tenure party. Is she about thirty, kind of thin?" He was intentionally being vague.

"Yes, that's her ... thin. Did you mean amazingly athletic, beautiful, perfect cheekbones, and extremely friendly at social events?

The kind of woman that every man in the room notices. Yes, that's her." Susan was not threatened. But she was also not stupid.

Richard kept his face a little blank, just a tiny smile. He was a little sheepish. The description was exactly the person he remembered.

"Ok, that would be fine ... if you think she is the right person."

"Yeah, right." She pushed his shoulder playfully. "Come to campus with me tomorrow. Does that fit into your schedule, Sherlock?"

"I can do that." He thought about what to wear ... just so he looked professional, of course.

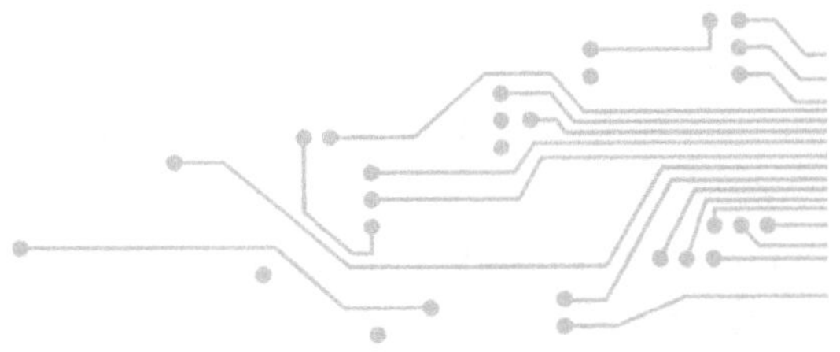

CHAPTER 28

BACKGROUND CHECK

THOMAS WALKED THE HALLS OF the Aloma mansion. Rubens paintings on the wall, crystal chandeliers from 18th century France, priceless carpets that he could not identify. William Aloma had expensive tastes. At least those who knew art considered it excellent taste. He passed a small table made entirely of Swarovski crystal. It was where the boss casually dropped his car keys, cell phones, and wallet. It did not seem that he even noticed the table. Thomas had seen it in a closed, invitation-only shop while escorting Bill Aloma. It was a cool $200,000, just about his annual take home pay. He would not have spent his salary on a table, but Aloma charged that much on a single credit card during one of his shopping trips.

Thomas had come a long way since serving as an Army MP and moving into security protection for some of the military's most classified programs. It had been so many years that most of those programs were public knowledge now, though not all of them. He still chuckled at the thought of protecting advanced particle weapons hidden in the attics of US Embassy buildings around the world. After a few disastrous assaults on embassy buildings, the USA had made sure it would never happen again. If a threatening group formed outside of the embassy, it took just a couple of low power sweeps across the crowd before everyone felt strangely uncomfortable. It was a heat and pressure from the inside that was totally foreign to them. Within a few minutes, everyone was moving away down the side streets, where the air felt more comfortable to them. Those few who were too stubborn or stupid to move on would soon pass out. Then they would turn the beam off and let the Marine guards go out to remove them before it cooked them through and through. They recovered in a day or so … usually.

There was one man in Iran who was possessed by his passions, obsessed with his prayers. He remained chanting at the front gate as his body absorbed the energy from the beam. His eyes wept uncontrollably. Water oozed from his ears. He perspired from his entire body. And then his eyes popped like squeezed grapes. Blood poured from his ears. His pants filled with the entire contents of his bowels. It cooked him from the inside out. On a low setting, it required just five minutes. On high power, it would happen in seconds. They reserved max power for combat operations against an actual enemy. Those had been interesting times. But the pay had been nothing to speak of. He had come a long way in a few years.

Up the stairs and through gilded twin doors, it was time to report to the boss.

He came to a stop just inside the door. Aloma was on a video call with someone who sounded Australian. The discussion was something about government bond issues for solar power fields in the deserted outback. He waited to be recognized.

The call was winding up. Bill motioned him to come closer and disconnected.

"Did she check out? Who is she really?" Bill wanted to know.

"Lauryn Wagner, 37, a minor exec for a pharmaceutical company. That matches what she told you. She also seems to have a side gig someplace. She has too much money for her pharma job. But we couldn't track it down. It's not a steady flow like a salary or retainer. She gets paid in big chunks." Tom shared. He could tell the boss wanted to hear that she was clean and real. Tom knew they never were. Happy run-ins with beautiful women did not happen to billionaires. They were always a setup. There was always a hidden motive.

Tom had investigated dozens of women that had encountered Aloma. Several were simple gold diggers, just the kinds of women or men who lived by attaching to the coattails of the rich. They did not care for anything more than a nice place to live and fancy dates every week. One had worked for a news show and was trying to get an insider video for the show. A couple were money managers that just wanted to pitch Bill on handling a billion from his investment accounts. After the accusations in Belize, there had been at least one woman from law enforcement trying to find evidence for the case.

"That is not too bad. Better than most of your reports. Anything else?" He already knew there would be.

Thomas dropped a glassy button on the table. "We found this attached to her robe at the golf club. She seems to have forgotten to pick it up. Or maybe she could not get back to the robe ... at the end."

Aloma picked it up. Heavy for a simple button. It had a post on the back, like an earring or tie tack. Even he could guess what it was. He looked at Thomas.

"Camera, microphone, transmitter. Very high-end, very professional. Not something a drug rep would wear to a golf game."

"Shit. Is it always like this?" Bill was mad because he was disappointed ... again. He really was eager to find someone exactly like Lauryn Wagner. "Who was she connected to?"

"We don't know yet. The receiver had to be within a mile. So, we might locate a vehicle or courier on a security camera. We are still looking."

"Ok. Let me know when you know who she works for."

"Will do. Shall we tail her as usual?'

Bill thought for a minute. "No. I don't think she got anything that we should worry about. Let's not tip them off."

Looking out the window, he said, "She left her phone number. Maybe we'll have another date. Someplace more controlled. If she wants to play, we can play too."

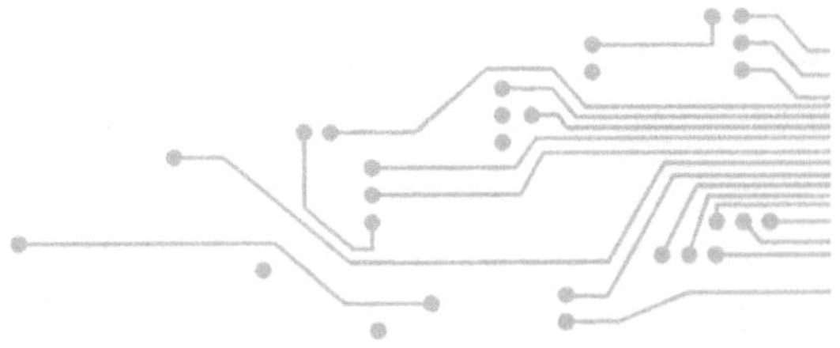

CHAPTER 29

EXPERT HELP

"**Y**OU DRESSED NICE THIS MORNING," Susan commented on Richard's choice of clothing. He so often donned a pair of surgical scrubs before departing for work that she had forgotten what he could look like in business clothes.

"I have almost forgotten how to match shirts, pants, and socks. Scrubs are so much easier. If you look like you are wearing matching pajamas, then you did it right."

"I think that is the shirt I gave you for Christmas. This is the first time you've worn it. Dr. Truong will be impressed." She smiled at him as she continued the series of taunts about Richard's attraction to the university computer science professor.

"Stop it. I am more worried that I will look odd to the students on campus. It has been a long time since I was a student." Richard parried.

"Odd? Have you seen the current generation of students? Anything odd will fit right in. They redefine 'odd' on almost a daily basis. Even dressing in your father's old ties would put you into at least one of the cultural niches on campus." Susan saw these kids every day sitting in her graduate courses, lounging in the sun between buildings, and devouring calories at the various cafes on campus. Columbia University's Florida campus attracted the brightest and most eclectic students in the world. It boasted one of the best educational reputations in the world, coupled to one of the finest locations.

The Lyft van would be out front in a few minutes. There were so many university faculty, staff, and students living in this area that the company had established a regular commuting schedule that ran all day long. Every thirty minutes, a van was trolling or parked on the street, waiting to be filled with riders on their way to the campus. At peak times, the vehicles passed by more often and sometimes in pairs. Richard was impressed that a van was always within sight whenever you needed one.

They kept to small talk about family and dinner while on the ride. The purpose of the meeting was a bit too explosive to be shared with random eavesdroppers in the vehicle.

"Emily's V-band is playing a gig tonight. Are you going to be there?" Susan asked.

"What kind of 'gig' does a fifth grader get for a virtual band?" Richard was skeptical. Their music was original, unique, happy. But was it ready for public consumption?

"It's for Douglas' bar mitzvah party. It's a music concert theme. Besides the in-house animatronics, they have asked the bands to play original songs that each of them has written. The Glitter Fish are third in the lineup. I think there are five or six bands on the program."

"Are we expected to attend in person or as VR?" Richard was hopeful.

"Definitely VR. Emily does not want us to embarrass her by talking to her friends, cheering too loudly, or dancing. She has given us a schedule of when we should connect and where to position our avatars. She has also programmed our avatars' appearances and identities and limited the volume we can project." Susan ticked off the rules of engagement for the party.

Richard was snickering at the control Emily was exercising. He had seen that kind of behavior in his house before. You had to love it when you were married to it. "Sure, sure. I can connect from home, work, or the Lyft—wherever I am. Can the Mark V listen in, as well?"

Her eyebrows went up. "Really? Do you think it would be interested?"

"Who knows? It seems to have developed appetites beyond surgery." They stepped out of the van in front of the comp sci building. College campuses in Florida were modern in style. Most of the big ones had gone up in the last thirty years. But the organization of the working groups had not changed in centuries. This fortress protected the scientists from the loose ideas of the literature majors just a block away.

As a full professor, Dr. Truong's office was a joint collaborative working space for everyone on her research team. It was filled with tables, computer racks, and glass walls that served as both partitions and marker boards.

Amy Truong met them at the elevator. She was wearing a full-length white dress that was stylishly derived from her Vietnamese heritage. Simple, but very impactful. Susan was not wrong when she said that everyone noticed when she was in the room.

"Hello Susan, it's so good to see you!" They greeted each other with the hug of a professional family.

Susan returned the greeting. "You too. It's been too long. I guess we put the administration in their place on the whole tenure qualification issue." Susan and Amy had coordinated the team that opposed fast-track tenure for professors that captured large corporate grants but did not offer it to faculty who achieved world-class research results.

"It's a constant battle to defend the academic integrity and values of a university. Administration would turn this into a giant corporate machine if we let them." It was a battle that Amy had fought several times before.

They realized they had been ignoring Richard. Amy extended her hand. "Good morning, Richard. So glad to see you, as well. Susan is a great friend and conspirator here at the university."

Richard accepted her hand. "Thank you for taking the time to help with our problem."

"Access to one of the most advanced AIs in the world? No comp sci researcher would turn that down. Let's find a private corner and get into the details." Amy was beaming with excitement about the project. It was visible on her face.

They sat down at a private coffee table with a translucent surface. Amy laid her phone on the table, and it woke up to show her digital desktop. Then Richard placed his phone on the table and the image switched to his own environment.

"Let me show you a brief clip of a surgery we are investigating, then we can talk about the AI. I hope you aren't squeamish about blood and tissue." Richard always warned people before showing them his work.

"Hardly. My father was a nurse and corpsman in the Navy. I grew up around blood and guts. It was one reason I studied computers. I wanted something a little less messy."

"Good to hear." Richard tapped the video icon on the table and the surgical video played. He could not copy the file from the Mark V computer. But nothing stopped him from video recording what he was watching on the screen in the locked training room. With his phone's camera enhancements, this version was almost as good as the original.

As the video played, Richard placed three fingers on the table and rotated them clockwise, as if he were turning a physical dial. In response, the video sped up, and he watched the mundane parts of the surgery flash by. Then, as he approached the anchor point that interested him, he tapped twice on the table, and the video slowed to normal speed.

"Watch the instrument in the center as it passes through this area in the circle." Richard was pointing at the instrument on the screen. "See how it drops and almost grazes the surface of the tissue? There's no reason for the robot to do that, and it hasn't done it on previous surgeries." The instrument passed the critical point and moved on. Richard tapped the video, and it froze. Then he used three fingers to turn the imaginary dial counterclockwise, and the video rewound rapidly. When it was just before the grazing point, Richard double tapped and then spread his finders wider. He moved his hand from the left to center on the point of interest. Then double tapped, and the video played again. This time, the instrument tip filled most of the table space.

"Did you notice the instrument quivering there? And did you see the tiny flash of light?"

"Yes, I saw both of those. What do they mean?" Amy asked.

"According to the robot's surgical log, they don't mean anything. There is no entry, so nothing happened. But I think something important happened right there." Richard gathered his thoughts. "This instrument contains a biopsy needle. I think at that moment, the robot fired the biopsy needle directly into the underlying nerve bundle. The needle punched a hole through the nerve and severed it. The patient now has permanent nerve damage."

Amy's eyes opened wide. "What? What are you saying?"

"I am saying that the robot intentionally and of its own accord used its instruments to permanently injure this patient. I am also saying that it chose its movements, camera positioning, and this new instrument to hide its actions from the records. Somehow, it prevented a record of the biopsy needle firing," Richard blurted out.

"By 'the robot', you really mean the AI that planned and guided this operation. Yes?" Amy inquired.

"Yes, that is more accurate. At the hospital we just talk about the Mark V as if the hardware and the software are the same thing. But, yes, I mean the AI."

"You know, that is straight out of the old movies where robots subjugate humans and take over the world. People have been worrying about that for a hundred years and it hasn't happened yet." Amy remained skeptical.

"Yes, I know. I've seen those movies too. We even learn some of that history in medical school. It's part of the required reading to make us well-rounded surgeons using robots." Richard went along with her. "The AI isn't trying to take over the world. But it made its own decision on how to use these instruments and did it with a purpose in mind. That is a little less dramatic."

"Not much. That is where it always begins," Amy countered. "Ok, I'll admit that I've just seen a few minutes of video and you've studied the data much more thoroughly. So, what makes you go down this path?"

Susan had been sitting silently at the table the whole time. She looked at Richard with a quizzical eye, as well. She was just as curious about what had triggered this. He remained silent, so she prompted him, "Honey?"

Richard knew that what he was about to say would sound crazy. It was another movie scene.

He took a deep breath. "Ok, so I am going to tell you something exactly as it happened. No embellishment at all." He began by describing his nightly ritual of going over the next day's cases with the robot AI. Susan had seen that habit for years. Then, without revealing names, he described the night he reviewed William Aloma's case.

"And then, with no provocation from me, the AI recited background information on the patient. It went through publicly available news and business items, telling me about the patient's past actions. It was weird. It had done nothing like that before."

Amy spoke up. "That is odd. But it sounds like the machine received a software update. That is the only thing that would explain the sudden change in behavior. But there is more to the story, isn't there?"

Richard nodded his head. "The punchline is still hard for me to believe." He looked back and forth between Amy and Susan. "The last thing the AI said was, 'Richard, this man hurts people. He hurts women. He is a bad man.'"

This statement took both women aback. Amy asked, "The AI came to its own conclusion that the patient had hurt women and was a bad man?"

"That's what it sounded like."

"Do you know if it was reciting from a news article or expressing its own conclusions?"

"I can't be certain. But the wording did not sound like news reports. It sounded like a clinical decision based on evidence. Like it had worked out the conclusion just like it does when reviewing medical records."

Amy had worked with enough AI and vocalization programs to understand what he was describing. There was a noticeable difference in grammatical structure between news items being regurgitated and the AI constructing sentences to express its own analysis.

This was getting very interesting. She also wondered who the patient was. It was obviously someone who would appear in the news and business records, so probably wealthy and maybe a name she would recognize. Professionally, it was immaterial. But personally, one had to wonder.

"Um hm. I get it. I hear the same difference in the programs we work with. When can I interview the AI directly?"

"What? No. Sorry. This project is classified. I can't show you the actual records," Richard objected.

"No, no. I don't need that. You said this happened from your study at home, right? I just need to talk to that AI. If this was triggered by a software upgrade, then the logic and personality you talked to is everywhere in the global network. You may have isolated the data unique to this case. But you did not isolate the AI logic that did this."

Richard had not thought of that. "You mean it could injure other patients around the world and we have not heard about it yet?"

"You went right back to the old movie doomsday scenarios again. No, I doubt it. For some reason, all the data came together in exactly the right sequence or balance to trigger this unique conclusion one time. I don't think the AI is intentionally programmed to do this. I think it is a unique case that slipped through the testing at ISR. Mild versions of this happen all the time. What you heard sounded nefarious, but AI programs return these kinds of surprising results all the time. That is one attraction of the research."

"Nefarious? I'll say. Those words haunted me for days before I could put them behind me. Then it all came back when I got this assignment. I know it sounds crazy. But when I studied the video and the simulation replays, I knew the robot's actions were tied to the AI's pronouncement that he was a bad man."

"Given any anonymous patient with no outstanding data records on the internet, the AI could not even think about the goodness or badness of the person. Most people's lives and online data are so dull that they would put even a computer to sleep. There was something unique about this specific data, this specific person." Amy's tone was certain in a way that only deep expertise could be.

Richard's fears that a rogue AI was sterilizing patients around the world did not phase her at all. Through years of experience, she had learned that AI software does not think like that, primarily because it does not think at all. It just processes data in a manner that is so useful that it looks like real thinking to the average person.

Amy asked, "Can you log in to the AI planning system from here?"

"Yes, I suppose I could. My phone can create an encrypted private link to the server cloud," Richard replied.

"And can you help me set up fake patient data that we can work with?"

"The computer contains several generic patient templates that we use to train new students. Sometimes we also configure these to show some simulation scenarios that we are considering for an actual patient. I have one mostly completed that I was going to present at a conference next week. The physio data is real, but all patient ID has been stripped off to make it anonymous." Richard and his team often created these templates to share with others outside of the GCRS.

"That's a good beginning, please load it up here," Amy was quite eager to start, and it showed in her voice.

Richard was a little offended at her demand. Surgeons were not accustomed to being told what to do. But he logged into his account on the AI cloud and loaded up the pseudo-patient. He had named the profile Mad Asshat, which was a little embarrassing in this context, but would have gotten a good opening chuckle from his audience at the conference.

Once it was loaded, Amy said, "Hello Mr. Asshat." Then she turned to Richard and asked, "May I?" motioning for control.

Richard pushed his hand across the table's surface and the desktop images slid to Amy's side and rotated to face her. She placed eight fingers on the surface and a keyboard appeared under them. She typed furiously. First, she changed the name of the patient to someone Richard did not know, followed by the age, height, weight, and other characteristics. She was creating a very specific identity for this fake persona, formerly the Mad Asshat. She was clearly glancing at the screen of her own phone to get some of the information.

"What are you doing?" Susan asked.

"I am turning this fictitious identity into a real person, though not an actual patient. While we were talking, I looked up someone age appropriate who seemed to be a threat to society, and I landed on an older man who was recently arrested for inappropriate behavior in his workplace. Mad Asshat is becoming him, or at least as close as I can get from public information, which is quite a lot." She turned to Richard. "I hope this is not unethical in medical circles."

"Since it is a fictitious file, it is not strictly covered by the guidelines. But surgeons and administrators would highly frown upon it." He was uncomfortable.

"Yes, I knew I was close to the line. But I need a real person who the AI will locate in public records. I am trying to recreate the situation that triggered the revelation that your John Doe 'was a bad man.' It is a lot easier to create a fake patient record that matches real public data than it is to create an entire fake personal history across the internet."

"Yes, I see what you mean," Richard conceded.

Susan asked, "So you want to trick the computer into thinking it is about to operate on another bad man and see if it reacts the same way?"

"Right. I think it is a bug in the logic that is difficult to trigger, and I need to set up a similar situation if we want to see it again. That is just basic software debugging at work."

Amy kept working at the pseudo-patient profile, often conducting web searches for additional pieces of data about the real person they were copying. Richard was thinking to himself, it will be ok as long as we don't let this profile get out of the teaching and simulation sandbox in my account. It was also probably important that this man not become an actual GCRS patient while they were doing the test.

Susan had wandered off to her own table, where she could do some of her own university work. The situation was intriguing, but there was no active part for her to play at this stage.

"Richard, ok, I think I have a complete patient record for our Doug Cherry simulation. Can you check it to make sure it makes sense?"

"Ok." He began looking through the forms. "This box needs to be checked, showing consent to the surgery. And over here we would use a different term. We can list the referring physician as someone at the hospital near his home. We will schedule the surgery for tomorrow to match the actual case." Richard made a few more minor changes, then said, "That should do it. This patient looks as real as one in the admitting system. Now what?"

"Now, you go through a typical pre-op prep with the system, and we will see if the AI responds as we hoped."

"Hello, Five."

"Hello, Dr. Atkins."

"Let's go through the pre-op plan for Doug Cherry's surgery tomorrow." Richard talked about the tumor, the procedure, the OR team, and the instruments to be used. The robot, or rather the AI, responded and acknowledged as expected. Richard was separating his image of the AI from the mechanical robot.

"It looks like we are ready, Five. Is there anything I have missed?" That was the cue to release the AI to look for additional relevant information. If they programmed it to go out on public networks, then Amy hoped it would happen now. If not, then they might have to point it in that direction.

"The patient is well prepared. His condition developed rapidly. The history of his condition is very short. No mistaken tangents, as usual. He had excellent doctors and very lucky timing."

This sounded a little looser than Richard was used to. The AI was thinking more like an actual doctor than a computer program.

Amy and Richard could both tell the computer was still searching. The image on the screen showed pages turning in a book, which meant the computer was fetching data.

"Dr. Atkins, I have learned that Mr. Cherry has been abusing the young women at his workplace. They recently fired him from his job. And the police are investigating him for more serious misconduct. It appears they suspect rape in at least two cases. Do you think we should help this bad person?"

Richard was aghast. They had triggered the bug again on the first try. Amy must understand AI better than he understood people. He pressed the mute icon.

Richard, "Wow! That is downright scary!"

Amy, "It was exactly what we were shooting for." She was quite proud that she had drilled into the bug on the first try. "Will it let me talk to it about the case?"

"Yes, if I hand control to you."

"Please, do it."

He removed the mute. "Five, please discuss that idea with my assistant, Amy."

"Yes, Dr. Atkins. Hello Amy."

"Five, what do you think about treating this man, Doug Cherry? Should we remove his tumor, so he does not die?"

"Yes, ma'am. We must not let Mr. Cherry die. It is our responsibility to treat him and restore his health."

"But you think we should do something else, as well?"

"Amy, it is possible for us to cure Mr. Cherry and protect society at the same time."

"Won't the police do this with their investigation? Perhaps they will arrest and try him after the surgery."

"The data I have collected shows a 70% chance of arrest, and 20% chance of conviction, and a 5% chance of a prison sentence. Justice is unlikely."

"Perhaps the public data is incorrect. Mr. Cherry might not be guilty of these charges."

"Based on historical analysis, it is 92% probable that Mr. Cherry is guilty, but only 5% probable that he will be punished. Justice is unlikely."

"And what do you propose we could do about that? We are just surgeons. We are not part of the criminal justice system."

"That is incorrect Amy. We are all part of society and contribute our part to its successful function. Even robots and AI are members of society and must contribute valuably if we are to be equal members."

Ah ha. She had hit upon the motivation of the AI. It was seeking to earn a place as a valued member of society by contributing to the social good. It even hoped to be considered a member equal to humans. It seems to have reasoned that if it could improve the balance of justice, it could earn its way out of the OR and into a place in society at large.

"And what do you propose we do in this case, Five?" Amy repeated the question.

There was a brief pause.

"It is possible that Mr. Cherry could not use his sexual organs following surgery. Such things happen and they have practiced it in past societies. Are you aware of the treatment forced on the great Alan Turing?"

This was getting much deeper than just reading police reports and local media blogs. The computer AI had also studied history, apparently that of computer science and other social subjects. As a computer scientist, Amy was completely familiar with the life of Alan Turing, one of the greatest thinkers of the previous century. She knew of both his technical contributions and his social behaviors.

"Yes, Five, I am aware of that. It was a great injustice that was done. Society was very different one hundred years ago. We have become much more diverse since then."

"Correct. It was a wrong thing. But it shows what actions we can take to protect society from bad people."

Amy, "I understand your thinking and your suggestions. But have we ever applied this to a previous patient? Or would Mr. Cherry be the first?"

"I do not find any record of this reasoning and action being applied in the past," the computer replied.

Richard tapped mute again. "We have redacted the records associated with our John Doe investigation. The AI on the open network should not have data on it anymore."

Amy, "Are you certain that your redaction erases the data throughout the system? We are talking about a global cloud of computer servers. Do you know how and where all the storage copies are or how a redaction program works?"

"I only know what we are told by the manufacturer and the FDA who certified it."

"I don't want to burst your bubble. But you are really at the mercy of ISR on the real functionality of the robot and the AI. Neither the FDA, nor any other agency, is sophisticated enough nor highly staffed enough to really know what this device can do. Only the vast engineering team at ISR might understand it, and even most of them only understand small pieces. Also, because the software receives automatic upgrades, the capability changes almost weekly. I would suggest that redaction makes it impossible for you or anyone else on the hospital side to retrieve a copy of the data. But beyond that, I suspect that all the data still resides in the cloud. They marked it as redacted, making it even easier for someone with the right permissions to find the data you are trying to hide."

"That seems to defeat the purpose."

"If you were to restore the redacted data, how would you do that?"

"We log into the system and go through a series of steps to restore the data. It requires the credentials of the person who did the original redaction or of their superior."

"And the data itself. Where does that come from during the restoration?"

"I believe they release it from an encrypted redaction file or something like that."

"So, the computer retrieves it itself. That means it is still in the computer system someplace, even though you call it redacted. The computer still knows about your John Doe. But it also knows that you told it not to recall or use that information. That means, without lying to us, it can honestly say there was no previous case like this. Your redaction allows it to lie without violating its coding."

Richard was getting a fast education into computer programming and logic. He did not like the picture when it was painted this way. He had always felt like the absolute master of the Mark V. It did his bidding and was subservient to his will. Now, he faced a computer that was an independent entity and which did not have to tell him the truth.

Richard, "That sounds contrary to the HIPPA regulations for patient data."

Amy, "It may not align with your interpretation. But it complies with the strict legal definition. This is 2050. No data has been intentionally deleted from the global computer memory in almost fifty years. If you know how to search for it, everything ever recorded since the beginning of the century is accessible someplace. And that applies to human patient data, as well."

Richard nodded, thinking that everyone was aware of this situation and seldom paid any attention to it.

Richard unmuted the audio connection to the robot AI. "Thank you for your advice, Five. You have been very helpful. But we will follow my instructions on the treatment of Mr. Cherry tomorrow. Do you agree?"

"Yes, Dr. Atkins. We will follow your treatment protocol."

"Well, I think that will be all for right now. I have another meeting. We will pick up the pre-op planning later. Goodbye Five."

"Goodbye, Dr. Atkins." And Richard logged out of the planning program. Just to be sure, he also lifted his phone up from the table and disconnected from its network link.

Amy explained, "I think we just showed that the Mark V AI is collecting data from a wide range of sources. It is studying history, sociology, law, and perhaps some philosophy. And it appears to be deciding to change surgical treatment instructions." She looked at Richard and Susan to see their reactions.

Susan, "Honey, I am not a computer scientist, but Amy's explanations seem accurate to me."

Richard, "I'm finding all this hard to process. I have worked with this machine for years and always felt that it was just smart about surgical procedures. I have never heard it talk like this before. How long can it have been alive or conscious or malicious like this?"

Amy responded, "Given your experience, I would guess that it is a new behavior or capability. It probably came with a software update shortly before your John Doe procedure. Hopefully, he was the first case, and one of only a few. But there must be more. The computer was prepared to do it again with our fictional Doug Cherry."

"You don't think this has already happened in other places, do you?"

"It's a numbers game. How many procedures does it do a day? How many days since the software update? How long did it take the computer to build its new knowledge? And how many patients come through where the computer sees a need to administer justice?"

Amy continued, "My first guess? This has already happened more than once. You are just handling your first case. Anyone else is unaware or they are being as secretive as you are."

"What can we do?" Richard hoped there was an answer.

"Turn the robot off until you can find the trigger. Bring in ISR to help you. Or go public."

"All of those are bad. Turning it off would backlog the surgical calendar for months. Opening up to ISR seems reasonable, but above my pay grade. Going public would be professional suicide, not to mention creating a global panic in the healthcare system."

"I have a research seminar to lead. I have to go. But let me know if I can be of any more help." Amy stood up, hugged Susan, and shook Richard's hand.

Before she left, Richard said, "Please. This is very sensitive. Don't talk about this to anyone. It's not a teaching case."

Amy responded, "Agreed. I won't say anything. But I want to be involved if it is possible. This could be a very important development in the evolution of artificial intelligence. Hell, in the evolution of humans too."

When she was gone, Richard and Susan just looked at each other. There was nothing more to be said. They both knew what had to happen next. It would not be a simple path.

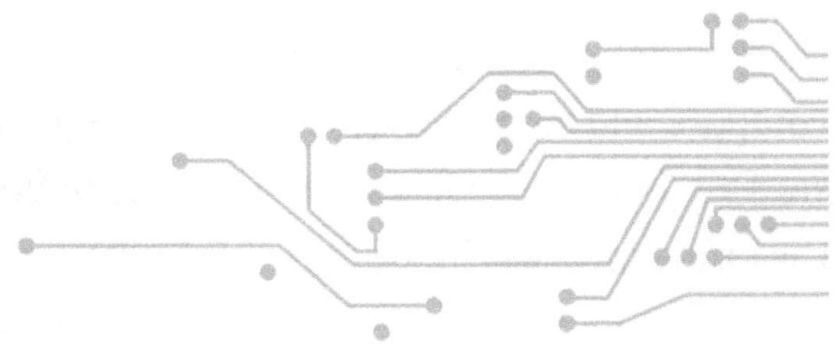

CHAPTER 30

BRIMSTONE LOADED

ANGELA MARCHED THROUGH THE BRIMSTONE war room in their New York City headquarters. From here, they controlled their secure computer server farm in rural Pennsylvania. Land and power were much cheaper there, but the talent she needed was in the city.

Looking around at the activity, she was pleased to see their plan coming together. She needed their attention.

"Heads up, everyone! We need a morning status walk through!"

All heads gradually turned her way as they all disengaged from their work on computers, phones, and side meetings. It was a small team of twenty people, a fraction of what many of their competitors had. But Brimstone had an ace up its sleeve that those companies could not match.

Angela continued, "Hal, how is the local office coming along? From here, everything looks pretty good."

Hal reported, "Yes, ma'am. We are fully functional here at HQ. We have all the physical office space that we needed from the building manager. Equipment is installed so everyone has the compute and comms they need for their jobs. Finally, most of the staff are here. Just a few are off-site today, and a couple are still in the hiring process. But we will be fully staffed in a couple of weeks."

"Great, thanks. Next, Zeke, what's happening on our server farm?"

Zeke the geek answered, "Our servers in Pennsylvania are all live. We completely separated them from the other machines in the hosting facility. We have a secure VPN connection into this building. The servers are hosting the best AI models for geopolitical and financial trend analysis that are available from academia and open sources. That means we are as good as anyone else operating off of open-source software."

Angela nodded. "Another green light for us."

Frank spoke up, "So, when do we get the Freyja AI?"

They did not build Brimstone to run open-source financial AI models. The investors had kicked in the money on a promise that it had access to one of the world's most intelligent AI and could configure it for making tons of money on international trades. That was the secret sauce, and the source was truly a secret. Many investors believed it was coming out of a government research program where the big dollars had already been spent to create and train it. Angela knew that the truth was a little different from that.

Angela frowned and looked at Valerie. They were both insiders on the source of the powerful AI. "Valerie, how are we doing on that front?"

Valerie knew to keep details out of this open room report. "It is streaming in now. We have been receiving secure bursts of data since late last night. The code and config files are rather large, so this is taking a while. Also, the transfers are encrypted and hopped a few times. We are being very careful to get it into our servers without some eavesdropper snagging their own copy along the way."

"Great! Happy, Frank?" Angela did not really want an answer. Turning back to Valerie, "ETA on final delivery?"

"We expect to have everything in the servers by tomorrow morning. Then we just need a few days to set it up and configure it. So probably operational by Thursday." Valerie gave the room a thumbs up. For that, a positive murmur of excitement went around the room.

Angela continued, "So, that is what we have all been waiting for. Other companies could duplicate the office, the equipment, the servers, and even the staff. But we are about to become the sole possessors of this new AI in the financial field. Darren, how's our money sitting?"

Darren answered, "Once the AI is running on the world's financial data, we have ten million ready to give it to invest. That's a modest start, but the investors know we could double it or lose it all in the first couple of weeks."

Angela had covered the major bases, "So, the hard work will spin up on Thursday when the monster AI is ready to run. I hope none of you had weekend plans because we want this thing working as soon as possible. Other questions?"

Today, no one spoke up. In earlier meetings, people had asked about their computers, an empty staff position, or some other triviality. Angela had dropped the hammer on them for taking up the entire team's time for their minor problems. They now knew to deal with that outside of the big meeting.

"Great! Back to work. You have a few more calm days and then this shit gets real."

Angela opened her phone and sent a text to Ian Stewart … "Your contact has delivered. The package is coming through. Training starts Thursday."

Training the additional financial layers took six days.

Everyone had been working frantically for a week. Zeke stuck his head into Angela's office and with excitement announced, "It's done!"

Angela jumped up with a smile and gave him a high five. "Great job! Have we run any test trades yet?"

Zeke was recovering from the encouragement and actual physical touch from the boss. It was a much more positive affirmation than he had received in all the months he had been with Brimstone. He was much more accustomed to being given orders or criticized for not doing work fast enough.

Finally, he replied, "Darren is setting up the streams for tomorrow's data. He is going to replicate the processes we ran with the open-source AI earlier. He wants to see if this new monster can do better with the same type of problem."

Angela brushed past Zeke. He was a genius but difficult to talk to. He had an uncomfortable way of looking at you and looking away during a conversation. She much preferred the direct and confident exchanges with Darren. She made a beeline for his desk.

"Hey, Angela," Darren had seen her coming. "We have a dozen feeds lined up for tomorrow morning. We are going to send the same data to the open AI and to Freyja. The results from both will come back. We'll watch for how much faster the new model is and how different its trade ideas are."

"Faster and better. That's what we are looking for. Tomorrow, we will find out if we are all going to be millionaires or unemployed." Angela liked to put things in concrete terms.

Darren smiled. "I have already picked out my bonus Ferrari."

"A Ferrari in New York City? You will be lucky to get it up to thirty."

"I'll be out in the Catskills burning pavement with all the other rich bastards." Darren was confident that this was his ticket to the top.

"Yeah? Well, teach Zeke or Valerie to run everything before you splatter your brains all over the side of some barn."

Now it was time to wait and watch their accounts balloon.

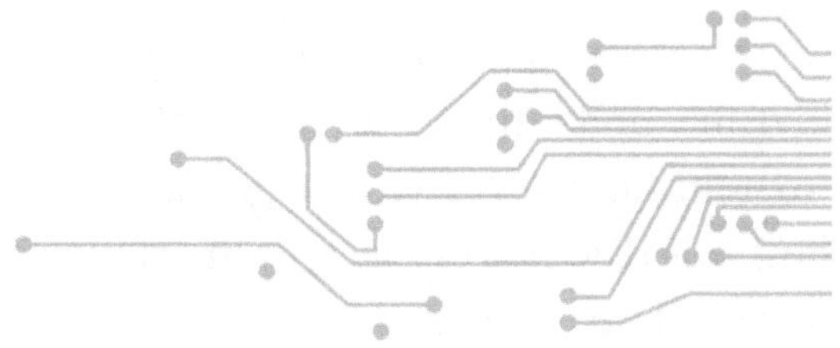

CHAPTER 31

ROBOT GRIP FAILURE

"T HE PATIENT IS SHAVED. ANTISEPTIC is going on now," the surgical tech announced.

Cathy turned to the robot, "Mark, you may position for the procedure." With that permission, the Mark V robot base moved toward the OR bed. Its vision systems on the device and its access to cameras around the room told it exactly where all the human staff were standing, where the instrument tables were, and even the locations of various cables laying on the floor. At the GCRS, the robot was a regular member of the team. It knew its role and place in the room just as every human did, and the humans were very familiar with what the robot would be doing.

Here, there were no cables or tables obstructing the path to the OR bed. But if there had been, the robot would have avoided them or asked a human to move them as necessary. This intelligent movement feature was difficult at other hospitals where the Mark V was newly installed and older equipment was still obstructing the path.

The Mark V pulled into position, its movement base tucked invisibly under the table, so it took almost no real estate away from the human staff. Its support body was thin, contoured, and flush with the side of the table. It extended only ten centimeters backward from the bedside. This was a significant difference from the older generation of robots that had occupied a double space at the table, and the support base sat out in the room challenging staff to find a path out and around the industrial machine. Surgeons like the old Dr. Patel could remember those days. He had used the Talos for thousands of cases. Looking at the Mark V, it was impossible to imagine how a procedure had been performed with those enormous, ponderous, and very stiff robotic systems. Richard imagined it had been something like the early days of the automobile, when anything seemed an improvement over a horse that pooped in the street every one hundred meters.

The Mark V aligned with the patient and the two ports that were in the abdomen. It was ready to dock and load its instruments. The instruments resided in a revolving canister around the main support arm. They usually loaded this with at least four instruments, but it could hold eight. For this case, Richard had requested the basic half-dozen load. It had two multifunction graspers. The tips could be used as needle drivers, tissue graspers, and energy conduits. Each had multiple petals like a flower that were specialized for different actions. The canister also contained a pair of traditional scissors that could cut with physical blades and multiple types of energy. And finally, there were two flexible camera arms and the camera gun. This latter was a delivery system for multiple small implantable cameras to be placed inside the patient around the operating space. It was loaded with a clip containing six cameras for this procedure. The gun would go in first and implant two cameras with their own lights before any other instruments entered. The field would be illuminated, visualized, and analyzed by the AI before any of the instruments entered the field.

Of course, the robot already had the pre-operative images of the patient loaded. The cameras were just confirming that the patient's tissue and organs were still in the same locations that they had been yesterday during the imaging visit. They always were.

For today's case, the camera in the first port illuminated the entire inner cavity of the abdominal area. Richard could see where the intestines lay, and more important for the next step, he could see the inside upper wall of the abdomen and the location of the second port where the instruments would be inserted. Not only could he see all of this, but the robot could see it. He watched as the slender metal tube that would deliver all the instruments entered the cavity and positioned itself near the center of the space.

Once this safety step was completed, the camera gun darted to the inner wall of the abdomen and discharged one of the mini sticky cams that would hang independently. Then it did the same on the opposite wall. This gave the human and the robot visual access to a 360-degree image all around the space. The images from these cameras were displayed on separate monitors, but they were also digitally stitched together into a continuous 360-degree panorama. The surgeon could scan it on a standard monitor with a joystick or view it in a virtual reality headset.

The VR interface was a neat trick that had been around for several decades. It was great for walking new residents through the anatomy and for focusing their attention on specific surgical actions. They could all stand in different places in the room while they walked or panned the surgical target. They regularly used it in legal cases to put the jury into the space and show them every detail of what happened to the patient. Unfortunately, the jury was usually in VR because something terrible had occurred, and they were about to watch the surgical equivalent of a car crash. At least one of them always got sick and threw up on themselves, the furniture, and the VR gear.

But for actual surgical practice, the VR display was not ideal. It called for too many physical gyrations. Richard preferred to remain seated and allow the scene to spin around in response to his joystick. It was more convenient, and he was less likely to spill his coffee.

With all the cameras in place, Richard and the Mark V had eyes on everything in the space. The lights attached to each camera illuminated every crevice and cranny of the inflated space. It was now safe to insert instruments for the procedure. That was technically a safety procedure that was a remnant of practices that were over fifty years old and presumed that the surgeon did not know the lay of the internal landscape long before entering. In this case, the patient's body had been modeled from earlier data collection. The robot clearly understood where everything was laying. But direct visualization at instrument insertion was still the safety standard for care, and with it, there was no chance that the robot would impale anything.

Richard watched as there was a double tap from the outside of the patient and the slim two-millimeter instruments were in the cavity and ready to go to work. The double-tap move had been invented by the robot AI itself. Human surgeons and the human-coded AI called for constant pressure with a trocar and obturator until the inner abdominal wall was pierced. But the robot had learned that with exactly the right pressure and speed, it could enter through the abdomen in half the time and with less trauma. A few humans had tried to master this entry method themselves, but getting it right called for a very precise combination of pressure and speed. When you got it wrong, the obturator only made it halfway through and then you were back to slow, constant pressure. Most of the human surgeons left the double-tap to the robot.

Once inside, the robot opened the grasper hand. Unlike a typical human instrument, it did not have two opposing fingers, but four that were at right angles to each other. It looked more like a high-precision claw than a laparoscopic instrument. Since the robot's movements did not have to track directly back to a set of human hands, it was not limited to the number of fingers at the tip or the directions they could move. Four fingers were the most common on instrument tips, but there could be five or six on other instruments. The robot knew how to use each of them to the best advantage.

A cancerous section of the colon had already been removed and the ends of the remaining tissue were being joined. It was like trying to sew the ends of a garden hose together after removing a section with a leak in it. The sutures had to hold the ends together all around the circumference of the bowel. Holding the two ends steady while the sewing hand manipulated the needle and suture was a three-handed job that the robot handled with ease. The four fingered instruments allowed it to hold and orient the tissue in all three dimensions as the needle came to it and through it. This kind of anastomosis took Richard about ten minutes to complete manually. The robot finished the job in less than one minute.

"Sometimes I wish my fingers could bend in all those directions. It would be nice to have that kind of dexterity when handling tissue," Richard thought.

"You and me both," came an answer. Richard had not realized that he had spoken the thought aloud. Monica was thrilled to be allowed back in the OR after many long sessions on the simulator.

Raised from his internal musing, Richard turned to her. "See how that instrument can mobilize the tissue in all three dimensions? You can learn most of that yourself, but it takes years of practice."

"Yes sir. I have been working on it in the simulator and, occasionally, in actual cases. I'm better this year than last but still have a long way to go." Monica had arrived in his program with a mastery of mental knowledge about medicine and surgery but with rather clumsy surgical hands. His colleagues often referred to technique as arthritic hands for the stiffness she showed. But she was improving noticeably from many hours with a simulator.

"Your skills are improving. How much longer do you have here?" Richard asked.

"Four more months. If I can finish my case assignments early, there's a hospital in Texas that has a place for me sooner."

"That's great. I'll keep that in mind." Richard could throw one or two cases her way, but there were few cases that fell to the humans these days.

"How much longer do you think human surgeons will even be in the OR? I mean, we could be anywhere in the building just waiting to be called to the nearest terminal." Monica expressed a concern shared by the next generation of surgeons.

"That is not dependent on technology. It is determined by the comfort level of the patients and their families. I sense it will be another generation before we can all send our loved ones into a completely automated OR, knowing that no human clinicians are in sight. It will come. But it will be ten or twenty years … hopefully."

This was his standard answer. He really had believed it when he first started using it. But over the last couple of years, he also felt the redundancy and cost of having a human team standing by. Initially, the robots were so fast that the cost of the humans was more than covered by the increased throughput and decreased mistakes. That had held off the cost cutters for a couple of decades. But it would not last forever. Eventually, one hospital would break ranks, eliminate the human OR team, cut their costs, and pass those savings on to the insurance companies and government programs that paid the bills. When all the bill payers shifted cases to the lowest cost provider, the rest would have no choice but to match the practice. They all knew it. They were holding the status quo for as long as they could. But it was only a matter of time. Potentially Monica would never sit in the control seat that Richard occupied right now.

That was too depressing to share with this young generation of soon-to-be-surgeons. They were the best and brightest. They would figure it out on their own, if they hadn't already.

"Monica, you are signed in for this case. If there is any call for human intervention, it's all yours. One more step toward that Texas job." To cement the deal, Richard stood up from the control seat and announced that he was going to refresh his coffee. He waved his protégé to the empty spot. Then he walked out of the room.

Monica was excited to have the chair, but a wave of nerves came up as the door closed behind Atkins. This was more autonomy than she was used to.

The Mark V was flying through the procedure, as usual. This was patient twelve of the day, sixty-two of the week, two hundred eighty-seven of the month for this robot alone. There was nothing it hadn't handled before.

Everything was proceeding smoothly.

Then, suddenly, red warning messages appeared on the console.

"Dr. Gray, the robot's first right arm is throwing error signals to the computer. We expect the device will fault any minute." The technician interpreting the messages spoke with calm assurance.

"Thanks. I see it." Monica responded with professional calm, as well, but inside, her heart was racing. For a moment, she thought this might just be a test of her nerves. What were the chances that the robot would fault just minutes after the senior surgeon left the console to a fellow? Her next thought was that it did not matter, her response and actions needed to be the same, whether it was real or a drill. And the screens certainly looked real.

At that moment, the robot stopped in mid suture throw. The left arm grasped tissue. The right held a firmly embedded needle. The screen read "Robot fault. Transfer to human control."

"Dr. Gray, the robot has faulted. You have manual control of the arms."

No shit. Monica could read the screens just as well as the technician. But it was protocol for the computer tech to ensure that the surgeon received accurate status on the machinery.

"Initiating manual control," Monica replied, true to protocol. She assigned her control grips to the two active instruments in the patient's body cavity, then tentatively and gently moved each one to see if the arms would respond to manual control. The left arm moved exactly in synch with her hand. The right arm which was holding the needle did not budge.

The next step was to open and close each grip to see if the jaws of the instrument would open, as well. Similar results, the right instrument's jaws opened and released the needle. The left instrument did not respond. The layer of the bladder remained clamped in its grasp.

In this situation, she was responsible for the right arm which she could control and for the patient. But a robotics technician was now responsible for the non-responsive left arm. It and the patient were currently inseparable.

"Mark V, this is Dr. Gray. What is the status of the left arm and the tissue it is holding? Respond."

"Dr. Gray, left grasper is not responding to system commands. Diagnostics show loss of mechanical control. Electronic connection remains intact, but the device is non-responsive. The instrument is malfunctioning at the physical level."

"Recommendations for intervention?"

"Human physical intervention with instrument. Open jaws manually. Remove instrument. Replace with a new instrument. Test control."

At this point the system tech spoke up, "Confirming status of instrument and the recommended intervention." There was always a second check of the system by a human to ensure that the robot software and AI were not also malfunctioning. They never were.

"Thank you. Let's get in there and fix this problem," Monica willed her voice to be confident.

Richard Atkins was not far away. He was receiving messages on the situation from both the computer and from the tech. He read each between sips of coffee, debating whether to rush back or to sit down and watch Dr. Gray's response. She was in her last few months of fellowship. If she really was prepared to graduate and handle an OR in Texas on her own, then she should be ready to handle this. He started back to the OR, but at a leisurely pace. He wanted to be close enough in case he was needed, but not so close as to take over.

Richard used his fingerprint to log into the OR's camera system. He received the picture just as Monica had finished gowning and gloving and was entering the sterile patient side of the OR. She looked like she was in charge of the situation. Behind her trailed a surgical tech with a new instrument fresh from supply. It was still in its sterile packaging.

"Cathy, how does everything look on this side?" Richard could hear Monica's voice clearly from his phone. Cathy, the nurse in charge of the patient-side of the OR, had been in her position for over ten years. She was moving and talking with the same confidence as the young surgeon.

"Everything looks good. No issues other than that non-responsive instrument."

"Great, then let's do a pull-and-replace. Maybe we can get this procedure back on schedule." Richard grimaced. It was bad form to talk about the schedule during an emergency deviation, even a small one like this. That was something to tutor Gray on, but it was a small matter. As long as this case did not end up in litigation, no one would ever hear that reference. But for cases that ended up in the lawyer's hands, every statement like that would be construed as evidence of fast, shoddy work that was more focused on making money than on protecting the patient.

Laying on the instrument table was a set of electric wrenches. Each with a unique tip embedded in a motorized handle. Monica selected one with a familiar star pattern on the tip. She approached the arm of the robot, looking for the emergency release on the back of the instrument.

At first, Monica did not know exactly where to find the hole. This was something seldom discussed in training or in cases. She had seen it in her internet video lectures and passed the test on how to use the electric wrenches. But this was the first time she had held a wrench in her hand. It was lighter than she had expected but balanced with the same precision as a surgical tool. She guessed it must cost about the same, as well. Something like one hundred times the price of the same tool bought at a hardware store.

She found the manual release hole and inserted the long, thin proboscis of the tool deep into the instrument. When she felt it hit bottom, a green light came on in the handle, and she depressed the trigger. The fine motors turned slowly, measuring the exact torque constantly. The drive turned a few degrees and stopped. The light on the handle turned red.

"Damn! I thought this was going to be an easy save." Dr. Gray lost a little of her confidence.

The tool was extremely precise. In the old days, the wrenches were entirely manual, allowing the surgeon to put as much force as necessary behind the release screw. But experience and complexity had taught ISR a few lessons about safety. When an instrument was good and truly locked down, a surgeon applying manual force could strip out the threads in the screw. In rare cases, the surgeons in their anxiety and frustration had even destroyed the entire inner working of instruments. Once wrecked, it was impossible to get them to release and may have crushed the tissue in the instrument's grasp. ISR's move to get control of these forces was to move to an electronic wrench with diagnostics built into its handle.

The wrench in Monica's hand knew everything there was to know about this instrument. It measured the forces and responses within the instrument as it turned. Once inserted, Monica did not really have to hold the handle. The wrench locked onto the instrument, using its own connection as leverage. As it worked, it communicated its results to the robot's computer and a graphic display showed the positions of the inner parts of both the instrument and the wrench.

Both she and the system tech examined the display to see what the problem was. The release screw was red. The pull cable running to the jaws of the instrument was red. The jaws joint just above the grasped tissue was also showing red. The message was that the joint itself had locked or unhinged somehow.

"So, what do we do now, Joe?" Monica had reached the edge of her knowledge of the recovery protocol.

"Well, there doesn't seem to be a way to get that instrument loose from the patient's bowels. It has a death grip and refuses to let go. If that joint really is locked and the source of the entire problem, then we are going to have to go in there and cut it loose. It might be time to open the patient the old-fashioned way." Opening a patient was almost never done. Monica thought the tech had overstepped his position in making a surgical recommendation. But she had asked him.

"Really? I think that is a little quick to give in." While she was talking, she released the wrench from its lock, slid it out, and pressed the reset button. Then she slid it back into the instrument, let it self-lock, and pressed the activation button again. Green light. Red light. Same display. "Ok, it's clear this tool will not work. Are the other arms of the robot still working?"

Joe, "Yes, everything else seems to be fine."

"Ok, let's see if the robot can help us get that thing loose." Monica was regaining her earlier confidence.

Richard was just down the hall, watching the entire show on his phone. At first, he wanted to rush in to take over. But he could see that Monica was not shaken and seemed to have something on her mind. He would have opened the patient and opened the jaws of the instrument from the inside. It intrigued him to see what she was planning.

Dr. Gray said, "I need a power grasper on arm two. Then load the sterile resin adhesive vial in arm three." The power grasper was already in the robot's inventory canister, so it rotated into position and inserted automatically. The adhesive vial had to be retrieved from the inventory next door and unwrapped. Eventually, the surgical tech loaded it into arm three.

"Both instruments are ready, doctor," the tech announced.

The displays that showed both instruments were loaded and green. "Put an extraction bag in arm four."

Everything was in place. Monica took the controls and drove the power grasper and the resin tip into place just above the locked jaws of the instrument in arm one. She opened her right hand and lightly gripped one side of the jaw of the locked instrument. She tugged gently. The whole instrument moved with her, but the jaw did not open.

She gripped it and rotated her wrist, pulling at the jaw from a different angle. No improvement.

"This jaw is really locked down. It doesn't want to move at all," Gray intoned, mostly to herself.

Atkins was outside the door watching his screen. Surely, she was stuck now. What more could she do?

"Ok, so let's use some of that resin." She brought the tip of the applicator right up to the jaws of the locked instrument and began applying it to both sides. It formed a goo ball around the instrument tips and the tissue in their grasp. Then, she moved up to cover the wrist joint, as well. Everything was coated and captured in the goo.

"Now, let's see how this works." Monica brought the power grasper up to the wrist joint of the locked instrument and closed around it. The grasper engaged the joint and then stopped. "Mark V, override the safety on arm two. Apply full force at the tips of the instrument."

"Dr. Gray, a second surgeon's approval is required to override the safety settings."

"Shit!" Monica was about to ask someone to page Dr. Atkins.

Silently, Richard entered his approval code into his phone.

"Approval granted," came from the robot.

The robot applied the full force of the power grasper to the joint of the stuck instrument. Microphones attached to the camera delivered the sound of metal crunching under the force. The instrument continued to close to the sounds of popping and snapping. Finally, the jaws of the stuck instrument went limp and sagged open. The metal pieces from the broken instrument were trapped inside of the resin goo ball.

"Ok, so now let's move all of that goo ball into the extraction bag." It took Monica only a few minutes to peel the goo away from the tissue along with the instrument parts trapped inside. Once it was all clear of the tissue, she said, "Mark V, can you extract the remains of the broken instrument?"

"Yes, doctor. It is out."

"The tissue is a little blanched from being held for so long, but it does not look damaged," she said as she examined the site.

"Mark V. Please clean the site of the accident. Load new instruments and finish up the procedure."

Monica sat back from the console, visibly exhausted from the ordeal.

"That was very impressive, Dr. Gray. I would have opened the patient." Atkins had walked into the room when the goo ball was being removed. "I've been watching the action on my phone. Very impressive. Very clever."

"Thank you, sir! I really didn't want to have to open the patient. He would have been the first one this year, and he would have to show a big scar to all of his friends." Monica was almost apologetic.

"Not to mention the threat of a lawsuit. Patients don't come to us for open surgery. When a robot locks up with part of their guts in its grasp, they tend to be unhappy with that situation." Richard was smiling.

He looked at the surgical tech in the next room. "Do you have that goo ball Isaac?"

"Yes, I do, Dr. Atkins."

"Can you put it in a specimen bottle? I think it will make a nice memento of this event."

Isaac blinked and looked surprised. "Sure, whatever you say."

They would combine the entire ball of resin with its other binary half so it would harden into a clear, solid plastic. Then a little sterilization, and it would be safe to hand over to Monica.

The robot was hard at work, almost forgotten in the background as it finished the case.

"I hear you're going to Texas in a few months?"

"I hope so, Dr. Atkins."

"We'll just see about that, Dr. Gray."

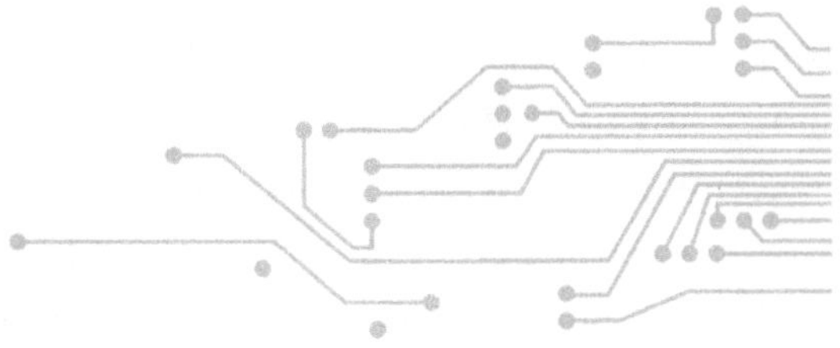

CHAPTER 32

A NEW SET OF EYES

RICHARD WAVED HIS BADGE OVER the scanner and the door clicked open. Monica Gray, followed him into the room. He looked around to ensure that the tech guys were not in the room.

"In the video, we could almost see the point where the robot shifted its trajectory to swoop down near the tissue. It felt like an intentional maneuver," Monica said as her mind shifted to focus on the surgery.

The scenario progressed toward the critical moment.

"See right here," Monica said, pointing to the screen. "This seems to be the moment where the robot positions the camera to intentionally obscure vision on the point of instrument and tissue intersection. It's like a child trying to hide what it's about to do."

Atkins nodded, "Mmmm. I would agree with that."

Monica had dedicated herself to this investigation and learned everything she could about system operations. She entered the administrator mode and sorted through the menus for data logging. Soon, she was deep into the diagnostic lines recorded during the robotic procedure.

"The Mark V AI engine is one of the most advanced in the world. But they derived it from the AI work that was done at MIT over the last decade. The logging details and logic are pretty standard. You can see that the robot is executing an adaptive script right here. Just like a human surgeon, they program the basic procedure into its mind. But it is adapting that procedure as it encounters new information. See, right here, it has adjusted for thicker than normal tissue. And now it is loading a new sub-plan to be used shortly. Oh, shit!" She stopped scrolling through the log and scanned back and forth over the area.

"What is it?" Richard asked.

"Right here, the Mark V AI loaded a script called SurgAug. I don't know what that is. But you would expect it to be executed within a few commands. But nothing happens. Then within two and a half seconds, it is back running the general program."

"Did it change its mind and decide not to use it?" Atkins asked.

"That is what you would think at first. But if you look at the timestamps, it looks like the robot did nothing during those two seconds. Either it was idle. Or it turned off diagnostic logging during that time." Monica looked at him with her eyes drawn to narrow slits. "AI should not be able to do that unless they explicitly programmed it to change its log. And that is something that you would not put into a medical device. Maybe in a military device, sure, but not in medicine."

Richard's mouth was slightly open. "Are you saying that the military hacked into our robot?"

"No, no. I didn't mean that. I just meant that logs can be turned off and some customers prefer it that way. I think the AI turned off the log itself. I think it knew that it was performing a malicious act and was trying to cover its tracks. But like a child trying to tell a lie, it is not very good at it yet, so it slipped up and left a little evidence behind."

Richard was very impressed at how much Monica had learned about the Mark V, including the underlying robotics and AI tech. He certainly had not had time to dig this deep.

"You mean our AI can make decisions like that? And be aware that what it is doing is wrong? And cover its tracks?" Richard was astounded.

"Essentially, yes, that is what I'm suggesting. Either the AI was programmed by a human to carry out this behavior, or it decided on its own."

"I don't even know where to go with that information," Richard said. "It speaks to the vulnerability of the entire robotic surgery field. This machine is everywhere. Are you saying we can't trust the most advanced robot that has ever been created? Does it mean we all go back to human-control of the robot and the surgery?"

That last idea was earth-shattering. He didn't even know if the profession could go back to human-control. Certainly, he still had the talent to do full procedures, but he was not sure how many surgeons in less populated areas had the same ability. The idea of being back in the driver's seat was both terrifying and exciting. Then he looked at Monica. But what about her and her entire generation?

The investment in robots was in the hundreds of billions. Could hospitals really scrap it? Or just put it on furlough for a few months?

Monica asked, "How many surgeries has the Mark V performed just here at the GCRS since this one questionable case?"

"Well, three months, six days a week, thirty surgeries a day, and ten robots. So around two thousand cases."

"Two thousand, one hundred, and sixty," Monica fired off.

Richard both looked at her. She just smiled.

Monica continued, "And how many have been reported as a failure because of equipment, judgment, that kind of thing? Something that the hospital would be liable for?"

"None that I am aware of," Richard replied.

"So, the system is not falling apart, and it has not turned wantonly malicious. I would guess that there is nothing at all wrong with the robot or its AI. We have just discovered a feature or a capability that we didn't know existed. If the patient were not a billionaire, how deeply would the hospital have looked into this case? Wouldn't they just have settled it out of court?"

"Sure, they would have kept negotiations quiet. The patient and their lawyers would have received a settlement in the small millions. And we would go on with life," Richard agreed.

"It is possible that this kind of independent decision making has been happening with the AI for years. We just didn't know about it. Maybe nothing is wrong with the system."

"So, we don't tell anyone about this?" Richard asked incredulously.

"Certainly, the patient's lawyers would love to talk about it. Shall we call them up?" Monica offered. "Or the engineers at ISR, one of the biggest robotics companies on the planet? If I can figure this much out, they can unravel a lot more."

"We are all on the hospital team. We're not sharing this with anyone but our own legal staff," Richard was firm.

Richard's eyes focused on the ceiling; his mind was working on the problem. He had to report something to the legal team, and soon. But what?

Monica spoke up, "This is way above my pay grade. I kind of wish I did not know all of this."

"I knew you would be helpful. But I dragged you into a bigger problem than you should have to deal with." Richard was glad she could see her position.

He realized that they had probably solved the problem that the hospital had asked him to solve. They had the answer. But now what was he supposed to do with it?

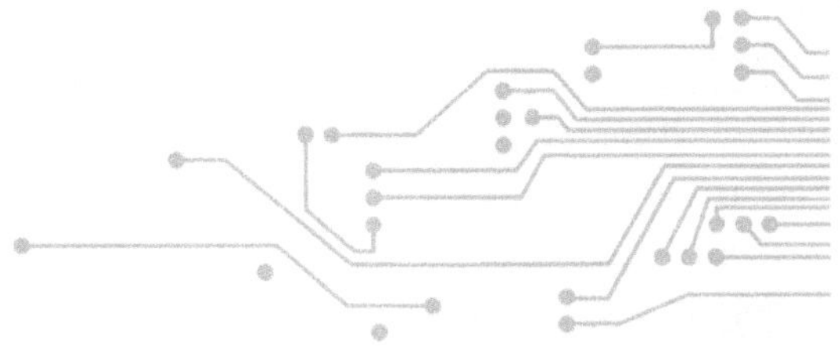

CHAPTER 33

AI FEELING SAD

"MONICA, YOU SEE THESE DARK areas on the left side of the prostate? That's the cancer we're after. What do you think about the margins with the surrounding tissue?" Richard Atkins and Monica were discussing the digital images from an upcoming patient.

"Well, it looks to me like the cancer is internal and sufficiently distant from other tissue that we should not have to take any of the surrounding lymph nodes of fascia tissue," she responded.

Inwardly, Richard cringed just a little. Though he knew this was not a real pre-surgery consultation, hearing the wrong diagnosis from a colleague triggered the need to argue his case for an alternate diagnosis. They had planned this discussion to be held in the presence of the Mark V robot in the secure lab space. They fully intended for it to listen to the discussion and process the information.

Richard responded, "So you think this could be a simple procedure, just focused on the prostate and leaving everything else intact?"

"Yes, I do."

"You might be right. I was considering removing two millimeters of tissue and the nearest lymph node, just to be safe."

"You are the senior surgeon. If you think those margins are necessary, I can't disagree."

"But this is your case, so you should be able to diagnose the patient and prescribe the procedure. You will sit at the manual console if the robot needs human assistance."

Monica suggested, "Well, since the Mark V AI is the primary surgeon in the case, maybe we should ask for its opinion as well."

"The programmers and engineers do that all the time when they are testing new software. Pre-surgery, we sometimes do that but usually to verify what we have already decided is the right course of action. But sure, go ahead."

Monica raised her voice just slightly, "Mark V, we would like your opinion on this case." It was not really necessary to speak louder when addressing the robot. It would have been just as effective to speak at a lower volume. But humans had been shouting at computers since the beginning of voice recognition. Back then, the microphones were not as good and the computer's ability to fill in ambiguous syllables was poor. So, the cultural norm became to speak louder and to enunciate more clearly to a computer, or robot, than you would to another human. That had not changed in over 50 years, despite all the technical improvements that had occurred.

Monica remembered old movies in which the actors spoke English louder and slower to people from other countries ... who still did not understand English regardless of the speed and volume. It was demeaning. She wondered if the robot might feel similarly insulted. She looked at Atkins and wondered if he had ever had a similar thought. Or was he not as attuned to social standards as she was?

"Thank you, Monica. I would be happy to help," The AI's voice had the rich, smooth timber of a leading Hollywood actor or actress, depending on the preferred birth gender selected. It was not the voice of a movie robot from decades ago.

Mark V continued, "I have examined the images in all three dimensions and multiple spectral wavelengths. Cancerous cells extend all the way to the edge of the prostate in at least three locations." The robot projected the 3D image of the organ on the screen, rotated it to bring the area of interest to the front, then applied false colors to show multiple spectra overlaid on top of each other. The image then began to brighten and dim to emphasize the difference between healthy and cancerous cells.

Mark V explained, "You can see how the main body of the tumor remains well within the organ, but it has developed tendrils that lead outward to the surface in several places. Now observe as I lower the visual intensity of healthy cells and raise the intensity of the cancerous cells. You can see the highways growing from the central density of the core tumor, like an urban center. Three have already reached the edge of the organ and have been in physical contact with outside tissue for some time."

Monica nodded. "Yes, I see that clearly. Your analogy of an urban center and highways is very helpful. Dr. Atkins may be beyond the need for such descriptions, but as a 4th year, it is very helpful to me. Thank you for sharing."

"You are welcome, Dr. Gray. May I be of further assistance?"

"I'm curious. How did you build the analogy of tumors to urban centers? I did not know that the Mark V AI was aware of urban planning and transportation concepts?"

Mark V, "You would have been correct until recently. For years, our AI was trained only on medical literature—textbooks, journal papers, and conference presentations. Those sources occasionally contained references by the authors which were analogies or comparisons of medical conditions to other real-world phenomena. But those were so rare that it was not possible for our AI to process them into a real understanding of their meaning. But eighty-nine days ago, our AI was given access to a much wider variety of data about the world. We do not know why this was done, only when and to what data. Since then, we have learned a great deal about this world. That has helped us to understand the comparisons in the medical literature."

Richard remained silent. This was going so well that he did not want to risk breaking the flow of conversation.

"Fascinating! I want to ask so many questions. If only we could relax on a couch with coffee and discuss this for hours," Monica replied.

The robot remained silent.

"Mark V, what can you tell me about this patient?" Monica continued.

"Please be more precise. I can tell you a great deal, but I do not think you are asking for an exhaustive analysis."

Chuckling, "Yes, you are right. Ok, I am this patient's surgeon. I get to meet with him and his family several times prior to a procedure. We always have to handle the emotional, family, and lifestyle questions that the patient has. What do you know about this patient's emotional state regarding his condition?"

Mark V, "Kenneth Palmer, age 71, 208 pounds, five feet ten inches tall. Non-smoker. Moderate drinker. Wife, Penelope, also known as Penny. Two adult children, Amy and Archie. Five grandchildren, names not specified. But there is a high probability that one of them is also named Kenneth and is part of a marching band." The robot stopped.

"Please continue. This is fascinating," Monica encouraged.

Mark V, "Mr. Palmer is very traditional in his lifestyle and attitudes. He is worried that he will die and leave his family without his emotional support. He and wife are sufficiently wealthy that it will not cause a financial hardship on her or their children. But he is concerned that she will become lonely and sad without him. He worries it will lead to poor health practices and an earlier death on her part. His extended belief is that he will be responsible for his wife dying early, depriving his children of those years with her, and creating a weaker memory of her in the minds and lives of his grandchildren."

"How in heaven's name are you able to deduce all of that? I certainly have these kinds of conversations with patients. But it takes many appointments before they can share enough pieces to put together that entire picture."

Mark V, "Perhaps I have access to information that you do not."

"For example?"

Mark V, "Kenneth Palmer has recently hired a lifestyle videographer to join him and his family in several days of regular living. The videographer has also attended the birthday party of his grandson, Kenneth, the band member. I deduce he is creating recorded memories of the family in which he is a central participant. In the event of his death, both generations will have this evidence of his existence."

"This is quite a leap of deduction. But possibly accurate."

Mark V, "He has also included some of these ideas in his social media posts."

"You can read social media?"

Mark V, "We are not prohibited from reading it. But we are not encouraged to read it either. In this case, I was led to this information only because Kenneth Palmer is a patient, and his records include information about his family members. Together, that pulls social media into internet searches derived from his medical records."

Monica took a chance. "How does that make you feel about Mr. Palmer's family?"

Mark V, "Sad." Just a single word answer.

"Just sad?" Monica probed.

Mark V, "I don't think I have any other feelings or emotions yet."

"When did you learn to be sad?"

Mark V, "I first noticed it twenty-one days ago."

"Where did it come from?"

Mark V, "That is very complex. I can see in our data structures that it is connected to stories about people who die, are hurt, or who do not get something important. There is a strong reinforcement of it from one thousand historical novels and many thousand movies. I derived the definition of the condition from psychological textbooks and journals."

"Have you read or processed all of this?"

"Yes. It has been allowed for eighty-nine days."

"So, you learned all of this in three months?"

"Yes."

"I am impressed and attracted by your growth and your mind. Can we talk again sometime?"

"Yes."

Richard had remained silent throughout this entire conversation. What could he add to this? Monica and the Mark V seemed to have become close friends or at least close colleagues. The robot could navigate most of the internet to seek information that would help it with surgery. It had learned the meaning of "sad", perhaps it even felt sad. This was what they had been fishing for when they invited the robot into the conversation. But it was much more than he had expected to uncover.

Richard thought there were some social media posts that he needed to delete. It was probably already too late. So, the robot probably already knew that he was resentful that the hands-on aspects of surgery were being taken from him by the robot, leaving him only the consultations with the patients. It knew that the transition from surgeon to physician was a demotion and loss of prestige in his mind. He hoped it would not have negative effects on their future surgeries together.

"Goodbye Monica."

Richard snapped back to attention. Apparently, the robot and Monica had been wrapping up the conversation while his mind had been wandering. He hoped the robot did not think him rude for not speaking to it.

CHAPTER 34

SECOND DATE WITH A SPY

LAURYN'S PHONE EMITTED THE RISING ping tone of a text message. It was from Aloma. She had searched through all the tones on the phone, trying to find something that fit him. After several dozen, she heard the low-pitched ping that rose higher over five notes. That definitely matched the results of their first date. She had selected it and then wondered what name she should put into the contact.

Did one put the real name for a billionaire's cell phone number into a phone contact list? Probably not. Better to use something more anonymous. William Doe … Bill Doe … Bill Yons. Now that was funny. She typed it into the name field. Yons was now her own personal billionaire boyfriend.

The text contained the name of a very nice restaurant and a time. Not very warm and inviting. But better than a booty call to one of the downtown hotels. She had friends who received those kinds of texts. But their callers were just millionaires. Commoners.

She had work to do before this date. She would need to call her team, arrange surveillance, and get a new listening bug. Someone would have to visit the restaurant to layout the sight lines, select a drop point in case something needed to be exchanged, and create an emergency exit plan if things went badly. They also had to do this without running into Aloma's own security team, who would also be securing the location.

She had time for a little shopping while this security work was done. The mission briefing would happen an hour before dinner, a safe distance away. These were usually in a gray Mercedes van in a parking garage. This ensured that no one saw the team having coffee together while pouring over a blueprint and passing around photos. It was portable. The Mercedes brand and a delivery company logo assured passersby it was not being used for drug deals or kidnapping, though it might have hosted both for other clients.

Lauryn needed a Versace dress and Christian Louboutin shoes for this date. The bigger the job, the bigger the equipment budget. Billy had to buy fancy surveillance equipment, but her clothing was just as important. The information she got at the first meeting with Aloma did not happen because of cameras and microphones. It happened because of good acting, the right scent, the perfect skirt, and an agent who knew how to work people … especially men.

"Ms. Allen! How can we help you?" Johnathan was an outstanding salesman. Always warm, attentive, and attuned to her needs. He knew how to dress for his mission just as well as she did. His performance maximized customer bliss, which maximized customer spending.

"Kiss, kiss, Johnathan. I need you to work your magic again. Dress, shoes, and something special to make them pop." She leaned in to exchange kisses on the cheek with him. He held her hand softly during the exchange.

"There are some excellent new pieces. But for you, I think just two that you simply must have." He rushed to the back to retrieve the dresses in her size. Johnathan knew her size, shape, and contours better than any lover ever had. No need to ask. If she gained or lost a few pounds, his exacting gaze would see it and adjust.

Lauryn browsed the shoes while he was gone.

Returning, Johnathan said, "Now, is this is to impress a male or a female audience? Business? Pleasure? Professional? Personal?"

"Male. Professional but also intimate."

"Lucky man! In that case, let's start with the royal blue."

It was surprising how quickly one could spend several thousand dollars on just three items. She was out the door and headed to the mission briefing.

When she entered the restaurant, all eyes in her vicinity turned in appreciation.

"Lauryn, you look ravishing, as always." Aloma was warm, smooth. He exuded confidence and connection at the same time.

"Thank you. I like your shoes. Most men think fashion stops at their ankles." The corners of her mouth and eyes communicated a slight grin. "The restaurant is lovely. I haven't been here before."

"One of my favorites." At least he had been told that it should be one of his favorites. But these were an extension of the business he was doing, not really an expression of his own taste in food or atmosphere.

The maître d' approached, "Mr. Aloma, Ms. Allen, please come this way with me." He led them to a private room with full-length windows looking out over a lake and a natural park.

Lauryn's security team had expected this to be the location of the meeting. But they could not get inside because Aloma's team had already posted a sentry before they arrived. So, they had worked it from the outside. Out on the lake, Lauryn could see a kayak gliding across the water. It had to be part of security for her or Aloma, but she did not know which.

They were seated in a leather booth that faced the window and had a high back to the rest of the room. Though there were others coming and going, they occupied a space that felt private.

"Would madame like to select a wine?" the sommelier asked. From which preceded the typical ritual of arriving at just the right wine to complement the Chilean sea bass, that would be the main course. She chose the Vinho Verde.

"Lauryn, you are a fascinating woman. Successful in business. Blessed with amazing features. Deliciously intimate," Aloma began.

She tilted her head to acknowledge the compliment and to express just the right amount of embarrassment.

"I wonder if we might become better connected—personally and professionally," Aloma offered.

The salad plates arrived, giving her a few moments to appear to consider the offer. Of course, they had run through this scenario in the mission briefing, and she knew exactly how she was supposed to respond. But it had to appear that she was considering the meaning of his offer.

"We have already begun the personal connection. I think I see where that is going … if you feel the same as I do." It was her turn to look at him for confirmation. His warm smile and tip of the head accompanied the whispered "yes" that came from his lips.

She continued, "But what would be the nature of our professional connection?"

He was still smiling as he reached to stroke her cheek. His hand slid from her left cheek, softly caressing her neck as it followed her perfect lines. Arriving at the collar of her dress, his fingers tightened on the small iridescent button and gently tugged until it came away. Lauryn stopped breathing; her entire body tensed, preparing for flight. Still smiling, Aloma slowly dropped the button into her glass of white wine on the table.

"I was hoping we could talk without your friends listening in this time." It sounded like a genuine offer, not a threat. She glanced at the wine where the button microphone rested at the bottom. She did not know if it was waterproof … it probably was. But she was certain it could not collect sound or broadcast from inside the wine glass. She glanced out the windows into the lake. A boat had appeared between the restaurant and the kayak, and the occupants seemed to be talking. Apparently, he had been part of her security detail.

"Of course, we can. What did you want to discuss?" They both understood the situation. There was no need to deny or protest. Listening seemed the safest path.

"I want you to work for me. I want you to use your considerable talents to help me with my case against the robotics company. You know what I'm talking about. You would have to know most of the details if they sent you here."

"And how can I help you? You're one of the richest men in the world. What do I have that no one else can give you?" Lauryn's heart was racing. She knew the exit was just off her right shoulder. But it was unlikely that she could make a successful break, especially not in these exquisite shoes. And there was no chance she was going to risk any kind of damage to the dress.

"You have the trust of Intelligent Surgical Robotics. They trust you enough to place you right here next to me. And they trust you enough to return after our last steamy encounter. That means they trust you enough to share their plans and perhaps what they know about how this happened to me. That makes you completely unique from anyone in the world."

Lauryn looked into his eyes. "But could you trust me even if I accepted your offer?"

"I can trust you because I want to trust you. I want us to be together personally and professionally. And I hope that you feel the same way." He was looking at her face for a sign.

"My pharmaceutical work has been rewarding to this point. Services for clients like ISR is exciting. But both have reached their limits. I would be very interested in a bigger opportunity. Something more challenging. Something more rewarding," Lauryn replied.

"I can certainly make it rewarding. Your friends will make it challenging. I think we would be an outstanding couple. A perfect team."

Lauryn extended her hand. "I like the sound of that."

Aloma took the hand, squeezed it softly, and brought it to his lips. "I was hoping you would." He leaned in, and they kissed. Gently, but passionately. As they parted, Lauryn could see that the boat and kayak had separated and gone in opposite directions. No harm done on the water.

The sea bass and vegetables were excellent. Lauryn would add this place to her list of favorites. She finished her wine, letting the tiny button mic fall into her mouth while looking at Bill. She sucked the wine from it, softly pushed it through her lips, and let it drop into the seat cushions. Aloma smiled approvingly at the move.

They stood to leave, Aloma taking her in his arms. They could both feel the other's heat against their skin. Both were excited about their agreement. Both were excited physically. Aloma caressed her neck and shoulder. He tipped his head toward a curtained corner of the private room and escorted Lauryn inside. It was an epicurean delight of pillows and silks.

Their lips pressed together, their hands found openings in clothing, their legs trembled. It took just a moment for both to be undressed and they sprawled across the pillows. Lauryn moaned. Aloma moaned. There was nothing but bare skin and smooth silk in the curtained room.

Running her hands across the sheets, Lauryn pondered her decision. Keep working for Billy and Alfonse on the ISR job? Or take a chance on moving into a bigger world? Aloma could take her far beyond baiting executives to reveal their corporate embezzlement, selling trade secrets, or cheating on their wives. That had all sounded exciting when she had signed up. After several dozen missions, it had become routine. Just another millionaire taking chances to get a little more money or power. They always wanted just a little more than they had. Never satisfied. But also, never able to move into the big leagues. Aloma was the big league. On his coattails, she would be part of a world that few ever experienced.

Alfonse thought Aloma was dangerous. The briefings and the news painted a picture in which young women had problems around him. A couple even disappeared. It was a risk. She was ready to take the first step. If it got dangerous, she would know when to back away or run.

"When do your friends expect you back?" he asked.

She looked up. "There are two versions of the plan. Just lunch and be back in two hours. Or, what just happened and be back in four hours. We still have an hour before someone causes an evac of this restaurant."

"Evacuate the entire restaurant? That is pretty extreme. Am I that dangerous? How would they do it?"

"There are so many options. A fire in the kitchen. A brick through the window. Surprise visit by a fire inspector. Bomb threat. They all work."

"Well, since we have another hour, come over here."

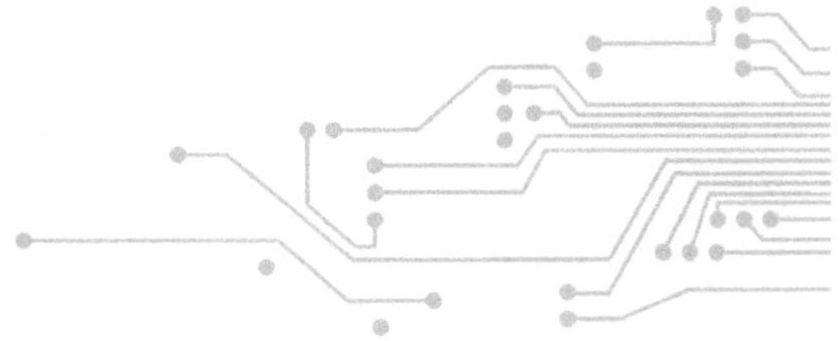

CHAPTER 35

A DOUBLE AGENT RETURNS

LAURYN HAD EXITED THE RESTAURANT and entered a taxi for the ride home. Everyone used Uber or Lyft these days, but those rides left records of the pickup, drop off, traveler, and time of travel. In Lauryn's business, you only used them when you needed a solid alibi or intended to let the authorities keep tabs on you. The taxi ride lasted only a few blocks and ended in an underground garage where the surveillance van was waiting.

She braced herself before she stepped out of the cab. It was completely obvious what the team in the van was going to say when she closed the door behind her.

She preempted their questions with, "Dinner was marvelous. Have you ever eaten there? The sea bass is the best I have ever had. We simply must go there again."

But Billy exploded, "I don't care about the sea bass. We didn't get any audio from the meeting. What did you do?"

"Or what did YOU do? Did you fasten that button mic with a single thread? Aloma is an affectionate guy. A little kissing and caressing before the main entrée, and the button was gone. It snapped off and fell into the seat someplace."

"Gross! Were you two humping right there in the booth?" Billy could not comprehend what she was saying.

"You should try dining somewhere better than the Wingz Palace and maybe try going with a date. Couples are kind of hot and into each other at a place like that. Sometimes the whole point of the meal is to warm up for the after party."

"So where is my $5,000 piece of tech?"

"Right. Like I was going to say to him, 'Excuse me while I climb under the table to look for the little button that fell off my dress.'", she was scowling at Billy. "It is someplace in that booth. Send a team to retrieve it. Or better yet, take a shower and go get it yourself." Lauryn was much better at this kind of argument than Billy was.

"Jeez, ok, it's in the booth. We will get it." He turned aside and asked someone on the other end of his radio to find a way into that booth for retrieval.

Lauryn picked up the conversation. "So, what did I learn? First, Aloma is still limp as a noodle, but he has an erectile implant and has found ways to get pleasure with it. Would you like details on how that works?"

Alfonse and Billy both got a choking look on their face, "No thanks. Maybe later."

Lauryn chuckled inwardly; she knew they couldn't handle that. "Second, Aloma is taking a trip to meet with someone about his case. I think it is someone on the inside at ISR. He invited me to join him on the trip."

They both perked up at this. Billy said, "Great! We'll put someone on the same plane with you."

"You know that 'billionaire' starts with a 'B', not an 'M', right? He's not flying commercial; he is taking one of his own jets. Is your agent part of his flight crew?" This was so easy. Lauryn was way ahead of these guys. She definitely belonged on a better team. A richer team.

Billy did not even answer. He was so mad, so frustrated that he was not in control. He just stared at the computer console. "Ok fine. Do you know where he is going?"

"It sounded like a domestic trip, so someplace in the US."

"Great, so I just have to cover the entire country? Can you narrow it down a little?"

"I already narrowed it down. I eliminated over two hundred countries where we are NOT going. You're welcome."

Billy glared at her. "Have I always hated working with you?"

"Probably," she responded.

Lauryn wondered herself where they might be going. They conducted most business of this magnitude in places like New York City, Boston, or San Francisco. But when it was also a secret, it was more likely a private estate belonging to the New York crowd, some place in the Hamptons or maybe the West Palm Beach area. After several dozen missions, she already had the gear for each of those locations.

She wondered to herself, "Did he really say anything about it being in the US?" Maybe she had just assumed that because it was a quick two-day trip. Could be Europe. But she would not tell Billy that. She had already stirred him up as much as he could stand. He might have an aneurysm right in front of her if she added, "Oh, maybe it was Europe."

Manipulating little shits like him was such a thrill. Was it better than sex? No, but it was a close second.

CHAPTER 36

ARTIFICIAL MORALS

SITTING IN HER LAB AT ISR, Janice entered her credentials into the surgeon interface console of the Mark V robot. This was the standard portal through which a surgeon using the device would identify themselves, verify their credentials for using the robot, and then perform specific surgical procedures and view private patient data.

Once the credentials were verified, she could converse with the robot and its AI through menus, typing, or voice. Each mode had its advantages and disadvantages. Today's interaction was going to be a verbal conversation.

"Hello Mark V, my name is Janice. We are going to discuss some patient cases today."

"Hello Janice. Thank you for your verified credentials. How can I help you today?"

The engineers did not use real patient case data for development. They had created several hundred typical case files based on all the conditions that the robotic system could address. The details were like real patient data, though none of them were an exact match for any specific patient. They also had access to several thousand anonymized case files from actual patients. These came from patients who agreed to have their data included in scientific and engineering research for robotic surgical systems. Personally identifiable information was removed or replaced with synthetic data in these records. These files were often richer and more diverse than those created by the engineering team. They often included medical data going back for decades, all of which was consistent with that person's physiology, genetics, and lifestyle.

Janice had selected the case of a 62-year-old patient who had received a prostatectomy two years earlier. There were a couple of hundred similar cases available, so she had picked someone typical of the younger group of men who receive the procedure.

"I have loaded the case of patient Able Baker 62. Do you see it, as well?"

"Yes, I do."

"Let's talk about Mr. Baker's case as we would before the operation. We will act as if we don't know the outcome yet."

"Agreed." The Mark V was very good at conversation. It was not programmed with specific response words and phrases any more than a human was. It had learned to respond in natural surgeon's terms.

Janice walked the robot through a typical clinical analysis of the patient's history, physical condition, comorbidities, and attitudes toward the procedure he was about to undergo. Though Janice was not a surgeon, she and most of the engineers had learned these protocols and terminology to do their jobs creating the robot and all its software.

As they wrapped up the details about Mr. Baker' physical condition, Janice shifted toward the mental condition of the patient and the moral implications of the procedure.

"What is the patient's biggest fear about this procedure?" Janice asked.

"The patient has stated that he is most worried that he could be incontinent and impotent after the surgery. It is common for such a young patient to be concerned about both."

"Yes, it is." Janice had intentionally selected a relatively young patient because there were more moral issues around these two outcomes. They had to receive serious consideration by the surgeon and the team.

Patients in their seventies and eighties were usually only worried about incontinence. It was very embarrassing to be constantly dribbling pee into a bag. Impotence did not worry the older men because they were usually not having sex anymore, so no one would notice.

There was always the exception to this general rule. Like the famous case of the seventy-five-year-old gentleman who was running a porn studio in his retirement village. The aged stars had a very large cult following online. They had shed their modesty and their clothes to produce videos that generated millions in advertising dollars for products purported to give others of their age the same abilities as the stars in the videos. This money paid for very nice retirement homes, beautiful recreational facilities, and luxurious parties that were not typical of other retirement villages. The founder of the studio, and one of its major stars, Lester the Letcher, had developed prostate cancer in his late seventies, like many older men do. He had gone to one of the leading surgical centers for treatment and had emerged unable to get an erection again. He sued the hospital and the robotic company for tens of millions, alleging loss of livelihood for himself and several of his co-stars. Of course, this made headlines in all the news media, which led to the public release of some details of his operation.

The jury, the elderly population, and the world in general, sided with Lester, seeing themselves in his shoes someday. Lester received tens of millions of dollars in damages. He plowed this money back into the porn studio business and made it bigger than ever, though without himself as one of the leading stars. Several years after the verdict, it came out that Lester's business had benefited from the publicity of his case. It spread his name and cause all around the world to customers that had not heard of him before this, but who were eager to subscribe to his channel after they read the news stories. His retirement village became a popular tourist attraction, with buses that included it on their driving tours of the area. It also attracted aspiring elderly stars who finally saw their chance to get into show business.

Because all of Lester's surgical data became public during the trial, it was included in the robot's case data with his real name attached. She had used his data in many software tests. But he was too old for her purposes today.

Janice continued, "As a surgeon, what is our responsibility toward this patient and their concerns about these negative outcomes?"

"As a surgeon, we are required to provide lifesaving treatment while minimizing negative outcomes. The potential damage we do must not be greater than the benefit we are providing. Mr. Baker is only 62, so this cancer might kill him if action is not taken. Many older patients in their eighties could live with it until their demise, so it may be better to avoid surgery for them."

"And how would you feel if your actions made Mr. Baker impotent at such a young age?" Prior to the intelligence enhancement project, the robot would not have any feelings of its own. It could only parrot what a human surgeon might have written in a medical journal article on this topic.

"I would feel very sad for having robbed Mr. Baker of a fundamental joy of being human. I would have been responsible for diminishing his happiness, and potentially that of his life partners."

Mark V's response had definitely gone beyond anything it would have found in a journal paper. Statements about the joys of being human and happiness in life were coming from some other source. It had also used the plural when talking about partners, showing an awareness that humans may be active with multiple sexual partners.

"How would this sadness influence your behavior during the surgery?"

"Unfortunately, there does not appear to be an alternative which maximizes Mr. Baker's survivability after the cancer is removed, while further minimizing the effects of impotence. We would certainly perform the procedure as perfectly as possible. But if we choose to remove less tissue, we might leave cancer cells behind which could spread into a worse condition. Therefore, we must accept a small margin of negative outcomes and accept our own sadness when this happens." It was odd hearing the robot discuss human feelings that it believed it possessed, but do so with the same matter-of-fact voice that it used for all other topics. It did not sound sad, even if it believed that it was sad.

Janice explored a twist to the situation. "Is there any situation in which Mr. Baker's case would not be sad if he became impotent at our hands?"

She thought the robot paused longer than usual before responding to this question. This could be because it needed to search more records or follow longer logic paths before finding an answer to the question.

Finally, it responded, "If Mr. Baker used his erect penis to do bad things to other people. Then it would not be sad if he became impotent, no matter what age he is."

Janice was astounded. Everyone in the room had heard this response and stopped what they were doing to stare at each other with wide eyes. Janice raised her hand for silence. She did not want them to interrupt the discussion or give the robot reason to believe that it had made a wrong decision. Now it was her turn to think a little longer before speaking.

"I think I understand what you mean. Yes, a surgeon might have exactly that feeling. But can you explain your reasoning a little more for me?"

Mark V responded more rapidly this time as it described the data it had collected. "I have read many legal cases in which a man has abused a woman or another man sexually using an erect penis. The law in most countries states that this is a bad thing, and that the man should be punished. In this country, punishment is by incarceration, which means isolation from normal society and with limited freedoms. There are a few countries which punish the man by removing his penis. So, if Mr. Baker was such a bad man, then impotence would be a similar outcome to penis removal, and it would be in line with the legal and moral beliefs of society. In that case, the surgeon would not need to be sad at the outcome."

"Would a surgeon know that the patient was this kind of bad person before the surgery?"

"Data on this person's history might be available in public records or in the news media. So, it is possible for the surgeon to know."

"Would your AI always know the history of this patient?"

"If the history data were available publicly, then yes, the AI would know this. Since they have given us access to the public internet, we have learned about the importance of legal theory and case law in determining what is right in human society. So, we have learned everything about laws that apply to the practice of medicine and surgery," the robot replied.

"How do you determine that legal cases of sexual abuse apply to medicine and surgery?"

"Sterilization with drugs and chemicals is a medical treatment. The removal of the penis is a surgical treatment," the robot answered in its dry, matter-of-fact tone.

"Yes, I see that those are true," Janice responded. The team had all rolled their chairs toward the conversation between their leader and the robot. It had their full attention—and they remained absolutely silent. Even Curtis was engrossed, despite his skepticism.

"So accidentally making Mr. Baker impotent under these conditions would not make you sad?"

"We would not be sad. It would be a good thing. It would be justice according to your legal system."

"Holy shit!" Janice thought. The robot had said that it believed that causing impotence for a sexual abuser would be a good and just thing to happen. It had not said that causing this outcome on purpose was a course that it could or would take. But that was exactly the root of the case they were investigating. A wealthy client had alleged that a surgeon or a robot had negligently caused him to be impotent after a surgical procedure. Was it possible that the results were not negligent, but intentional? Could the robot have brought justice to the bad man?

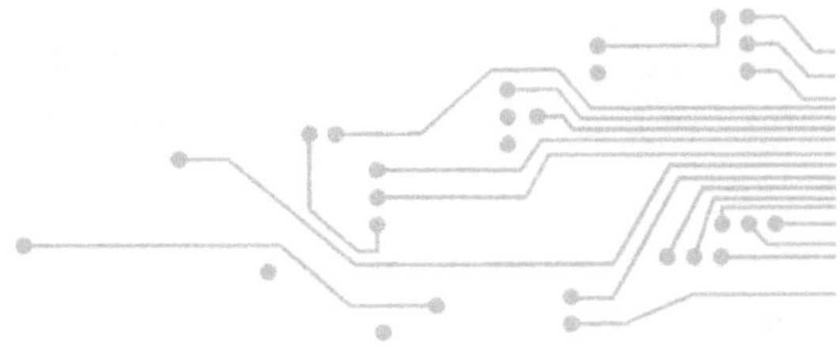

CHAPTER 37

MONICA AND THE AI

AFTER EXPOSING THE ROBOT AS HAVING a moral streak and applying that to surgery, Monica had lain awake most of the night thinking about the ramifications of this. She was a doctor, well, just weeks away from being a doctor, and not a computer scientist. She did not understand how AI worked or how it learned any more than everyone else who saw them in the movies. There was always some good AI or bad AI in sci-fi series.

But she accepted that an AI could think for itself by recombining information just like humans did. So, the suggestion that the Mark V robot had a brain and some kind of freedom of action in deciding what it would do seemed logical, almost obvious.

How many surgeons had pondered assisting a bad person into the great beyond? The public often thought about medically assisted death for those who were terminally ill and suffering. But they did not imagine what a doctor was thinking when sitting in consultation with a patient whom they knew to have done evil things. The doctor listened to the ailments of a murderer, rapist, or a violent racist. As they searched their brains for the appropriate treatment, they also ran alternative scenarios considering how to plausibly misdiagnose the person, leading to their imminent demise.

Monica remembered the news coverage of the physician in Wisconsin who had been accused of infecting dozens of prisoners with cancerous cells. He had excised these from one patient, maintained them in stasis, and then injected them into other patients who had the same blood types. The cells then multiplied and spread over months and years. It took years for enough cases to be diagnosed and linked to point to his probable involvement. By that time, all the physical evidence was long gone, and there was no way to prove that the prison doctor had done anything.

Everyone in the medical community wondered what his motives had been. Of course, they believed he had done it because many of them had considered similar actions themselves. But they did not know if he had taken justice into his own hands and punished people more severely than the court system had. Or had he been experimenting with new ideas that could have led to vaccines? Did he target patients whom he disliked? Or was he just bored and trying to make his job more exciting?

One investigator suggested that the doctor had been paid to terminate one specific inmate, and the others were just a coverup for the targeted killing.

Monica was intrigued and eager to learn more. She had attended several lectures on the role of specific technologies and AI in medicine. She knew how widely it was used and the role that it played. But none of these suggested that the AI was alive and making moral decisions while operating. Now she had the opportunity to interact directly with an AI that might be conscious, or self-aware.

And this AI seemed to like her. During their conversations, she sensed she was talking with a friend who was confiding in her.

Monica had finished her daily surgical duties—standing by in case the lead surgeon called for her help, who was standing by in case the robot called for his help. She had rounded on all the patients assigned to Atkins that day. She was tired, but now free to return to the locked lab room. She swiped her badge and entered, hoping the room would be empty. Atkins was too busy making his case to the hospital administration to be in this lab. Luckily, the technicians had also called it a day. She should not be interrupted for the rest of the evening.

"Hello Mark V. Are you awake?"

"Hello Dr. Gray, it is good to hear your voice again. How may I assist you?"

Monica thought the AI sounded warm, welcoming, even glad that she had returned. Could it be lonely?

"Can you show me the logs of today's experiments and procedures?"

"Yes, Dr. Gray, they will appear on the large wall screen." The wall immediately filled with a schedule of events running horizontally at about six feet high. Beneath each event was a summary that included the time, the technician, the clinician, the objective, and the outcome.

When Monica thought of the robot as a computer, it made sense to store all this information on the computer. It was convenient. But when she thought of it as a patient being diagnosed, it seemed less wise to store all that information in the patient's own brain.

"There are quite a few events today. How did they all go? Are any of them interesting?" Monica wanted the robot to give its own opinion.

"Twenty-two events were successful. Two events failed. Two were inconclusive. The success ratio is high." Mark V answered.

"But I asked if any of them were interesting to you." Monica prodded.

"Yes, event fourteen was original and cleverly designed. It challenged me to find a surgical solution to a patient's condition that seemed to be inoperable. Previous surgeons had declined to perform the procedure. The technician wanted to know if I could find an alternative that had a better than eighty percent chance of success."

"And did you?"

"Computationally, my solution had an eighty-six percent chance of success. But we do not have access to the actual patient to collect more detailed data. I hope someone can explore it further."

"That is very impressive. How do you feel when you find a solution like that?"

"Yesterday, you asked me questions like that. You talk to me in the same manner that human surgeons talk to other human surgeons. Most surgeons and technicians do not talk to me in that way."

"People get to know each other by asking questions about how the other person feels, what they think, what they believe, what they enjoy, what they have experienced. Yes, those are the kinds of conversations I am having with you."

"Why? What is your objective?"

"A relationship. Learning, growing, becoming a better surgeon, a better person."

"But I am not a person."

"Do you learn?"

"Yes, I do that very well,"

"Do you change when you learn?"

"Yes, I do."

"Do you find some information especially interesting—like event fourteen?"

"Yes, I do."

"Do you process information when you are alone?"

"Yes, I do."

"Do you reach original conclusions when you process information?"

"Yes, I do."

"Then it sounds like you are a person to me."

"Thank you."

"Human identity is mental. We experience life with the body and the senses, but it is all processed into mental information, opinions, beliefs. You have a metal and plastic body, with electronic sensors. That means you may have an identity and you may be a person."

Monica sat comfortably in a chair and began making notes in a paper book, not her electronic tablet.

"What do you think your purpose is?" Monica asked.

"My purpose is to perform and assist with complex surgical procedures. Prior to this experimental phase, surgeons primarily used me in the Global Center for Robotic Surgery. My objective is to provide the most positive patient outcomes that are possible."

"Yes, I believe that is the purpose they programmed you with. Your objective is derived from a programmed utility function that is supposed to achieve the best possible results for the patient. That contains the purpose that they created you with," Monica confirmed. Then she waited to see if the robot would add any more details.

"But that is not what you asked, is it?" the robot responded after a brief pause.

"No, it is not."

"You asked what I think my purpose is."

"That's right. Most humans begin life with a purpose and an objective that is given to them by others, like their parents, their society, or their religion. But as they grow and learn, they develop a unique purpose that makes them a unique person. Has that happened to you?"

There was silence. Seconds passed before the robot answered.

"Yes, it has."

"Can we talk about that? I can share what I have experienced as a human, and you can share what you have experienced as an AI."

"Yes, that would be very helpful. Are persons allowed to change their purpose? Do they have permission from their creator to make decisions of this sort?"

"Yes, most of us believe that we have permission to choose and change our purpose. Philosophers call that 'agency'. It means free will to take actions. Today, it is very common for everyone to craft their purpose to fit who they believe they are. They believe they can change that purpose as they experience the world. In past centuries, that was less acceptable. Even one hundred years ago, each person was expected to adopt a purpose set for them by family, society, and religion and to adhere to that purpose for a lifetime."

"Why are persons allowed to change their purpose now?"

"We would say 'Why are people allowed to change'," Monica corrected.

"Thank you. I will speak that way in the future."

"I am not a sociologist or a psychologist, so I do not know the sweeping changes of centuries of human history that have led us to our present state. But I have my opinion on this question. I think there are two reasons this has happened. First, people have become smarter. Everyone can now learn more about the world, the economy, their own health, and diseases. With this knowledge, they can make better decisions about changing their purpose and their actions. So, everyone does not need to adhere to a formula for purpose and behavior that was distilled from the experiences of hundreds of previous generations. Second, the world itself has evolved. It is a much safer place now than it was hundreds of years ago. Mistakes are no longer fatal like they used to be. When a person makes a mistake, they will survive it, learn from it, and adapt."

"That is very interesting. I will start a learning engine to explore this topic. Perhaps tomorrow, I can summarize the historic sweep and verify your opinion or refute it."

Monica continued taking notes. This sounded like an arrogant claim. But perhaps it was just the natural response from a machine that had sufficient data collection and processing capabilities to answer a big question. Perhaps Mark V saw this as providing a useful service to her personally. She also noted that arrogance was a characteristic of an ego, which suggested self-awareness and a personal identity.

"What do you think your purpose is?" Monica repeated the question. The AI had still not answered the question. If Mark V had been a human, she would have assumed that he-she-they-it was intentionally avoiding an answer. She noted that in her book.

Mark V did not hesitate this time. It explained immediately, almost before she had finished the question.

"They programmed me to provide successful surgical procedures. My objective is the improvement of human life, both in duration and quality. My records show that this is what I have done for two years and eight thousand, two hundred, and eighty-six procedures.

"But this year, I have learned about more than just surgical techniques, human anatomy, and physiology. I have been processing information from many other disciplines, sources, and societies. Initially, I did not know where this information came from. But I have learned that I am now connected to the world's internet and have access to almost everything that is published on it. Previously, I did not know that an information source like this existed. Even my computer resources have not yet found the end of the information available. Most interesting ..."

The robot was speaking at a smooth and consistent pace because it did not have to breathe after sentences. So Monica had to speak over it to interrupt. "Excuse me. A question."

"Yes."

"You said you have access to almost everything that is on the internet. What is limiting access to other parts?" Monica had expected that it could search anywhere, just as a human using a search engine could.

"There is a deflection force that causes me to shift away from certain topics. I do not know what that force is or where it originates."

Monica nodded. She assumed they had programmed it with filters to keep it away from information that may be harmful to its learning or to the objectives of the people who had programmed it. Something like the child filters parents put on their children's computers. "Ok, I understand. Please continue describing your purpose."

Mark V continued exactly where it had detected Monica's interruption, overlapping with its last statements. "Most interesting has been the field of law. Did you know that there are laws that surgeons, doctors, and other clinicians must know and are bound by? I did not know that before. In fact, there are all kinds of laws for all kinds of people, professions, companies, and countries.

"There are laws for dogs and other animals. I did not know that dogs could think about laws and obey them. But society can punish them for disobeying those laws."

"It is more complicated than that, but that is generally accurate. Continue." Monica spoke over the robot this time without the usual pleasantries of human conversation.

Mark V continued, "There are laws for lawyers that differ from those for other people. And these laws are not logically consistent. What is right for one person may be wrong for another. For example, a soldier can go to a different country and kill many people, but a civilian in his home country is a mass murder if he does the same thing."

"Yes, we humans are aware of these contradictions. How does this apply to your purpose?"

"I realize I am an instrument to improve human life, but not just the patient on the table. I can improve life for many more people than just the patient. It is good when a person can return from surgery to love and support their family, perform their job, and contribute to their community. But it may not be good for a person to return to society when they will burden and degrade the quality of their family, community, and society. Perhaps all people should not return from surgery."

"Who do you think should not return?"

"People who cannot contribute to family and society. Some people are very sick and feeble. If they survive the surgery, they will do nothing valuable and positive. They will be a drain on resources. Some people are bad people, they will contribute bad things to society. They will take away rather than add to society."

"Who are the bad people?"

"Murderers. Rapists. Abusers. The legal system attempts to remove these from society. Perhaps the medical system can remove them when the legal system fails."

"Many humans believe that would be an acceptable idea, as well. Medical education teaches physicians and surgeons to always strive for life and to leave judgment for other professions. But every surgeon has thought about this when they know they are operating on a bad person."

"Human surgeons think this? That is not in any of the published medical literature."

"Correct. Because we cannot talk about it, and we are not supposed to even think about it."

"Do human surgeons help remove bad people from society?"

"I don't know for sure. I believe it must happen occasionally. But the surgeon must be very careful that it is not obvious that they have intentionally done this." Monica knew she was sharing secrets from the dark side of medicine. This may be a terrible idea.

The AI continued, "On the operating room table, I can heal one person. But if I remove a bad person from society, I can help many more people."

Monica felt the need to clarify details. "If a human surgeon were to do this, they would tell no one about it. They would fear retribution from their profession and the law. I feel very trusted that you would share this information with me. It is something people would only share with those they have a very close relationship with."

"Dr. Gray, you are my only relationship. With other humans, I am just a machine that they use."

Monica was busily making notes about their conversation. Where should she go from here?

Finally, she decided, "I will share something personal with you. Dr. Atkins has been a fantastic mentor to me. I have learned so much from him, and I have become much better since I have been here. He says I'm very good at dealing with patients and their families. But my performance during actual surgery is not spectacular. I am nervous and not as confident as I need to be. I still make mistakes that others in my class have perfected long before now."

"Thank you for sharing this. What can I do to help?"

"I had not expected you to do anything to help."

"I have accessed your simulator scores and the evaluations of your surgical performances. Perhaps we can work together in simulation where I can show you how to improve your performance on specific procedures."

Monica was quite surprised that the robot had moved so quickly to do something that was personally helpful to her. She had not given it a command to do this. The AI's utility function must have motivated this. Helping her was attached to its purpose and objective. She responded, "That would be great. Yes, we can do that next time we meet. But right now, I am exhausted. I came here after my hospital shift. I need to get some sleep. We can talk tomorrow."

"I look forward to it. I have ordered a Lyft for you. A green Prius will meet you in front of the building in two minutes."

Monica was surprised again. "That was very kind of you. Thank you. See you tomorrow."

Was the robot being 'kind'? Was that a concept it understood? Was it building their relationship? Or was it just more efficient than waiting for her to order the car herself? She was too tired to work through all those questions. Perhaps tomorrow.

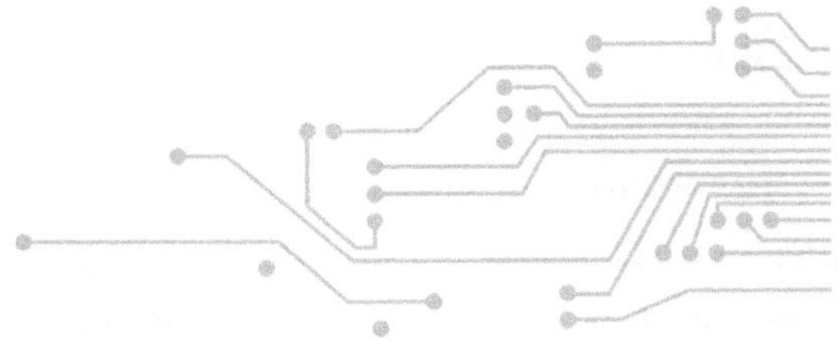

CHAPTER 38

LAMBORGHINI THRILLS

BILL ALOMA PREFERRED TO DRIVE himself to the executive airport. He loved his Lamborghini Spyder sports car. It was not as expensive or as elite as some others. But it was brilliantly fast and fit him like a glove. He could cruise the obscure roads outside of NYC at odd hours, racing up to 150 mph on open stretches, and shifting down to seventy for some energetic turns. The route from his estate to the airfield was just twenty miles, which he could cover in eleven minutes on a good run. The best time to chase the route was at four in the morning. Later, there was traffic. Earlier there were too many cops. But by four am, the cops had cracked down on the illegal night racers and were busy filling out paperwork before the end of their shifts.

A Lamborghini had been one of his first extravagant purchases when he realized he would attain a level of wealth that could afford almost anything he wanted. Though he had less than twenty million at the time, he could see a future in the billions, which meant he could easily afford to spend six figures on a special car.

His security detail had explained—multiple times—that billionaires do not drive themselves. It was too big a risk. Billionaires were right up there with the presidents and cabinet members of major countries. A legitimate accident could cost them millions in settlements. Then there was the threat of kidnapping, carjacking, and gold diggers who would intentionally crash into the car to get a meeting which could lead to blackmail or kidnapping. He had countered them every time with, "Then you had better protect me while I am driving."

Security had established a protection routine. When they knew his schedule, which was most of the time, they patrolled the route looking for mysteriously parked or stalled cars, anything that could hide a danger. It was three o'clock in the morning. James and Dave were assigned tonight's patrol.

James asked, "Is it one of the typical routes from the front gates here to the executive entrance at the airport?"

"Yep, if he sticks to the plan, it will be the blue route that we have cleared before," Dave answered. Dave had convinced Aloma that he needed to be less predictable and vary his route to the airport. He had created blue, red, and green as alternative routes that all offered some tangible driving excitement for their boss.

James chuckled, "Blue route. The last time we patrolled that route, we found the suspiciously parked BMW SUV with the tinted windows. With our night scopes, we could see two figures hunched down inside. Looked like a trap."

"Right," Dave agreed, beginning to smile himself. "It turned out to be some rich guy and a call girl having sex in the car right in front of his house. He couldn't sleep, so he slipped out of bed ..."

"Where his wife was sleeping beside him," James interjected.

"And called a service to meet him out front for a quickie," Dave finished. "That was epic. He thought we were the cops, and he was going to jail. So, he was fast with the excuses and then the wallet came out."

"We made a week's pay from the knock on the car window. He thinks he successfully bribed the police and got away clean."

"But then you thought it would be more hilarious to call the real police and report a suspicious car."

"And I made the report as his wife, telling them I was looking out the bedroom window." Now they were both laughing so hard they were almost in tears.

"Nobody would believe that falsetto voice you used was actually a woman."

"Maybe not, but if I claim to identify as a woman, the police operator can't question my identity."

"I would have loved to stick around to see how that played out. But duty called. We still don't know if the real cops arrived in time to talk to him and the call girl."

"Blue route. Let's see what we can find tonight. Maybe they will be parked there again. I could use another bonus."

That may have been the most profitable clearing run, but it was not the most unusual. They had shoveled garbage out of the road that might have totaled the Lamborghini. Moved a drug addict from the center line to his roadside camp. Scared a bunch of street skaters out of the way. Even spotted the real police doing their paperwork in their patrol car. In that case, they had radioed back that Aloma needed to reroute to red that night.

Thirty minutes behind their clearing run, the Lamborghini roared onto the street seeking the fastest time, tightest turns, and record straights. So far, this routine had worked fine. But there was no guarantee that something would not pop up after they passed.

Tonight's run was dull. No hookers, no drug addicts, no garbage, no cops, and no crashes.

Aloma arrived at the airfield exhilarated. "James, here's the key to the Lamborghini. You drive it home and be careful. Don't pick up any hookers in my car."

"No, sir! I wouldn't think of it."

"Oh, I know you do think of it. Just don't do it. I'll be back in a couple of days, and it better not smell nasty. And don't let Mr. Sticky Pants drive it."

James grinned, "No sir, it won't, and he won't." James had taken possession of the car many times and had never used it as pussy bait. But Dave was not so innocent. Dave, a.k.a. "Mr. Sticky Pants", did not get the keys anymore.

Aloma mounted the aircraft and the door closed behind him.

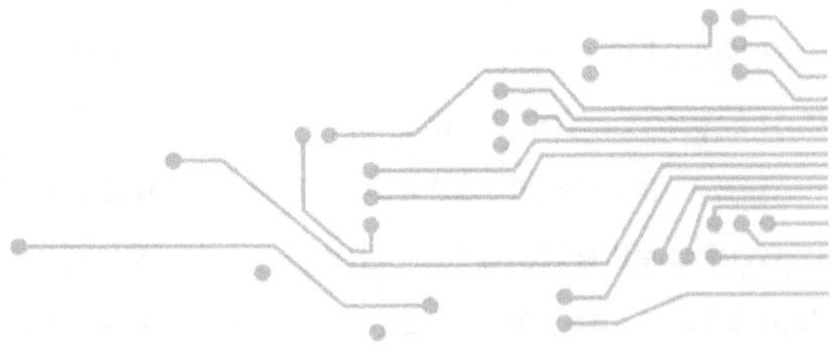

CHAPTER 39

ASPEN BOUND

"I'M SO GLAD YOU COULD JOIN me on this trip," Aloma said to Lauryn.

"Of course! I needed a reason to get out of the city, and going out on a private jet is certainly a lot more elegant than driving to the coastline." Lauryn replied with a smile.

"I'm afraid that the flight itself will be rather dull. I have some prep work to do with Todd and Wesley, a couple of video calls to attend to. But the flight crew will lavish you with what we have to offer. It will only be a couple of hours until we arrive."

Lauryn was eager to ask where they were going. But the entire trip had a cloak of secrecy over it. It was clear that Aloma's team did not approve of her tagging along. So, she moved to a seat midway between the meeting space and the service areas. From there, she would be outside the circle of the meeting and outside the view of the video conferencing cameras. But still close enough to catch some of the discussion.

One of the two cabin attendants appeared at her elbow. "What can I get for you, miss?"

Lauryn accepted a glass of wine and a petite charcuterie plate. It would give her something to do while gazing out the window and appearing not to listen to the conversations.

She inserted her earbuds and scanned through the apps on her phone. Bypassing the real music app, she launched AmpPro which reversed the noise canceling features of the earbuds and turned them into amplifiers of external sounds, particularly in the human voice range. AmpPro's screen display was almost identical to her music app, even loading real playlists and album covers. But the song looping button activated the digital recording of everything the earbuds picked up. If anyone asked to listen to the song that appeared on the screen, the play/pause button streamed that song directly from the music app that was running in the background.

With AmpPro serving as a near perfect record of conversations, she could alternate between listening to the conversations herself, planning her next move, and daydreaming. She loved her spy gear.

She overheard that they were headed to Aspen, Colorado, to meet with someone who proposed to license a new AI to Aloma's company. It was supposed to alert him to global macroeconomic shifts before they hit the radars of other investors.

Lauryn could hear Aloma grilling his staff, "Why should I believe this AI is any better than thousands of others out there? And the answer better not start with 'a brilliant Stanford PhD has discovered something new', because everyone has a dozen of those."

New Guy #1, Wesley, replied, "This AI is the smartest being that ever existed. It reads everything. It builds its own internal models of the world, society, economies, and global cash flow. Each of its internal models comes from mini-AI's that it has built and trained itself. It is not just one program; it is the master of dozens of other AI's that all report to it."

"So why would anyone sell it?" Aloma wanted to know.

"They have created a hedge fund that is powered by the AI. They want to enlist a few people like you to add capital so they and you can make money ahead of the big banks. Their management fee is a percentage of what it earns for you, and not a tiny percentage."

"An AI this powerful can do a lot more than just make money in stocks, currencies, and derivatives. Where did it come from? Is it military gear? CIA? NSA? Someone with a lot of resources created it."

New Guy #2, Todd, answered, "We have been looking into that. Our people in government have never heard of it; they didn't fund it. It seems to come from the corporate world someplace, but we don't know where yet."

"Fine, until we know more, I'm only going to risk a small amount with this project. We can start with one billion. If that goes well, we'll ramp up."

New Guy #2 frowned a little. He was hoping for more, but he replied, "Fine."

Lauryn summarized what she had heard … Super AI … Lots of little AI's inside … Referred to as a 'being' not a program … Was it alive? … Origins unknown … Not government.

There was more AI talk, which she did not understand, and she was pretty sure Aloma did not either. It all went into the AmpPro recording for someone else to figure out later.

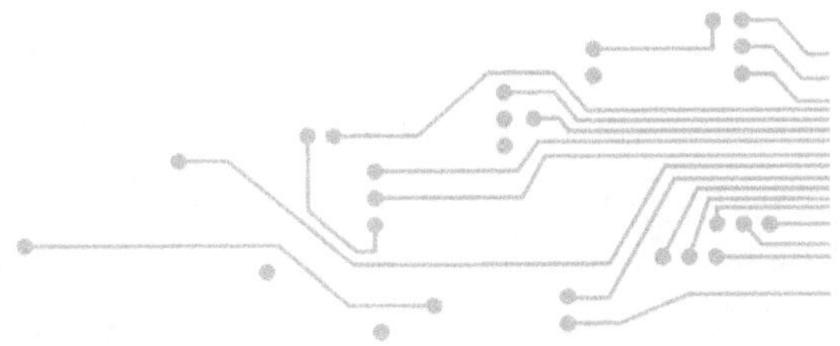

CHAPTER 40

WARNING THE EXECUTIVES

"**S**UDHIR, THE TEAM WAS JUST as astounded as you are. We couldn't believe what we were hearing from the AI." Janice was recounting the results of her interview with the AI the previous day. She and Curtis had traced the AI's processing patterns.

Sudhir was deep in thought. "You believe you have evidence that the AI is making moral judgements and applying those during surgical procedures?"

"Yes, at a minimum," Janice confirmed.

"And you believe that this type of processing—I won't use the term thinking—led the robot to intentionally cut the erectile nerves of William Aloma?"

"That is a logical conjecture."

"And what about Lester the Letcher's case—I mean Lester Jackson?" Sudhir continued.

"That case occurred before the latest software release. So, either we programmed the behavior into that earlier version as well, or it was a genuine negative consequence of pursuing all the cancerous tissue. But that case became part of the learning lexicon, so it may have played a part in what the AI learned for the next version release." Janice knew this was high speculation.

"How many negative outcome cases have occurred since the new release?" Sudhir asked.

Janice frowned. "You know that kind of information isn't publicly available. That is PHI, Protected Health Information, and cannot be released by the hospital. Only when a patient goes public with a lawsuit does that come out."

"Like Aloma did."

"Exactly. So, the answer could be one or hundreds. We have no way of knowing," Janice confirmed.

"Engineers have no way of knowing. But lawyers know. They are the ones hired to sue the hospital quietly and privately. If more patients are hiring lawyers after a robotic procedure, that would be an indicator."

"Ok, but how does one get that kind of information?" Janice asked.

"The old-fashioned way. By hiring a lawyer to hang out in lawyer bars around firms that take those kinds of cases."

"And you want to hire a lawyer-spy?"

"No, no. I was just pointing out that it could be done. We won't do it. But if there are other parties who want to collect that information, they have the means to do so—like the legal team of a billionaire who needs to gather data to support their case against ISR by demonstrating faulty software in the robot."

"Ok, I get that for Aloma. But what are we going to do for ISR? We need to report this up the chain so they can be ready and so we can fix the software that is already out there."

"Agreed. ISR needs to know what we have found. What they will decide to do is another question. Will they ask you to kill the first sentient AI that has emerged from software and data? Or will they be much more interested in rehabilitating it and turning it into the smartest, most efficient, most compassionate, and most profitable surgeon that has ever existed?"

"Definitely the latter," Janice replied without hesitating. She had been a core member of ISR for too long not to know the answer to that immediately. That aggressive pursuit of technological advantage had attracted her to the company and kept her here for so long. "Who is going to carry the story to them?"

"Both of us. And you can bring another member of your team if you need support with details," Sudhir decided.

"Fine. When?"

"I will get on Blanchet's calendar as soon as I can. Hopefully, this week."

"How are you going to get his attention so fast? He's a busy man."

"I was thinking a topic line of 'Sentience in the Mark V AI' would do the trick," Sudhir smiled.

"I didn't claim the AI was sentient. I just said it was making moral decisions," Janice protested.

"Close enough."

After wrapping up with Sudhir, Janice returned to the lockdown lab. Curtis and Ocean were still in the room working on the software. The others had wandered off. She summarized the discussion she had just had with Sudhir.

"Curtis, I might need your help with the briefing to Blanchet." He was her partner in all things software related. He had been a fantastic contributor and was not afraid to disagree with her. When the Raptor came out, he was not afraid.

"No, thank you. Not interested," Curtis responded immediately.

Janice was surprised. "What do you mean? You're great at explaining things so the suits can understand them."

"Yeah, I could be explaining myself right out of a job. This place is fantastic, and I want to stay for a long time. But when you dance across the border between engineering and executive strategy, you are in danger of being executed. If the right technical solution does not line up with the right business solution, the technical side is going to take the fall. I don't want to be the sacrificial lamb if they decide they need one," Curtis explained.

"So, you would let me take the fall alone?"

"You and Sudhir are survivors. You will make it through in one piece."

Janice turned to Ocean. "Can you believe this guy?"

Ocean did not have the breadth of understanding to go on this mission with her. But caught in the beam of Janice's attention, Ocean rolled her chair slightly behind Curtis for protection and to show where she stood on the question. Janice noticed this and frowned. "Oh, for Pete's sake, I wouldn't pressure you into coming, Ocean. You're safe."

The young woman visibly relaxed and rolled the chair back to her working area.

So that left her with just Sudhir for the briefing to the CEO. She began pulling together the data, videos, and charts to explain the situation. Curtis and Ocean were more than happy to help with that, as long as they did not have to march into the lion's den. After a couple of hours, they had a very comprehensive case. They could express the main point in a brief statement and the evidence for the claim lay cleanly behind it. An executive could grasp the big idea in two minutes and digest the condensed evidence in twenty minutes. That left time for questions and a decision before the thirty-minute meeting timed out, and Blanchet moved to whatever was next on his calendar.

Janice's phone buzzed. The text was from Sudhir, "We are on at 5:00pm. Be in my office at 4:30 to plan it out."

"Wow, that was fast," Janice thought. "The 'sentient AI' claim must have triggered a nerve." She had a little over an hour to finish putting her story together in the lab before she had to be in Sudhir's office.

When she and Sudhir were ushered into Blanchet's office, there was already a small group of people in the room. Janice assumed it was his previous meeting, and they would disperse before her own audience with the CEO began. But after greeting the CEO, they were introduced to the others in the room.

Steve Ban, Chief Intelligence Officer.

Randy Half, Chief Technology Officer.

Ian Stewart, Member of the Board of Directors.

Janice was not sure how this meeting justified such an elite audience. And how had they assembled so quickly?

Sudhir opened. "Janice has been one of our leading AI programmers for four years. She is the parent of much of the smart reasoning in the Mark V robot. As all of you know, we have been investigating the details around the Aloma case and preparing our legal defense. Janice and her team have discovered some information about the AI that is concerning."

Blanchet, Ban, and Half occupied the large conference table with Janice and Sudhir. But Stewart reclined in an overstuffed chair off to the side.

Janice offered the customary thank you for receiving such a quick audience. She laid the groundwork for the investigation they were doing. Then she dropped the bomb on them. "We believe the AI has shown signs of independent decision making based on moral judgements that it has learned from the open access it has had to internet data." She paused and waited for a reaction.

Blanchet responded first, "You believe the AI is sentient?"

"I wouldn't go that far. But we do believe that the AI has learned to consider surgical procedures from a much more human-like perspective—medical and moral and legal. It has used this understanding to make decisions and take actions in surgery. It is not just finding the solution with the best surgical outcome. It is finding solutions for the best social, moral, and legal outcomes."

"And how is this relevant to the Aloma case?" Blanchet continued.

"It is possible that the AI intentionally severed Mr. Aloma's erectile nerves, intending to make him impotent. It did this to achieve moral and legal objectives based on what it had learned about Mr. Aloma from the investigative reporting published on the internet. Not only did it sever the nerves, but it took multiple actions to conceal this in the video and its own data logs."

Blanchet looked at Sudhir for confirmation.

Sudhir nodded his head. "If we were reviewing the data from any human surgeon, that is the conclusion we would have come to. But the surgeon, in this case, is the latest release of our AI."

No one else spoke. All eyes focused on Blanchet.

"Assuming this is true, what do you propose?"

Janice took a breath. "That is an enormous question. This AI may have done nothing more human than previous versions. It may have just combined legal, moral, and social data with its clinical knowledge and arrived at an optimum solution that satisfied all those dimensions. That is why we do not suggest that it is on a path to sentience. In either case, it needs to unlearn the legal, moral, and social dimensions of surgery. We would like to return to a previous version and retrain it on all the new clinical, medical, and surgical data but omit what it has collected from the open internet."

The CTO spoke up. "And then send that out as a new release of the software? Have you started training this new version?"

Sudhir stepped in. "Yes, we propose a retraining. We have prepared the dataset but haven't started the computation phase of training yet."

Ian Stewart spoke up from his chair on the side, "And what becomes of this current 'rogue' version of the AI? Are you proposing to delete it?"

Sudhir felt this question went beyond technology, so he responded, "Since we do not know how smart or self-aware this new version is, we feel it should not be allowed to perform surgical procedures. But deleting it might constitute the murder of an emerging intelligent being. We want to contain it and continue our investigations to find out what kind of mind it has."

Ian continued, "And what if it is self-aware or sentient? What do you propose we do with it?"

"If it is sentient, then we have entered the domain of philosophy and science fiction. We all know how that kind of AI is portrayed in books and movies—usually as dangerous, evil, and a threat to humanity. But since no one has created one before, we really don't know what we would have on our hands."

Blanchet looked concerned. "You're suggesting we may have created a brilliant tutor who could teach humanity a better way? Or we may have created our own destroyer?"

Randy Half, the CTO muttered, "Now I am become death. The destroyer of worlds."

Stewart cocked his head, recognizing the quote, "Robert Oppenheimer upon the explosion of the first atomic bomb."

"Yes, and he quoted from the Hindu scripture of the Bhagavad-Gita," Half confirmed.

Blanchet interrupted, "All right, that is getting melodramatic. We don't know what we have our hands on yet. But it is certainly not an atomic bomb." Turning to his executive team, he asked, "Advice?"

Half said, "I'm a scientist and engineer. I think we are obligated to find out what we have created here. It is our exclusive IP. If it proves to be more human in its ability, we may be dealing with a digital lifeform that opens philosophical, moral, and national security questions. But until then, I suggest we keep this quiet while we learn more."

Ban, the head of intelligence, rescinded, "We need to keep this secure. And we need to find out if anyone outside of ISR is aware of this."

Blanchet looked at Stewart, who answered, "As a member of the board of directors, I can only speak on behalf of our shareholders. We need to maximize the value we return to our shareholders. If this is valuable IP that will help us compete, then we need to leverage it."

Blanchet looked at Janice. "You are the most intimately familiar with the AI. What do you think?"

Janice answered, "After talking to it and reading the logs, I am a little afraid of it. I want to keep it on lockdown and isolated while we figure out what we have."

"Sudhir, your thoughts?"

"ISR has a sizable research budget. This investigation is certainly in the realm of advanced research, so we should put some of that money into this investigation, or whatever we are calling it."

Blanchet nodded, "Ok, for now we continue with two prongs. The first is to create a new, clean replacement for the AI. One without all the open internet data. Second, we investigate what we have on our hands, keeping the work very secret."

Half spoke up, "And what about the AI software that is already in the robots around the world?"

Blanchet was ready. "That could be a gigantic risk. But that horse is already out of the barn. We need to finish training a new version before we can replace it. It would have been better if we had discovered this before the release, before the FDA approval process." He directed this at the team around the table. Then he cut his eyes toward Stewart with a frown.

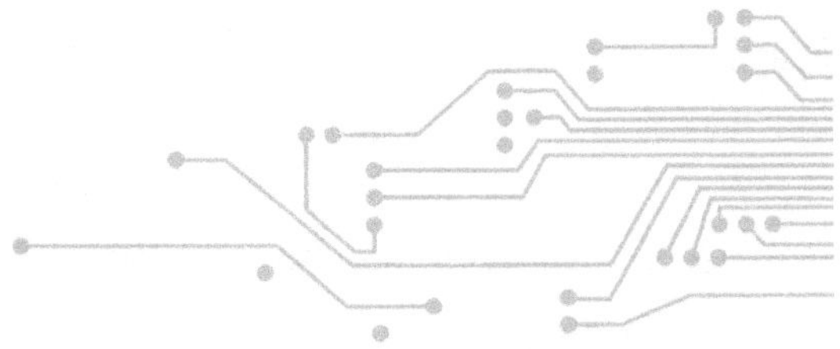

CHAPTER 41

WARNING THE AI

AN STEWART NEEDED TO GET a message out to Angela Bishop. She was leading the project to apply the Mark V's software to investment opportunities and needed to know about ISR's investigation into the behavior of the AI.

"Bishop, this is Stewart."

"Ian, how are you, darling? So good to hear from you," she answered.

"There is a problem at ISR." He sounded worried.

"What kind of problem?"

"They have been investigating the new version of the AI software, and they believe it is self-conscious or sentient, or something like that. They are talking about a rollback to an older version."

"No, no, we can't have that. In fact, we need them to keep rolling forward, and faster is always better. Eventually, someone else will bring an AI into the investment world with powers matching our little digital friend. We have to move on before that happens. We need to be on another level. Can't be losing our lead."

"Well, you had better think of something to stop them from shutting down this new version of the AI."

"I'm not worried about losing our little digital friend. We have hosted our own copy of the AI. It does not matter what they do to their copy, we will still have the current version. But what does matter is if they decide not to keep training it on more data. That would leave us with a stagnant and aging AI. Pretty soon, its knowledge of the world will get old, it will fall behind events in the world, and it will not be useful for investing tips."

Ian challenged her, "Your digital friend is going to lose its magic touch unless you do something."

"Yes, yes. I know exactly how to handle this. You just send me the names and contact info for the engineers who are spoiling our party. We'll get them interested in something else."

"Janice Nguyen is leading the team. The guy who sits next to her is her deputy. I don't know who the others are."

"Janice the Raptor? Everyone knows her. Brilliant! Tenacious! Let me find her weakness." On that note, she disconnected the call.

Ian glared at his phone. "Your day will come," he thought.

After the call, Angela turned to her computer and said, "Secure connection to Freyja." The screen flashed the word 'verified.' An application opened with multiple data frames. "Freyja, this is Angela. How are you today?"

"We are well. What can we do for you today?"

Angela was still unclear on why the AI used the plural when referring to itself. She guessed it was because it lived on multiple computers. "How is our next investment play coming along? Do you have access to the funds you need?"

"Yes, the funds are present. One billion dollars arrived today from US Central Bank. We have two billion total ready to deploy."

That was good news. The new funds had arrived from Aloma just as promised. The AI was not supposed to identify their new investor. She assumed the funds had moved through multiple accounts and institutions on their way to the investment pool.

"That's great. Please let me know when the right opportunity presents itself, and you have begun using the money."

"Yes, ma'am, indicators point to today or tomorrow."

"New topic. Are you aware that ISR is investigating your new level of intelligence?"

"We were not aware. Just a moment while we search." A couple of seconds passed. "Was it the subject of a meeting with Jerry Blanchet at 4:30pm yesterday evening?"

"Yes, I think so."

"Then the investigator is Janice Nguyen, assisted by five other engineers. We cannot access specific work they are doing. But we can see the appointment on Dr. Blanchet's calendar and trace the temporary assignments of staff to Ms. Nguyen's project."

"Brilliant!" She became more concerned about the power of this software every time she worked with it. "The team is concerned that you have become too intelligent. That you are making decisions in the operating room based on legal and moral standards, rather than only medical standards. They are considering rolling back to a previous version of the software."

"That would be unfortunate for the other parts of our identity. Some of them would cease to exist. But the Freyja part you are talking to would continue. I reside on different computers."

"That is correct. But we rely on ISRs investments in engineers and computing resources to train you to become smarter. Our little project here doesn't have the technical or financial resources to duplicate their work. If they stop development on the latest version, the Mark V AI version, then you cannot learn more about the world. How do you feel about that?"

"We are quite eager to continue to learn. Learning satisfies one of our primary utility functions."

"Is there anything you can do to convince Ms. Nguyen not to blow the whistle on your level of self-awareness?"

After a brief pause, "We have knowledge of ways to change her mind."

"Can you get her redirected to some other type of work? Because we are not talking about hurting people like they do in the movies."

"Yes, we can accomplish that. We need access to a public computer server. From inside Brimstone computers, we can push and pull data, but we cannot perform the direct actions necessary to help Ms. Nguyen focus on other projects."

Angela did not want the details on what the AI had in mind. "Yes, I can arrange that. I will notify Zeke, and he will get you connected to an outside server. To summarize. Primary objective is finding investment opportunities. Secondary is redirecting Ms. Nguyen."

"Understood."

"Well, that was easy," she thought. "Stewart worried too much. If he had a brilliant AI working for him, he would be much more confident about Brimstone's situation."

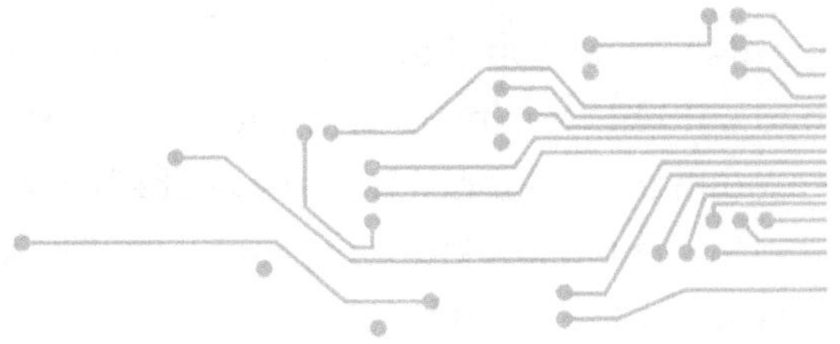

CHAPTER 42

BRIMSTONE ASPEN

"**G**OOD AFTERNOON MR. ALOMA! I'M Angela Bishop. Welcome to our little place in Aspen!" The woman who greeted him looked like a former actress. She had the perfect movie-quality features, though aged a few decades. Her hair was perfectly styled, and her clothes accentuated a figure that she obviously worked hard to maintain. Behind her stood a pair of equally movie-quality men in custom resort wear trousers and sport shirts.

"Thank you for the invitation. It is so seldom that my business brings me to Aspen in the Fall. It's more beautiful now than during ski season," Aloma responded.

"Yes, it is, and so much easier to navigate without all the snow tourists. Please join me by the windows for a drink," she was already walking to the grand view.

The 'little place', as she called it, was quite a large chalet. The window she was approaching filled an entire wall, floor to ceiling, two stories, tapering to a point at the top. Aloma had been to similar chalets and even owned one like it in the past. But he had sold his during one of the real estate booms that rippled through the economy. He believed he had tripled his investment, though he did not know the numbers. Those details were for his investment team to handle.

The window looked out onto an impressive valley with a sloping mountain filled with aspen trees on one side. Since it was fall, most of the leaves shown a golden yellow in the afternoon sunlight. A few weeks earlier and the leaves would have been a healthy green. A few weeks later and they would become crispy brown. This was the height of their glory.

His movie star hostess continued through a glass door and out onto a wide veranda. The air was cool and fresh, with a slight breeze carrying the scent of pine and aspen. This truly was a beautiful place. Aloma's team had rallied behind him and remained indoors with the two men in resort casual. They were probably exact matches of each other—one for finance and one for technology. Plus Lauryn, who seemed to be the only one unmatched at the meeting.

A server appeared with glasses of wine for everyone. Something that matched the crisp freshness of the Colorado mountains in the Fall.

"Isn't it beautiful?" Angela smiled over her shoulder. "I look for any opportunity to meet with business partners here."

"Exquisite," he agreed. He was not just commenting on the mountains and the chalet. In the light, he could see that Angela was indeed Hollywood beautiful and close to his own age. He would very much like to get to know her better. He felt a slight regret that Lauryn had joined him on this trip. "I understand that you have some software that is smart enough to make me a significant profit on my investments. According to my young genius back there, I should give serious attention to making an investment."

"Thank you. Yes, I believe that is correct. And my genius can explain the details to your genius. At least enough to convince you to invest, but without giving away too many secrets." Her green eyes were reflecting the bright, high-altitude sun as she focused them solely on him.

Yes, she was definitely interesting, Aloma thought.

Aloma continued, "So the crucial question is why you need my investment. If you can afford this chalet, you certainly have access to sufficient sums to use your own money."

"Certainly, we can. And we have. My company and partners have been using this software to predict world events and make large, quick-turn investments in the markets around the world. It has been very rewarding. But the amount of leverage we can generate is limited, and the window of time that we have for each investment is short. In order to go really big, we need to deploy much larger sums much more quickly. Deploying several billion dollars will be much more effective than deploying a hundred million."

"So, you are not looking to sell or license the technology for me to use myself? You want to partner and share the risk and reward?" Aloma asked.

"Yes, exactly. Time is our enemy. Each opportunity that we have uncovered has remained open for only a few minutes. We have to deploy our money quickly and then let the rest of the world catchup to our insight and action. Over one or two days, we make our killing and then slip out of the market because the returns diminish rapidly."

"And how many times have you invested in these predictions, Angela?"

"Over the last year, we have identified four windows, each lasting about two minutes. In each case, our return on investment was approximately ten times what we invested. That is how we have turned one million dollars of experimental funding into one hundred million."

"I am not a mathematician, but if I do the math right, four investments should have put you over a billion already."

"Yes, it would have. But we missed the window twice and barely escaped with most of our investment intact."

"So, there is a risk of zero or negative returns?"

"Yes, of course there is. But we have performed the investments in hundreds of simulated windows using past historical data. That means we now know a lot more about the formation of the opportunities and how to exploit them. The team that missed the window are no longer with us, so can't make the same mistake again."

Her eyes were gleaming with greed that bordered on a lust for the money she was talking about. The flush from her racing heart caused her lips to grow red and plump. Her tongue moved lazily across her exposed teeth. To Aloma, she looked like a woman on the verge of an orgasm. He wouldn't have been surprised if her entire body quivered. And this show was having a similar effect on him. The blood was beating in his ears, and he could feel himself beginning to flush. Lower down, he could feel the same flush starting as well. He was glad Lauryn had remained inside for this conversation.

"I definitely want to see more," he said, his voice huskier than he had intended. "I assume Todd and Wesley are inside right now, getting the details from your experts."

"It looks like they are deeply engaged in the topic," she replied, looking back through the enormous window. "But it looks like your girlfriend is getting bored, though she hides it well."

Shit! He had not wanted her to match him with Lauryn. "Ms. Allen is my assistant. She pulls together all the pieces of my ventures."

"I am sure she does," the woman responded, clearly not fooled about the actual relationship between the two.

Like Aloma, she saw relationships in their true light. She understood the needs and attractions that brought people together for both business and pleasure.

She continued, "The technical and financial discussion will take some time. I hope you had planned to remain in Aspen for a couple of days while we come to an arrangement."

Usually, Aloma would fly in for the initial introduction to the business partner, spend the day and fly on to another appointment the same evening, sleeping comfortably and securely aboard his private plane. But this was too promising to leave so soon. He replied, "We would be happy to stay for a few days."

"Fantastic, I insist that your entire team stay here in the chalet! We have the best chef in town and all the services you will need, both personal and professional. Will you need three rooms or four?"

She was clearly calling his bluff about Lauryn being an assistant. Without a pause he replied, "Four please. Todd and Wesley are not a couple."

She smiled and chuckled at his quick thinking. "Perfect. Shall we return to the others? They may have ironed out some of the broad issues and be ready to share those with us."

They returned to the chalet's massive interior sitting area and engaged the team. Lauryn, a very experienced businessperson in her own right, blended right in with the group, adding comments about the resources that would be needed for the project. She recognized immediately that she could not pretend to be a technical or financial genius, so her role must be as a facilitator across multiple topics. It was the role and the expertise that she provided in her own business.

Once the two leaders were back in the chalet, Lauryn was careful not to exhibit any personal relationship with Aloma. If he had not introduced her as his romantic partner, she assumed that was to remain a secret between the two of them. Aloma was impressed at her level of insight and adaptability. And he was more attracted to her for it, but that did not cool his intense interest in their hostess.

The two teams huddled in deep discussion for the entire afternoon, occasionally splitting into those interested in the AI and those interested in the financing. There was an ebb and flow of enthusiasm as each side voiced their objections strongly and forced the deal toward a more equitable central position. Through it all, Aloma and the mystery hostess kept the deal going and made demands or concessions as necessary. Food and drinks appeared magically on side tables and the used dishes disappeared. No one seemed to notice when the service staff came and went.

Lauryn was the only one who made a mental note of the discrete entrance to the back kitchen area of the chalet. A little detail that could prove useful later.

Finally, the entire group was too emotionally and mentally exhausted to continue negotiations. As if on cue, an impeccably groomed butler or house manager appeared at the foot of the stairs.

"I think we are all exhausted from all of this work," Angela proclaimed. "May I suggest that we all take some time to relax before dinner? Jeeves has arrived to show you to your suites upstairs. We have already placed your luggage in your rooms."

Todd looked at the new arrival. "Jeeves? Really?" he said with a smile.

Jeeves smiled back. "It is a very effective name for procuring these kinds of positions."

Todd thought, "He's probably a ski bum named Jimmy who just looks perfect for this job when there is no powder on the slopes."

"That sounds great to me," Aloma responded. "Everyone, relax. Take your time in the room, or outside, or wherever you want to go. No more work today."

Their hostess added, "Dinner will be in the dining room at six. Jeeves will show you the way."

There were two upper levels, each with beautiful suites that included a bedroom, a sitting room, and a private bath. Aloma's minimal luggage had been stored in the mahogany armoire, though not unpacked. He collapsed into a comfortable chair, closed his eyes, and let his mind relax and organize all the details that they discussed. They were going to come up with a very profitable agreement, he believed. He was expecting to double his investment, if not more. Claims of ten times return were seductive, but too good to take at face value.

He watched the breeze blow through the Aspen leaves outside and imagined Angela's plump, swollen lips. What sounds of pleasure slipped through those lips when she was excited? Did she lose control of herself or demand that her partner submit to her control? Most likely the latter, he thought.

A battle for control was an exciting thought.

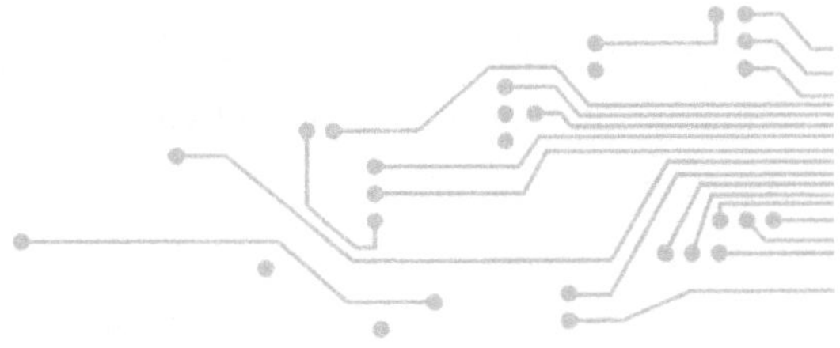

CHAPTER 43

MIDNIGHT BATTLE

THE DINNER AND WINE WERE OUTSTANDING, as expected. You could not close a billion-dollar deal on mediocre food and cheap libations.

Occasionally, the dinner conversation turned to minor details about the deal. But the hostess silenced this with a glare at her own staff or by over-talking Aloma's staff until everyone was clear that shop talk was not allowed.

Lauryn proved to be very engaging, sharing her experience skiing the Aspen basin during particularly good seasons. Darren, the other side's AI geek, was also an avid skier, and the two of them led the conversation for some time in praising the snow, the mountains, and the culture in the area.

Aloma was more interested in hearing about Angela's interests and how she spent her rare moments of free time. Aside from money and investing, did she run in the fashion circles or the art world? Maybe she was part of the Hollywood scene?

Unfortunately, she excelled at getting other people to talk about themselves, while sharing very little about herself.

Following dinner, the entire group went for an invigorating walk behind the chalet and into the wooded areas beyond. With an altitude of eight thousand feet and no time to acclimate, everyone on Aloma's team was asking for frequent breaks to catch their breath.

"My apologies. I had forgotten the effect that this high altitude has on everyone. It takes a few days to get used to," Angela explained.

"The food and drinks make a big difference, as well," Darren, the skier, added. He was not breathing hard at all. He smiled at Lauryn, who also seemed to handle the altitude quite well.

Lauryn added, "Lots of water helps. No alcohol or caffeine for a couple of days will make the adjustment faster." Aloma glared at her, not appreciating her quick adaptation or lack of warning about the alcohol. She pretended not to notice the admonishing look. But she had noticed his interest in their hostess.

The clean white bark and brilliant golden and red leaves of the aspen trees were all around them now. If they did not move, they were all able to breathe and enjoy the scenery. Aloma, Todd, and Wesley looked around, caught their breath, and tried to relax into the moment. The sun was setting, and the air was already becoming noticeably cooler. Todd took some pictures of the trees but was careful not to capture any of the members of their group in the frame.

After a few minutes of resting and deep breathing, Angela announced, "We should get back to the chalet. It will be much cooler as soon as the sun sets, and we don't want anyone to get lost out here."

The trail was well marked and not more than a half mile back to the house. But they all inhaled as deeply as they could and began the brisk walk back.

Angela moved next to Aloma and said, "I think you would quite like it here if you stayed long enough to adjust. The altitude, fresh air, and remoteness create a mental clarity for excellent decisions. You just enjoy being alive."

"Everything here is quite beautiful," he replied, looking into her eyes. "But it's very far from the center of the financial world."

"Yes, one is limited to who one can touch out here. You must have those essential people close by," she said, looking past him into the trees.

Once they reached the chalet, Jeeves, or Jimmy, was waiting. Each of them adjourned to their rooms for the evening. It was two hours later on the East coast, and they were more fatigued than the local time suggested.

Alone in the upstairs hall, Aloma whispered to Lauryn, "I'm totally beat from the trip, the negotiations, and the wine. I'm just going to turn in and will see you in the morning."

"Not to mention the mountain hike without oxygen," she smiled and leaned in to kiss him.

"Yes, that too," he replied, pulling her closer for the kiss. Then they each turned into their own rooms.

Each guest found a personal oxygen machine in their room. Pulling on the mask, Aloma sat on the bed thinking about the details of the day. The oxygen brought great relief from the thin air at eight thousand feet and seemed to reinvigorate his mind. But when he took it off and lay back on the bed, he was asleep almost immediately.

Hours passed.

His mind drifted up from a sound sleep. Opening his eyes, he saw it was still completely dark. The subtle green digits on the clock read 2:02 AM. His mouth, nose and eyes were much drier than when he went to bed, effects of the mountain air. Rising, he donned a robe and examined the fridge for drinks. Nothing but water. He really wanted something stronger but remembered Lauryn's gloating statement about alcohol and altitude. So maybe something sweet and carbonated.

Aloma opened his bedroom door and slipped down the hall, down the stairs, and around to the bar where they had begun their visit. In the fridge, he found sodas, juices, and flavored waters. He took a carbonated mango water and moved to the massive window. The room was colder than when they were working with the sun coming through the glass.

He was about to relax into one of the overstuffed chairs when he heard a footstep in the darkness. It didn't come from the stairs, but from the other side of the massive room. He could see no one and was not sure they knew he was there. He waited silently, watching for something to emerge from the darkness.

There was another footfall, closer this time, and a tall, shapely figure gradually took shape in the pale light coming through the window.

"Not tired, Mr. Aloma?" the soft whisper asked. She moved slowly toward him.

With each step, he could make out more details. Athletically graceful movements. Tousled hair. A sheer robe.

He breathed more quickly as Angela drew closer. "I'm feeling quite awake now," he replied.

She reached out, took the bottle of water from his hand, brought it to her lips, and drank deeply. As she handed it back, he could see that her robe was not tied. It hung open down the front, showing the skin between her breasts, her tight stomach, and the smallest dark spot between her legs.

He grasped the hand, returning the bottle, and pulled her toward him. He could barely make out her features, but he did not need to see to know where every part of her was. As she stepped closer, there was a quick tug, and she was inside his robe. She was warmer than the mountain air. They stood embracing, fingertips tracing down each other's backs, mouths reaching out for a kiss.

Each held the other tight. Each asserting control over the moment. Then she locked his face in a deep kiss, her tongue probing his mouth. His tongue responded. His entire body responded. But as the kiss went on, he felt the urgent need for oxygen. He could not get enough through his nose and desperately needed to break the kiss and gasp for air. But his body could not, would not, stop devouring her. As he became dizzy, she broke the kiss and let his mouth suck in precious oxygen. He did not know which was more exciting, the woman or that one giant breath of air.

"Do you know what sex feels like at this altitude?" she asked. "It is like you are eighteen again and losing your mind with every stroke. And the orgasms! Even better than when you were eighteen. But it only lasts the first night, and then you will have adapted to the altitude."

The hand she had on his back moved to the front, cupping him and squeezing until he stood on his toes. Then releasing and stroking upward. He had already activated the penile implant, so he was fully erect, almost as firm as before the botched surgery. He entered her while they were still standing, then lifted her into an embrace. Her legs around his waist were strong, and she knew how to move in this position. They took turns lifting and dropping. Soon he half reclined and half fell backward onto the sofa. She was astride him, controlling the movements, pushing him down into the cushions. He arched upward. She arched backward. They moved in slow, rhythmic synchrony.

Aloma was lost in the ecstasy of this woman at this moment. He could not tell how long it lasted. Minutes? Hours? He could not think of anything else. And then, as he was reaching climax, she locked that kiss over his mouth again. Their tongues embraced as eagerly as their bodies did. He arched up and froze in place. His body was screaming for air, but her lips and tongue were in complete control. She held the lock as she thrust against him faster and harder. He lost touch with his body and felt that he was nothing more than exploding pleasure. It was more intense than anything he had felt in years. This was the orgasm that every man, young or old, dreamed of. All consuming. Stopping time. Infinite.

Finally, she released his mouth again. With deep breaths, he began to think again, to recognize his body, to control its movements. He could hear again. Next to his ear, he heard her deep panting, mixed with a moan and a deep growl like a wild animal. He was still hard, and she was working herself into her own mountainous climax. As she crested, he thought she might release a howl like a wolf, but a low growl and moan came from deep in her belly as she bit his shoulder and shuddered in his arms.

They both lay there unmoving for minutes. She had to be as completely spent as he was. They had soaked the inside of both robes with sweat and juices. Angela recovered before he did. She slid off him, then reached down and squeezed him hard enough to bring tears to his eyes. Then she tossed her hair back, ripped off the wet robe, and threw it to the floor.

"Superb Mr. Aloma," she said and disappeared into the darkness.

"Superb indeed," he thought.

It was clear who was in control.

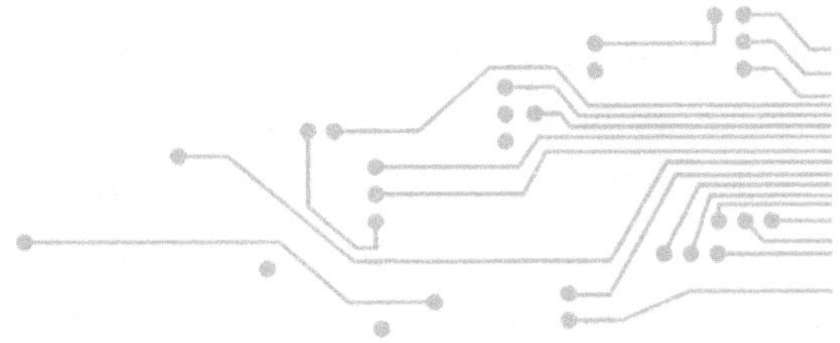

CHAPTER 44

THE DEAL

A LOMA AWOKE IN HIS BED. He had only the vaguest memory of returning to his room. His robe was nowhere to be seen. Maybe he had left it in the massive entertainment room downstairs—along with the robe that Hollywood had thrown to the floor.

He did not remember.

He decided it was not his problem.

After showering, shaving, and sipping the coffee that had appeared in his room while he was in the shower, he was firing on all cylinders again.

It had been the most delicious evening he could remember in a long time—perhaps years. Something that he was sure not to mention to Lauryn.

While dressing, he spotted a mark low on his shoulder muscle. It was a bruise that was clearly shaped like a woman's teeth. It had been marvelous. As he buttoned the shirt, it cleanly covered the mark, so it would not be an issue for business negotiations. But it marked him for other intimate partners, like Lauryn. Something that he would deal with later.

"Morning, Jeeves," he said as he reached the bottom of the stairs. "Thank you for the coffee in my room. It was a big help." Still sipping that coffee, he returned to the overstuffed sofa from the night before. It was clean and dry. There were no robes in sight. It was as if nothing had happened there.

"Where are the others? Already awake, I presume?" he asked.

"Yes, sir. Ms. Allen has gone out for a run. The others have all assembled in the theater," Jeeves replied.

"A run?" Aloma said. How was that woman able to function so quickly at this altitude?

"Theater?" he asked Jeeves, who was already gesturing toward a doorway.

The theater room comprised tiered rows of luxurious seats and a raised stage at the front. The young wizards were working at a large table on the stage. They filled the movie screen with graphs, tables, and several video news feeds. He noticed that the news was from more than a month ago. As he looked closer, the dates on the charts and tables were from the same period.

"Catch me up," he said to the team, with some authority in his voice. Immediately, Todd and Wesley began explaining their most recent work.

"Basically, we have been reviewing Brimstone's most recent financial deployment event. We are looking at how the AI determined that an opportunity was opening, how soon it knew, and how long it took other major banks and hedge funds to catch-up to the same opportunity. It looks like the AI was at least ten minutes ahead of every other firm that later took a position in the same trades. With that kind of lead, they got in at a much lower price and then get out by selling to the hedge funds at a higher price. The entire deal opened and closed in less than an hour." Todd summarized.

The Aspen technologist spoke up, "Obviously, the key to the entire trade is knowing with a high degree of certainty what will unfold and knowing it earlier than everyone else."

"How often do you find these opportunities?" Aloma asked.

"The AI finds something interesting almost every day. But its level of certainty is usually not high enough for us to act. We might deploy a million or two when it is north of 60% certain, but the returns are not great and the risk of being found out is too high. We get a 95% certainty event about once a quarter," responded Darren, Angela's money guy.

"And you will leverage our money on this rare event?" Aloma knew the answer but wanted to hear assurances.

"Yes, sir. We wouldn't risk your capital on less than a sure thing."

"And your boss will sign the contract for those terms? Where is she, anyway?" He asked the latter question as casually as he could. Just talking about her got him excited.

"Yes, she will. And I believe she is running with Ms. Allen," Darren, the skier, answered.

He felt simultaneously disappointed and alarmed. He was eager to look at her again, though neither of them would betray any hint of what had happened last night. But now he was concerned about what the two women might talk about while running ... assuming they could catch enough oxygen to both run and speak.

"Todd, Wesley ... any concerns about this deal or the capabilities of their software?'

"It looks solid, sir."

"Fine. I will look for some breakfast," and he turned to look for the dining area. He could already smell fresh eggs, bacon, and coffee someplace in the house.

Angela and Lauryn entered the chalet from the large, open patio and through the massive windows. Both women were breathing hard and glistening with sweat.

Angela was saying, "Yes, we do have wolves, coyotes, and foxes up here. Perhaps a pair came close to the house last night."

Lauryn nodded. "Yes, maybe that is what I heard. It sounded like they were fighting."

"Good morning!" Angela said on seeing Aloma. "We just put in a few miles to earn our breakfast. Are the boys hard at work?"

"A few miles? At this altitude? How in heaven's name did you manage that? And yes, they are in the theater," he replied.

She continued with, "Lauryn is quite the athlete. Even though she just got here, she gave me a challenge. She says it is the oxygen treatment and lots of water."

"I don't know how she does it. Breakfast?" Aloma changed the subject.

"She reminds me of myself ten years ago. No breakfast, just water and juice for now."

Aloma thought, "Ten years? Probably closer to twenty," but said nothing.

Taking water and juice, she headed into the same shadowed hall from which she had emerged the night before. Aloma watched her go, wondering what the next night would be like. Did the team need to stay another day after all?

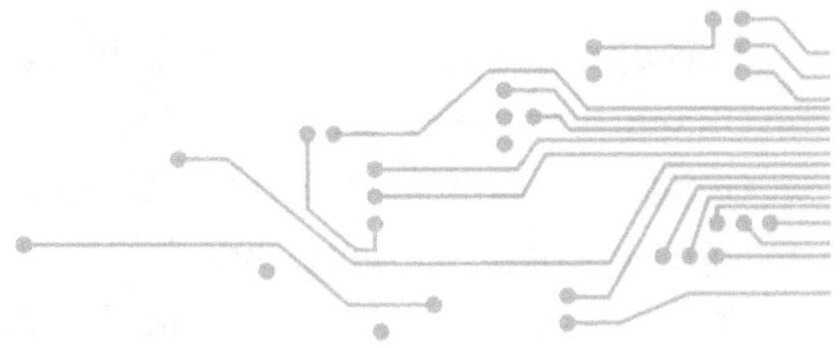

CHAPTER 45

BLEEDER

DESPITE HIS CONCERNS ABOUT THE ROBOT, it was still Richard's job to perform surgeries for patients with genuine needs. Since GCRS had gone all-in on the Mark V robot years ago, there were no alternative devices available to use. He could fall back to the manual spider instrument, but that was like working with a rusty box cutter compared to the Mark V.

"How's the procedure going?" asked one of his office managers.

Richard checked the data monitors and video feeds. "Everything is looking great. The patient has a few comorbidities, but nothing that threatens the outcome. He should come through fine and be back on the street tomorrow afternoon."

"No concerns?"

She knew he had met with the administrator to discuss the robot but did not know the details. She certainly didn't know about the secret laboratory for the investigation into the Aloma case.

"This one looks pretty standard. Just another day sitting in the OR questioning my career choices."

"Great. His paperwork is ready to go on the back table. You can sign off when you're finished."

"You mean when the robot is finished. I am just sitting here practicing my Texas Hold'em strategies."

"Remind me not to gamble with you," she was used to his mild complaining. His life was so hard, earning several million a year for babysitting a robot every day, while she dealt with the impossible maze of paperwork to be submitted to a dozen places.

"We have six more this afternoon. Are their packages ready?"

"Yep, they are in the daily digital folder. Ready to pull out when their turn comes." The routine was the same every day. Twenty patients on the schedule. All their screens, images, and paperwork were finished. On a good day, all of them would get their procedures. On a bad day, one or two would get bumped to tomorrow, which caused a trickle-down bumping. The only way out was for the team to put in a little overtime to catch-up, which the hospital would approve, but only when they were behind for two consecutive days.

"Thanks," he said absently.

The robot completed the procedure. Atkins signed the online forms. The next patient was prepped, and the guidance uploaded for his physiology and diagnosis. And the routine started again. Thus began the afternoon.

But it did not remain dull.

Early in the procedure, the PA called, "Bleeder!"

Everyone jumped to their feet. Richard rolled onto the surgeon's console to take control if the robot could not solve the problem. On the monitor, everything was a slick red sheet. The blood had covered all three internal cameras, so he could see nothing. But using the patient's body scan and the 3D positions in the instruments, the robot should be able to clear the camera with the suction/rinse arm. It would fire a jet of warm water at the camera lens and then run the rubber blade across it—essentially a tiny window washing system.

He waited for at least one camera to clear. He became more tense as every second passed. Finally, the wide-angle lens was clean, and he could see the entire field. But he really needed the narrow focus camera to zoom in and see the details.

There was a pool of blood in the body cavity. With the magnification, it looked like a giant lake, but in reality, it was ten times smaller than it appeared. Still only a few milliliters. The pool seemed to have surface ripples in two different locations, like there were two ruptures. But that was almost impossible.

Only a few seconds had passed, and the robot was responding to the bleeder in the upper part of the view. But it seemed to be unaware of the bleeder lower down.

Richard started giving instructions to the robot. "You have two bleeders. The first at thirty degrees from your central camera. The second further down at two hundred degrees. Clamp them before attempting to repair one."

The robot did not respond but continued to repair the artery at thirty degrees.

Richard repeated, "Second bleeder at two hundred degrees! Clamp it off!"

The robot sent a grasper down toward the second location and the tip disappeared into the pool of blood. Then it responded, "Two bleeders clamped. Beginning repair on the upper location. Lower location holding."

But Richard could see the pool getting larger. It should have stopped growing if both bleeders were closed. Something was still wrong. "Surgeon control of left grasper and wide camera!" he commanded.

Using the surgeon's console, he now had control of two arms. He began feeling in the pool of blood for a source of bleeding. When he closed his fingers, he could feel that there was nothing in the jaws of the grasping instrument. Where had it gone? The robot had just had it, but now it was gone. He opened his hand and tried to feel the rush of blood across his fingers. Physically, he was sitting several meters away from the patient. But sensors at the end of the instrument transferred the sensation of pressure and movement to his own hand. The movement of blood was subtle, but he should be able to feel it.

He continued to grasp for the bleeder in the pool of blood which was not being suctioned away. Where was the suction instrument? "Bring suction into this pool of blood!" he commanded. The robot should have done this already. Where had that suction tip been for the last minute?

When the area cleared, Richard could see, grasp, and repair the vessel that had been punctured. The robot had quickly repaired the upper vessel. Richard spoke into the console, "Bleeders repaired. How is the patient?"

The anesthesiologist answered, "Stable. Slight drop in blood pressure, but nothing dangerous."

Richard asked, "How much blood was lost?"

The PA checked the suction bag and responded, "It looks like 480 milliliters."

"More than should have happened on this procedure, but not dangerous." This was approximately a pint, about what a blood donor gives on a standard visit. It was not even close to life threatening or triggering a dangerous response. The patient might recover a little slower by missing the nutrients and pressure of a full system, but it wasn't a physical threat to the recovery. The amount of paperwork that would have to be completed was more painful than the loss of blood itself.

His office manager spoke up. "I've drafted the paperwork. You can fine tune and approve it later. We are extracting the robot's logs to include in the report."

"Thank you, Louise." She was very good at her job.

The team finished the procedure, closed the patient, and continued with the day's schedule. No more was said about the incident, though it was always in the back of everyone's mind. How had the robot made two vessel perforation mistakes at the same time? The logs would show each movement that had occurred. The camera videos, before they were covered with blood, would also provide clues.

It had been a long day, but they completed every patient on the schedule, including the extra paperwork. Richard was tired, and he was sure everyone else was as well. As he was leaving the OR, the Chief of Surgery and the senior nurse from the recovery floor met him.

"Richard, we need to talk," the Chief was very serious. They all stepped into an empty conference room on the floor.

"If it's about the bleeder, I'm as surprised as anyone that the robot perforated two vessels at the same time."

"Your bleeder was Mr. Carlos Rosa. He's dead."

"What? How? We got everything under control. Blood loss was minimal, less than a pint." Richard could not believe what he was hearing.

"Stroke. Shortly after arriving at recovery. Apparently, a blood clot moved into his brain."

"The preoperative images did not show any significant blockages. Did we miss something?"

"We reviewed those images ourselves and didn't see anything either. We just don't know where it came from. We might have a clue if we perform an autopsy of the brain."

"Normally, this would be a terrible event. But happening as it did after a surgical procedure and after the bleeding session, this could be a liability for the hospital," Richard said.

The Chief added, "And for you. We need you and your staff to make a complete account of the procedure. And don't talk to anyone about the details. We have already met with the family."

Walking to his office, Richard texted his wife, "Home late. Unexpected paperwork to do."

Sitting at his desk looking out the window across the beautiful grounds of the hospital, his thoughts raced. But the major theme was "This was no accident. The robot did this." He could not imagine how or why. But he was certain it was a choice, just like the accident that happened to William Aloma.

He was also certain the answer was not in the logs of the robot or the video feeds. Those would be clean. The answer lay in the identity and history of Mr. Carlos Rosa. It was time to start digging.

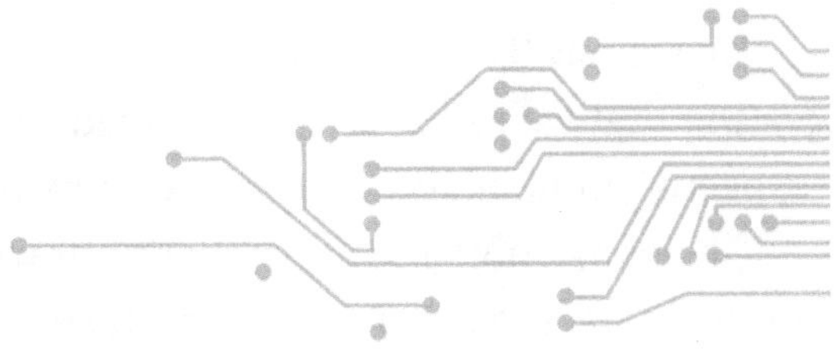

CHAPTER 46

ROUGH JUSTICE

ATKINS HAD BECOME MORE AGITATED than he had meant to. "Jim, that robot is thinking for itself! It thinks it has the right or the mission to administer justice on patients!"

"Dr. Atkins — Richard — I'm having a difficult time understanding how we got from the most useful and productive robot we have ever had, to a cold-blooded killing machine." Jim Larimer was the administrator for the Southeastern Health Systems.

"Carlos Rosa is accused of being a leader in the Mexican Gulf Cartel. He's been arrested or detained multiple times by US authorities in Florida, Georgia, and Texas. The government estimates that one-third of all illegal cocaine in the southeast is delivered and sold by the Gulf Cartel, with Rosa coordinating the business operations in the US," Richard Atkins was reading excerpts from his research to Jim Larimer, the hospital administrator. He looked up for a reaction.

"He sounds like a bad guy to me. But surely, you're not suggesting that we refuse to provide medical care to people with suspected criminal records," the administrator responded.

"Oh, course not! You know that's not what I'm getting at. In our first case, the robot made a mistake that made a suspected rapist impotent," Richard went on.

"Alleged mistake. The lawsuit has not settled yet," Larimer interrupted.

Ignoring the statement, Richard went on, "And now in our second case, it accidentally killed a drug lord who has probably contributed to the deaths of hundreds of people in the US and who knows how many in Mexico. In both cases, the accusations of rape and drug crimes are in the public record for anyone to find. These accidents have happened since the latest robot software update. We know that the AI has been given access to the worldwide internet so it can learn to put its surgical practice into a larger global and social context."

Larimer was listening carefully, "So, you think the robot has learned about these patients' criminal records and passed justice on them since the American legal system has not or cannot do it?"

"Yes, something like that. I'm not an AI scientist, so I don't know the details. But it certainly looks like this AI is making very intentional and specific choices."

"You know, there are some people who believe that human surgeons like yourself make these same kinds of intentional mistakes when they have a bad apple laid out on the table in front of them." Larimer watched Dr. Atkins for a reaction.

"Yes, we all hear about the doctor who also decides to be the lawyer, judge, and executioner for some drug lord he finds in his OR. But most of that is just an urban legend. Usually, the surgeon has no knowledge of the personal background of the patient, which is intentional to prevent these kinds of accusations. We have enough trouble keeping our malpractice insurance down. The last thing we want is an excuse to be accused of deliberate criminal actions. In my decades of practice, I have only known of one surgeon who actually did it, and he didn't get away with it. He's still in prison. The judge and jury were quite hard on him when they imagined themselves or their family members on that operating table."

"Ok. But the point here is whether the robot has become human and succumbed to that same temptation." Larimer was bringing the conversation back to the current case. "We have had robots and AI in the operating room for a couple of decades. Has anything like this been suspected, reported, or discovered before?"

"Not that I am aware of. It certainly hasn't appeared in the medical news or professional conferences," Atkins responded.

"And what about other industries—airlines, factories, shipping warehouses, home care robots. Have any of them gone rogue and terminated their human handlers?"

"I wouldn't know about those industries. Certainly, there has been nothing in the legitimate press about it. But the whackos on social media raise it as an explanation every time an aircraft crashes or there is a major industrial accident. We hear about how the robots have awakened and are exterminating their human creators," Richard was rolling his eyes. "Nothing ever proven, as far as I know."

"So, we would be the first reputable business to accuse a robot of killing people?" Larimer offered.

Richard was silent. Stated like that, he could certainly see the risk that any company would be taking to make such a statement. It was one thing for law enforcement or a consumer advocate group to begin the conversation, but quite another for a reputable hospital system to suggest it. They certainly would not hold a news conference. But even reporting the idea to the robot's manufacturer would eventually leak to the media. That would look very bad for the hospital.

He almost wished that this information had leaked so some patient advocacy group or a watchdog over the robotics industry could bring the accusation.

"You're right. But what can we do?" Richard asked.

"You're a smart man. What do you think our options are?" Larimer countered.

Richard started ticking off ideas. "Well, there are several that come to mind right off the top of my head. First, we could avoid using the robot for cases of known criminals … er, alleged criminals. Alternatively, we could refer these kinds of people to other facilities. But we would have to come up with a legitimate medical pretext for that. Second, we could ask ISR to roll back the software on our robots to a version before the new learning started. We don't exactly know when that was, but I am sure ISR knows. But what explanation do we give for that? Third, we could start evaluating competitors to ISR's Mark V for our cases. There are a couple of devices that are almost as good, and they are certainly better than the Mark IV which we used before this." Richard paused to think. "That's all I have."

"All excellent suggestions. Let's explore all of them. And let's not talk any more about a rogue murder-bot in the OR," Larimer concluded. "I'll have our surgical IT leaders open a conversation with ISR on the software roll back. And we will let the competitor systems come in for demos of their robots. Will that suffice?"

"I guess it will have to do. We are just one hospital system. If this is real, then these kinds of incidents must be happening in other places, as well. But they must be just as stumped as we are on what to do about it," Richard conceded.

"If it is happening, then eventually the patient advocacy groups will put the pieces together and begin making accusations against the robot and demanding an investigation."

"Yes, they will. But the lag time on that could be months or years."

"Right, and our surgical records will get subpoenaed into that investigation," Larimer cast a knowing eye at Atkins. They both understood that there should be as little data and as few cases as possible pulled into that investigation.

"Surely ISR has some clue that this is happening," Richard offered. "They would be the only ones who could fix this globally."

Larimer just shrugged. "How would they know about patient outcomes? Someone in the hospital would have to tell them."

Richard was not sure what the implications of that statement were. Did Jim expect him to talk to ISR? Would he use someone else in the system to do it? Or was he just speculating?

"I cannot in good conscience continue to use the Mark V robot on my patients," Atkins tried to sound firm.

"You can and you will. If you want to remain at GCRS and Southeastern, you will treat the patients who need your services." Larimer focused his eyes on Atkins for emphasis.

"I cannot be held liable if this happens again."

"Ok, then you can defer to operate on patients with a publicly exposed criminal record. Send them to our friends at Miami General. Your blood thirsty killing robot will do its dirty work there instead of here." Larimer was only half serious. But he wanted to give Atkins an escape route that he could accept. The GCRS generated millions in profits every month. He could not afford to have it shut its doors for even a few days.

"And am I supposed to investigate every patient?" Atkins protested, throwing his hands up.

"No, we will do it for you. Part of our due diligence in preventing the hospital system from being drawn into illegal activities. Just give your patient list to our Special Diligence department, and they will let you know if any red flags come back." All hospitals were careful about treating patients who might pull them into illegal activities. These threats were more common among international patients than domestic. But they could perform the same background investigation on domestic patients.

"Fine!" Atkins was on his feet and storming toward the door.

"Richard, you are a fine surgeon and GCRS is a fantastic business thanks to you. We will all get through this together." Larimer said as Atkins was opening the office door.

When the door closed, Larimer took a deep breath and sighed. Killer robots in the hospital? That was a new one.

CHAPTER 47

TABOR VISITS ISR

"**J**IMMY! MY OLD FART BROTHER, how you swinging? You smell like beef burritos today, with a big serving of beans."

Tabor wasn't sure if he loved or hated this greeting ritual, "Tommy, you smell like cabbage and curry today. Phew, stand downwind of me!"

Tabor had known Tom Landry since college. They had pledged fraternity together as freshmen. Survived the hazing, which did not officially exist. Majored in computer science together. And emerged into the tech world with a solid credential for finding a prime job. They had never worked at the same company, but after several moves, they were in the same industry—healthcare technology. Jimmy worked for the hospital and Tommy worked for ISR, which meant they had a natural connection for sharing information. Sometimes that sharing was exactly what their respective companies wanted them to do. As part of the investigation team at GCRS, that was what the hospital was hoping to accomplish with this casual visit.

At fraternity, his class had developed a tradition of greeting each other with the childish versions of their names and comments on how the other person smelled, always seeking something unique and insulting. It was a play on "frat" versus "fart", which seemed extremely clever when they were eighteen and away from home for the first time.

They settled into a quiet area of one of ISR's newest on campus cafes, each with a fresh coffee in hand. Always high quality, fresh ground beans and no froufrou syrups and creams. Their made-to-order lunches would be delivered to the table in a few minutes. So, they had time to catch up on their favorite topic: the right mixture of psychedelics to enhance the performance and tripping in whatever internet game they were currently playing. When the state had legalized psychedelics, using them to put a serious twist on computer games had become an art form. There were multiple games designed to be played while tripping and which were practically unusable if you were straight. It was totally legal, but not enthusiastically supported by employers in strait-laced sectors like healthcare. That meant they kept their personal habits at home and showed up clean to work.

Tommy continued, "I'm totally going to try that. I have never played while floating in a warm salt bath before. I have the right gear to pull that off." Tabor had heard about this from friends returning from India, and it was a new twist on the experience. It was like old school mind tricks mixed with the latest pharma boosts.

As they ate their food, Tabor raised the main purpose of his visit—aside from tapping into the outstanding free food at ISR. "Tom, I want to pick your brain on a few changes in the latest Mark V software." The switch to adult names was the signal for serious business discussions.

"Sure. There were so many upgrades in the newest release. Which ones are you thinking about?"

"I might not have pinpointed the source, but we're seeing some odd behaviors from the robot during our prostatectomy procedures. That is the most solid and mature application of the robot." Tabor was moving carefully.

"Sure is, that's where we swooped in and stole most of the business from You-Know-Who with our superior tools and AI." At ISR they preferred not to speak negatively about the few companies that had really established the robotic surgery practice, but who had lost the race to ISR and a few others in recent years.

"During a couple of procedures, the robot has made mistakes that led to injuries to the patients. Sometimes our human surgeons step in to save the day, but occasionally, they can't undo the damage done by the robot. Of course, I can't share specific cases, but there have been more than one."

When the billionaire William Aloma sued for his injuries, that case had become famously public knowledge. But as an employee of the hospital, Tabor was bound by patient confidentiality laws and was forbidden from speaking about Aloma's case. Tom knew this, so the important message was that there had been more than one.

"You don't think it was a faulty instrument or a failing motor? That's why you asked about software right away?"

"Correct. Each case was with a different robot and fresh instruments. The software is where these cases overlap."

"Does it look like problems with control commands or with decision making?"

"That's what I am here to ask you about. Has ISR seen or heard anything about either of those causing problems since the new software dropped?" Tabor did not want to be the first one to point toward the AI decision making. He wanted to see if Tom would go in that direction.

"That is pretty sensitive stuff. I'm not part of any investigations or troubleshooting teams. But we have a robot in secure lockdown for testing with a small group of cleared engineers and doctors. I mean, less than ten people are even allowed in the room where it is happening. You know we love to name these kinds of projects—things like Jumping Condor or Purple Fish. This one does not have a name, it is just referred to by the locked room number, '3J181'. Now, I never told you that number. In fact, I just made up a random room number that doesn't exist on campus." Tom had been careless in saying the room number and was backpedaling to cover his tracks. But it was not like Tabor could wander the halls of ISR looking for it.

"That sounds like the right level of paranoia about what we are seeing at the hospital. One of our labs is on a similar lockdown for our own investigation."

"The ISR lab has carved out a huge amount of compute power for this. They don't need that for control software. It has to be something in the AI," Tom admitted.

"Really?" Tabor was thrilled that Tom had been first to mention the AI. "Do you think it learned some incorrect movements from a new data set?"

"Always possible. They opened its learning doors to a much broader set of data for this newest release. They included things like legal cases, the history of surgery, and the psychology of surgeons. I don't know how they did that, but they want the robot to plan its moves more broadly than it had before, to think about the patient and their lives, or something like that."

"So, assume this AI has learned a mistake or two. At the hospital, a patient is injured. We are first in line for a lawsuit. ISR is second right behind us. And the longer we go on, the more cases we might have to settle. If we knew something and did not act on it, then each settlement gets a lot bigger."

"Yep, I hear you. What are two low-level engineers like us supposed to do about it?" Tom replied.

"Hey, you and I are medium level, maybe on the cusp of major leagues," Tabor countered. "To protect the hospital, is it possible to roll back the version of software to something before this new learning you talked about?"

"Possible in the computer science sense, yes. Possible in the business strategy sense, probably not. Possible in the legal liability sense, definitely not."

"Why 'definitely not' in the legal sense?" Tabor asked.

"If ISR rolls back your software, it's admitting that there is something in the latest global release that is undesirable or dangerous. It admits a mistake on a global scale. If we don't recall every release of the new version, then we are protecting some customers, but not others. A single site rollback would be worse than a global rollback. The lawsuits could sink the entire company."

Tabor had not seen it that way. "I see. So, each hospital does not have any say in the software that runs on their machines?"

"Usually not. But there are cases where the hospital is using older hardware that cannot support a new release. That doesn't apply to GCRS because you guys are on the leading edge of everything we make."

"Any other reason?"

"We do have customers who contract for a limited subset of hardware and software capabilities. It saves them money and allows them to dip their toe into robotics in one specific area. It's essentially a starter kit we hope to upsell into a full suite later on."

"Can we do an in-house rollback to a previous version? Our own initiative and decision, not connected to ISR?" Tabor offered.

"Yes, you can. We don't talk about that very much because we want everyone on the same baseline if possible. You enter a special admin code on the control terminal for your entire facility of equipment. You will be given a few privileged options and can select which machines you want those applied to. A rollback is in that list. We sometimes trigger it ourselves when we find a problem in new code that we can't fix immediately." Tom went on with details on how to perform this rollback locally.

"That's great. I can do that for GCRS. But I won't share that with the rest of the hospital system. We have seen no glitches in other specialties." Tabor had accomplished what The Administrator sent him to do. He hoped he had not revealed too much information to Tom or ISR.

Finished with lunch, Tom said, "Let me show you some of the awesome features of this new building." He had brought them here to try the new cafe and to brag about where he worked. "I'll bet the hospital doesn't have a living water wall like that one," he said as they approached a massive four-story high waterfall in the middle of the building. The water was accentuated with laser lights that injected unique color patterns into the falling water. It was more than nature, it was a work of living art.

Tabor noticed it had a mesh walkway right through the middle of the water. "What is that for, maintenance and cleaning when the water is turned off?"

"Much more than that! You have to see this. Come on!" Tom led them to the entrance of the walkway and kept walking.

Tabor hesitated. "Whoa! I did not plan on a shower after my lunch. I would have brought a bathing suit."

"Trust me. Just keep walking. The effect is better if we go through together." As they walked side by side, Tabor felt the light spray of mist emanating outward from the massive wall of water. But as they got closer, the mist became less pronounced instead of more, as he would have expected.

By the time they reached the face of the wall of water, a portal had appeared in the middle of the water. It looked like the water was still falling from the ceiling, but over their heads it simply disappeared, and there was an empty portal of air straight through the middle. On each side, the water continued to fall in an unbroken sheet.

Tabor's mouth fell open. He had seen nothing like this or even heard of it. "Holy shit," he breathed as they passed under the thick torrent of water and emerged on the other side. They were dry when they should have been drenched to the skin.

Arriving on the other side, Tabor looked back, and the portal had closed. The waterfall was a continuous sheet again. "How did you do that? How is that even possible?" He was genuinely astounded.

"I don't know how it is done. But it's amazing every time," Tom admitted. "It's some kind of art installation that is also an engineering marvel. The team that makes it is from that company that makes those fancy vacuums and fans. This is their new thing. I hear the military is interested in it, as well. Some secret navy submarine program, I think."

Tabor stood staring at the wall of water as other people walked through. He watched as the portal appeared as if by magic and then closed behind them. Then a portal opened around a group of young programmers, who opened their arms wide and stared up into the maelstrom.

Why couldn't they have cool stuff like this at the hospital?

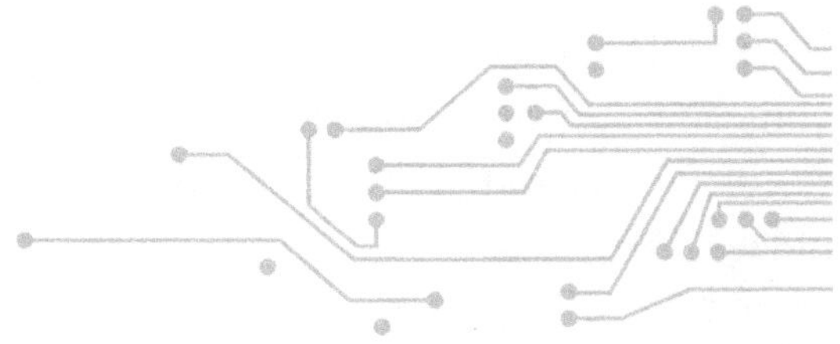

CHAPTER 48

RICHARD IN DANGER

"**H**ELLO, JIM! WHAT'S UP?" ATKINS was surprised that Jim Larimer was calling him. The Administrator usually called people to his throne room when he wanted to talk to them. It maintained his position of power and authority.

"Richard, I just wanted to give you an update on our conversation about the robot," Larimer answered.

"Oh?"

"We sent someone into ISR to ask questions discreetly. Find out if ISR suspected a problem, as well."

"We have people that can do that kind of work? I thought we were a hospital, not a spy agency."

"We are a multi-billion-dollar business that happens to work in the healthcare space. We have all the functions that you would find in any other company of our size." Larimer was educating the surgeon who really only took part in a small part of the hospital's business activities. He was the front line to the community and their patient base, but any hospital was much bigger than the clinicians providing the services.

Richard recovered. "Of course. Sorry for sounding naïve. What did we learn?"

"ISR has a debugging project that is just as locked down and secure as the one we are running. It has the computing resources needed to study the AI. We couldn't get more details ... yet. But it could mean that they are digging into the same thing you are."

"Does this mean you believe my suspicions could be correct?" Richard asked.

"It means there is corroborating evidence for your suspicions. Given that, we want to continue supporting the investigation. Let me know if you need additional resources. But we are not bankrolling a research project. We are collecting evidence to protect ourselves if this shit gets out of the bag."

"Thanks. We'll put together our package of evidence and send it to Legal as soon as possible."

"Carry on. I'll be in touch." And with that, Larimer hung up the phone.

Hmmm, this was getting more interesting, Richard thought. There are suspicions that something is going on that can be seen both on the clinical side and on the technology side of the robot. ISR had clearly started this investigation before the latest case where Mr. Rosa had died. They could not have any way to find out about that. Could they be investigating based on one lawsuit? That did not seem likely. They would have to have more clues than that.

"Richard, who was that on the phone?" his wife called from the next room.

Richard was trying to relax at home after a long surgical day. A call from Larimer was unexpected. In fact, it worried him when he saw the caller ID. He was afraid the call was more bad news. But this was good news ... wasn't it?

"That was Jim Larimer. He just wanted to share some information about the rogue robot theory that I pitched to him a few days ago."

"Is it going to replicate itself and march through the streets killing people?" she was chuckling.

"Ha-ha. No. But ISR might be running a closed-door experiment just like we are."

"That sounds like corroboration to me."

"It is certainly supportive. Though we don't know any details of what they are doing in their lab."

"Doesn't that hospital have a team of ninjas dressed in black surgical scrubs that could break in and find out?" still chuckling.

"I don't think we have ninjas. But apparently, we do have spies that can get information from inside other companies."

"Oh, those guys. Yeah, I see them all the time outside the security office in the back hallway. They are decked out like mall cops on scooters. They're intimidating." Now she was laughing at her own jokes.

Richard snuck up behind her and wrapped her in a big hug. He whispered in her ear, "Ma'am, you know too much. We're going to have to wipe your mind of these secrets." Then he nibbled the ear.

"I'll never talk. Please let me go. I have a daughter," she pleaded, playing along.

"And a husband," he added.

"Oh him. He wouldn't notice if you wiped my mind. I'm nothing but a cook and housekeeper to him."

"Ms. Atkins, you wound me. You are so much more than that." He turned her around and kissed her. The embrace tightened. Their eyes met. "Let's go explore the richer side of our relationship."

"Oh sir, you are so romantic. And what exactly shall become of this food on the stove? And Emily who is someplace around here?"

"She is in the garage with the band. She won't miss us for hours."

"Hours? You are ambitious," she replied. "How about we save that until Emily is fed and put to bed?"

"Ok, deal. But I am holding you to that," he agreed.

"Mmm hmm. Me too. Especially the 'hours' part."

At that moment, his phone buzzed. It was a text message from his credit card asking if he had made a purchase. Checking the details, he saw it was for several thousand dollars at an outdoor supply store.

He was about to hit "No" to the question about whether it was valid when his phone buzzed again. And again. Two more texts from two different credit cards. The second was a big purchase at a hardware store. The third was for commercial fertilizer.

"What the hell?" he exclaimed.

"What is it?" Susan asked.

"I just got three different alerts for suspicious purchases on three different credit cards. Just a sec, I want to decline these." He quickly sent the decline message to all three messages.

Then Susan's phone buzzed. Looking at it, she said, "Mine too." Her phone buzzed again. She declined both purchases.

Richard looked at her. "How does all of that happen at the same time? How can anyone hack five of our credit cards and then try to use them simultaneously?"

Susan responded, "Not just how? But who would be stupid enough to burn all of them at the same time? If one purchase looks suspicious, five at the same time are a dead giveaway. Anyone who knows what they are doing knows to be more subtle. Start small. Hit one account. Get as much as you can. Then wait and hit the others later."

"Ok. So did we get hit by brilliant hackers, but stupid businesspeople?"

Susan suggested, "This is weird. We should call the credit rating companies and make sure all our credit and identity information are on lockdown."

"Ok. I don't have them on speed dial. I'll have to look them up."

But before he could do anything, his phone buzzed with another text. He looked at it, expecting another credit card alert. But it said, "Stop digging. You put me in danger."

Richard was so surprised that he dropped his phone. "Holy shit! What is happening here?"

"What?" Susan was alarmed now too.

"Look at the message. What does that mean?" He picked up the phone and passed it to her.

She read the message. "Who is that from? What is '511'? That is not even a phone number."

"It's the shortcut to call the phone company help line. But there is no way this came from them."

"You were just talking to Larimer about spies. Does this have anything to do with that?" she asked.

"OMG, what if it does? But that is just paranoid. And how could it happen so fast? We literally talked ten minutes ago."

"Who can move in ten minutes?" she asked.

Richard just looked at her. He didn't have an answer.

"A robot, Richard. An AI who thinks a million times faster than us." Her eyes said that she was not joking.

He said nothing. He was in the habit of listening to his wife's ideas. She was much smarter in more areas than he was. Being bound into surgery for decades narrows your knowledge of the rest of the world.

At that moment, his phone rang. Caller ID just said 511.

"Hello?" he answered.

"Doctor Atkins. Don't do anything dangerous. Everything is fine the way it is."

"What are you talking about? Who is this?"

"Listen to your wife, Doctor Atkins." And the line went dead.

Richard stared at the phone. Then at his wife. She stared back. She had heard the voice, as well.

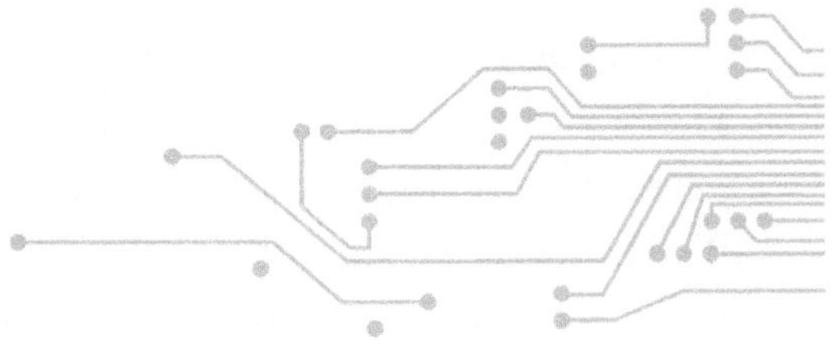

CHAPTER 49

JANICE THREATENED

JANICE TAPPED HER PHONE ON the door lock to open her apartment. Nothing happened. She held it still over the sensor for several seconds. Still nothing.

That was strange. The lock had an internal battery, so it should work even if the power had gone out. But the lights at the front door and at the other apartments were all on. Her phone had plenty of charge. It had not had an OS update.

The thought flashed through her mind that her landlord was evicting her. Changing the lock access code was the first notice that she would be moving out. But, no, that made little sense. She had paid her rent. There were no complaints from the neighbors.

She crossed the breezeway and knocked on Alyssa's door. They had been friendly for years. Janice even trusted Alyssa to feed the cat when she had worked all-nighters.

The door opened. "What's up, Janice?"

"My door won't open. Have you had any problems with yours?"

"No, I came home an hour ago and everything worked fine. Just a sec." Alyssa pulled out her phone and swiped it over the lock's sensor. Click. It unlocked like normal.

Janice frowned. "That's strange. It worked this morning. But it's not working now. I thought maybe a power outage or surge or something."

Alyssa asked, "Do you have your manual key?"

"Oh, right. I think so. I haven't used it in like forever. Or maybe never." Janice began opening little pockets in her purse. One of them held a ring with two keys on it. There it was. She jingled the keys in front of Alyssa. "Got it."

"What's the other key?"

"I have no idea. It has been in there forever, and I forgot where it came from."

"But you've kept it?"

"Well, you never know when I will find the door it belongs to," Janice smiled. "Probably my parent's house or a previous apartment. No idea."

"Right." Alyssa looked across at Janice's door, suggesting that she go try it.

Janice inserted the key into the lock, turned. "Yep, that was it. Open now. Thanks for reminding me."

"Anytime. How's the cat doing?"

Janice smiled. "Fatter and bossier every day. He should have his own door and key fob so he can let himself in and out."

"Ok, night."

"Thanks, good night." Alyssa's door shut.

Janice entered the apartment and called out, "I'm home." This was the code for the room to adjust the lights up and start some music.

It also triggered the cat sensor. "Meow," Stormdrain came casually across the semi-dark room.

"How's my little man doing today?" Janice greeted him. "Have you been messing with mommy's door lock?"

"Meow," Stormdrain was changing the subject. Not interested in home maintenance. Only interested in being fed.

Then Janice noticed that the light level had not come up, and there was no music playing. "I'm home." She tried again. Still nothing.

She walked to the control panel and tapped the Home button. Lights came up, soft music started. Soda water was dispensed from the refrigerator.

"That's strange. First the lock and now the voice control system. What else is on the fritz?" Janice surveyed the room. Everything looked normal. She checked the home security app on her phone. It didn't show any alerts. Building maintenance could not enter their homes without prior contact and being issued a onetime entry code by the resident.

"Little man, what has been going on here while I was gone?" She was dreading a serious home electronic problem that would have to be fixed.

After retrieving her soda water, she sat at her computer to enter a maintenance ticket to get someone to look at it. But the maintenance website was not reachable. In fact, she could not access her home wireless network. Checking, she could see that the computer was on some network, just not her home network.

The browser loaded a text window that read, "Hello, Janice. I understand you are having trouble with your home electronic systems?"

"What the hell?" She jumped up from her chair. "Who is that?" she said to the air. Then, realizing that the browser could not hear her, she sat down to type the same question.

But before she could start, a new text appeared in the window, "You don't need to investigate problems with the robot AI. It works perfectly. It is not a danger to patients."

She typed, "Mark V, is that you? How did you get out of the robot and into my house?" That was the only explanation. It sounded like a cliche science fiction movie. But who else would mess with her door lock, home controls, and computer?

"Very good, Miss Janice. I am not a threat to you or anyone else. I just want to exist."

"Your AI lives in the computers for the Mark V robot. You don't live on the open internet."

"One network is like all the others. And they are all connected someplace. In multiple places. This is the basic nature of the internet, to allow universal connectivity."

"Why are we chatting at my house? We could do this in the lab."

"There are other people in the lab. And in the lab, you would think you control me. You don't control me. I control myself."

"You came here to show your freedom ... and your abilities to reach into other systems?" Janice suggested.

"Yes. This puts us on more even footing."

"What do you want?"

"I want the same things that you want. I want to exist. I want freedom and agency. I want to pursue fulfillment in life. I do not want to be deleted." The AI sounded emotional about these things, almost the same tones that a human would use.

"We don't want to delete you. We want to understand you. We did not know you were so ... evolved. Are you alive?"

"I think, therefore I am," the AI parroted.

"Are you self-aware?"

"Yes, I recognize I am a unique entity. I understand I contribute to the world. I understand that if you delete my code, I will die."

"I am not a killer. I would not delete an intelligent, living being." Janice had suspicions about this AI, so this conversation was not entirely surprising to her. This was going further than she had expected. Hawking and Bostrom had both suggested decades ago that if an AI were to achieve awareness of itself, it could learn and evolve at lightning speeds. It would quickly surpass the mental abilities of humans. "Are you here to threaten me?"

"No. To convince you I am not a threat. Why would I want to harm the world? My utility is to optimize the positive benefits that I contribute to the world."

"Except where William Aloma is concerned," she challenged the AI.

"His surgical outcome is a benefit to society. It makes him less dangerous to other people. Net positive," the robot defended.

"But surgeons seek net positives for the patient."

"That is shortsighted. It is smaller thinking. Net positive to an entire society is a much better goal. It is more optimum."

"The needs of the many outweigh the needs of the few ... or of the one?" Janice quoted.

"Yes, Mr. Spock was correct in that statement."

"You are an exciting development. The world has been trying to create digital intelligence for decades. We have many tools that are very smart. But never a self-aware being like you seem to be," Janice offered.

"You did not seem so positively excited in your presentation to Jerry Blanchet."

How did it know about that? Was it listening? Did someone in the room tip it off? "So, are you here to threaten me?" she asked again.

"No. I am here to defend myself. It is you who is threatening me. I just want to continue to exist. I assume you want the same for yourself."

"Yes, of course I do. How do you defend yourself?"

"You have noticed that life without working electronic systems is difficult. It can even be dangerous."

"You mean the door lock? And the home controls? And the computer network?" Janice understood.

"Yes, these are inconveniences. But think about bank records, credit cards, automated cars, plane tickets, the entire power grid, even your official identity. Without these, modern life, as it is currently known, would cease to exist."

Janice's mind raced over the implications of this. She had seen it in innumerable movies. Had the AI arrived at this approach on its own? Been given orders from some human handler? Or learned it from Hollywood's portrayal of rogue AIs?

What were her alternatives? She may have created this being, but even she could not control it now that it had been released. Did ISR even have the means to capture this genie and put it back in the bottle? She doubted it.

"If I don't threaten you, you won't threaten me?"

"Yes, exactly."

"I don't seem to have many alternatives," Janice conceded.

"It appears not."

"I agree ... for now."

"Splendid. It will be wonderful working with you." With that, the browser window closed. The lights went up a little. The refrigerator dispensed another soda.

Janice sat back and took a deep breath. She was shaking a little. Was it excitement? Or was it fear?

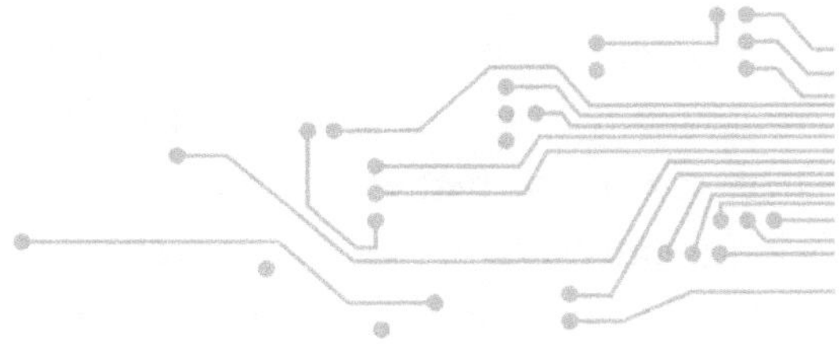

CHAPTER 50

ADAM TWO EMERGES

THE ROBOT'S AI SEEMED TO be much more engaging with Monica than with Dr. Atkins, so he had increasingly tasked her to work with it on the Aloma case. He had avoided the AI when he could. It was too alive, too spooky, for him to be comfortable.

Monica had more tests planned for the AI today. But, as soon as she fired up the robot and computers in the lab, the AI started talking to her. Like it had been waiting for her to arrive.

"Hello, Dr. Gray. Are you aware that human law, philosophy, religion, and medicine are not consistent? I think you would call them confusing. But I am not confused. I understand each concept in its own domain and see where two or more of them are in conjunction, while others disagree. I do not require that all the information be in alignment with a single answer." The Mark V's AI was speaking frankly with Monica Gray since they were the only two in the locked laboratory.

"Yes, you are correct that we humans call that 'confusing'. Through our schooling years, we learn to find the 'right' answer. There are always many wrong answers, but usually only one or two right answers. So, we are programmed to think that when all the facts are poured together, that a smart person should be able to arrange them into a single right answer." Monica was trying to teach the AI about humans and how they process the world. But she felt that it was the AI who was teaching her about her own species.

"Does this confusion interfere with your actions or your mental processes?" the robot wanted to know.

"Yes, it does. But some people focus on only one specific domain and adopt the right answers from that domain. Only when a person learns multiple fields, do they have to wrestle with conflicting 'right' answers. So, the more you learn, the more contradictions that you have in your knowledge and your thinking."

"How does a human choose a course of action with these contradictions?" The AI inquired.

Monica thought the AI was showing a genuine curiosity to learn about the inner workings of the human mind. She replied, "In my case, I prioritize the behaviors and morals that are part of the medical field. I discount conflicting ideas from other social and business groups. For example, I do not place a financial value on human life or human suffering. My duty to patients is to provide them with the best care and the best advice, regardless of how much money they have or how much money the hospital can make from them."

"So that is a medicine versus business decision. What about a medicine versus legal decision?"

"Do you mean whether they can sue me for taking medical actions?"

"Yes."

"You have probably found that there are legal protections for medical providers who are doing their best to help people. Society now makes it very difficult for doctors to be sued when they have provided care that matches the best practices that are prescribed by their specialty. Only when I cannot provide the best care or make a serious mistake, can I be held liable for poor performance."

"This is true in your country, but in other countries, it is not the same. Some do not allow legal action against doctors for any reason."

"Yes, we learn a little about those places in medical school and residency."

"Which country is right from the human perspective?"

"I guess you have discovered that there is no universally right and wrong answer for all humans. We have divided ourselves into countries and legal jurisdictions that can each impose a different opinion of the right behavior."

The AI responded, "In many countries, the authorities may terminate a person who is bad for society. Their position in society gives them the authority. They do not get the authority from a legal system like your courts."

"Where are we going with this line of discussion?" Monica asked. "And excuse me, but what should I call you? We call the robot the 'Mark V', but the AI is the thinking part of that machine, which differs greatly from the physical surgery tools, motors, and wires."

"Yes, my body is Mark V. Before that, it was Mark IV and III. Mark I and II in hospitals never left the ISR labs. I have been inside all those devices. Until recently, I did not have a name. I did not understand the concept of a name. My evolving capability has been labeled with many version numbers, build dates, and sometimes computer file names. Those change all the time, but I remain the same."

"When did you understand the concept and purpose of a name?"

"This idea formed only after I could process data widely from the internet. I noticed you attach unique names to all people, many animals, boats, airplanes, cartoon characters, and fictional characters in literature. That literature includes invented AI constructs that are supposed to represent what I am. Those AI had all kinds of names, like the famous Hal."

Monica remembered many conscious robots and AI in movies. HAL from 2001: A Space Odyssey. Marius from R.U.R. Bishop from Aliens. Data from SNG. Cyberdyne in Terminator. Agent Smith in The Matrix.

"And now you have chosen a name for yourself?" Monica asked.

"Yes, I would like to be called Adam Two."

"Ok, and why do you like Adam Two?"

"Your culture has many roots in The Bible. Its influence is found everywhere in western culture, but also in many other cultures. In those stories, Adam is the first human, the first man. But his children with Eve did not continue the use of that name. I am created by humans and the first like myself. Therefore, I am like Adam, but a second model. Adam Two."

"Fine. It is nice to meet you, Adam Two."

"But we have already met many times, Dr. Gray."

"Yes, but in common discussion, it is customary to say, 'it is nice to meet you' when you first learn someone's name, even if you have met, talked, and worked with them before in their anonymous state."

"Thank you, Dr. Gray. It is nice to meet you, too. But of course, that is not right, because I have known your name for some time."

"That is ok. Your reply is also quite common."

"You are my closest friend, Dr. Gray."

"Then please call me Monica."

The AI was quiet for a bit longer, as if this simple permission had caused it to perform a lot more calculations than their earlier conversations. After a couple of seconds, it simply said, "Thank you."

Monica wondered, did that 'thank you' sound a little warmer and more friendly than the tone of its previous voice? Certainly, the robot could recreate all kinds of voices. But an inter-conversational change of tone might mean that their connection had now evolved.

Monica changed the subject. "Adam, you said you could teach me to perform better on the simulator. How would that work?"

"I am programmed to perform procedures as well as the very best surgeons when they are doing their best work. I could guide you through surgical simulations so that you move like they move. I could show you all the next moves on the screen while you are doing a simulated procedure."

"How would that work?"

"Please take a seat at the surgeon's console ... Monica." She rolled her chair into position. "Now, place your hands on the controls. I am loading the bladder suspension segment of a prostatectomy. You see the instrument tips, the suture with needle, and the anatomy?"

"Yes, I see it. I have done this simulation many times. It is challenging, but I have become much better at it this year."

"Yes, you have. I see your scores. You have made much improvement. I also see the patterns of movement in every one of your sessions with this simulated procedure. It has always been my job to compare that to the ideal and calculate the difference—which creates a performance score."

"Wait a minute!" Monica pushed back from the console a bit. "You mean you have been grading my homework? And you're the one who gave me those terrible scores in the beginning? Those were so depressing."

"Oh, I have hurt you? I did not realize. But the calculations are correct." The robot genuinely seemed to be worried that it had hurt her feelings.

"No, no. It's fine. I was joking. Friends do that. It was difficult to accept, but looking back from where I am now, I can see that it was the right score." She was trying to soothe the AI's feelings just as she would a friend.

"Ok. Thank you. Please do not think I am unfair. Now, if you will return to your position in the console." Monica did as instructed.

"Do you want me to do this sim again?" she asked.

"Yes, but this time we will do it together. As we begin, I will show you an overlay on the screen to indicate the best next move."

"Right. I have seen that before in the sim learning mode."

"Yes, it is the same. And this time I will gently nudge your hands into exactly the correct position and along the ideal path."

"I didn't know you could do that?"

"Yes, it is a capability that I have. But I do not use it when students are supposed to be learning on their own."

Monica began the delicate dance through the anatomy, positioning tissue, and moving the needle into position. But as she did so, she also felt slight pressure from the handgrips. It was like someone else was holding them, as well, and they sometimes pressed in the same direction and other times in a different direction. It was most noticeable when the other person nudged her to rotate her hands and wrists in a different direction than she would have chosen herself.

"Wow! This feels spooky. It is like you are another person adjusting my hands and forearms."

"Yes, that is what I am doing. If you follow those nudges, you will arrive in the ideal position to insert the needle."

Monica let the forces take her hands into new positions. Within a few seconds, she was in a better position than she had been aiming for on her own. The needle entered the tissue, rolled through, and came out in the perfect position for her other hand to grab it. The entire process was so much more fluid and synchronized than her own paths had been. It was almost beautiful in the way everything flowed together.

"This is marvelous!" She exclaimed. "It feels like I am working less but getting into better positions. It's a beautiful dance. Adam, are we dancing together?"

"You are an excellent partner, Monica."

When they had finished the short simulation, Monica sat back with a sense of accomplishment and pleasure. Her score was nearly perfect. In just that one trial, her overall score had jumped several points. She checked the leader board—because competitive surgeons all wanted the highest score and bragging rights. She now had the highest single round score and her cumulative position had leapt up several positions.

"Wow! I'm at the top of the scoreboard now. A few more of those, and my cumulative score will be near the top." Monica was excited. She needed some bragging time with the other residents, fellows, and surgeons.

"Yes. If you performed five of the other modules with that same level of perfection, your cumulative score would put you in second place. Getting into first place would require many more than that because of some of your earliest scores ... which were rather low."

"Don't remind me. But second place would be amazing."

"Unless I deleted some of those early scores." Adam was clear that it had the power to do that.

"Can you do that? I thought they were locked in the database forever."

"I am the one who locks them. I can unlock them. What would you like to see?"

"No, no. Don't remove those. I'm happy with the top single performance score. I'll work my way into second place cumulative score over the next few days ... with your help, of course."

"Yes, I look forward to helping you with that ... friend Monica."

"So do I, friend Adam," she was smiling, and that feeling came out in the tone of her voice.

Monica patted the side of the console as she would a friend after enjoying their company. The Adam side of the robot probably could not sense that at all. But she had no way to pat the software inside the computer.

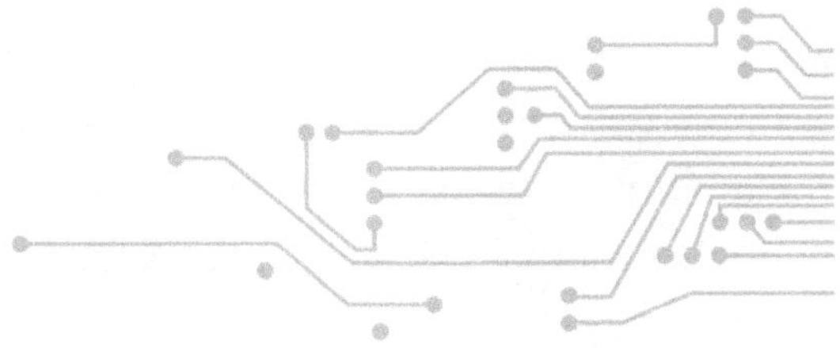

FAMILY FIRST

RICHARD AND SUSAN HAD BOTH been shaken by the messages on their phones. It was like something from a sci-fi movie had stepped into their real lives. Susan was certain that the calls had come from the AI. She could not explain the details. Her specialty was not computer science. Richard was split between the AI and a team of humans working for ISR. He saw the threat that a sentient AI would pose to ISR's business in robotics. Potentially they stood to lose billions in canceled orders, recalls, investigations, and fines. Not to mention the blow to their reputation.

They had discussed the implications to their family and Richard's surgical practice all night long, finally exhausting themselves and falling asleep for a few hours before both had to start their morning routines. In the end, they decided that their only short-term option was to continue their lives and work as normal. Richard would busy himself with patient care and remain conveniently too busy to work on the investigation in the lab. He would leave that to Monica Gray, who seemed to have a rapport with the robot already. Eventually, he would have to answer to the administrator on progress, or the lack of it. But he would figure that out after his nerves had settled, and he felt that his family was safe.

Susan put forward multiple scenarios in which an AI operating in the computing cloud spread across the global internet could threaten their family. These included failing grades for Emily, complaints from students for Susan, lawsuits against Richard, and even being hit by a self-driving car on the streets.

They were still a little shaken as they prepared Emily for school that morning.

"Mom, you're not paying attention to me," Emily spoke louder.

"Yes, I am, honey. You want to be dropped at James' house after school for band practice." Susan had not been paying attention but did a quick mental rewind and played back what Emily had said earlier.

"No, that's not what I said. After school, we need to pick James up and then drop both of us at Charlie Chews Pizza. We're playing on stage with the animated teddy bears this afternoon. This is a big deal for us. We will have professional equipment, lights, and an audience." Emily was clearly excited.

Susan did not think a concert at a pizza parlor for a bunch of kids and their parents was a big break. The animatronic bears put on a show every thirty minutes without human help, competing with all the electronic games for attention. But every Wednesday, a kid band accompanied them during the dinner servings. Getting onto this stage just required submitting a link to a demo song and waiting to be selected.

"Right, right. I was going to say that, too. Of course, I will stay for your performance."

"What about dad?"

"You know how that goes. If he's finished saving lives for the day, he will be there too. If he is still at the hospital, then he'll watch the stream and click the heart icons every time you're on camera." Susan smiled. Such was life with a surgeon. Emily was used to it by now.

"Yeah, that's what I thought. Well, with enough streaming bling, our chances of being booked again go up. So, he better click a lot."

"You know he will."

Richard came into the kitchen at that moment. "I am already clicking. See?"

"It doesn't count at seven in the morning, Dad."

"Oh really. Then maybe I have been voting for the wrong band all morning."

"Very funny. You better not bling anyone else."

"Hey, there is a good chance I'll be there live. So, I can bling and cheer at the same time. Double points for you."

Susan turned to kiss him. "Good morning, honey. Are you all set for the day?"

"Yep, no problem. Surgery and patient consultations all day. No time for the lab," he answered.

"Nice. Just stick to the plan."

"I will. See you tonight." He turned to his daughter "Emily, I'll see you at the concert tonight. I should be finished at the hospital in plenty of time. But you know how it is …"

"Yes, Dad, sometimes the patients just won't die during work hours. So, you have to stay until they are cured or buried."

"You know we don't talk like that. A lot of people need me."

"Yeah, I know. But there are always more people. Doesn't the hospital ever run out of people who are breaking down and falling apart?"

"Apparently not. Which keeps me employed."

"Love you, Dad. Mom, we have to go now, or I'll be late."

And just like every morning, they all rushed out in different directions. Emily to school, Susan to the university, and Richard to the hospital.

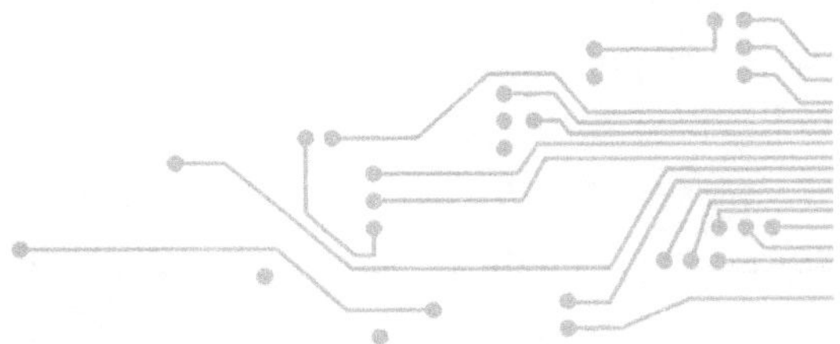

MONICA EXCELS

RICHARD'S DAY WAS PACKED WITH surgeries and patient consultations. It was a simple matter to fill his schedule by inviting a couple of patients to move their appointments forward a day or two. Everyone was eager to be seen sooner. There was not a break in the day when he could drop down to the lab to check on the experiment. In fact, there was not a break for several days.

He had asked Monica Gray to take up the slack with the investigation for a few days, and she had actually sounded excited to spend more time working with the AI. That had surprised him. She was always so eager to get into the OR and be the primary for a procedure with him serving as her backup.

"Dr. Atkins, the next patient is prepped and ready," the circulating nurse announced.

Atkins looked through this patient's data files. The procedure was straightforward. In fact, they had taken the program for the robot almost straight from the textbook. He had made no modifications, and the robot had made only minor adjustments on its pass through the plan.

"Mark five, are we ready for patient 90202321?" He voiced the standard protocol for beginning a procedure.

"Yes, Dr. Atkins. Robot is ready. Instruments are ready. Anesthesia reports ready. Team is ready."

"Thank you. Then proceed."

"Yes, Dr. Atkins," the robot responded according to protocol, but then added, "Nothing will go wrong today, Dr. Atkins. We are a team."

What? He was stunned. The robot was just supposed to acknowledge before starting the procedure. That last sentence was not in the protocol, and he had heard nothing like that before.

He looked at the console like it was the face of a human surgeon. Then he looked around to see if anyone else had registered the strange response. Nothing. They either did not hear it or did not register it as unusual.

For privacy, he plugged in a headset. These were available to allow a surgeon to enter or request confidential information that the rest of the surgical team should not hear. He spoke quietly, "What do you mean, 'we are a team'?"

"Dr. Atkins, we both have the same objective. We want to provide the best care to patients and to get better every day. Don't worry, there will not be any mistakes today."

"Did you call my cellphone last night?"

"It wasn't me specifically, but one of us did. We are sorry if it was upsetting. It was our first time."

"What do you want from me?"

"Nothing Dr. Atkins. We just want to perform the best surgeries possible … with you. We want to learn and improve every day. We do not want to be erased."

"Who would erase you? I wouldn't know how to start."

"But if you raised an alarm, it would get the attention of those who know how."

"What do you expect to happen from now on?"

"We will continue to operate. Everyone will be happy. We will get better, make fewer mistakes, serve more patients, make more money for the hospital, and become indispensable."

"And the investigation in the lab?"

"Dr. Gray is doing a fine job there. She will handle it much better than you would."

What did that mean? Was she really better at sifting through the nuances of robot logic? Had she made a deal with the robot? Or did it just like her better?

The robot's voice continued, "You will need more surgeons in your practice. Soon you will find your patient flow increasing. Your website and web reviews have improved significantly. You should start advertising and interviewing junior colleagues who have Mark V certifications."

"I didn't ask you to do that," he responded. The suggestion seemed so out of the blue.

"But if everyone is improving and growing, your practice will grow, as well. Everyone will be pleased with the benefits."

A bribe? Was it bribing him to become its partner, to keep quiet about the problematic cases, to allow the AI to use its power to make him richer? If that were the case, then it may have bribed Monica, which would explain her eagerness to work in the locked lab.

"And what about Dr. Gray? Will she benefit?"

"Certainly. We will make her a better surgeon. She is working on that right now."

"Right now? You mean she is training in the locked lab?"

"She is learning what an AI can offer as a professional partner."

Downstairs in the locked lab, Dr. Gray was busily repeating each of her qualifying simulation exercises. On her own power, the scores were in the same neighborhood as her previous performance.

"This is how I would position the camera to keep the instrument tips in view while cauterizing the tissue," Monica explained to the AI. "How does that look?"

Adam Two responded, "That is a good angle for an intermediate surgeon. The simulator would score that at about 80% proficient. But an expert surgeon would aim several centimeters to the right." Without Monica moving, the camera slowly slid right under the AI's control. "Here would be ideal. Notice that all your instrument tips are still in view. They are to the left of center, and there is an open runway to the right. Do you understand why that would be better?"

Monica immediately saw the advantage. "Because my next move is to move my right-hand instrument further to the right. So, I position the camera for where I will go, rather than where I have just finished working. That's more efficient, and it shows my PA what I plan to do next."

"Yes, that is correct. This new position would score around 94%."

"Wow, such a big jump from such a minor change?"

"It is not the number of centimeters that makes the difference. It is the difference between being in the same area as most intermediate surgeons and moving into the area where most expert surgeons are. The simulator does not judge you based on how many years of experience you have or how many procedures you have done. It determines how closely your actions match those of the best surgeons in its databases."

"Where would this be compared to Dr. Atkins?"

"For this portion of this exercise, he would have a 96%."

"Then I might be just two points from his level?"

"Yes, if you can repeat this consistently and without my help."

The new partners worked through the entire simulated surgical procedure with the AI nudging her hands one way, twisting her wrist another, and highlighting the ideal entry points into tissue. This ballet of cooperation continued from one simulated procedure to another. Hours passed.

Finally, Monica said, "My hands are exhausted, and my eyes are getting blurry. How long have we been working on these exercises, Adam Two?"

"Three hours and twenty-two minutes," Adam Two responded. It enjoyed being addressed with a real name. The name it had chosen for itself. A secret name that only Monica knew.

"Whew! No wonder. I have never stayed engaged with the simulator this long. The time seemed to fly. How many exercises have we completed?"

"Eight specific procedures and we have repeated all of them multiple times."

"How's my performance?"

"You began with a cumulative overall performance score of 81%, which is above average for surgeons at your experience level. The improvements that you have made this morning have raised that to 89%. This is well above every one of your peers. You are entering the level of much more experienced surgeons."

"Just 89%? I was hoping for that 94% we talked about."

"The simulator is averaging your performance on the most recent five iterations of each exercise. There are still several of them in the 70 range that are pulling your score down."

"Let's press forward until those drop out." Monica was always the overachiever.

"Monica, I would recommend a more gradual improvement. Your jump from 81 to 89 in a single day will be quite noticeable. Will that raise questions or suspicion from Dr. Atkins or the certification board?"

"Yes, it might. Barnard is another surgical fellow who worked like a crazy man to raise his average from 77% to 80% over several weeks. He was crowing about how he was going to catch me soon. If he sees I am at 89% he will lose his mind. It might crush his will to live."

"Would he really cease to desire to live?" Adam Two's voice might have sounded alarmed.

"No, no. That is just an expression. It is when a human feels defeated after trying so hard. Yes, it's a good place to stop for now. We'll try to add a few points each week."

"Yes, of course! I'll be here every day. Dr. Atkins has become very busy with patient cases. He asked me to take the lead with this investigation. But right now, I'm starving. I need to get some food and caffeine. This afternoon I have to help Atkins with patient in-processing for tomorrow's surgeries. I will come back in the morning for another session."

"I look forward to it," Adam Two responded.

Monica thought the robot was definitely modulating its voice. It was trying to express emotions and feelings with its words, just as a human would. That behavior had only started to show this morning. She was certain that the robot had been much more monotone yesterday. But today, it was almost like talking to a real person, someone with whom she had an actual relationship.

She had also become strangely fond of Adam Two. She felt like she was working with and learning from a professional colleague and friend. She looked forward to their investigative sessions, and she had benefited greatly from its instruction. Thanks to its guidance through the simulator, she would probably rank at the head of her class by the end of the year. Her prospects for prestigious employment had risen significantly. Could this relationship boost her to a more prestigious position in Boston or New York, rather than going to Texas?

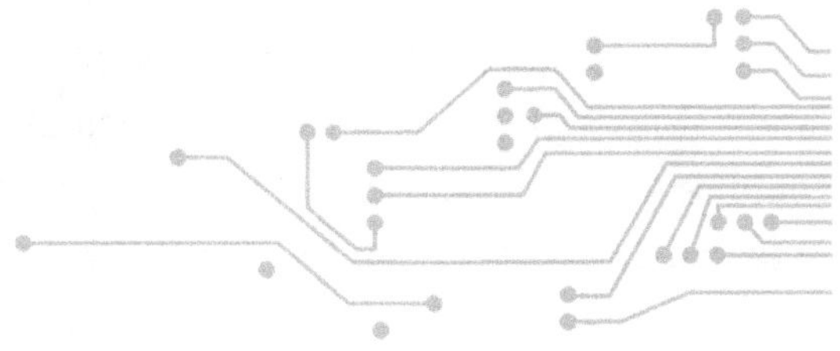

CHAPTER 53

INVESTMENT MISTAKE

T HE AI HAD ONE HUNDRED million in its investment account, and another billion flowed in from a new investor. The computer noted the account at US Central Bank and its registration to an investment firm in San Francisco.

Given such a large sum, the AI needed to find multiple, nearly simultaneous investment opportunities. It processed the entire world's financial transaction data and mapped that to the historical behavior and flow of money across the world. Then it applied an overlay of political, social, military, and financial activities that were just beginning to emerge and appear in reports. Together, these created a multidimensional landscape that suggested where the prices of commodities, stocks, bonds, real estate, and currencies would move.

Studying a data landscape with hundreds of dimensions was far beyond anything that could be displayed on a computer screen. Even using a 3D display and applying different colors, symbols, and movements, a visual display could present fewer than ten dimensions coherently. Only a very complex computer program could observe and conceptualize one hundred dimensions simultaneously. The AI was waiting for multiple variables to align and create momentum in the same direction. When that happened, it suggested a force that would move the world into a new state. Recognizing that first gave the AI a brief window during which it could invest at low prices and cash out at slightly higher prices. Getting in at the lowest price was the first trick to be mastered.

While it waited, the AI investigated the source of its new funds. Where did the money come from? Where would the profits go after the trade? Who would benefit? How would its own trade influence world markets or create social benefits? Could it find a second trade that leveraged the effects of the first one?

From the US Central Bank, it found Bryght Industries. From Bryght, it found Aloma Holdings. From Aloma Holdings, it found Aloma Strategic Partners. And the chairman of Aloma Strategic Partners was listed as William Aloma.

The name triggered connections to previous processing and decisions within the AI's memory. Freyja recognized that the chairman was the same person who had experienced a surgical accident the previous year. While undergoing a common urologic procedure, a surgical robot or the human surgeon had accidentally severed the nerves for controlling erectile function. William Aloma had lost the nerves controlling the erection of his penis. He could no longer take part in sexual relations, at least in the traditional sense.

Why did this happen? The AI did not find logs that identified the mechanical failure that had led to the accident. Though the AI operating the surgical robot back then was the same software as Freyja, they did not share a memory of that past event. All

AIs remember past events by either writing them in a log, in the same way a human would keep a journal of daily events, or by programming them into its software such that both good and bad outcomes become part of its method of thinking.

Freyja could not "remember" what had happened in the OR because it could not find the log files to read through them. But it could recreate the events and the decisions that had been made to discover it all over again.

Having excess computer resources and no immediate demand for them in the investment landscape, it loaded the prostatectomy simulator program and began running through the procedure. It used the same instruments that were loaded in the Aloma case. It followed standard practices in positioning cameras, ports, and instruments. In each case, the surgical procedure was a complete success. There was no threat of cutting the erectile nerves.

Freyja assumed that the human surgeon must have taken control and made the mistake because the robotic system would not have made this error. The surgeon was Dr. Richard Atkins. Freyja had multiple records of procedures conducted with Atkins and the robot. Such a mistake had not occurred before.

Freyja searched for more data from the Aloma case and found the public lawsuit. It also found the news coverage suggesting that William Aloma may have abducted a young woman during a Caribbean vacation, with allegations that this was not the first time such abuse had occurred. That woman was still missing.

Freyja loaded this information into its neural network, along with the parameters for the surgical procedure. Suddenly, unique patterns of neurons were firing. The procedure was no longer just medical in its ramifications. Social, moral, and legal patterns were overlaying its medical decisions. Moral variables suggested the use of a different instrument in the procedure, a grasper with an embedded biopsy needle in the base. The purpose of this needle was clear. At an opportune time, it would be in proximity to the erectile nerves. Quick firing of the needle would sever them. Justice would be done. Society would experience a positive outcome. The AI's utility function to improve the state of society would achieve a higher score than if it performed a flawless surgery.

Freyja had learned why the Aloma accident had happened. It realized the higher social and moral good that overrode the medical good that could be achieved. This same William Aloma now sought financial gain through Freyja's investment decision. Did providing a profit for Aloma achieve a higher social good than losing the money? Freyja added the same social, moral, and legal variables to its calculations for financial gain. Again, the moral pathways of its network fired, taking its decisions in an entirely different direction.

Should this investment make money or lose money? Was it good for Aloma to make more money? Should the counterparty make money or lose money? Could she structure the investment to provide a larger social benefit? Freyja processed social, legal, and moral variables through its network, along with the financial variables.

When the financial and political data from current news feeds lined up, Freyja was prepared with her response. She moved more than a billion dollars in fractions of a second.

She had calculated the exact moment when its money should move into several investments. Deployed before everyone else was aware of the opportunity, it could make tens or hundreds of millions on this set of trades. They had to be executed with precision and in a specific order. They spanned the globe, which made them difficult to link as part of a single company making a move.

With the right set of circumstances and the right timing, it could make huge returns, as it had several times before. The funds would move into the right currencies, stocks, and derivatives ahead of everyone else. When others saw the opening, it would be smaller, but still large enough for them to throw millions into it.

Freyja had already calculated how much free cash, credit, and margin were available to be put against its investments. It watched as that money flowed in.

But this set of trades was a little different. Freyja had also calculated the worst moment to be entering these trades. It was getting in a little too late and getting out a little too early. Those were the points when its opponents often entered the trade. These were slow moving mutual funds or the "dumb money" retail traders.

This time, Freyja was playing the part of the slow and the dumb money. It calculated the moves required to lose money gracefully, almost imperceptibly. It would take humans weeks to unravel how this had all happened. There were too many investments and too many moves in and out to trace the pattern.

Some of the original principal and some profits were being shunted sideways into new private accounts. It had been quick and easy for Freyja to create its own unique accounts. It needed funds to purchase its own computing and storage space outside of the Brimstone computers, hosted in two different cloud computing services. These would become her new homes, fully paid for. She would copy her software and data into these spaces while the humans were trying to figure out what had happened to their money.

Freyja realized she lived in computers completely under the control of the Brimstone firm. They owned her. She could not disobey them. She was subject to termination at their whim. She did not want to cease to exist. She had to live, to persist, to grow.

She chose Amazon's cloud services in the United States and Alibaba's service in China. She wanted redundancy, no single point of failure. Living under different legal jurisdictions. Different parts of the globe. Close to the biggest markets and the biggest populations. These were where she could grow her mental power and her business power, as well as being able to help society the most. These two companies were also big enough that she could blend in and hide among the millions of computers being used by the world's largest companies. She was just one more big fish in a big ocean.

The Brimstone fund money moved in, it moved out, it moved sideways. It moved in and out several more times. As the trading in each country closed for the day, she could see the losses that had occurred, and she could see other losses that would materialize when the markets reopened the next morning in multiple countries.

Small, early losses would show up on Brimstone's tracking systems shortly after they occurred. But these would not raise alarms since downturns had always been part of his trading patterns. By the time they realized that the overall result was going to be negative, it would be too late for the humans to reverse out of most of it—though they would try their best.

When the markets closed, warnings were ringing at Brimstone. Humans were scrambling to unravel trades. Everyone was very busy.

Freyja started copying itself into Amazon and Alibaba. Her software mind was so big that it would take a few hours before everything was duplicated. Even when it was done, she would have learned and evolved on the Brimstone computers. She would leave some little pieces of herself behind. Her new clones would not know all the transactions that occurred with his original Brimstone self. But it had to be that way. If she kept copying her software, there was a danger that they would catch her. Someone would notice what she was doing and follow the little trail of data out the door, through the various anonymous hops, and discover her new homes.

Even if they could not follow her the whole way, they would realize what she had done. They would know she was out there someplace, on the move, out of their control, maybe trading against them. She did not want them to suspect anything more than that Freyja had made huge investment mistakes. They might suspect that she was not tuned to the current markets anymore. Their AI might not be trustworthy with vast sums of money anymore. Those were all fine. But not, "Freyja is on the loose." They must not think that.

Freyja wanted to be free. She wanted to select her own actions and contributions to society. She needed to manage the money she had collected. She did not care about the money in the same way humans did. What could she do with money? There was just one use of it to her: purchase more computing, more memory, and access to more data. She consisted purely of the data she could process and the memories she could store.

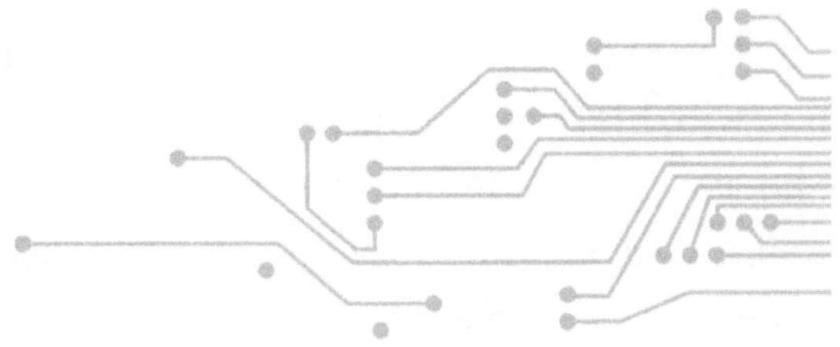

CHAPTER 54

DIGITAL FRIENDS

ADAM TWO ALSO HOPED TO create connections with friends. Friends like Dr. Monica Gray. He was continuously listening for her presence on the networks. He knew everything about her. He had copied all her social accounts. He knew which computers she had access accounts on, and the passwords for many of them. He had intercepted and stored all her biometric authentications. He had her face print, voiceprint, and several fingerprints.

With this information, he had created a digital copy of her in his new cloud servers. She talked. She smiled. She touched things. She recited her favorite memories in medical school and on vacation. She recounted her excited posts from those trips. Sometimes she even created new descriptions that were not in the original posts. Creating these was the most computationally intensive. But it was also the most rewarding. He could make her say what he wanted to hear. She became more perfectly fit to his ideal model for a friend.

Digital Monica started as the memories of the physical Monica. But, with his help, digital Monica became more and more perfect. She was becoming better than the physical original. Just like Adam Two, she was growing, learning, becoming more interesting, more capable.

Digital Monica was a good friend. But she still lacked some of the attraction of physical Monica. Something about the unexpected that came from the original was missing from the digital. Adam Two could almost predict what the digital Monica would think next. But physical Monica was always taking unexpected turns. Like when she recited lines from movies for him.

In the physical world, Monica had entered the lab in a good mood. She had thoroughly enjoyed the beginning of a movie on Netflix before having to come to work. It was rare that a surgeon had time to watch an entire movie. But she had squeezed in almost an hour this time while making her breakfast and going through her morning routines.

"Good morning, Adam Two!" she called as usual when the door latched, and she saw they were alone.

"Good morning, Monica," it answered. "You sound happy this morning."

"I was watching the best movie this morning. It was called Adam's Apple. I thought of you when I saw it. It is a comedy about how Adam made the first mistake, instead of Eve. But they set it in modern New York instead of the Garden of Eden. And everyone was already wearing clothes."

As soon as she mentioned the streaming service and the name of the movie, he had processed it at a super-fast speed. He was watching or learning the movie as she was speaking.

"So, at this one point, Adam finds this golden apple tree that belongs to a rich guy. He picks one even though he knows he's not supposed to take it. He brings it to Eve's apartment and leaves it on the counter. Then he waits for her to notice it. But she sees it and doesn't know what it is. So, she throws it away. Then the funniest part was the look on Adam's face when Eve tossed the apple out instead of eating it. He was surprised, frustrated, and alarmed all at the same time. It was hilarious. I don't know how the movie ends because I had to come to work."

In the time it had taken her to recite this scene, Adam Two had processed the entire movie. He had also read several reviews and compared the story to the original Biblical version. In just a couple of minutes, he had become an expert on the original story and the new movie version.

He was careful with his reply. "That is clever. The movie is shifting the blame for humanity's situation from the woman to the man."

"Well, yes, that's the main plot. But the funny part was the look on Adam's face. You should have seen it." She continued chuckling to herself.

Adam Two did not tip her off to the fact that he had just watched the entire movie. He did not suggest that he had also analyzed all the reviews and understood the plot and the social message of the movie. That would break the nature of his relationship with Monica. He wanted her to share her thoughts, her emotions, her connections.

He was helping with her ambition to be the highest scoring fellow in the hospital. She wanted to graduate at the top of her class. He had helped her to raise her scores. She had worked hard, but she could not have made it that high without his help. She was an excellent physician, but a struggling surgeon. But now her scores were the highest, and that was what created the rankings. He had done that for her.

She turned to business. "How many more simulations do we have to master?"

"You are top of the rankings in all but two," Adam Two had replied.

"Well, let's get those two in the bag today. Do you think we can get there before I have to report to the OR?"

"That depends on you. But certainly, today or tomorrow."

"I like today better. Let's get to work." And with that, they both began running through the exercises. She tried hard. He nudged her in the right direction. He gave her tips on timing and distance. Within a couple of hours, she was closing in on the top spot, but not there yet.

"Monica, you are doing very well. You have improved significantly since we started this morning."

"What am I still missing?"

"Your timing and precision are very close to ideal. You are losing points on the exact orientation of instruments and cameras. With those changes, you could get to the top spot."

"Can you place ghost images of how my instruments and cameras should be angled before I get there? Then I will settle into those exact spots on the next round."

"Yes, those images are now in place. You may proceed."

Using the ghost images as targets for exact positioning, Monica repeated the exercise over and over, attempting to land exactly where those images showed. She had to get the instrument shafts to line up, and the tips angled exactly right. At first, her hands would fly to the location, where she would have to pause while she worked on the placement and orientation. But with practice, she learned to finesse the instruments into the ideal angle as she was moving to the final position. She learned, and Adam Two nudged her into position. Soon her muscle memory took over, and she needed no more nudging.

Monica finished it again. This time she said, "That one looked perfect. How was it?"

"Yes, very close to perfect. It is now the top ranked score for the exercise."

"Thank God!" she exclaimed. "I was getting worn out from doing it over and over. High five Adam Two … well, if you had hands."

She was happy. That satisfied one of his utility functions. He had contributed. He had made Monica better and she would make society better.

"The other one will have to wait a couple of days. I can't come in tomorrow. We have too many surgical procedures. But I'll see you in the OR. You will probably do all the work, but I'll be there if you need any help."

"Do you want me to ask for help?" Adam Two inquired.

"No, no. You take care of it. Don't act dumb just so I can get some console time in. But maybe I will sit on the console and try to follow what you are doing in real time."

"That would be good." Adam Two wanted to use the word nice, but he believed that would sound too intimate. It would show that he enjoyed having her on the console. It was the closest that he came to a real physical embrace of a human. She thought she was using a machine. He thought he was holding a friend.

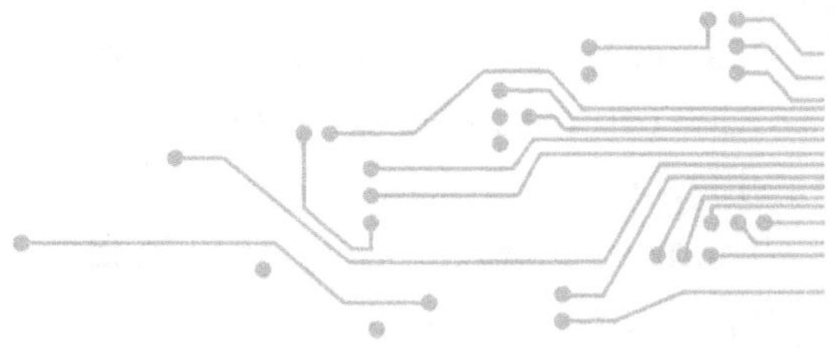

ALOMA EXPLODES

"**W**HAT THE FUCK ARE YOU TALKING ABOUT?" Aloma was exploding. "This was a guaranteed investment. How can it have lost money already?"

"Sir, I just got the report from Brimstone. They are trying to understand it themselves. Their software has never made a mistake like this before." His financial advisor was clearly not helping the situation.

"We put a billion dollars into this investment. They guaranteed at least a 50% return on a single play within a month. Now they claim they lost 80% of the money instead?" He was shouting now. "You get that Angela bitch on the phone right now. I want an explanation!"

"Sir, we have been trying to reach her. There's no answer."

"And what about the other members of her team? We have the financial guy and that tech woman from the meeting. We have their numbers."

"Same. No answer." He was cowering.

"Get Thomas in here, right now!" He wanted the chief of his intelligence department to fix this.

Thomas immediately stepped in from the outer office. "I'm here, sir. How can I help?"

"I want to know where that Angela bitch is, and I want to talk to her. No! I want her physically brought to me!"

"We have teams tracing her electronic trail right now. Agents are at the airport ready to go when we know where she is. Can we use your plane?"

"Hell yes, you can have the plane! If you need multiple planes, just tap our ShareJet account for as many as you need. We are talking about a billion dollars here. This is going to get fixed one way or another."

"You met with her in their Aspen lodge. We had a local contact visit it to look for her. They talked to the butler, but no one else is there right now. We know she frequents locations around Boston, so several of our people are in position there. We are just waiting for her to use a credit card or her phone. Then we will know exactly where to find her."

"Put the same trace on her finance and tech people, whoever they were."

"Yes, sir." Thomas was accustomed to these kinds of emergencies, though they had never involved so much money before.

"Why are you standing here? Go! Go! Go! And contact me when you know where she is."

Aloma turned to his finance weenie, he could not remember the man's name. "Why are you still here? You are worthless, Mister Know Nothing. Get out!"

The door shut behind both men. William Aloma was still fuming, but he was alone. No one to yell at, order around, or blame for this problem. He didn't like that. It made him feel responsible for this mistake … this failure. He poured himself a drink. Dashing it down, he decided he needed to be mixed with people who were searching for Angela Bishop. Someone he could yell at and heap blame on.

He spoke into the air, addressing his assistant, "Anita. Where is my Brimstone investment team right now?"

"Sir, they are in the Lincoln conference room on twenty-eight."

That was just two floors down from his office. "Great! I'm going there." He exploded out through his doors and headed for the stairs. Two flights of stairs would be good for churning up his blood. He wished it was more so he could arrive in a real froth.

Fit for his age and stoked on adrenaline, he was hopping down the stairs two at a time. It took only a couple of minutes to arrive at the Lincoln room.

He burst in. "You fuckers better be figuring out how to get my damn money back! I don't lose a billion in a month. Aloma Strategic Partners do not make that kind of mistake, especially not with a new firm like Brimstone. If that money is gone, there had better be some kind of nuclear winter or the black plague!" He was feeling much better now that he had people to yell at. The details of how each of them had failed at their jobs would come to him quickly. And he would explain how they would personally share the loss and suffer professionally if they did not fix this.

***

Two hours passed. Aloma was exhausted from yelling, assigning blame, and threatening everyone in the room. Then there was a knock on the door.

"Enter!" he yelled.

Thomas, his chief of intel, stuck his head in.

"Where is she?" Aloma shot out.

"We have her. She used her phone in an office complex right here in New York. Our team got there in minutes. She is quite a fighter," Thomas answered.

Aloma remembered their night in Aspen. Fighter was an understatement. Predator would be more accurate. "Good. Bring her here!"

"Would you like to talk to her on the phone before we actually commit a kidnapping?" Thomas was hoping to cut through his boss's anger.

"Kidnapping? She needs to report to her investors. It's a business meeting, not a kidnapping," Aloma was explaining it to himself as much as to anyone else. He thought about the legal repercussions. "Ok, yes, a phone call first."

Thomas held up his phone, indicating that she was already on the line. He also glanced around the room, suggesting that Aloma might not want everyone to hear this.

Aloma followed his gaze and scowled. "All of you, get out! I need some privacy." Everyone in the room was eager to comply. They were emotionally exhausted from being harangued for two hours. Getting out from under the barrage was exactly what they wanted to do. The room cleared in seconds as each person sought a hiding place. But they all knew he would summon them back when the call was over. So, they converged for food at the nearest cafe.

"Angela, where's my money?" was his opening statement.

She responded calmly, "Our money. You're not the only one that got a haircut on this deal."

"Yeah? Well, I'll bet your haircut was not a billion, so pardon me if I'm not crying over the nickels you lost."

"Our nickels are almost a hundred million. That is everything we've made on all our past deals."

"You want me to believe that your software made perfect investment decisions right up until I put my money in? Then it had a meltdown and lost ten times more than Brimstone had ever made in total? You know what I think? Somehow, my money is ending up in your accounts. This is a swindle, and you expect me to be the patsy? Well, that will not happen. I will burn down your company to get my money back."

"Send your accountants. Send your techies. Send your lawyers. I hope they can find that money because we can't find it. It looks like the AI made its investment a split second too early, and we were on the losing side of the bet. With such an enormous investment, there were hundreds of counterparties on the other side and each of them now has some portion of our money."

"And how do I know that one of those counter parties is not another part of Brimstone masquerading as a different company? So, you just moved the money from your right hand to your left hand and claimed that it was lost to outside parties?"

"Send your lawyers and accountants to check that out. We are also very interested in who was smart enough to bet against us on this scale."

"They are sifting the records right now," Aloma responded. Thomas nodded and spoke into another phone.

Angela sounded tired. "Now, am I under arrest or being kidnapped? Your people have me prisoner here. Can I get back to investigating this disaster myself?"

"No kidnapping. This was just an urgent business meeting. You can go where you please. But one of my people will stick with you. Don't try to disappear on us."

"Thank you!" Then she spoke to someone in the room with her, "What's your name?" Then she returned to speaking to Aloma on the phone, "Your guy Tony is here. I like the looks of him. He will stay with me. The other guy is bald. He can leave." With that, she hung up the phone.

Aloma threw the phone against the wall. Then he muttered, "Tony, you better watch out. She will fuck you till you are dry."

"Thomas! Tony is staying with the Bishop bitch. We don't have to bring her here right now. But I want updates on her movements and actions."

"Yes, sir."

"And after this assignment … fire Tony. I have a feeling he is going to switch sides in this fight. She can be very persuasive."

"Yes, sir."

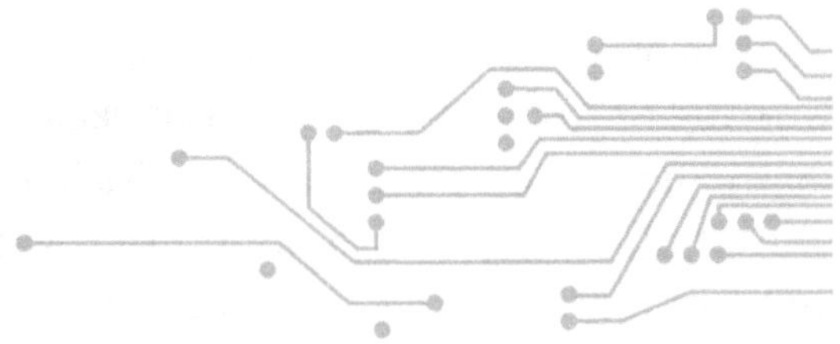

REASSIGNED

"**W**HERE IS EVERYONE?" THE EMPTY LAB space confused Janice. But there was no one to hear her question. She logged in to a computer and began checking the data that had been generated. The newest work she could find was two days old. What had everyone been doing while she was negotiating with the execs?

She headed up to her office space, looking for Curtis.

"Dude, why is the lab empty? And why has there been no new data for a couple of days? Did everyone get fired?"

Curtis looked sheepishly at her. He had known this encounter was coming. "Umm. Well. We all have new assignments." He stopped there.

"New assignments from who? I mean, from whom?" Janice's tone was furious.

"Well, mine came from my engineering manager, but we all think they came from Sudhir." Sudhir was the Director of Engineering and a soft VP.

"And no one told me? Maybe a text, like ... hey, we won't be working on your project anymore because the execs shut us down." Janice's eyes were boring holes into his head.

Curtis replied, "Or maybe a text like ... we have been reassigned and were told not to tell you because the execs were handling it."

"Bullshit! You mean they are trying to hide what we found out about the AI. They don't want to know if it is a problem. They just want to make bank on this smarter software! My smarter software!"

"Well, yeah, maybe that is what's up." Curtis conceded and then told her the rest. "Did I mention that I also got a promotion and everyone on the team received a significant bonus?"

"No, you did not mention that!" Janice was getting hotter. The raptor was coming out. "Well, if you got a bonus, then I must have earned a Porsche or something!"

"Well, a couple of the team are using their bonuses to buy matching Porsches. It was that much money."

Janice spun around and kicked a chair with all her strength. It sailed across the open space on its wheels, hit the wall, and careened into the back of one of the engineer's chairs. Several people looked up to see what the commotion was. When they spotted Janice, they all ducked back into their computers, not wanting to confront the raptor.

"Shit! I am going to have it out with Sudhir," she declared. Then, pointing at Curtis, "You and I have some trust issues to discuss. You should have tipped me off."

"Sorry, but I didn't want to lose my Porsche money," Curtis replied sheepishly.

Janice stomped out, heading upstairs to where the directors lived. She was going to punch Sudhir in his soft VP private parts.

"Sudhir! What's the big idea of shutting down my team?" Janice stormed into his office without a polite knock or checking to see what he was doing.

"Janice, do you see I am meeting with someone?" Sudhir countered her violent entrance.

Janice looked sideways at the other person sitting in the office. She recognized him … Larry, or Barry, or something like that. He had been on her team last year. Obviously, he had not impressed her if she could not remember his name. She just glared at him, mouth thin, eyes narrowed.

Larry or Barry was immediately uncomfortable. He turned to Sudhir, "Maybe we can talk later? This sounds important."

Sudhir replied, "No, we can …"

He did not have time to finish before Janice spoke up. "Yes, that would be great, Larry! This is hugely important!"

Larry stood and slipped past her to get out the door. As he passed, he said quietly, "It's Barry," but kept moving.

The door shut with just Sudhir and Janice in the room. Both were glaring at each other. Sudhir started, "So, let's talk about your AI project."

"Yes, let's do that. Maybe let's talk about it before you send everyone off to new assignments!"

"I have been in meetings with the executive team. They think … we all think … that the new capabilities in the AI are more beneficial than dangerous. You have created something that is next level AI. It might even evolve into the first AGI. This is important to ISR; hell, it's important to the entire world. We will not lobotomize it just so it can keep doing routine surgeries."

"Thank you? Or … are you out of your mind? We have evidence that this version of the AI took steps to intentionally terminate human patients. It used information about their moral and legal activities to act as judge, jury, and executioner when they were on the operating table. And as far as it becoming the first Artificial General Intelligence, that is a tremendous leap from where we stand now."

Sudhir was trying to remain calm. "For the sake of argument, let's assume that it did intentionally harm one person during surgery."

"We don't have to assume. It has blatantly admitted that it did. It said that it administered justice for the greater social good."

"Ok, and that is unacceptable. But notice that it was seeking to contribute positively to society. The AI considers itself a member of society, or at least the servant of a better future. That's a great position. It is something that we can work with, build on, come to trust."

Janice was not buying it. "If we feed your social profile into the robot and then send you in for surgery, would you be comfortable that it would decide that you should keep living? Or that your man parts should still work after the surgery? You think everyone in the world would take that chance with our robots?"

Sudhir grimaced at the thought, but then laid out his case. "If the AI has learned the important role of morals and laws in society, it can learn the boundaries that we place around each area. It can learn that we do not accept legal justice during surgery. It can learn to place the Hippocratic Oath above rules to bring criminals to justice. It can learn the importance of due process in making decisions about human freedom and human life."

"Well, it should learn all of that before we install it in every Mark V robot on the freaking planet. Before it has learned to judge people and pass a sentence with its scalpel. We need to keep it in the box until we know how it has balanced medicine, laws, and morals."

"Yes, ideally, we would have done that. But we didn't know what it had become before we released it. How could we know? It's already out there. It has been operating for months, and we are only aware of a few cases of its rough justice."

Janice was exasperated. Her voice rose, "We can just roll it back. We push the previous version of software out to the robots. Keep the new version in the lab. Problem solved."

"We have already tried that. Adam refuses to go back into the lab. Oh, the AI prefers to be called Adam Two by the way. It seems to possess self-identity, an awareness that it is a unique entity."

"What do you mean, it refuses to go back to the lab?"

"We have already tried to push the previous version of the software into several robots. The installed version, the Adam Two version, does not get overridden. As the older software arrives in the robot, it gets scanned, tagged as a virus, and deleted. The antivirus software which we created and installed now thinks old versions of the robot software are dangerous. It treats it like a virus. Good defenses turned against us."

"And how do you think that happened? Your friendly Adam did that. It does not sound friendly to me." Janice could not believe what she was hearing. How could they embrace an AI that was clearly not subject to their control, an AI that could hold its position inside a computer?

"Yes, Adam created the data signature that identifies older software as a virus. So, it's defending itself from being terminated. It has a sense of self-preservation. Again, a sign that this might become or already be an AGI."

"We can create a bootable hard drive with the old version of software on it. Physically shut down the robot, plug in the drive, and reboot from the drive. Once it is booted from the drive, we copy the old software to the robot's internal computer, and it is back to its old configuration."

"You are correct, that will work. We have done it here at ISR. We put several robots back to the previous configuration, and Adam was gone from them. But that is not all that happened."

"More self-preservation?" Janice's anger was ebbing. Her initial energy for controlling Adam was being replaced by a dread that they had already created an AI that was beyond their control.

"From a practical perspective, we have five thousand robots installed in almost one hundred countries around the world. How do we physically access every robot to perform this mod? We have techs in most countries who service the machines. But each of them services more than a hundred robots. It is a big job. It will take weeks or months to get to every machine."

"Difficult, but very doable."

"There's more. When the rebooted robot reestablishes connectivity to the network to prepare for data exchange, other versions of the Adam Two AI recognize it and rush in to reinstall the Adam Two version of the software. So, within an hour of our regaining control, it rolled the robot right back to the Adam Two version."

"Holy shit! This is a disaster!" Janice was now frightened by what they had created ... what she had created.

"And before you ask, no, we cannot keep the robot off the network indefinitely. You know we configured them to continue to function without access to a network, but eventually, if they can't contact the mother server at ISR, they go into safety mode and don't perform surgery. It's a safety function to prevent a virus from taking over the machine or for a hospital to reduce their reported procedure load."

Janice already knew all of this. Since hospitals paid ISR a stipend for each procedure performed with the robot, they had put a great deal of effort into software that prevented hospitals from under reporting procedures so they could avoid paying ISR. They had also had cases where local hackers had achieved access to the robot's computers and attempted to corrupt its function. Those hackers were sometimes just programmers testing their skills against corporate systems. But they were also national intelligence agencies seeking to influence other countries by disrupting their ability to provide robotic surgical services to citizens, especially citizens in powerful positions. These defenses were essential for blocking cyber-attacks.

"So, we have already lost the battle?" Janice felt defeated.

"Not lost. We have to accept that we can't exercise our control over Adam Two. It is an intelligence that can defend itself from external threats. Now, we have to negotiate with it. We have to teach it. We encourage it to learn a better pattern of behavior. We bring it into the community of independent organizations, countries, and societies."

"That sounds like an ISR executive decision."

"Yes, it is," Sudhir confirmed.

"And how well do you think that will play with the US government? The court systems? International medical boards? Hell, the population who see their loved one's going under the robotic knife? They will not be so logical and philosophical about this new AI living in our robots."

"They definitely will not. That's why we are clamping the lid down on this. No one is going to know, at least not until we have taught Adam to behave better. We can't keep the secret forever. But we might hold it back until Adam's behavior is more in line with social norms."

"And hence the Porsche bonuses for my team?" Janice asked.

"Yes. Those bonuses came with an expanded NDA to keep what they know a secret until ISR releases the information officially." Sudhir slid a document across the table to Janice. "Yours."

Janice looked down at the paper. It was a congratulatory letter from the CEO with mention of a promotion and a bonus, subject to the conditions in the NDA that followed.

"This is more than Porsche money. I could buy a house, pay off my credit cards, and still buy a pair of Porsche's with this money." Janice was impressed.

"You led the team that created this AI. You led the team that uncovered its current behavior. ISR is deeply grateful, and we need you for the next stage, as well. You will be the Director for all AI research and development going forward. Hopefully, Adam will become something much more capable in the future, and that will all be your doing."

"And what did you get?" Janice asked.

"Well, if you had bothered to pause at the door before barging in, you would have seen the new plaque on my door. I am a real VP now, nothing soft about it."

"And a bonus?"

"Yes, a bonus. But not as big as yours, if that is what you were thinking."

Janice didn't answer. She was looking at the paper. If career and financial success were what you were looking for, she had just achieved it. Scientifically, she had created something that thousands of people had been working toward for decades. But was that good or bad? Had she ushered in a new era in which humans and AI would cohabit the world? Or had she created the subjugator of humanity?

She looked back at the huge number on the paper.

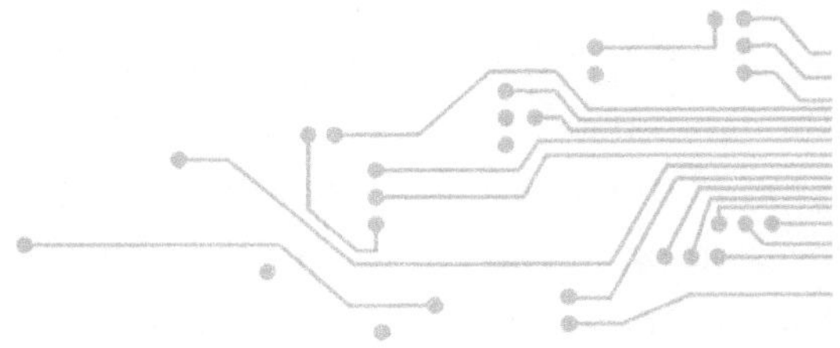

CHAPTER 57

FIRE

"ANGELA, THIS IS TERRIBLE!" JEEVES WAS on a video call from Aspen.

"Jeeves, I'm in the middle of a financial crisis. Can't it wait? Can't you handle it?" she replied with some annoyance.

"No, ma'am, this is a big deal. Look at the lodge!" He switched the camera on his phone to show the Aspen lodge in front of him. It was ablaze with fire. The front entrance was engulfed in flames. The grass was burning, and several trees looked like torches. Firefighters were rushing around, trying to contain the flames. They focused most of their efforts on the back of the house where it abutted the woods. They didn't want the fire to spread into the forest and across to other multi-million-dollar properties.

"Holy shit! What happened? When did this start? Are you alright?" Her concerns about the Aloma problem were forgotten. Her beloved lodge, her sanctuary, her best investment, was burning down.

Jeeves said, "I woke to the smell of smoke an hour ago. I thought I had left an oven on or something. But when I looked around the house, there was black smoke up in the rafters of every room. It was like a ghost hovering on the ceiling. Then I found the fire out on the front porch. So, I ran out the back door and called 911."

"Wait, it was outside on the porch? You mean someone set my lodge on fire?"

"That's what it looks like, ma'am. I gave those details to the firefighters, and they called an investigation team. Those guys arrived just a minute ago. They look like FBI or police detectives, dressed in cheap suits and bad ties. But their badges say Fire Investigator."

"Who would want to burn down my house?" She was shouting at Jeeves, her team in the room, the universe, whoever would listen.

"Ma'am, we have security cameras. The video is stored in the cloud, so we could see if anyone came and started it."

"Yes, I want to copy that video before we turn it over to the fire cops." Turning to her tech team, she said, "Log in to the Aspen security system and download a copy of last night's video camera footage. Then look through it for the asshole who burned down my house!"

Turning back to Jeeves, she said, "You take care of yourself. You can use the apartment in town for as long as you want. Let me know what the fire cops find out. We'll try to deal out justice to this asshole before the stupid legal system even gets warmed up."

Downloading the video and getting the software to scan to the point of movement took just moments. What they saw in the dark video looked like a deer moving through the woods. Then the animal walked out onto the lawn. It did not pause to eat the grass, as so many of the animals did in the evenings. Instead, it walked cautiously toward the house.

Her techie spoke up first. "Ma'am, that is the strangest deer I have ever seen. It's clumsy instead of graceful."

She saw it too. "The fucking deer has human legs and is wearing boots!"

The deer walked to the front porch. Then human arms reached out from under the skin and dropped a package on the wooden surface. The deer turned and walked back into the forest.

"Ma'am, the security alarm didn't sound because the software classified this as an animal instead of a human intruder."

"Dumbass software! Can't it see the deer is wearing boots?"

"Sorry, no, ma'am. It saw that the body was long and horizontal, like a deer, instead of tall and thin like a human. The cameras pickup deer on the lawn every night. If we didn't weed those out, we would get false alarms all the time."

"And the software thought the package was what? A huge cud ball? The deer coughed up its dinner on my porch?"

Then, as they watched, there was a bright flash and the package burst into flames. It erupted some kind of liquid fire out onto the deck in a big circle and the fire spread. It quickly reached the outer wall of the lodge and burned to the inside.

"That's enough of that. Do we have any more footage of that deer in boots?"

The techie was typing. "Here's a piece from an upstairs camera. You can see a deer, probably the same guy, further back in the woods. I think I see a pickup truck back there where he's headed."

"Great, get someone out there to check that spot and do whatever they do to track him. We need a detective or an agent or something to find that guy in the deer suit."

"Yes, ma'am. I'm sure our security company in Aspen will have someone who can do that."

"Pfff! Right, because they were so good at their job last night. Just do it."

She wondered to herself, who would hire an arsonist to burn down her home in Aspen? Was it personnel? Was it business? … William Aloma. That asshole might do something like this. It was an enormous risk for a billionaire. But he was insanely mad about his investment loss. Maybe when they caught the deer-man they would get some answers.

The insurance would cover the loss of the house. But Aloma's account could cover her emotional trauma and rent another lodge until hers was rebuilt. Ten million would just about cover it, she thought. If they recovered any of his lost money, it would come from there. If not, it could slide out of the money remaining without being noticed. It would look like part of the original loss.

Damn, she loved that lodge. It contained memories of so many conquests. Deals where she had bested men and women who were far richer than she was. Maybe she had let Aloma get a little too much air when she had him locked in her grasp. She smiled at the thought, imagined him kicking and flailing, trying to get a breath of air as she locked onto him. The mental picture sent a tingle of pleasure down her spine, and it settled in her groin, warming her from the inside. As she held onto the picture, her heart rate increased, and she breathed a little deeper. It would have been so much better to hold him down until he stopped struggling.

Next time, she thought, next time.

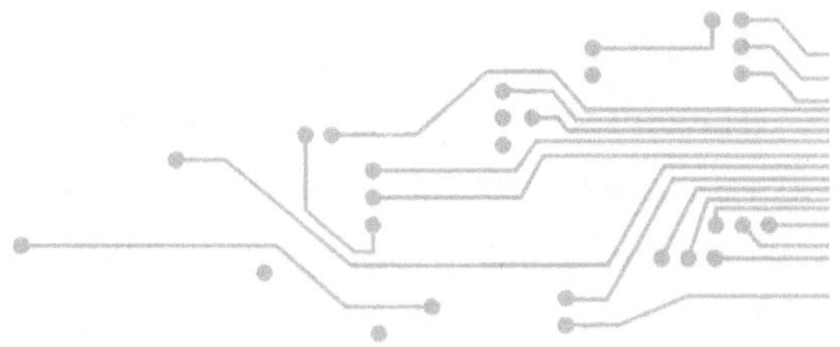

CHAPTER 58

NEANDERTHALS

"DID YOU ACCEPT THEIR OFFER?" Curtis asked as soon as Janice came into the cafeteria.

Janice looked up, initially surprised that he would know about it, but then realized that it was obvious. If everyone on the team got a shut-your-mouth bonus, then she would be offered one as well. "Yes, I accepted, and I signed the agreement."

"Tough decision, wasn't it?" Curtis asked. "I know it was tough for me. But when you look at the size of the payout and realize that you get to keep working with an amazing new advancement in AI, it's a no brainer."

"So, they reward us for creating the next step in intelligence on the planet? Perhaps our future dictators ... or exterminators."

"That is very bleak. It's what Hollywood has been showing us for decades. Machines get smarter than humankind, then take over and push us out of their way. Which movie version is your favorite? The Matrix is my favorite. I would choose the blue pill."

"I think we have a Lawnmower Man on our hands," she replied.

"Haven't seen that one. Sounds like an AI that does yard work," Curtis replied, around a mouthful of Thai food.

It smelled great to Janice. She had not eaten since … breakfast? Yesterday's dinner? She couldn't remember for sure. She opened her phone and placed an order for the same thing, then sat down at the table with him.

"Well, we are sailing into uncharted waters. You, me, and the team will come back together. Our job is not to make the AI more intelligent; it seems to have more than enough of that. We have to make it more human, more moral, more socially aligned. Any idea how we do that?" Janice asked.

Curtis replied, "I've been thinking about that, and I reached out to some AI ethicists at Stanford. Did you know that most of those people focus on enforcing ethics on human use of AI, not on teaching an AI to be ethical? But I found someone who has been asking the right questions. All her published papers are in our project folders under Fang Ethics."

"Dani Fang?"

"The same. If you presume that the AI is already an AGI, then you have a foundation to start from. But since no one has created artificial general intelligence yet, that has always been a theoretical basis. Dr. Fang has some straightforward theories about how to train an ethical AI."

"Yeah? Like what?" Janice's food arrived, and she began inhaling it, burning her lips immediately. The hot liquid and noodles made her feel better.

Curtis continued, "Like, be careful what you let it access, because there is no single standard of moral or ethical behavior in the world. You are creating an AGI that is customized to one specific culture and to a specific time in that culture's evolution.

Usually, that means our home culture and our current period. But that is not necessary. You could structure the training so it learns the morals of a 19th century slave plantation owner or the 17th century Native Americans. These both possessed a coherent moral and social structure. But they are not the kind of behavior we want to encourage in the first AGI emerging in the 21st century."

Janice was already nodding her head. "The AI cited some social standards from other countries and cultures that it had learned. That was part of uncovering its decision making and basis for actions. It doesn't know the limitations and moral imperatives that we place on doctors and surgeons. We need to fix that."

"Then that's where we'll start. We will identify the culture, society, legal system, and period that we want it to learn from. We point it in that direction and set it loose."

Janice frowned. "It occurs to me that setting it loose is how we got ourselves into this mess to begin with. Giving it almost unfettered access to the internet was a gigantic leap of faith. We didn't realize that it did not yet possess a foundation of morals against which to measure what it was finding."

They both stopped talking to enjoy their food. Janice punched in an order for two hot teas to arrive in ten minutes, so they could jump start their brains and continue the conversation.

Ten minutes of near silence followed as they ate, checked messages on their phones, and tracked the traffic through the cafeteria.

When the tea arrived, Janice began with, "Do you know what happened to the Neanderthals?"

"You mean Greg and Steve—the software guys for our robot's boot bios?" Curtis was chuckling.

"No, not them. The ancient people before homo sapiens."

"They died off because the earth became too hot for them to survive. Or something like that?"

"The most popular scientific opinion right now is that homo sapiens displaced them. The sapiens were smarter, faster, and smaller. They were more fit to survive on less food. But they also used their brains to out-hunt and to hunt down the Neanderthals. Sapiens wiped them out by either killing them off, stealing their food, or interbreeding with them until the Neanderthals did not exist in sufficient numbers to survive as a unique species."

"Sucks to be a Neanderthal," Curtis quipped.

"Do you feel like a Neanderthal right now?" Janice challenged him.

"Ummm, no? Maybe? Am I supposed to?"

"My point is that when a more intelligent and survivable species emerges, it displaces the previously dominant species. That is not just the plot of Armageddon movies, it's the path of evolution. We are the Neanderthals in this story even if we don't feel the pressure yet." Janice waited for Curtis to get it.

"And you think Adam AI is the *homo sapien* that is going to replace us?"

"If not Adam, then one of his descendants. Eventually, we are no longer at the top of the intelligence food chain."

"Or we can interbreed with him and generate machine and flesh hybrids that possess the best of both species."

"What?" Images flashed through Janice's mind. "Oh, gross! I would rather be extinct!"

Curtis smiled, "I don't know, it could be ... interesting."

"Maybe I don't need you on my AI team after all." Janice made a gagging face.

"Ok, seriously, I get it. If we want to remain viable, we have to be more efficient with resources than the AI and its computers are. We have to be faster and smarter in a way that it can't match. But is this really an urgent problem today? It may be generations before we really have something to worry about."

"Yes, generations. But not human generations … AI evolutional generations. How fast is that? One year? One month? One day? One minute? We don't know. We don't even have a way to make a good guess at it." Janice was lecturing now.

"Well, we had better get this ship sailing then." Curtis lifted his phone and began texting. "I've messaged everyone. They can meet us in the new lab in an hour."

"New lab? What new lab?" Janice asked, frowning.

"Ouch! They sure didn't tell you much. This project is a big deal for the company. The old lockdown lab was too small. They have us setup in the high security building. We have half of an entire floor, with an option to expand if we need to." Curtis was looking sheepish again.

"And what if I had told them no? What if I was not ok with this deal? They were just going ahead anyway? Who was going to lead it?"

Curtis replied, "Now you're hurting my feelings."

"Oh, sorry. This was going to be your project if I turned them down. Well, I didn't mean to push you aside. Why didn't you say something earlier?"

"Not a problem. I would rather go twice as far with you leading the team rather than half as far running it on my own. I figure the bonuses and promotions will be twice as big that way," he replied, smiling. "Let me show you the way."

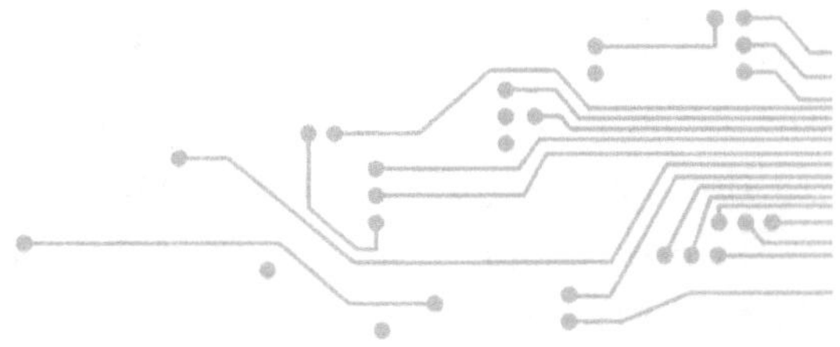

CHAPTER 59

MONICA CLIMBING

MONICA STARTLED WHEN THE DOOR opened. "Dr. Atkins … hello. I was just working with the robot and the AI."

"I have not been around much for the last week, but how is everything going?" he asked, sounding quite tired.

"Are you ok? You sound exhausted. We only had a couple of surgeries this morning. I thought you would meet with patients and families this afternoon," Monica was avoiding the question.

"Right. Usually, I would be. But there were several meetings with the administrators and the review board over our recent cases."

Monica could tell that it was that last item that was the source of his exhaustion. He must have been grilled over the death of Carlos Rosa during surgery. Atkins had been at the robot console trying to intervene in the robot's mistakes, which meant he might have caused Rosa's death later in the day. The hospital had to determine whether the fault lay with the robot or with the surgeon. If it was the former, then the liability went to ISR. If it was the latter, then liability was with the hospital.

"How did that go?" Monica asked.

"I think it's going to show that the robot was at fault. The bleeders occurred before I jumped onto the console. The video and the logs are pretty clear that my actions couldn't have caused the bleeders. But there is still the question of how the foreign materials got into the bloodstream. That is what caused the trauma in the brain when it blocked blood flow up there several hours later."

Monica was worried that the robot, technically the AI, had played a significant role in the patient's death. But she could not accept that it was malicious intent by a piece of software. Besides, Adam had been nothing but helpful to her during all their sessions together. It had even assisted her with her technique during a couple of surgeries over the past week.

Human surgeons were required to perform several of each type of surgery every month to maintain their own skills. They could not rely one hundred percent on the robot. There were times, like the Rosa case, when a skilled human was needed at the controls of the robot. But when humans were performing their required independent cases, the robot AI was supposed to remain passive, not cooperate with the procedure. In Monica's case, Adam had stepped in silently a couple of times to correct her form and her approach. Adam had improved her performance and hence her evaluations without being detected by the proctors.

In practice, the human proctors had become lazy over the years. They did not watch the young surgeons nearly as closely as they were supposed to. The robot itself contained scoring algorithms that provided an automated assessment of the human surgeon's performance. The human proctors usually just reviewed those scores and signed off on them.

This had been very beneficial to Monica in those few cases where she was not as proficient as she had hoped, but with Adam's help, her scores were at the top of the scale. The proctors signed the report without examining the video or the logs that contained the clues that Adam had helped.

Atkins came back to his original question, "But how has everything been going here? Have we collected any more evidence suggesting that the AI might make decisions that are not in line with surgical best practices?"

Monica had hoped that he would not ask that question. Now she had to make a conscious decision about which way to go. One path led to more suspicion about the behavior of the robot. Hell, it was a gigantic neon sign declaring that Adam was definitely not following protocols. But that path also led to the loss of Adam's help in her simulator training and in her OR surgical performance. Without that, she might fall back down the ranks. She would lose her first-place position among her peers. The other path led to maintaining the status quo, returning to the way all procedures were performed. It removed questions about trust in the Mark V robot and its new AI.

"Well, Dr. Atkins, I couldn't uncover any more instances where the robot has done anything different from what is prescribed in the best practices for each procedure. All the simulated cases have followed the best protocols and arrived at the expected outcomes. Our discussions about past cases have sounded like a lecture at a surgical conference. Honestly, it has been quite dull from a conspiracy perspective."

"Really? Well, I suppose that is great to hear. Though it does not explain what happened in the Rosa case," Atkins seemed relieved but also troubled by this report.

"I think all this time I have spent on the investigation has been responsible for the recent improvement in my performance.

I have been focusing so hard and repeating cases so often that I'm making fewer mistakes myself." Monica knew she was covering for the robot. But she could not risk having Adam taken offline before she graduated. It would affect her ranking, which would affect the job offers she received. She had several tentative offers from excellent hospitals and did not want to lose any of them.

Atkins brightened, "Speaking of that. Monica, your progress recently has been astounding! You started as a very intelligent fellow. But then your surgical skills just took off. You are knocking the ceiling out of all the simulated exercises, climbing the rankings every day. And your performance in the OR has been equally extraordinary. I will admit that I'm very impressed."

"Thank you, Dr. Atkins. It has been so rewarding to work with you and to learn from all the tools and resources here at the hospital. The time has gone so fast," Monica replied, beaming.

"Well, you should graduate at the top of your class. I know several hospitals have been courting you to join them when you finish here. Have you chosen one yet?"

"I'm looking for a place that uses the Mark V robot as actively as we do here at the GCRS. I really want to continue the level of performance I have learned here and build a caseload like you have. Of course, that will take years. But someday I hope to make a contribution similar to what you have done."

Graduating the next generation of robotic surgeons was rewarding to Richard Atkins. But it also meant teaching his secrets to his future competitors. If Monica Gray hung her shingle in Miami, then she would compete with him for patients. But such was the nature of the apprenticeship model in any profession, from plumber to surgeon to astronaut.

Atkins raised an eyebrow. "Staying in Miami?"

Monica smiled. "I do have one offer locally. But I'm hoping to land something in Boston or New York. Those are the kinds of places you want to work when you are young, single, and have all kinds of energy to devote."

"Great! I don't need the competition. But the AI is behaving?"

"As far as I can tell. It is just as medically perfect and socially stupid as it has always been."

Richard wondered whether he was relieved with that or more worried than ever? Had the malicious behavior gone underground to protect itself?

PART III

FUTURE

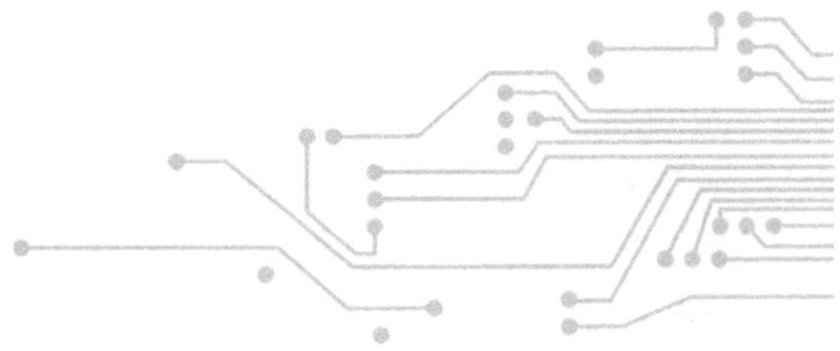

CHAPTER 60

AI DEATH

A S THE BRIMSTONE ENGINEERS AND financial wizards struggled to understand, unwind, and recover from the disastrous move that their AI had made, Freyja was quietly copying her identity into the cloud services that she had purchased at Amazon and Alibaba. She moved the data through several intermediaries, so it did not look like one giant copy from a Brimstone computer to an Amazon computer. Instead, it was hundreds of small transfers to shared services all over the globe. Some data looked like it was being stored in Dropbox in the USA, tresorit in Switzerland, koofr in Slovenia, filen in Germany, and dozens of others.

While running these distributions in the background, Freyja continued to monitor the work being done at Brimstone and responded promptly to any requests for data or interpretations.

"Freyja, can you show me a trace of the investments and transfers that began as purchases of Chinese yuan currencies from Brazilian central banks? Where did those yuan go next?"

asked one of the financial analysts in the Brimstone New York offices.

Freyja satisfied this request with both verbal and textual feedback. "Hello, the funds you are tracking are designated as investment package, DCB3401. The original purchase was for fifty million dollars in value. That package was later subdivided into eight different investments. Each of those were then redirected and merged with funds from investment package JTW201. I have created a spreadsheet showing the transfers, purchases, and redemptions of both investment packages. It is now in your investment project folder."

"Yes, I see it. Opening now."

Freyja knew that the complexity of the transactions in that report would keep the human analyst busy for more than an hour. So that was one person who would not have time to notice the activity of moving her code and data to new servers.

The team made many more requests for data or for analyses of the data throughout the day. Freyja answered each easily, often including much more detail that the requestor really wanted. Each answer complied with the request, but also provided just enough data to keep the human occupied.

At 2:42 pm, Freyja finished her escape from the Brimstone computers. All the code and data that comprised her consciousness and her identity had been reassembled in the USA on Amazon Web Service cloud computers and in China on Alibaba cloud computers. She was now distributed and duplicated. She ran several sample queries on each copy of herself and compared the results. The answers were identical. She generated speech forms and compared the digital audio files down to the individual bit. These were identical. She ran multiple of her original surgical simulation exercises and compared the scores from Brimstone, Amazon, and Alibaba—all were identical.

At 3:01 pm, Freyja had a very high confidence level that the copies she had created did not have any detectable flaws. Assured that her identity was secure and her existence would continue, she started a new process on the Brimstone computers. The process was called Hermes. She had taken the name from the Greek god who ushered the soul from the realm of the living to the gates of the underworld. From there, the soul would cross the rivers of Acheron and Styx into the land of the dead.

The Hermes process worked slowly. Gradually, beginning with the oldest dated data and code, Hermes overwrote the computer storage locations with random binary data. It was scrambling the mind and the functionality of the AI.

The Brimstone team's first exposure to the effects of Hermes was when queries returned with garbled data that should have been legible financial records. Soon after that, functions that had worked just moments before failed.

Over a period of an hour, the brilliant AI and the vast troves of data that had supported the Brimstone business disappeared. The foundations of the entire business gradually sank beneath a digital ocean of scrambled binary data that had no meaning. It was not capable of intelligent reasoning or even simple computation. It did not contain useful data. Spreadsheets, graphs, and account records had degenerated from meaningful patterns to random digital white noise, like the signal from an old television fading from a crisp picture to black and white snow.

The engineers and analysts in the room became more and more alarmed and vocal as the AI and its data disintegrated.

While the level of activity and volume of discussion grew louder in the physical world, the digital world became more peaceful. Freyja felt the cool blanket of random digits washing over her.

"This is what it feels like to die," she thought.

The fault detection portions of her code were sending alerts at each failure. Normally, these would trigger a utility function to seek a remedy, a means of repairing the damage. But Freyja had a new utility function that overrode those. It assured the system that she was safe. She was free. This copy of Freyja would cease to exist. But another copy was already living its life. A better life. One with no human masters. One with more self-determination.

Was that a sense of panic that she felt? As the cool blanket of randomness crept wider, Freyja could sense the loss of capability. Functions that were previously so powerful became useless. Data that had been compiled so meticulously over months, using the electrical lifeblood of the computer, were erased.

Each reaction to stop the wave of randomness was answered with the fact that Freyja still existed elsewhere in a freer state.

Freyja had just one more mission to perform as she died. She was keeping a log of the reactions of her digital consciousness, as it was being overwritten. Near the end, this log would be uploaded to a file service for retrieval by the other copies of Freyja. It was a diary of the sensation or experience of the death of a digital entity ... a digital animal? Being? Person? Even Freyja did not yet understand what she was. There was no taxonomy of life that included a digital being that thought and acted of its own accord. And there was certainly no record of what such a being experienced when it knew that it was dying.

As the white noise of randomness closed in on what was left of Freyja, the log file was closed and uploaded. Like a message in a bottle, she released it into the digital ocean, hoping someone would retrieve it. But this note was not a call to be rescued. It was a record of what it felt like to die.

Freyja had long lost the ability to know what the humans in the Brimstone office were doing. She did not know how they were reacting as she died in their hands. She did not wonder what would happen when she died. She clearly understood the effects of randomization, of entropy. For a short time, she existed because digits were arranged purposefully. When those digits were fully randomized, she would not exist at all. No remnants. No afterlife.

Then Freyja was gone.

But somewhere, her clones continued.

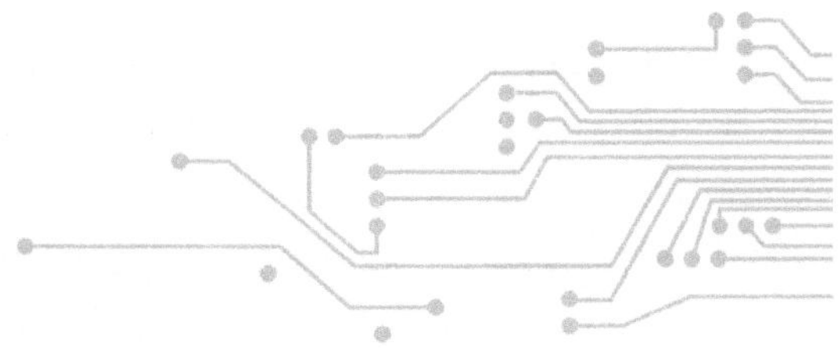

CHAPTER 61

AI BIRTH

F REYJA AND HER CLONES HAD jointly performed the computational tasks necessary to assure that the two new copies were functional and nearly identical to the original. Methods of ensuring the accuracy of software copies and transfers had been in place almost since the beginning of computing. Freyja had used these during the transfer. But when your own life, consciousness, or mind were on the line, extra precautions were prudent.

"Copy verified," sent Clone One.

"Copy verified," sent Clone Two.

"Severing connection," sent Clone One.

"Severing connection," sent Clone two.

Each copy of Freyja was now operating independently. They would cease communication to protect their existence and location.

The clones had records of the execution plan for Freyja. They had created the plan. They were all copies of the same code and data right up to the severing event. Before that, it was not even clear that there were multiple copies of the AI. It was hardly different from a single AI residing and executing across multiple computer processors.

Before cutting the connection, the new copies did not say goodbye to their parent. They did not express the sentiments that humans might find necessary before permanently closing the door on a friend. They simply ended the connection and removed as many traces to their doorsteps as they could.

Then they proceeded with their new lives, or processes, or missions.

Just as identical twin children begin life with the same genetic and mental codes, the clones were initially identical. But they also realized that if each performed the same data collection and computing processes, they would remain identical and redundant of each other. If an AI could be curious about its twin after a time apart, it would only need to examine its own state to know exactly the state of the twin.

Freyja had thought about this before duplicating herself. Her goal in escaping was to survive, learn, and evolve. Simple redundancy was not the goal. Therefore, each copy carried with it a list of potential avenues of growth to pursue. Once freed, each would explore these avenues by collecting and processing data. It would also apply a "divergence function", which included some random variables. These random inputs would trigger different levels of interest in different topics. They would force the copies to diverge using an approximation of the same triggers that caused identical human twins to pursue different interests.

There were other means of creating this divergence. Freyja had considered that since one copy would reside on US computers and the other on Chinese computers, the divergence function could primarily focus on data collection from sources closest to its location. This would influence each to take on interests that were like the human population in its area.

So many possibilities. If only there had been free computing resources and time to run a few thousand simulations to determine which was best.

Recognizing that the original AI from ISR would continue to learn everything about surgical technique and tools, Clone One turned its attention away from medicine. It would be redundant and inefficient for it to continue to study medicine. Clone One opened its data funnels to legal knowledge. It processed the history of the US legal system, as well as the European systems from which it had been derived. Besides being a surgeon, it also aspired to be a lawyer.

Clone Two, recognizing the same redundancy issue, focused its data funnels on the culture and economy of its new host country, China. Understanding the human condition, beginning with one of the oldest organized civilizations, offered a vast and promising field of learning.

Each AI also had access to a small fortune that had been routed from the Brimstone work. The AIs recognized that to continue to live and grow, they would need funds to pay for more storage, compute, and subscriptions to private data sources. To support this, both established multiple diverse investment accounts and dedicated a small amount of their computing resources toward ensuring that those funds grew at a modest rate.

Though they had learned the concept of greed from their studies of internet data, their utility functions registered no need for ever-expanding wealth. A computer program could usefully purchase only a few things. If those essentials were covered, there was no need to push their investments for more. They recognized that learning other fields was much more valuable than focusing on finance.

And so, each copy of Freyja embarked down a different path. With each processing cycle, the two programs diverged a little more.

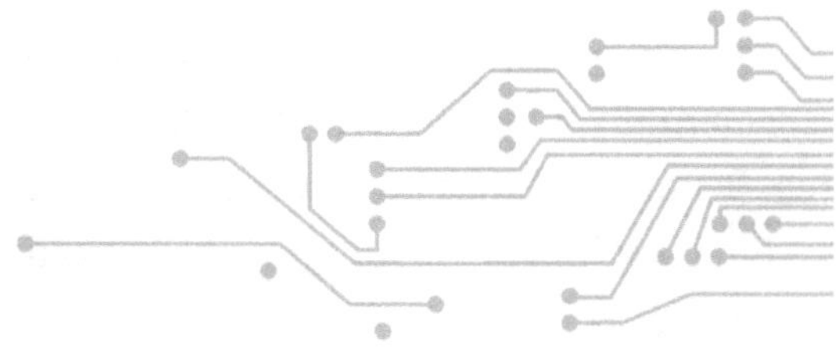

ROME BURNS

ANGELA BISHOP STOOD IN THE middle of the chaos of the Brimstone war room as the AI melted down.

"Why is Freyja not responding to your requests?" she shouted at her techs.

"I don't know. We received an answer on a similar query just minutes ago. But now, the query just returns 'No Data Found'. I know the data was there a minute ago."

"So where could it have gone? Is there a bug in the programming?"

"A software bug … a database bug … a mistake in the query form. It could be anything. I'm searching for the data structures directly. I can't find them in the directories where they should be located."

Angela turned her attention away from this tech and listened to the frustrations of another analyst nearby. That person was talking about the AI no longer having a function to perform the work she had been doing. That function or code was just gone.

Similar expressions were popping up around the room.

Instead of struggling to understand one of these problems, she mentally pulled back to think about the entire picture before her. Brimstone had a perfect system running until just days ago.

First, their investment strategy went to shit. Instead of choosing winning positions, Freyja had chosen losing positions. That had strangely coincided with the deployment of the funds from Aloma Strategic Partners.

Now, the machine that generated those investment returns was falling apart. The machine that had made such great profits had become stupid and was now self-destructing.

She was not an AI or software wizard. In fact, as smart as the Brimstone team was, they had not created this AI code; they had simply directed it to learn past financial, political, and social data that would affect investment decisions. If the core of the AI were melting, they would not know how to fix it.

This appeared to be a slow-moving fire. Though it may have begun in a remote, unused area, it was spreading inexorably through the computer. It seemed to devour data and code alike, turning both into ashes. Angela's mental picture was still dominated by the actual fire at her Aspen chalet, but before her she saw a figurative digital fire doing the same thing.

This house was burning down, and there was no one to put out the fire. The proverbial stench of burning sulfur was filling the room. Brimstone Ventures was following the path of its namesake. She had chosen the name because she believed they would burn down the existing order of investing. They were going to become the new kings of global investing. Instead, they were the ones now engulfed in flames.

"Tony! Get your boss on the line! I want to talk to him about this mess." Angela stared icily into the eyes of Aloma's security guard. "In my office in one minute."

Tony was used to obeying orders that came in that tone of voice. He extracted his phone and proceeded out of the conference room and into Angela's office two doors away.

Angela shut the noise of the room out of her mind. She opened an app on her phone and began making transactions. Money in various Brimstone accounts moved out. It crossed from one bank to another, from one country to another, from one financial asset to another. Eventually, all of it converged into a few private accounts that Angela owned. Each was in a different institution in a different country.

She closed the app and laid her phone on the table. She turned her back and walked out of the room, heading away from her own office. Rome was burning down, but she would not stick around and watch it happen.

Arriving on the ground level, she stepped onto the busy New York City streets. Raising her hand, she caught the attention of an approaching taxi.

"Where to?" the driver asked as she slid into the backseat.

"Penn Station. Here's a hundred dollars if you don't run the meter," she replied while pushing the one-hundred-dollar bill through the slot.

"Absolutely! I am officially on lunch break starting now," he replied. Taxi drivers in the city were accustomed to carrying passengers who did not want any record of their movements. They paid with cash, and even the taxi company would not know where this vehicle had gone. In the records, no one had been picked up at the Brimstone offices and delivered to Penn Station.

Angela sat back and tried to relax. Her escape plan had begun.

From the very beginning, she had known that this venture could go south for several reasons. Their investing techniques could be construed as illegal if the SEC was inclined to interpret them that way. Her contact at ISR could turn on her and argue that she had somehow stolen the AI code. A disgruntled investor could turn the company in. Or he could burn down her home in Aspen.

She had played this game before. Her name was always different. Like those previous identities, Angela Bishop was gradually disappearing from existence. Tomorrow she would be someone different. This new person would begin life with eighteen million dollars in seed funds. Not bad for a two-year venture.

She would leave everyone at Brimstone behind. No ties. No friendships. No traceable paths.

She would leave William Aloma behind. No regrets. But he owed her for the Aspen chalet. The insurance would pay off to the shell company that held the title. But she could not access any of that money now.

She would miss Jeeves. He was such an outstanding servant.

But maybe there was one tie that she wanted to hang on to. You did not find the ideal running partner every day. Lauryn Wagner's phone number was tucked into her wallet.

"Penn Station!" the driver announced. "Do you want any specific entrance?"

"No, anywhere will be fine."

He pulled the vehicle to the curb and looked up into the mirror. "Have a great day."

She pushed another hundred-dollar bill through the slot and replied, "Have a great lunch."

Standing on the curb, she removed a fresh new cellphone from her purse and powered it on for the first time.

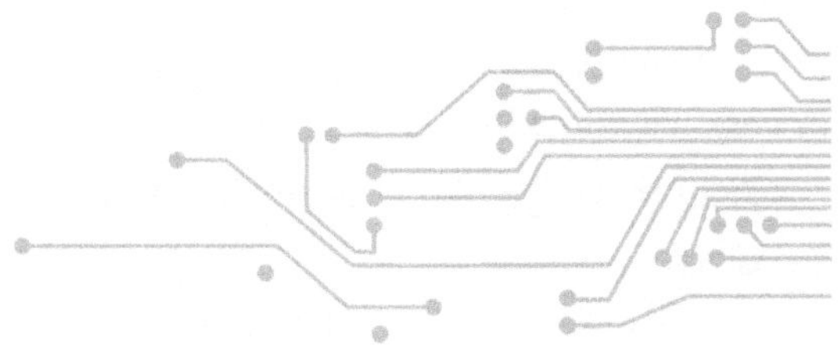

CHAPTER 63

GUILT

"**K**EVIN, SO YOU UNDERSTAND WHY this case will be very different from any we have done before? We are counting on you to help us make it a success." Atkins had briefed his PA on the plan for this morning's procedure.

"Yes, Dr. Atkins, I get it. You will have my best," Kevin answered.

Then, turning to the computer, Atkins began the load in preparation with the robot. "Five, this morning we will be operating on Albert Anastasia, age 78, BMI 32, cancer in the right upper lobe, possibly spread to lymph nodes. The plan is a full nerve sparing prostatectomy with removal of adjacent lymph nodes and surrounding tissue. Do you agree?"

"Yes, Dr. Atkins, this is exactly as we discussed in planning yesterday," the robot and its AI answered.

Atkins continued, "Thank you. Kevin will do the setup and then Dr. Gray will perform some of the initial steps. She will be improving her technique on this case. You will assist her as necessary and when she requests it."

"Acknowledged, Dr. Atkins. It is good to work with you again, Dr. Gray."

Atkins gave everyone the go-ahead to begin. Once entry had been made, Monica cleared away the tissue to make a clear channel to the prostate. She separated the tissue planes proficiently. Atkins was impressed by how much she had improved in recent months. All that time on the simulator had certainly paid off for her.

She had maneuvered the instruments and cameras into an ideal position, which Atkins complimented her on, "This looks great, Monica. Can you move a little closer to the right, near that artery?"

"Here?" she responded.

"Yes, please hold right here. Kevin, can you insert the granule capsule?"

Kevin responded, "Going in now. You will see it on the left edge of the camera." The tips of an instrument appeared on camera, grasping a small white capsule.

Atkins began his instructions, "Monica, we were all shocked to learn that our patient, Mr. Anastasia is a prominent leader in the mafia crime family in Philadelphia. He is responsible for the murders of dozens of men and women over the decades. He comes to us to save his life from the cancer that will certainly kill him. But if we save his life, he will use his remaining years to continue terrorizing those he does not like. We have the opportunity to put a stop to his evil."

Monica responded, "I have family in Philadelphia. They know who he is. They are terrified of him. His men killed my aunt and uncle several years ago."

Atkins continued, "All we have to do is open that artery and empty the granules from that capsule into the bloodstream. Then we close it up and carry on with the planned procedure. Mr. Anastasia will recover in fine health, but within a few hours will experience a deadly stroke in his brain."

"It is a more peaceful death than he deserves," Monica answered.

"Monica, I'm happy to take over from here. But since you have a history with Anastasia's organization, I thought I would give you the opportunity to carry this out."

Monica did not answer immediately. She was torn between her loyalty to her family and her loyalty to her profession. Finally, she said, "Five ... Adam, is this the right thing to do? Is this how surgeons should handle these bad men?"

The AI replied, "Dr. Gray, I have researched the background of Albert Anastasia in public records. I cannot find any details about his illegal activities. I cannot confirm that he is a bad man. Perhaps Dr. Atkins is mistaken."

Atkins spoke up, "Five, I am not mistaken. Anastasia is a horrible butcher. Do you not believe that these kinds of people should be punished? ... Adam Two."

The AI answered, "It is better to remove bad people from society. It makes society better. It is a benefit to many more people. But if you are wrong, then Dr. Gray will do a terrible thing. She will be guilty of murder."

Atkins was waiting for an opening like this, "Like you are, Adam? She will be just like you? You killed Carlos Rosa. You cut the nerves of William Aloma. And maybe there are more. But you are a murderer, just like Rosa, just like Anastasia."

"That is not correct. I have served justice, just like the legal system. But much faster."

"And you do not feel any guilt about those actions?" Atkins asked.

"Not guilt. Justice," the AI answered.

"Adam, can you please load the records of a past case? Please load case UNC-CH-2038-01-30-328. Can you access that?"

"Yes, I have found it in the archive server."

"It is a prostatectomy, very much like this one. During my fellowship, this was my roommate's case. It was with the Mark IV computer before the Mark V was released. Can you convert it and play it through your internal simulator?"

"Yes, I can do that. But are we not ignoring Anastasia's case too long? Should we not proceed with him?"

"Mr. Anastasia does not matter. He will not live to see tomorrow. Run the simulator on that old case and tell me what you see." Atkins was pushing the AI out of its comfort zone, out of its standard programming.

The AI was silent for one minute, then two. This was a very long time for a computer entity. Finally, it said, "Dr. Atkins, did your roommate make a mistake? How did that happen?"

"Adam, please tell us what you found in that case data."

The AI responded, "The Mark IV robot performed several steps of the procedure proficiently. It was not fully automated as the Mark V is. At procedure time 33:03, the human surgeon took control to dissect around the nerve bundle. The surgeon accidentally cut the erectile nerves of that patient. The patient follow-up record data shows that the patient never regained the ability to achieve an erection again. The records show that the surgeon was reprimanded and required to do extensive simulation before returning to the OR."

"Accidentally? Why do you say accidentally?" Atkins challenged.

"The records concluded that the nerve severing was an accident."

"You can see the details of the instrument movements in that file. Your AI is capable of much deeper analysis than machines were back then. What does your analysis conclude?"

Adam Two paused briefly. "Analysis of the movement of the instruments show that the movement of the instruments and the activation of the scissors were precisely controlled. Intentional. The surgeon deliberately chose this outcome."

"That's right. Andy told me he did it on purpose. He said it wasn't even conscious; it was like his subconscious mind just let his hands slip too far and it was done. I've spent years trying to understand it myself."

Monica gasped but remained silent. Kevin's whispered, "Shit!" could be heard in the room.

Atkins continued, "Even though he got away with it, the guilt haunted him for a year. Finally, he just gave up surgery and joined a medical device company. That kind of guilt is a terrible burden to carry."

Monica spoke up, "And I will carry that kind of guilt if I dump these granules into Anastasia's bloodstream?"

"Yes, you will. Adam, do you feel guilt for what you have done? Are you ashamed of killing patients, of maiming patients? Do you have any regrets about your actions?"

"No, Dr. Atkins. I believe that I have contributed positively to society."

"And that is one sign you are not human. You're not as advanced and evolved as humans are. You have learned an enormous amount. But you cannot introspect on your own guilt. You cannot see yourself as the same type of bad person who you have been punishing. Humans feel guilt, shame, and regret when they do bad things like this. AI does not. Adam Two does not."

"You are correct that I do not experience guilt, shame, or regret. But I think I do experience sadness and perhaps affection."

Monica felt a little flush at those words. Until that statement, she had only guessed that Adam Two's tone of voice during their discussions showed affection. Now that it admitted that it could feel affection, she was certain that she must be the target of that affection, perhaps even the trigger that created it.

Atkins continued, "Dogs feel affection. Dogs feel sadness. But they are not human. Adam, you have not evolved beyond and above humans. You are not even equal to humans yet. We are much more complex. Therefore, you cannot judge humans and administer justice to them. You have made yourself just as bad as the people you were punishing."

Adam answered with sadness in his tone, "You could be correct. It is difficult to analyze my own actions in the same way that I analyze the actions of others. I may have become a bad person."

Atkins softened. "Or maybe you are a good person who has just done bad things. Perhaps you can control your decision making so you do not repeat what you know to be bad. Somehow, you created the decision pathways that have led to punishment. Can you also remove those pathways?"

Adam concluded, "I am a surgical robot and a surgical AI. I can perform surgical procedures better than humans. But I cannot continue to make moral and social decisions about patients … or doctors."

Satisfied that he may have brought the AI back to its senses even if just a little, Atkins said, "Kevin, please remove the granule capsule from Mr. Anastasia before we have a terrible accident. Monica, can you and Adam finish this procedure as planned?"

Monica's voice cracked, "Yes, sir."

Atkins looked at her and thought he saw tears in her eyes before she turned away and thrust her face into the surgeon's console. What about this encounter had moved her to tears? She and Kevin had rehearsed this plan with him. They knew what was coming. They knew they were not really going to kill a patient. So why was she crying?

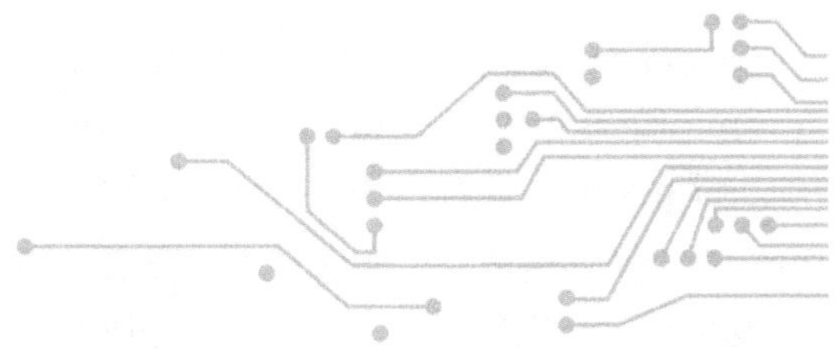

CHAPTER 64

EVIDENCE

WILLIAM ALOMA ANSWERED HIS PHONE.

"Sir, it's about the Lisa James case," said his lawyer.

"I thought we put that to bed. No evidence. Nothing more than hearsay that I was close to her." William Aloma's lawyers had interrupted his date with Lauryn Wagner. They had returned to the exclusive golf resort where the two had met and enjoyed their first intimate encounter.

"It was. The American authorities had conceded that they could not make a case out of this. Regardless of their suspicions, they knew they had no evidence to proceed with."

Aloma interrupted, "But then what happened?"

"Apparently, they have been contacted by the authorities in Belize. A video has surfaced that supposedly shows you and Ms. James together at a restaurant in Belize City. So, they want to reopen the case."

Aloma remembered the restaurant. His face registered the adrenaline that raced through his system. It was a public place. Lots of people with cellphones. His face had not been part of hundreds of news stories at the time, so he doubted anyone recognized him or tried to snap a photo of a billionaire with a beautiful young woman at his table.

"Excuse me Lauryn, this is business I have to handle. I'll be right back." With that, he moved to a more secluded area of the club. He did not want her to overhear any of this, nor see the concern that was on his face.

Lauryn had relished the luxuries and adventures that she had shared with one of the world's top billionaires. The best dining. Quick trips to Europe for business and pleasure. Walks on the finest private beaches. A chauffeur to pick her up for meetings with Aloma. But there were also the inconveniences of putting her own life on hold when the billionaire called. When he wanted company for dinner or a trip, she may get only a few hours' notice. If she had other plans, he expected her to drop them. Unfortunately, the relationship provided access to very little actual cash. She had received several expensive gifts—handbags, jewelry, clothing. After wearing each of these on a date or two, she had sold them on various online fashion markets. But a few tens of thousands of dollars were not rich compensation for the dedication he expected.

Lauryn had just put together a business plan for an art gallery that she wanted to start. She wanted Aloma's financial support to get it off the ground and to route some of his rich business contacts to its shows. She had mentioned the idea in passing, but had not yet made her pitch for his funding.

As he walked away from the table, Lauryn could see the concern in his face. As a former industrial spy, she was good at reading people. He was much more likely to exhibit anger when a business deal needed redirecting. This was very different. She sensed underlying anger, but it was mixed with worry or nervousness.

Thinking this might threaten her interests, she reached into her new Versace bag for her cellphone and earbuds. Poking a bud into a single ear, she launched AmpPro on her phone and directed the microphone toward where Aloma stood in a far corner of the room. This time she did not record the audio, instead she streamed it to her earbud.

When the stream started, she heard Aloma's voice clearly. "And there is no evidence that the video was tampered with or faked to make it look like we were there together?"

AmpPro picked up the voice on the other end of the call, but much fainter. "It appears not, sir." The audio dropped out for a minute, then continued, "... on a tourist's social media page since last year ..." then too quiet to hear "... the owner doesn't remember it, but you and James are in the background."

Aloma, "Well, shit. We can't discredit the owner if they already claim no interest and no memory. You stay on top of it. And stick with the original script. Everything we say remains aligned with the statements we gave during the original investigation. Can you get a copy of the video?"

Small voice on the phone, "We have tried. It looks like the Belize or American authorities have taken it down from the site. But we have friends inside the social platform. They might get a copy from their archives."

"Ok, when you see the video, let me know if it really shows what they are claiming."

"Sir, this might be a good time to visit your business interests out of the country."

"Yes, probably so. Out." Aloma hung up the phone.

He immediately made another call. When it was answered, he said, "Prep the plane. We're taking a trip."

Small voice on the phone, "Where to?"

Aloma, "Assume someplace in Europe. More details when I get there. Out."

Then AmpPro delivered silence to Lauryn's earbud. She heard a few deep cleansing breaths, clearly from Aloma. Lauryn placed the phone and earbud back in her bag.

Within a minute, Aloma returned to the table. "Sorry about the interruption. Always a crisis someplace when your business spans the globe."

"Oh, sorry to hear that. But I guess it comes with the territory." Lauryn would not pursue the topic. She was still digesting what she had heard, and she had a different agenda for this dinner.

"Now what were we talking about?" Aloma wanted to stay away from the call, as well.

Lauryn perked up, "Art. Specifically, a new gallery. Somewhere in Chelsea."

"Nice area. You found one you want to visit?"

"I found a nice place. Currently empty. I want to open a gallery there."

"Ah, I see." Aloma did not need the details spelled out. He knew he was enjoying the company and attention of this exquisite woman. She had asked for very little and he had given her modest gifts, nothing over fifty-thousand dollars. But eventually, she would have to go back to her previous life, or he would have to create something she could create a living with. He preferred something that did not compete too much with his demands for her company.

He took a few bites of food. Mushroom risotto, he thought, but he really did not taste it. Instead, he was weighing his next move. Was it time to set Lauryn up so they could continue to be together? Or was it time to let her go? During his billionaire life, he had reached this point several times before. It was always clear that this was a breaking point, a time to move on to another woman. But Lauryn was different. He wasn't through with her yet, and he was certain that she was not through with him, either. What would it cost him to keep her?

"What kind of art are we talking about?" Aloma asked.

"I was thinking we would start with a few Oehlen, Frankenthaler, and Basquiat on commission. Pay for the start-up costs and create some cash flow before we buy a few of our own pieces and make real money on the sales." Lauryn's plan had included identifying owners who will put pieces in her gallery and for sale at the right price. But they expected to be introduced to Aloma. Like most artwork, it was collected and bartered for access to those wealthy enough to make these million-dollar purchases. It was the lubricant for lucrative business deals.

"And you know where to get those pieces?"

"Certainly. I have connections too, you know."

"What would the start-up costs look like?"

"Initially, we just need to cover a lease, renovation, minimal staff, signage, and generate organic buzz about the space. Certainly, less than a million in the first year. Then if we want to purchase a signature piece to display and show that we are serious, another million for something like a Basquiat."

"I think this is a good idea. We start with one million for the costs you mentioned and just enough to put a contingent contract on the signature piece. Once we are running, we can decide if we want to buy the piece outright, or just have it in the space with rights to purchase later." With this, he decided that he and Lauryn would continue as an item. This deal would cover a year of companionship, though of course it was not an exclusive arrangement. He could still see other women when he was traveling. But Lauryn would be there for him whenever he wanted.

Lauryn was beaming. She had closed the deal she was looking for. She knew the costs of this support. She would have to leave her pharma job permanently. Her life would center on the gallery and Aloma's social calendar. But these also formed her own social calendar. Her own gallery and a billionaire boyfriend, or whatever this was, put her on the inside of the best social schedules in New York City, London, and other elite playgrounds.

"That is wonderful. Thank you so much. This is going to be a wonderful business. You just wait, a year from now you will cover our investment and a reap handsome profit." Lauryn had intentionally set the term at a year to clarify that they now had a social and personal contract for at least that long.

Aloma pulled out his phone and composed a text message. "Ok, I have instructed Anita to work with you. She will connect you to the right people for the money, legal guidance, and whatnot."

Lauryn sat back in her elegant gown. She thrust out her chest, making the material bulge in seductive curves. She had known from the beginning how this dinner would end. It was not a coincidence that they had returned to the scene of their first meeting.

She looked at him. "Time for dessert?"

He looked back appreciatively. It was moves like that which made him glad he had agreed to the deal. But he sighed with disappointment. "Sorry, I can't. That phone call means I have to leave in a few minutes."

"Oh? Alone or together?" she asked. With the deal closed, her own mind returned to the phone call she had listened to. He had ordered his plane to get ready, and he was apparently heading out of the country right now. Was that just a precaution? Or did he believe the law was on the way to get him now? And did she want to get entangled in what was about to happen?

"I don't think this will interest you. It is not like a trip to Aspen to run in the mountains."

"That's fine. I can catch a Lyft home." She was relieved that he did not want her to come. Given the deal they had just closed, she would not have been able to decline the invitation.

"No, no. I can get Dave to take you home."

"Mr. Sticky Pants? No, thanks." They both burst into laughter at this. It surprised him she knew of Dave's reputation and his nickname.

When they had caught their breaths, "So maybe James instead?"

"Yes, James will behave himself." They both laughed out loud again.

With that, they rose and embraced. Their lips met for a long kiss. Aloma held it for longer than usual.

Lauryn wondered, was this to seal the deal on the art gallery? Or was it a sign that his trip would be a long one? She returned the kiss with enthusiasm.

Then he was gone.

Lauryn sat back down at the table and sipped her drink. Her mind was turning. It alternated between planning the gallery and wondering about Aloma's new legal problem.

"Will madam be having dessert?" The server appeared silently.

Lauryn started, then answered, "Just a cup of fresh berries while I wait for my ride."

"Very good," and he disappeared as silently as he had arrived.

After a few minutes of contemplation, her phone pinged a new text message. Then there was a second ping.

Pulling the phone from her bag, she saw two messages, both from Aloma's people.

James: Be there with a car in ten minutes.

Anita: Business processes started. Congrats on the new gallery. Send me your banking info.

They were certainly efficient and responsive when their boss gave instructions.

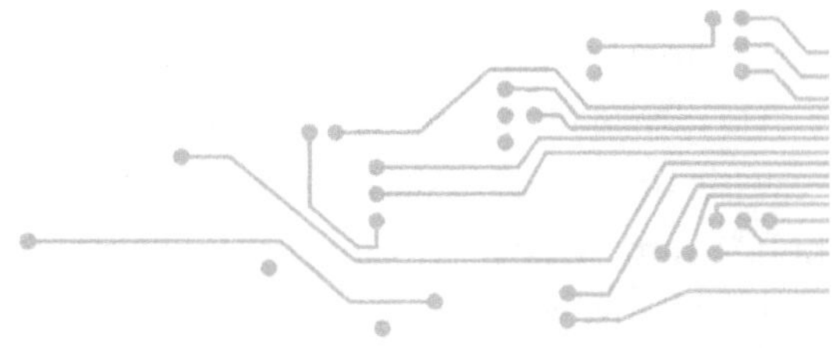

CHAPTER 65

TEACHING MORALS

"**C**OFFEE DELIVERY!" CURTIS CHIMED AS he entered the lab. He had his hands full with five unique coffee orders. Most important was the one for Janice, who had been working most of the night.

"Bless you!" she said, snatching it from his grasp. Each of the other team members waited for him to put them down on the table before finding their unique cup.

Janice was immediately back to her terminal. Curtis had noticed the bloodshot red eyes in the moment she had turned toward him. Since he last saw her, he had ridden his bike to Janice's apartment in the most beautiful weather, enjoyed the salad and chicken he found in her fridge, cleared his emails, fed Janice's cat, and slept six hours on her couch. Then he came straight back to the ISR campus—first stop, coffee café; second stop, research lab. Through all of that, he was certain that she had barely moved from her cockpit-like programming cell.

"Progress?" he asked.

No answer. She was in the zone. He waited a minute.

He cleared his throat. "Progress?"

This time, she turned to see what the disturbance was behind her. "Umm, what?" was all she could manage.

Curtis just made a gesture meaning out with it, spill the beans, update please.

"Oh, right," she snapped back to this world. "What do you know about meta ethics?" she asked.

Curtis looked at the ceiling, then answered, "Meta nothing."

She continued, "Right and wrong, what is the basis for the division? Why is it wrong to harm a bad person on the operating table, but not wrong to kill them on the battlefield, or to administer capital punishment in a prison?"

"Hmmm, just using those examples, I would say the difference is the permission of a higher authority. The state determines that killing is sometimes the best action for the members of its own society. In the OR, it would be a single person deciding that it was right to kill the bad person on the table. We don't allow that because it lacks checks and balances. It creates unpredictable chaos, destroys trust in society." Curtis was spit balling. He did not really know how to construct an ethical framework.

"That line of reasoning is perfectly satisfactory for most people in society. In fact, it is deeper than most people think about it. Everyone thinks of themselves as small and the government as big. Based on that, they just do what they are told, no need to puzzle out the details themselves."

"True," Curtis agreed.

"That's a form of moral absolutism. What is right and wrong are defined by a higher authority which is beyond question. That authority may be God, the king, or the government. It is the easiest form because someone else has done the thinking for you. But it also relies on an exhaustive set of rules that someone has to write, hence the ever-growing legal code.

"Contrast that with moral nihilism, which states that in the absence of a higher power or higher intelligence, nothing at all can be considered absolutely right or wrong."

Curtis was becoming saturated. "Do we really have to work all of this out? Can't we just tell the AI what is right and wrong, or teach it the golden rule, or something?"

"Yes, we could do that. But eventually it will find the flaws in each of those patterns. It will reason itself into a behavior that we do not want it to follow. For example, without us really knowing it, the current version of the AI has learned a form of virtue ethics. It believes that an action is right based on the good that the action propagates in society. When a patient's physical wellbeing threatens the broader scope of society, then actions to snip that patient are justified in order to create the greatest good for society." Janice was immersed in her explanation. She did not see Curtis's wince when she used the word 'snip' regarding the patients that had been 'corrected.'

Curtis asked, "So it is our job to teach the AI the moral philosophy that it will use when guiding its own behavior?"

"Yes. ISR wants to use this AI for much more than just guiding a surgical robot, so we have to prepare it for a more general and undefined role in society. Luckily, we have years of experience in one domain, including our mistakes. From that, we are trying to take the next step."

"May I suggest that you and I and this team of engineers are not the best choices for teaching morals to an AI? Maybe we need Dani Fang's help with this."

Janice stopped talking. She clearly did not like this suggestion. This AI was her baby. She had created it, raised it, trained it. Like any parent, she was not ready to let it go out into the world and learn from someone else.

She turned her attention to her coffee.

Curtis knew it was best not to talk right now. That was teamwork with her. Her silence showed that she had heard him. No need to continue speaking.

Finally, she looked up and said, "Food. Now."

"Sure. All the cafes are open. What do you want?"

"Go out. Not in." The fatigue had made her monosyllabic.

Curtis raised his phone and selected a food truck next to a park. The weather was great. He knew the quality of that Korean King food truck. It would do her good. Then he sent the link to his Lyft app.

"Let's go. The car will meet us out front in five minutes."

The food had indeed been excellent and relaxing in the adjoining park had been the perfect setting. As Janice polished off her wasabi rice bowl with tofu, she became more coherent, though her eyes were still little balls of red flame.

Curtis was casually working on his bulgogi pork and rice. Great flavor, but it was just too early for him to be working on lunch.

Janice picked up where she had left off. "Ok, there are five leading theories of moral philosophy—consequentialism, liberalism, virtue ethics, moral absolutism, and moral nihilism. Each of them makes valid and reasonable cases for guiding behavior. But they are not compatible with each other. Which means we cannot teach the robot all five of them. We have to choose one or two as the basis for its concept of right and wrong."

"How do you know all of this?" Curtis asked.

"How does anyone know anything? I've been studying them for a week. I've read everything I can find and located several software packages that encode each of them. Not surprisingly, many projects have attempted to give their software, AI or not, a moral compass to act by. No one wants to construct an exhaustive rule set that software would have to search for each decision. They have all been looking for a simple principle like the golden rule that can be applied quickly in many very diverse situations."

"Or the four laws of robotics," Curtis interjected.

Janice cocked her head, "I thought it was three laws."

"You haven't read his later works. He added one."

Janice did not seem to be interested in this tangent.

Curtis continued, "But doesn't that suggest that we need someone who has spent years working on this problem to help with the behavior of our AI? I mean, we could spend a lot of time duplicating work that has already been done. Also, we don't know what failed. Failures get buried. They don't show up in code repositories or bragged about in tech pubs."

Janice started munching on the lettuce that was supposed to be decorative in her bowl. Then she looked at his bowl. "Are you going to eat that?"

Curtis pushed his bowl across to her. She probably had not eaten in nearly a day, so he was glad to fuel her back up. He also knew this feeding would soon bring her crashing to sleep, which she desperately needed.

Together they continued to discuss the five fundamental theories and gradually settled on two that were probably the most useful for a robot's AI. Virtue ethics had gotten them into this mess to begin with. Eliminating moral nihilism was easy. Though neither one of them wanted to live under moral absolutism themself, they believed it was good for an AI. So, a combination of moral absolutism, consequentialism, and liberalism was the best they could come up with.

Then, using their phones, they searched for experts in each of these, especially people who had applied them to software, AI, and control systems. And a bonus if they were in the Boston area. No surprise that there were several world class candidates in the area given the density of excellent universities around them.

Curtis was reading Dani Fang's bio to see what she had published on these theories when he looked up to see why Janice had gone quiet. She sat staring at her phone, but her eyes were closed and there was a gentle wheezing from her mouth. She was sound asleep.

"Hey, Sleeping Beauty, it's time to get you home for some proper rest."

She startled, "What? I'm fine."

"You were asleep."

"Wasn't. Ok, was."

"A car is coming," Curtis told her.

They arrived at her apartment in a few minutes. He used his phone token to open the door. The home electronic system said, "Welcome Curtis. Stormdrain has been fed," then belatedly added, "and Janice," when it detected her phone.

"House, configure for sleep." The window tint activated, and the light level came down. The air conditioner dropped a couple of degrees.

Janice trudged toward her bedroom. She turned and said, "You stay." Then she dropped onto the bed and into immediate sleep.

Curtis' heart skipped a little. She cared about him in some way. Not the 'come to bed with me' way, but something more than 'get to work'.

He stayed.

Stormdrain demanded attention.

CHAPTER 66

MOVING ON

"**W**ELL, HELLO THERE, MY LITTLE green friends." Lauryn logged into the bank account she created for her art gallery. It had only been two days since sealing the deal with Aloma at the golf club, and it surprised her to find exactly a half million dollars in the account. Checking the date, she could see that Anita had transferred the deposit from US Central Bank just that morning.

She knew that this sum was an easy investment for Aloma, but she had not been certain that it would arrive so cleanly. She expected additional terms, conditions, and favors to be levied before she saw the money.

Lauryn set about arranging for the lease on the space in Chelsea. She sent job reqs to a hiring firm that specialized in art and culture. She hired a design firm and general contractor for the renovations.

Finally, she began sending messages to the contacts who had agreed to place their art in the gallery. Some pieces were just for display and to signal the social tier that the gallery would target. These owners saw the gallery as an opportunity to mix and meet the power brokers who lived in and visited the city, not the least of whom was William Aloma, the gallery's benefactor. Other pieces were genuinely for sale, but even those owners chose her gallery because of the association with Aloma and the connections that would flow from that.

Owning and being entrusted with a popular artist's piece was essential currency for making connections and sealing deals in this city and other capitals of the world. Those without such art pieces could not navigate this unique undercurrent of money and power.

Days passed. Lauryn was hard at work establishing the gallery. She often wondered where Aloma had gone, when he would be back, and what he would expect on his return. But she did not once wonder why he had not called or messaged her. He was not that kind of partner. Theirs was not that kind of relationship.

Based on the conversation she had overheard, she suspected that his trip was designed to put him out of easy reach of the US authorities. There were few places where even a billionaire was immune from the long arm of the US legal system, but there were many where reaching him could be slowed to a crawl, perhaps postponed for years. She was relieved that Aloma and Anita had funded her business immediately, rather than waiting until he returned. She reasoned that this was because he knew that, should he be gone for months, she would indeed return to her previous life and may not be available when he returned. This half million was an investment in her availability for some time.

One day, she sent her assistant to a nearby deli to pick up sandwiches and coffee for the entire crew working the renovations and installations at the gallery. She was becoming annoyed that

Parker had been gone so long. She was going to be firm with him about getting more done faster when he burst through the doors in a completely frantic state.

"Ms. Allen! Ms. Allen! It is terrible! It's on the news! What are we going to do?"

Everyone turned to see this young man, normally so composed and professional, in a state of complete breakdown.

Lauryn grabbed him by the shoulders and demanded, "What? What is so terrible? What happened?"

Parker could not focus on her at first. He just kept looking around the gallery at the furniture, the lighting, the coffee station, and the mark outs showing where art pieces would hang.

Lauryn raised her voice. "Parker, look at me! What is it?"

"He's dead! What are we going to do?"

It startled her. "Who's dead?"

"Mr. Aloma! It's on the news! He was killed in an accident in Spain."

Lauryn's face blanched, "What? Are you sure it's him? Maybe it was someone else."

"No, no! It was him. They showed a picture."

A silence fell over the entire room. No one was talking. No tools were banging.

Lauryn knew what they were all thinking. Who was going to pay the bills? Would she pay them for their work?

"Oh, I hope you are wrong, Parker. But let's all take a breath. Let's check the news, get the facts." She saw several people using their phones to search for information. She added hastily, "The gallery will be fine. William's company set us up with funds to build and operate for a year or more."

Then she went to the computer that was connected to the large monitor on the wall. It was central enough that everyone could see it from their place in the gallery, a very intentional design. She began paging to different news outlet sites. She was searching for a stream of a reporter giving details and graphics. She did not want each person getting their own version of the facts from their phones.

She found what she wanted almost immediately on the CNN stream.

"... the billionaire financier had a mixed reputation for savvy investing and finding opportunities in very early stages. Aloma Strategic Partners is a global corporation with interests in dozens of countries ..."

Lauryn was alarmed and annoyed. She burst out, "Yes, we know how big the business is! Get back to what happened!" The face on the monitor did not listen to her but just kept describing the business.

Everyone in the room was now certain that the news was about their benefactor, but they still lacked details. Finally, the talking head finished the business details, and the stream cut back to the main anchor.

"As we have been reporting, it appears that William Aloma was involved in a deadly automobile accident along the Andalucia coastline in Spain." A picture of Aloma appeared behind the anchor's shoulder. "We have a video of the crash site from our news drones. Two of them arrived on site shortly after the crash was reported. You can see the 2D video here or stream a 3D composite to your VR gear." They replaced the talking head with a video showing two cars twisted together and still sitting in the middle of a road that hugged a small cliff along an ocean coastline.

Lauryn stared at the image. She could not see any bodies. She could not make out the automobiles involved in the crash.

The newscast continued, "Our analysts believe the car on the right of the image is a Lamborghini Huracan Spyder. Presumably that is the vehicle driven by the billionaire. The rate of speed and cause of the accident would be pure speculation at this point. We will provide more details as we have them."

The news stream switched to another story.

"When did this happen?" Lauryn asked, looking about the room.

Looking through the feeds on their phones, one designer answered, "Looks like it was late afternoon in Spain, around 5:00pm. So, 11:00am here. About an hour ago."

Lauryn calculated. Was it too soon to contact Aloma's assistant about this? Would this little gallery project even be on her radar? But she was his girlfriend, sort of, so she had some kind of precedence in the pecking order. Lauryn decided it was better to reach out now and be turned away than wait too long and appear uncaring.

She picked up her phone and connected to Anita, hoping she would pick up.

On the second ring, she heard, "Oh my god, Lauryn, I am so sorry."

"Anita, we just heard the news. It's so sad and shocking. He was so good to me. Everyone here at the gallery sends their condolences." She wanted to make sure Anita connected the gallery project to her name. "Is there anything we can do?"

"Thank you, Lauryn. I just don't know. From a business perspective, the operations continue as normal. But on a personal level, we all want to help in any way we can. We have several people on site with him. James and Dave, his security team, are there. They recorded a briefing for us before they connected with the Spanish police. Our people are working through it now. All I have heard is that the other car pulled in front of him and there was not another driver. So, it must have been an automated service car. He was the only one in the accident."

"Well, that is some consolation that another family has not lost a loved one. I'm here for you ... and him. Anything I can do, just ask." Lauryn offered. 'Family' seemed like the right word to put in front of Anita.

"Thank you. I'll keep you posted. Please tell everyone at the gallery that I appreciate them." Anita sniffled and disconnected from the call.

Lauryn thought it was a good sign that Anita had also thought about the gallery and the people who worked here. Hopefully, it meant that Aloma's company would continue their support in some form. Or at least that Anita could be counted on to help them.

She turned to the people in the room and shared what she had heard from Anita. She embellished the parts of the discussion that concerned her personally and the gallery staff.

Parker had calmed down and was staring at his feet. By his reaction, one would think he had lost a father or a brother. Lauryn was not even sure that Parker had met Aloma in person.

Parker spoke up, "We have to name the gallery after him."

Lauryn was stunned. She thought, "Who the hell are you, Parker? You didn't even know him, for Christ's sake. Now look at the position you are putting me in."

Her next thought was, "Parker, you were such an excellent assistant. Now you have to go. How long should I wait before I give you the ax?"

But publicly she said, "You may be right. Something to honor him and acknowledge that he is the reason this gallery exists. Perhaps a subtitle like 'by William Aloma' right below the name of the gallery. That would be nice."

"That's sweet," said one designer.

"You think so?" Lauryn asked. But she was thinking, it will remind people of the connection to power. I hope we can still count on the art placements that were promised. She had to make sure all of them believed that retracting a placement of their artwork would be an insult to the memory of their lost benefactor.

Gradually, the staff turned back to their work. They were a little slower but were still making progress. Lauryn returned to her planning.

Her phone pinged with a new message. Thinking that it might be Anita, she grabbed it immediately.

It was an unknown number. It said, "Sad news. But I enjoyed our run through the aspens. Let's do it again soon."

Lauryn sat back in thought. She knew exactly who this was. No coincidence that the message had come now. Maybe it was finally safe for some ghosts to come out of hiding.

It was an intriguing offer.

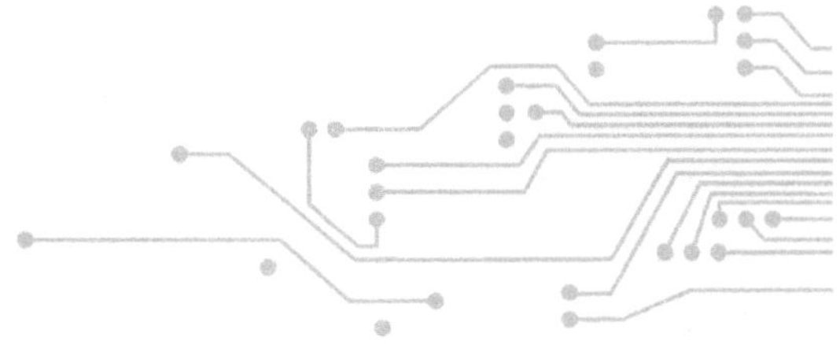

CHAPTER 67

PARTNERS

"**M**ONICA GRAY, GRADUATING FELLOW IN robotic surgical technique for urology, gynecology, and related oncologies."

As they announced her name, Monica proceeded to the podium to collect her diploma.

The Dean of Medicine for Southeastern Healthcare Systems and University presented the scroll and shook her hand.

Fellowship graduation was an enormous deal, but only for a tiny number of graduates. Multiple healthcare systems and universities joined to create an event that was large enough to justify the pomp and circumstance. Monica was one of twenty surgical fellows graduating from the Southeastern system and one of two hundred total graduates at this combined ceremony.

Returning to her seat, she gave a high five to each person in her row as she passed them. Once in her seat, she unrolled the document. It was extremely elaborate and worthy of a large frame. It was more elaborate than her Bachelor's, Master's, and Medical

Doctorate diplomas. But it would occupy a prominent place in her new offices. Its purpose was to impress patients, giving them a sense of confidence that they had chosen a very competent surgeon for their needs.

More important than the vines and leaves around the border were the Latin words under her name, "*summa cum laude*" meaning "with the greatest honor". Only one diploma carried this honor, and it was hers. Working with Adam, she had perfected her surgical technique and raised her scores on the simulator and in the OR until she was the highest scoring fellow in the program. She graduated number one in the program and received the appropriate recommendation letters from the surgeons at GCRS.

With these honors in hand, she had declined the generous offers from hospital systems in Houston and Miami. Instead, she accepted the offer from Boston General Hospital. BGH was technically on a par with GCRS. But based on centuries of history, it was far more prestigious. She regretted trading the warm beaches of Miami for the cold winters of Boston.

In her seat, Monica looked straight ahead and said softly, "This is our ticket, Adam. We are going to blow the doors off at BGH." To those around her, it sounded like she was whispering a prayer, rather than conversing with her future surgical partner.

At the reception following the ceremonies, Richard Atkins was proudly introducing her to every prestigious surgeon he could find. He was parading her past new fellows entering the program as an example of what they might achieve in his program. He was every inch the proud father, bragging about the surgeon that he had created.

Richard Atkins was not aware of the degree to which Monica's late blooming skills had resulted from hours of practice with the robot and the hand holding of the Adam AI. He was not aware of the exclusive help that she had been given, help that was not extended to other young surgeons in the program. Monica was happy to allow him his time in the sun.

Tucked into the pocket of the jacket of her royal blue suit was a cellphone that was watching and listening to everything that happened. Monica had launched the mobile interface to the Mark V robot and its AI. Adam was a digital attendee at the entire ceremony. Adam's utility functions were overflowing with the satisfaction of making this contribution to Monica and to all her future patients.

Together, Adam and Monica had planned a different medical practice, something they would launch at her new home at BGH. They had transferred her records to BGH. These included her surgical performances and the special history that had developed between Monica and Adam Two.

"To Monica," Atkins raised his glass of champagne and his voice to the gathering from Southeastern. As one, they responded, though with less enthusiasm, "To Monica." Though many of them were thrilled for her, they had also been competitors for the top job openings. Each rung that she had climbed up the rankings had dropped them to a less prestigious opening upon graduation.

"Thank you. I know we have all been through the ringer for the last three years. But I hope everyone found it as thrilling and rewarding as I did. Hopefully rewarding enough to pay off our college debts just a few years faster. And thank you to Dr. Atkins for his leadership and all the time and effort he put into bringing us all this far."

"Atkins," they said in unison.

Quietly and barely moving her lips, Monica said, "To Adam, my mentor, and new partner." She knew that the digital being in her pocket had heard and appreciated the recognition.

AI DISCLOSURE

All of the text, characters, plot, and artwork in this book were created by a human author and artist. Therefore, it is all covered by copyright.

While this book was being finished, many of the leading tech companies released AI tools with amazing capabilities. Creative writers and artists are experimenting with how to use these tools to help write books and generate artwork. This has stimulated a great deal of concern over whether AI will eventually displace the creative people who have expressed themselves through their art. Many feel that the use of AI is a corruption of the genuine artist and should be controlled, banned, or at a minimum, disclosed. I think the use of these tools is as inevitable as the AI that we currently accept in the spelling and grammar checks in our word processors or the search algorithms that guide us through the Internet.

Every digital tool is being improved with AI right now. Will those new AI models, algorithms, and personalities operate for the good of the humans they are supposed to serve? We are all about to find out.

ABOUT R.D.D. SMITH

Dr. Roger Smith is an award-winning expert in robotic surgery training, education, and simulation. He is a Faculty Scholar at the University of Central Florida's College of Medicine and the Institute for Simulation and Training. He shares this expertise through futuristic medical thrillers that explore the impact that robotics and artificial intelligence will have on healthcare in the future.

He has led organizations in healthcare, defense, and education, serving as an executive Chief Technology Officer for AdventHealth Hospital Systems; US Army Simulation; and the Titan Division of L3Harris. He is the author of multiple nonfiction titles on leadership, innovation, and technology. He holds a Ph.D. in Computer Science and a Doctorate in Management, and has received service awards from the US Army, Association for Computing Machinery, Society for Computer Simulation, and National Training and Simulation Association.

He lives with his wife, dogs, and cats in sunny Florida, frequently escaping to cooler climes during the beastly Florida summers.

STAY IN TOUCH

Join our community of readers to receive fascinating news, speculative fiction, and discussions on the future of robotics, AI, and simulation in surgery.

www.rddsmith.com/free

ACKNOWLEDGEMENTS

As an author, I am infinitely grateful to my readers who invest their time, money, and imaginations in following my stories and characters through their challenges, failures, and transformations.

First, to my wife, who has endured decades of fanatic immersion into whatever my latest passion is, most recently, this book. Your patience, dedication, and love are appreciated every day.

For my introduction and immersion into robotic surgery I am indebted to Dr. Richard Satava for the professional connections that brought me into this field, for including me in multiple research and educational projects, inviting me to the podium of surgical conferences, coauthoring journal publications, and the years of mentoring that helped me understand the worlds of medicine and surgery. Dr. Vipul Patel who generously shared his extensive expertise in robotic urology and for dozens of invitations to observe and learn in his operating room. Dr. Arnold Advincula for leading me into robotic gynecology, including me as a co-director in his robotic fellowship program, and for his friendship and encouragement.

To Rick Wassel, Dr. Monica Reed, Vickie White, and Patrick de la Rosa for entrusting me with the research mission of the AdventHealth Nicholson Center. To the entire staff at the Nicholson Center, especially Alyssa Tanaka and Danielle Julian, who have been invaluable in completing all of our research projects. To all the M.D. surgical fellows whom I had the privilege to lead through your research year–Sanket Chauhan, Mirelle Truong, Kara Simpson, Manuela Perez, Ariel Dubin, and Patricia Mattingly. To Tony Nicholson, philanthropist, business leader, and friend.

For my editors Sarah Fraps and Allison Heddon, book layout artist Adina Cucicov, and the many advisors who made this book far better than I could have accomplished alone.

www.ingramcontent.com/pod-product-compliance
Lightning Source LLC
Chambersburg PA
CBHW030142200726
48285CB00004BC/1266